GARNET AND SILVER

Legal

The following is a work of fiction. All characters are fictitious, including the ones implied to be making brief cameos. Any similarities to any real persons, living or dead, are completely coincidental.

GARNET AND SILVER

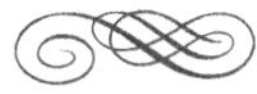

A Faerie Tale

Black Unicorn Books

Dedication

This book is dedicated to my sisters Ali and Katie.

Keep raising those little warriors right.

Contents

Legal — iii
Dedication — vii

1 Realm — 1

2 The Strange Familiar — 9

3 For My Lady Fair — 23

4 Pearls — 39

5 My Best Friend's Keeper — 48

6 Pixie Sticks do not Equate to Pixie Dust — 82

7 The Faerie Kingdom — 94

8 The Prince's Castle — 100

9 The Prince and the Weavers — 107

10 The Hunters of the Wood — 135

11 To Dance no More — 147

12 Heart of Stone — 159

13 On These Broken Wings — 187

14 The Night Garden — 192

15 Faerie Queen — 207

16 Flight — 216

17 The Sorceress of 27 Foxberry Bay   229

18 Night Mares   255

19 The Crowned   272

20 Return   288

I

Realm

The court of the eldest surviving prince of the realm had been stagnant for the past two centuries. When the youngest prince and his men approached from a distance the castle appeared spectacular; a white gem gleaning against the blue-gray mountains reflecting the crystal waters but as they neared, Prince Altroine's dormant palace revealed quiet ruin. The prince's party rode past crumbling statues; what little remained of the vegetation in the area was harsh brown and brittle, breaking under the silver hooves of the riders' mounts as they crossed the narrow bridges over rushing waters.

Prince Nyveo had his company halt before the main bridge leading into his uncle's fortress. There were no guards seen from the high walls or the gates and no one appeared to announce them. The young prince dismounted and had only his personal guard Moaz follow him across the long stone bridge, to the open gate that held no bars. Moaz hesitated slightly as they were to enter through the main arch leading to the white marble castle, but mostly kept in his lord's wake. Advancing on foot through the stone gardens, devoid of plants and animals, save for those of a variety of rock ignored or shattered. They heard the sound of harps, small drums, and flutes; songs that were old centuries before the youngest prince was born. They followed the music inside.

Prince Altroine's servants were not bound as their master, but they too lived in squalor. Broken pieces of the castle's walls littered the floor. Perhaps Altroine liked it better this way, but Moaz and the young prince remembered when the castle was the most beautiful place in all the world; several, for that matter. Some things didn't change; light flooded the old halls, memories of better times whispered despite the ruin. To eyes that had not seen the young prince's castle, perhaps they would still think the prison magnificent.

The dancers were varied in looks and talent, not even changing their costumes in the past two decades. Prince Altroine didn't seem to notice them spinning before him. He lounged on his throne, his brow in his left hand and his eyes downcast, as if the beautiful music and performance was an annoyance. He remained still when his nephew and servant entered the vaulted-ceiling ivory throne room. Moaz and the younger prince watched the dancers for a moment. Several small pixies flittered from their hiding places, from sills and ripples in the aged curtains and cracks in the marble walls, flying towards the younger prince, only upon realizing who he was, to flit away, out of the old shabby throne room. When the pixies fled, the other servants of Prince Altroine acknowledged Moaz and his master, bowing, seemingly reinvigorated by new eyes and ears. The music became more lively, and the dancers, both human and of the immortal races, began a much more intricate display of their abilities. The younger prince kept his eyes on his uncle's throne. Altroine's silver eyes finally moved and acknowledged the younger prince, though Altroine remained as a statue on his silver throne.

Nyveo motioned for Moaz to remain behind, and descended the slight decline of steps onto the dance floor. Once his boot stepped from the stone steps to the pale marble floor of his uncle's court, the lighting in the castle changed, and at once the music and dancing stopped. Moaz halted while his lord did not hesitate, and his uncle's servants parted before Nyveo. Finally, Altroine stood.

"You are bold, son of Kylreas," Altroine said. Altroine looked like a beggar, his dark beard unkempt, his red and gold clothes fringed and appeared baggy on his form. While his toys watched anxiously, they appeared clean and however stagnant in costume theirs appeared tailored.

"It is your cage, uncle, not mine," said Nyveo. "I trust you are well?"

Prince Altroine motioned with a quick raise of his chin, and his servants left the throne room, most did not even cast a hazarding glance at Moaz. When the elder prince stepped down its rust lifted. Though he was the oldest-lived of their race, he was smooth-cheeked and appeared no older than forty. "Has it been ten years already?" he asked.

"I've not visited you in more than twenty," said Nyveo, never catching his uncle's gaze for more than an instant. "Your castle appears in ill repair. Have you need of more servants?"

"A cage remains a cage if it is the finest one in all the world," said the tall and lean prince. "Do not bore me with small talk. State your business."

"I brought you a present. Allow my men inside, and they shall bring her."

"How very kind of you to ask permission this time," Altroine said.

Moaz stumbled backwards as the castle suddenly shifted. Loose stones fell from the ceiling, and Altroine's toys squealed and ran for cover. Neither of the princes appeared upset by the falling rocks. The only one the spell was designed to imprison was Altroine. After his nephew failed to back down, Altroine relented, the castle became still and the prince and allowed his nephew's men to enter. After a few moments Nyveo's men entered Altroine's court and bowed, though kept their distance, as if suspecting treachery, and remained on the far side of the room, before the marble floor where the two princes of the sidhe stood.

Ten years Nyveo's princess, ten years his prisoner, she was physically seventeen and still the girl struggled against the two guardsmen who held her arms. They needn't tie her hands together, although the humans grew taller in some parts of the world in the past century, physically they were weak. Despite spending more time in this kingdom than her own world, the scent of her mortality was evident, like a fresh breeze in a tomb.

"I don't like humans from this last century," said Altroine, hardly casting a glance at her. "They are too feisty and think themselves learned."

"You consider yourself wiser than I," said Nyveo. "At the very least, you can use her to help with the local vegetation. Your mortals can't even make the grasses grow."

"What care I for grasses if I cannot walk upon them?" Altroine asked before descending the cold steps and walking towards the girl. This one only had rage in her eyes but not aimed at him. "Marry one of your mortals, and return to their world," he told his nephew. "You will be free to come and go as you please."

"I will not do that while you and Bulgorio have claim to the throne," the younger prince said, before adding quietly, "in addition to my half-brother."

"Sylavanos could never claim the throne," Altroine said with a laugh, before looking at the girl. "What is your name?"

The girl hesitated. He took her chin, and had her look at him. "Wyvarre," she snapped.

"Not the one he gave you," Altroine said. She tried to look away, but Altroine knew how to handle mortals, and dug one finger under the angle of her jaw. "Who *were* you?"

"Consuela Dorez," she held his gaze firmly. She'd forgotten fear.

"And where were you from?"

"Hamilton, Ontario."

"What were you going to be," Altroine asked, "before you were stolen?"

She broke free from the hands of one of the sidhe guardsmen that held her and struck Altroine. Altroine almost flinched but he didn't seize her arm and with a gesture ordered the other release the human before diverting his gaze to the human again. "Consuela, I am not a young prince," he said quietly. "My age was ancient when your world was new. I have destroyed greater worlds than yours over less. Consider yourself lucky that I am bored and bound; my brother Bulgorio would turn you into a bovine for sport and if he was feeling kindly, he'd kill and eat you afterwords. What were you going to be, before you were stolen?"

She looked distant, and for an instant, her defence broke. Her eyes watered, before she drew on her hate once again. "I'm going back."

"Did anyone come for her?" Altroine asked his nephew, not breaking her gaze.

"None," Nyveo said.

"You're a liar," Consuela said lowly.

"We have a difficult time not telling the truth. We've centuries to remember the lies we've spun."

"You twist words," Consuela said. "Same thing. They looked. Just because they couldn't find this place didn't mean they didn't try. You hide away things that are not yours. If you had an ounce of courage, you'd let mortals walk this realm. You may be physically stronger then us, but we defeated your kind before."

For a moment there was an eerie silence. Finally, Nyveo cocked his head. "If we were to send you back, you'd not belong to your world."

She moved suddenly, and taking Altroine's sword, poised it at the youngest prince, tip at his neck. Feisty *was* too weak a word. "You deserve to die, but I'm not convinced this will do it." She looked to the older prince. "What magic binds you?"

"You would release me?" the older prince asked with a muted chuckle. "Interesting."

"Altroine," Nyveo said, no fear in his tone, but it was betrayed by his eyes.

"I'm so very tempted," said Altroine, "however, you see, dear girl, I need my wretched nephew alive for the time being."

The sword burned white suddenly. Consuela screamed, dropping to her knees she tried to release it, but the hilt remained in her grip. She fell, and the younger prince stepped back, his fear still apparent as his uncle stepped over the girl, who lay still, pain still etched onto her brow. When she no longer moved, the sword stopped, and it slipped from her grasp, clanking unceremoniously on the floor.

"She lives?" Nyveo asked.

"Not for my love of you, nephew," Altroine said, taking his sword. He stooped, picked her up and cradled her, not unkindly. "I could have killed you a hundred times by now. I will not have a mortal deny me the pleasure."

He turned from his nephew, and walked up his steps, and placed Consuela down gently on his throne.

"Does she please you?" his nephew asked.

"You gave her to me, if I wish to curse her or crown her that is no longer your concern. Or have you attachments to your mortals?"

"It is my kingdom, Uncle. I am the only one fit to rule. I have the blood of the one responsible for your ruin in my veins. "

"If you are king, let me see your proof," Altroine said.

"You live. Renounce all claim to the throne and I will release you in an instant," said his nephew, "and you would be the second most powerful in the land."

"I already am that, and more," Altroine said. "Release me, and take me with you to the world of the mortals. You need me or I would not still be here. I will find a mortal who can wield Silver. We will take back the kingdom. I will give you half to do with as you please."

"So you might marry the human and then crown yourself?" his nephew asked with a laugh. "What will you do with this girl?"

"I shall send her to find the staff," Altroine said.

The younger prince sighed before replying, "And when she fails? She cannot wield the staff."

"So the dragon kills her. Perhaps I shall train her to kill your men." Altroine smiled at his nephew. "I fear that you are more my son than Kylreas' – pity your mother slew him before you were born. Let it be as it was, I will not hold your prideful youth against you."

His nephew smiled. "Yes you will. I would not prefer you to Bulgorio if you did not."

"Imagine if Bulgorio had his way," Altroine said mostly to himself. "The Empress would prefer him on the throne to either of us. We need one another, nephew. Don't let me send her back to you with knowledge to use that sword."

"Who would free you, once I am slain? You need me more than I need you. You would not be so kind towards my... insolence. I know you, uncle. Yours is the old way, with the old weaknesses. It has been defeated. I am new, and part of that world. It is only right that I assume the throne of both."

"How much longer, nephew?" Altroine said. "You've been at this for two centuries without my help. You'll never find one who can wield Silver. Is it not better to share power with me?"

"So that I may bow before you?" Nyveo asked, not masking the laughter in his tone. "My dame's birthright draws close, uncle. You've a choice; and it seems you need ten years more to reconsider. It would be a shame if the next mortal made me king, and you were unable to join me."

Altroine grabbed his nephew's arm when he turned to go. "You'll never wake the kingdom. You play these games, but there are too few real princesses left. You'll never be king. Not without my help."

"Our kind are all but spent because of the foolishness of my father," said the younger prince. "Was it not his brothers that led to his downfall, and the slumber of our race? You would cling to that remnant – that legacy. I will bring us into a new age, into new glory. When you walked into the world of mortal men, they were mostly savages. You think she is learned?" He gestured to the sleeping Consuela. "Every ten years I return, they have changed a hundred times. *Feisty.*"

Altroine gave his nephew a mocking laugh. "They are mostly savages still," he said, letting go of his nephew. "Little more than the dust on my boots. Be gone from this place – I lack the power to bind you, but not your men. If you find a mortal who could wield silver, the Empress will tear out her throat before she comes near the staff. You are as much a prisoner as I. We need one another to escape our shackles, else you would have slain me centuries ago."

The younger prince strode from the court of his uncle, his servant Moaz followed quickly behind him, in silence, not glancing back at the small eyes of the pixies or the dancers and musicians waiting in the hallways.

"He seems in a better mood than last we saw him, my lord," Moaz offered as they made their way across the long bridge, to their mounts. The once-horned unicorns bowed their heads when the prince and his servant walked past them. "He will never revoke his claim and now the girl's gone and shown that she knows how to use that sword."

"She will keep him out of our hair," his prince replied.

"You should have both of your uncles destroyed."

"And what happens when the Empress learns that I am without allies?" asked the prince. "They have their uses, however limited. Are you ready to return to the human world, Moaz?" He mounted his brilliant white charger, who went to speak, but the prince pulled back on the unicorn's bit and silenced him. "Hurry beasts – to the castle. You'd like to go the land of mortals, and have one of them remember you, wouldn't you?" he asked. "You'll see some live ones, I promise, but they'll be in no position to restore you – much less, you them."

2

The Strange Familiar

"Why are we in separate chemistry classes again?" Chloe asked as Jane forced her pre-calculus textbook onto their shared shelf.

"Because you take band," Jane reminded her. "Everything revolves around band."

That wasn't quite true: Jane could have taken chemistry with her next semester if she didn't insist on the extra gym class. Chloe waited for Jane to grab her old lunchbox and they walked through the forum to get to the basement cafeteria. Chloe tried not to be jealous of the cheerleading gaggle from their grade who got to sit in the forum with seniors and eat their lunches. Janice Ilkes had a dark tan; she probably went on vacation or spent the summer at the beach. Chloe overheard Vanessa Purret tell Freddie Shewertz that her parents took her boating all summer. Chloe tried to think of something wonderful to tell anyone if they asked what she did, but she and Jane were almost ignored as they made their way through the forum.

"Hey, Jane!"

Chloe didn't much care for Natalie Frites. Natalie smiled at Jane but rolled her eyes when she saw Chloe wait for Jane at the top of the stairwell. Natalie looked like she still belonged in Junior High, with her hair in a ball cap and wearing some purple sports jersey three sizes too big.

"You up for rugby this year?" Natalie asked, not stepping a foot outside the open gym doors.

"I just got my braces out last year," Jane said, shaking her head. "My mom'll kill me if I mess up my teeth."

"Come on, Jane," Natalie whined. "I need at least four more people or we won't even have a team this year."

"You got pre-cal and chemistry this semester, plus soccer," Chloe said. "I don't know about you, Jane, but I'd need to study those two subjects every day, let alone the rest of your classes."

"I didn't ask you, Princess," Natalie snapped. Chloe wondered when *Princess* became an insult. "Come on, I've got the schedule just inside the gym. Let's see if it interferes with soccer before you tell me no."

Jane began to follow Natalie.

Chloe was tempted to stay with Jane, but decided there was nothing she could say that would help Jane dodge the call. "Jane, I'll wait for you downstairs," Chloe said.

Jane nodded. Chloe made her way downstairs to the noisy cafeteria and looked for someone friendly to sit by. She saw Bethany Pelshmidt at an otherwise empty table and plopped down across from her. Bethany played with a strand of her frizzy blonde hair and smiled, but just as quick went back to whatever screenplay she was working on. "How was Toronto? " Bethany asked eventually, blowing a purple bubble and offering Chloe a fresh piece.

Chloe shook her head. "Okay, I guess. Just did the family thing, like every summer for as long as I can remember." It sounded cool to go visit family around the Toronto Hub, except that Chloe wasn't allowed to go to anywhere worth going unescorted. Nothing screamed *loser* like being driven around by grandma. "As exciting as visiting family can be, I guess. How about you? I haven't seen you since July."

"Been out at the cottage whenever I'm not ripping tickets. Todd and I are shooting a zombie flick," Bethany said. "You wanna be in it? We need some victims."

Chloe didn't know why she nodded her head. "What's it about? Beside zombies?"

Bethany smiled, looking overtop of her glasses and Chloe looked over her shoulder to follow Bethany's gaze. Bethany's boyfriend - Toby? Todd? He sat down and pulled out his paper bag lunch. "Hey Bethany. Chloe." He didn't even give Bethany a quick peck on the cheek, he started to eat some monstrosity on white bread.

"Chloe agreed to be a victim for us!" Bethany said.

"Cool. We can discuss different ways for you to die while we try this really cool card game I picked up," he said, whipping out some cards.

Chloe could have swore she saw her little cousins watching the cartoon with the same characters on the cards and the oldest cousin into it was in middle grade. "I'll go ask Jane if she wants to die with me," Chloe said, standing when she saw her best friend. "Don't let us interrupt your couple time."

Jane didn't see her, or at least only had milk on her mind. She waited in line and jumped when Chloe clapped a hand on her shoulder. "Rugby?" Chloe asked.

"Not a chance," Jane said. "I told her that I was up for a soccer scholarship and she believed me. Nat's holding a spot for us."

Chloe bit her tongue. "Their table already looks full," Chloe said, and a wicked smile crossed her face. "Bethany's still with whatshisname. They're playing cards."

Jane made a face. "We'd only be spoiling the fun."

"You know, we could go sit over there, with Michael and Trevor," Chloe chimed. "Michael's got a nice tan this year, doesn't he?"

"They look like they're busy," Jane said.

Chloe looked. It was just the two seniors at the table, and the only thing they seemed to be busy with was stuffing their faces and goofing off. The table was by the exit. She and Jane could always bolt if it got too dangerous. "Come on, Jane. They don't bite," Chloe said, and sashayed to the table.

Jane almost forgot to get the change for her milk. They sat on the opposite end of the otherwise deserted table, and Jane looked ahead, or away from Michael Benton. Chloe saw them check them both out when she checked her make-up with her compact mirror. She cringed at the potential thoughts Trevor might be having, but got over them quickly. Chloe was sick of being quiet, so she said, "Bethany and Steve–"

"Todd."

"Are making some zombie film, they want me to be the star," Chloe said, dipping her fork in her salad dressing before spearing her tomato and cucumber.

"You'd be a zombie?" Jane asked flatly.

"You can't make the zombie the main character!"

A granny smith apple rolled between the two girls and off the table. Jane caught it just before it hit the floor. Chloe knew she couldn't catch anything if her life depended on it. "Toss it back," Trevor said.

"Nice throw," Mike said after Jane threw the apple to him. "You sure you're a soccer player?"

"She plays badminton too," Chloe offered.

"Not really," Jane said. She had an annoying way of playing with her single braid when she got nervous. Chloe wanted to smack her hand. "Badminton's just at lunchtime. I'm not very good, though."

"No, you're terrible at badminton – just like you're terrible at basketball, volleyball, tennis, and soccer." Chloe smiled, foraging through her salad for the fixings. She wanted to kick Jane under the table, but there was a solid barrier between them. All she'd accomplish was scuffing her shoes and taking out the much-needed heel.

"What, you don't like hockey?" Trevor asked.

"I love hockey," Jane said, "I hate waking up at five a.m."

That wasn't the real reason. Chloe finished eating her salad in her preordained order and threw out the twin cream cookies her mother had snuck into her bag as the three talked about hockey. Last Chloe checked, Mike and Trevor weren't on the school hockey team. Now they were about – lacrosse? The boys had moved over to their half of the table and were talking about Trevor's Dad's season tickets to the Winnipeg Jets while it was still football season. Bored, Chloe's eyes wandered about the room. *If those two were good jocks, they'd be in the forum,* she decided, before she saw the most gorgeous guy – ever.

She wasn't the first to spot him. A lot of the conversations had dwindled since he entered the cafeteria with two others. His face was very angular, but in general his features seemed more boyish than mature. The age was in his eyes, which were a cold grey. He was pale, but not like a basement dweller. He had nearly bleach-blond hair, but no freckles blemished his skin.

The others he walked with were also good-looking. The blond must have easily been over six feet tall, but the two were almost a full head taller than him and were dark haired. Despite their baggy coats, their black t-shirts gave off a presence of musculature, especially for teens, though Chloe thought they must be at least in college. The blond spoke to one of his friends, who nodded and got in line. He and the other friend kept walking around the room, taking in the students as much as the students were taking in them.

He caught her eyes and Chloe looked away and down. She didn't dare look up in his direction again. She worried who saw, who whispered, who laughed. Chloe retreated to Jane's conversation. She didn't find a good place to interrupt, so she packed up her lunch and got up. When Jane didn't take a hint, Chloe put a hand on her best friend's shoulder. "I'm done. Let's go to the library."

"In a minute," Jane said, shrugging off Chloe's grip.

"Let's go," Chloe said.

"Let's finish eating outside," Mike said, grabbing his apple and soda. "I'm told to shut up all day. I don't need that during lunch."

The trio kept talking, oblivious to Chloe. Chloe looked over her shoulder as they made their way out of the cafeteria. He was speaking to his friends, but caught her eyes once more. She couldn't look away, until he smiled at her. She tripped into Trevor. "Watch it! Dumb girl, throwing yourself at me!"

Did he have to be so loud? Chloe could only save her honour by being louder. "Not if the human species depended on it!" she shouted.

She could hear people giggling – no doubt at her – so she quickly left them all behind. They could go outside and get all sweaty and get second hand smoke all they wanted. She made her way up the stairwell and through the forum and was about to go upstairs when she heard Jane's voice. "Wait up!"

She waited for Jane to catch up. "Don't you got real friends to talk to?" Chloe asked.

"You're the one who wanted to sit with them," Jane said.

Chloe looked around her friend. "Mike's still looking, by the way."

"Is he?" Jane asked.

"Hands off the braid," Chloe said. "The things I do for you. Hey, Jane, did you see that guy in the cafeteria?"

"Guy?" Jane asked. "I think half of everyone in the cafeteria was-"

"New guy," Chloe said, "with grey eyes, and had a bomber coat on."

"Grey eyes? You probably don't even know what color my eyes are," Jane said. "I don't know who you're talking about. Mike's still waiting. Come with me. Please."

"Oh, alright," Chloe said, rolling her eyes. They started back but Mike and Trevor were with their other guy friends. One of them had a football, and they seemed to be laughing, and walking towards the main entrance. Chloe felt Jane's eyes on her. "You didn't have to chase after me."

"I won't next time," Jane snapped. "You worry too much about what other people think. And, if you wouldn't wear those shoes, you might not fall into people all the time."

"They make me average height," Chloe stated.

"For what, a model?" Jane asked.

"Don't you want to go talk lacrosse with Mike?" Chloe asked.

"Mike yes, Trevor no," Jane said. "Come on."

~*~

It was supposed to get easier, doing your own thing in High School, not having to worry about anyone else's schedule but as Jane got more choices, she also found that it was hard not to feel alone. She and Chloe tried to take as many things as possible together, but in their first semester, the only classes they had in common were Pre-cal and Spanish. It wasn't like Chloe was her only friend, but Jane had a hard time fitting in and just talking to people – something Chloe never had a hard time with.

Last class of the day, Jane hoped they'd spend the first day just talking about the wonders of Spanish and how it would help when they traveled. "How was band?" she asked when her best friend finally made her appearance.

Chloe stuck out her tongue.

"They making you take extra classes during lunch again?" Jane asked.

"I hope not. I'm already playing for church," Chloe said. "My parents think I have nothing better to do than to plan for when I'm old."

"Speaking of, can I come over tonight and do Pre-cal with you?" Jane asked. "My brother's starting up a garage band – again – and if I have to escape to the library one more time I'll go crazy."

"It's my uncle's birthday today, so we're going to his house. I can give you my house key," Chloe offered. It wasn't like they hadn't done it before. "Just don't let Shiloh take up all your time."

Jane couldn't help it – she escaped to Chloe's house all summer under the pretence of taking care of her bichon frise puppy while Chloe's family was out of town. Shiloh was with one of Chloe's cousins on the other side, and Chloe was really only gone for two weeks, but that was besides the point. "When will you do your homework?" Jane asked.

"I'll get it done somehow," Chloe said. "You wanna come?"

"Nah. I've got an assignment for my journalism class," Jane said. "Besides, if your grandparents see much more of me they'll think I'm one of their grandkids."

"My inexplicable Metis twin," Chloe giggled, and Jane couldn't help but join her.

"Hey girls," Janice Ilkes said, plopping down beside Chloe. "Chloe, is that a new jacket?"

"Yes it is," Chloe beamed.

Janice smiled at Jane briefly. Jane wondered if Janice knew what her name was. They'd only been in school together for the past decade.

"You look like you spent the summer at the beach," Chloe said.

"I did! My sister got married in Jamaica three weeks ago!" Janice said, "I had to get tanned to make sure I didn't look all funny in the dress she picked out! She picked the most hideous thing she could for the bridesmaids to make herself look good…"

Jane wished she could contribute but she'd never been a bridesmaid. Chloe had last summer, for an aunt. It looked like fun, even though Jane's older sister Carol, who had, said it was a lot of work. Jane had been invited to that wedding as Chloe's "date" and the most work Chloe did was point out that the bride's bouquet was starting to droop and then Jane and Chloe had to rummage around the hall basement for matching vases. Jane politely tuned out of the conversation until she heard her name.

"Actually, Jane and I are planning on traveling before we start University," Chloe said, whacking Jane's arm. "Isn't that right?"

"Together?" Janice asked. "Like, backpacking across Europe?"

"We're planning on Australia," Jane said. "Chloe wants to stop at Hawaii for a few nights but I think if she stops there for more than a day a volcano will erupt."

"Well, I'd like to go to Paris too," Chloe said, and then laughed. "Actually, I'd like to see the entire world. But yeah, Australia before University, and then, who knows? I need to take Jane with me to France so she can translate."

"Glad to know I have some purpose in life," Jane said. She and Chloe giggled.

"I've been to Australia," Janice declared, "and it wasn't that good."

"The entire country?" Jane asked.

At first Jane thought Chloe and Janice were raising eyebrows at her, but their eyes went past her. Jane knew she couldn't turn around without making it obvious, so she took out her binder and pretended to be a keener by writing the date and class and teacher.

"Is it safe to look back now?" Jane mouthed to Chloe.

Chloe nodded, looked ahead, and proceeded to powder her nose using her very special mirror.

Jane pretended to need to need to get into her backpack on the back of the chair. She didn't see anything special. A few new students, though

Chloe probably didn't want to look lame in front of one of the seniors trying to make easy grades. Turning back towards the front of the class, there was a note on her desk. Chloe was an expert at passing notes, but Jane wasn't so good at giving them back. Mrs. Hojensil entered the room and gave her a knowing look. Jane tried to keep from blushing, and stuffed the note into her notebook, and waited for her to start to orally test someone at the back of the room before reading it.

The guy in the blue jacket, is he hot or what?

Jane looked at Chloe, then over her shoulder. There were three blue jackets.

The blond one. The new note had an angry-frowny face. *Stop staring!*

Jane offered a nod. Jane sneezed and when she opened her eyes, a new note was on her desk.

I knew this year would be different.

Jane glanced back at him when she heard his smooth voice perfectly utter the phrase Janice just struggled with. She was bilingual with French, (her dad's side), but she found Spanish easy, but was far from perfect. He and the two he was with looked too old to be in High School, but not so old that she would think twice about it. The other two wore the same jackets and were darker haired, taller, and they too had no problem speaking *Español*. Jane generally preferred boys that were at least 6', with height guiding her preference, but the blond's face was easily the most attractive. Beautiful, even. Beautiful wasn't a word she'd use on a boy, but it seemed to fit.

Jane felt self-conscious, and looked ahead, staring at common phrases she'd never use because she'd never make it to Mexico, much less Spain. Australia was a dream. She wouldn't amount to anything unless she went to University, and that was where all her money was going to go. Chloe no doubt knew his name, his sign, his clique, so Jane knew she'd hear about it later. As the class reviewed the basics from last year, Jane busied herself with reviewing trig, and hoping she wouldn't have to spend near as much time studying as she had last year. Languages were her thing, she wished hanging out with Bethany would help her pick up the math so she wouldn't have to spend so much time on it.

Class ended before Jane learned much of anything besides how silly other girls sounded sometimes. "Did you see the way he picked up his pen?" Janice asked.

Jane hadn't.

"Oh, and for a moment there I thought he had a Spanish accent!" Chloe said.

"He doesn't look Spanish," Jane said.

"He's in my French class too," Janice said, "He must be like a genius or something! I think I'm going to Polo Park tonight, Chloe. Want to join me?"

"I would love to come shopping with you, but I have a family birthday I can't ditch," Chloe said. "Jane?"

"Homework," Jane said. "Have fun, Janice."

"I will," Janice said, stopping off in the forum to use her locker.

"How did she get a locker in the forum?" Jane demanded as they trudged down the hall, towards the band room.

"Just let it go," Chloe said, "I'm working on raising our popularity a notch. If she asks you to go shopping, go."

"She didn't ask me," Jane said. "She probably thinks you always have access to your parent's car."

"I walked today," Chloe said.

"I know. I walked with you." Up until they went to Oak Park High School, they made almost the entire walk together. They went their separate ways too early now, a problem they didn't have on their walk to the elementary and middle school. Jane was tempted to invite herself to Chloe's family gathering but she walked home, promising herself she'd only to go Chloe's house if the noise got to be too much.

Jane could hear the noise radiating from down the block. Her older sister Carol was arguing with their mother about tuition and taxes while her younger brother Paul and two of his friends were in the living room, playing video games and the odd man out was on his phone, eating the last of the chips.

Jane looked in the fridge and found the good leftovers already gobbled up, but there were no shortage of apples from their tree, so she went outside and plucked a couple. She'd make herself a treat of apple crisp before dinner if she wasn't so sure the cretins in the other room would steal it all. Her brother had somehow inherited a set of drums from one of their cousins, so every attempt at a garage band came to their house. Paul was a half-decent drummer, much to their parents' dismay. There was some cheese the horde hadn't descended upon yet; it would work. Jane took a bite from her apple and a voice made her choke. "I thought soccer try-outs were today. Jane, are you alright?"

Jane didn't know which was more embarrassing: doing abdominal thrusts on herself, or spewing the chunk of apple onto Mike's forehead.

"Jane! Jane!" Mom and Dad squealed after the problem was fixed.

"Ew, gross," said Willy Isliefson.

"I've had worse," Mike said, plucking the blob of chewed apple off his forehead.

"Jane, if you hate our music so much you can just say so. Stop hucking up on my friends," Paul said.

"Sit down, have a drink of water," Mom ordered.

"Choke on an apple," Willy laughed. "Come on, guys, let's leave Sleeping Beauty and go practice."

"That's Cinderella, dumbass," Trevor said as the posse made their way to the garage.

"Serves you right for eating before dinner," Carol said.

Jane knew her sins, she could smell the fish fingers and chips in all their glory. Jane would have to go punish herself by raiding Chloe's family fridge. Much later, after her face stopped beaming red and she came out of her room. By the time she turned thirty-two seemed about right.

"Are you sure you're alright?" Mom asked.

"I'm fine," Jane said.

"You never choked on nothing before," said Dad.

"Dad, proper English is-" Carol started.

Jane was ignored as Carol continued bickering with their parents. Wondering if it was possible to change schools, Jane looked over her sister's first year textbooks and glancing at the bill for used books, wondered if there would be any money left over for when she got to go to school. *Chloe won't settle for a day trip to Brandon, and that's probably all I can afford.* Jane cut the apple into small pieces and chewed visibly so her mother would stop nagging her. Before she could begin to graph on her overpriced calculator she heard a dog bark – seriously, who brings their dog with them to visit? And a trio of boys, one barely off his skateboard rushed in, followed by their ballooning mother.

"Your sister and her kids are over again?" Dad asked.

Mom ignored him and kissed Jane's aunt's cheeks and then happily wiped the snotty nose of the current youngest, and brought out the hidden stash of cookies not meant for immediate family – Jane got some anyway – and the TV was back on and instead of video games it was some cartoon with the volume reserved for the elderly. Jane shared sentiments with Dad.

"I don't know how we can get these girls educated with all this racket!" Dad gave Carol the keys because her education was being directly paid for. "Here's some cash for some dinner."

Not much cash in hand, but enough for a burger, Jane still felt jealous. Jane knew a little white lie of, "Dinner at Chloe's," wouldn't hurt with her cousins and Paul's friends over. If she hurried, she might even make the birthday party, and she and Chloe could have a legitimate excuse to escape and do their homework at their own table. She opened her mouth but Mom said, "Jane, can I get you to shuck corn?"

The good stuff always gets broken out when people you care about visit, Jane figured as she exiled herself to the back porch.

"Go away," she told her aunt's dog, an overweight golden retriever who snuffled for something to mooch.

"I thought we were getting along nicely at lunch time," Mike said from back door.

At least she didn't choke. "Not you, the dog," Jane said. "Sorry about earlier."

"That's gotta be the cleanest vomit I've ever had thrown up on me," Mike said. "Sorry I didn't help you." He sat down on the step beside her. "Want some help now?"

There were only three cobs left, but Jane nodded. "They all laughing at me?" she asked.

"That was really cool," Mike said. "Most girls would have freaked out, and probably fainted."

"Most girls are stupid." She didn't mean to say it like that and regretted the words as they came tumbling out.

"Yeah. Unfortunately the only guy I ever saved was a big fat guy," Mike said. "I could barely pull him out of the water."

"What happened?" Jane asked.

"I'm a new lifeguard, so I think I just get to watch girls in their bikinis at the Pan Am Pool. This giant hairy fat guy decides to jump off the high board – the ones restricted to professional divers, right? He sinks like an anvil to the bottom of the pool." he started to laugh when Jane laughed. "The senior lifeguard's smaller than your friend Chloe, and I mean tiny little walking mouth, can swim like a fish, and she had to dive twice to grab him, took three of us to tow him in, they're looking at me to do the lifting. We get him to the side and there's an instant crowd, and our shrimpy senior lifeguard wouldn't go get the mask. She said she'd do compressions and my work-buddy is all, 'I dunno where they keep the gloves.' Nastiest thing I've ever had to do."

"Aren't you glad they don't make us write those stories down anymore?" she asked. "What I did on my summer vacation?"

"I think Trevor caught it on video," Mike said, "not the fall or the rescue. He ran to the locker room and caught some of it on his phone: us arguing about getting him out of the water, and him throwing up into my mouth."

Jane laughed, then said, "Did that really happen, or are you telling me this so I don't feel so bad?"

"You think in the garage I'm telling them it was some chick with big boobs?"

"Chloe would drown, too," Jane said, "if she knew where the cute lifeguards were."

"I'm not cute?" Mike asked.

"Yes, well, no – I mean – Chloe does that sort of thing for attention,"

Jane said. "I just want a job that pays better than babysitting and won't make my skin break out."

"If I were you I wouldn't work unless I had to," Mike said. "All my money gets sunk into my truck. If you can, be a lifeguard. It would be nice to work with someone who hasn't favorited that video."

"Maybe I will if I ever get a cellphone."

"You don't have a cellphone?" Mike asked.

"Can't afford it without a job. Can't afford the certification to be a lifeguard to get your job," Jane said.

"Sev' at the top of the street," Mike said. "They only get shot at."

"You have to be eighteen," Jane said. "They sell cigarettes."

"McD's?"

"Okay," she said, "maybe I can work at the one near the Pan Am Pool. Give the fat guys in speedos a little extra special sauce."

He laughed. Jane was surprised he kissed her, but only at first. They got squirted by her little cousin's water gun, followed by, "Ew! Mom, she's sucking out his brains!!"

3

For My Lady Fair

Chloe squealed like Jane broke her foot when she found out. "You waited until morning to tell me? When are you going out? Has he got you a promise ring?"

"We're going to a movie Friday," Jane said, "and no, I don't know to which one yet."

"You should go see something classy," Chloe said. "So what do you have before lunch, anyway?" Chloe asked as they made their way to their locker.

"Drama," Jane said, "You should take it."

"Dad says it's a useless course," Chloe said. "When are they making you take history?"

"Next semester," Jane said.

"Chloe!" called one of the girls from the forum.

"What is it?" Chloe asked, and abandoned Jane to the squealing.

Probably about that new boy, Jane thought, sighing. She normally would have gone through the forum, but to avoid being one of the sheep, instead went to the nearest stairwell and made her way up to journalism. "Hey Bethany."

"Hey Jane," Bethany said. "Who did you fictionally interview?"

"The devil."

"Ain't you Catholic?" Bethany asked.

"Metis Catholic is way more fun then French Catholic, I'll be forgiven," Jane said with a smile. Bethany and Chloe were some sort of protestant, but they still sometimes snuck off to each other's churches for the youth groups and sleepovers. "Besides, it's the little devil on my shoulder. You?"

"Dracula, Vlad the Impaler." Bethany posed before she took off her glasses and cleaned them on her shirt. "Inspired by every girl in the school's latest crush."

"Who?"

"Some new guy. You seen him around?" Bethany asked. "Blond guy with the two thugs. I'll admit he's good looking, but he's white. Really, really white."

That was rich, coming from Bethany. She was covered in freckles, they were forming together to form some semblance of a tan. "Huh," Jane said. "I think I saw him in my Spanish class. He was okay. Heeey – ! Guess who asked me out for this Friday?"

Bethany didn't have the annoying habit of squealing.

~*~

Jane didn't know why she bothered some times. Chloe acted normal during pre-cal, but as soon as lunch rolled around she was with Janice and Vanessa and other girls that never spoke to Jane unless it was to express their annoyance at her existence. They went outside because that's where *he* was. Jane wanted a name, but as soon as someone mentioned *that guy* she knew who they were talking about. Jane could stomach Janice, but there was only so much concentrated stupid she could handle. Jane knew in a week all his secrets would be spilled and they'd discover that the bigger two were probably his parole officers.

"So how does this game work?" Trevor asked Todd in the nearly abandoned cafeteria.

"Nerds," Mike said, fully immersed in the game. "You gotta put this down first, I think."

"How long have you been playing?" Todd asked.

"Since I got stuck behind the desk," Mike said. "I started playing when I found a deck at the lost and found."

Bethany put away her screenplay when some of the hummus from her pita dribbled onto one of the pages. "Quiet in here today," she said. "Everyone's outside."

"We're not," said Jane. "Hey Bethany, have you ever been anywhere?"

"What you mean?" Bethany asked.

"Traveling?" Jane said.

"No, not really," Bethany said, "Todd's been to the states a few times. Texas, I think," she said, and poked her boyfriend. "Where have you travelled?"

"Texas and Florida," he said, "I got family in BC, but we haven't been there in ages."

"I got Newfies for family," Mike said. "Trevor, where's your family from?"

"Here," Trevor said, "but he's giving me a ticket to Europe as soon as I blow this joint. He wants me to get some Scandinavian culture. Like we don't have that around the house. I'd rather go see Iceland. Why?"

"Just curious," Jane said, sipping her milk.

Bethany leaned in so that the boys couldn't hear. "Chloe's just hanging out with Janice because she thinks Janice is going to open the door to a whole new world," she said. "Besides, I mentioned tagging along on your little trip to Australia and she said she'd have to talk to you." She looked to the guys. "I'm done. Want to go outside, or will you guys explode in natural light?"

"We can shoot hoops in the gym," Mike suggested. "I think they're doing volleyball in the other half, so if we're there early we should snag half the gym to ourselves."

Jane smiled, and even Todd put away his card deck for a little three on two.

~*~

"How goes the stalking?" Jane asked when Chloe and Janice sauntered into Spanish.

"Quiet, he's practically right behind us," Janice said, "and it's not stalking. It's becoming informed."

"You're all sweaty!" Chloe said to Jane.

"We shot hoops during lunch," Jane said. "So what's his name?"

"As if I know!" Janice said. "Patricia Mistlebacher tried to talk to him yesterday and he totally blew her off!"

"Patricia Mistlebacher?" Jane asked. "Isn't she a model?"

"For Walmart," Janice said, rolling her eyes.

"He didn't blow her off," Chloe said. "She asked if he had a name, and he said, 'Yes, I do.' I think he's foreign. I *love* accents." Jane was pretty sure Chloe made fun of Mike's Newfie accent when he moved to Winnipeg five years prior.

"Did you see his motorcycle? Foreign and loaded," Janice said.

"Foreign and loaded and gorgeous," Chloe agreed.

"Foreign, loaded and gorgeous is in the room," Jane quipped.

Janice and Chloe sat at their desks and looked ahead like studious little scholars.

"Wanna do pre-cal together tonight?" Jane asked Chloe.

Chloe looked to Janice, who didn't acknowledge the question. She looked back at Jane. "Alright," Chloe said. "Do you want to study with us, Janice? My place? You can see my puppy."

"Maybe some other time," Janice said, "I have it on good information that you-know-who is going to be at a certain coffee shop near the park – apparently he's been there for the past three days, reading *Chaucer*."

"*Chaucer?*" Chloe squealed.

"*Who?*" Jane asked as class started.

~*~

"Come on Jane, at least think about it!"

"I have!" Jane laughed as they made their way from the gym. Last class, Jane got all sweaty at lunch, took a break for Spanish and was sweaty again – the first two and last two classes of the day would flip-flop, so some days, she wouldn't even get that break in Spanish. Jane and Mike lucked out – his phys-ed leadership course corresponded with her gym class, and as luck would have it, their teachers made them go outdoors. Jane snuck away from ultimate Frisbee to play lacrosse with the older grade. "Chloe's a singer and a musician, not me. I'd attract the wrong crowd."

"Guys come to see girls on stage," Mike said. "Well, if you finish your homework early, give me a call. We're not meeting at your garage until next week."

"Alright. Hey, you wanna go bowling or something instead of going to a movie?" Jane asked.

"Your choice," Mike said. "Can I walk you home?"

"Do you mind waiting for Chloe?" Jane asked.

"She doesn't deserve a friend like you!" Mike said. "Nah, I don't wanna smother you before our first real date."

"Alright." He gave her hand a slight squeeze before making his way to the forum, where he shared a locker with Trevor. Jane listened to the band continue some rendition of one a song she recognized but couldn't name before remembering Chloe brought her parents' blue Toyota Corolla. Jane quickly decided, she'd wait to tell her that she was going to walk home with Mike. The Queen of Notes wouldn't stand being ditched by one. The last bell hadn't quite gone yet, but Jane opened her locker and threw in her gym clothes and began to round up her homework and lunch box. Jane wished she was musically talented, especially if her boyfriend, brother, and the other two managed to make it big. She felt someone touch her ponytail.

Jane always felt self-conscious about her hair – it was thick and coarse, it was easiest to pull it into a braid or ponytail, stylish buns would start to unravel and if she cut it short it would just poof out and make her head look gigantic. She quietly envied her sister who always complained about her fine hair. Jane subconsciously moved her ponytail over one shoulder. "Sorry if I hit you with it," she said, before glancing at the figure. It was the new guy Chloe was stalking.

"You didn't," he said. "Gym class?"

"Yeah." Jane tried to free her mother's Tupperware from Chloe's history textbook. "We're in Spanish together, right?"

"That's right," he said, leaning against another locker. "You're name is Jane, isn't it?"

"How'd you know that?" Jane asked, before being startled when he put a hand on top of hers, and proceeded to lift the chemistry text. "Thanks," she said, freeing the container.

"You're welcome," he said. "Mind if I help you out a little more?"

"Huh?" Jane asked. He ran a hand past her ear. He helped himself to her scrunchie. Jane smoothed back her hair – she'd ran comb through it after she'd changed from gym, but she was still sweaty.

"It's prettier down," he said, arm against the wall, as if blocking her. "Though you could go with a cut that would flatter your face, I think." He touched her jaw, as if examining her. Jane quickly jerked her head from his hands. "I don't bite."

"Don't touch me!" Jane snapped, dodging under his arm. She was only half-surprised that Mike was in the hallway. She caught his eyes. Mike's expression went from confusion to anger.

"Hey!" Mike shouted.

Jane hurried to Mike, only wanting him to put an arm around her shoulder, but he moved past her. "What was that about?" he demanded at the new guy.

The blond didn't reply, just looked at Mike as if in amusement.

"I'm talking to you," Mike said.

"I gathered."

"Stay away from Jane," Mike snapped.

"Or what?"

Jane was surprised at her own yelp when Mike threw the first punch. Mike was half a head taller, and muscular. She didn't see the new guy move, but Mike sunk his first into the locker. The new guy had dodged behind Mike. "Are you sure you want to do this?" the new guy asked. The bell rang. Class was over.

"Mike, calm down!" Jane shouted as Mike tried to punch him several times, but each time the new guy managed to evade Mike. There were people in the hall. Jane heard shouts from the forum and from down the hall, to the math wing. "Fight!" sounded, and blood sprayed the tiled floor. Mike clutched his face briefly, Jane couldn't see where he got hit, but he knocked the other guy on his back when Mike hooked his leg, but he got up just as quick. It seemed Mike finally landed a punch, and then he clutched his wrist, as if he'd snapped it.

"Alright, that's enough!" one of TA's Jane didn't know shouted. He was late-twenties, shorter than both teenagers but thick, though not as solid as Mike. He stood between the two as Mike's friends rushed to his side.

"Mike, Mike, you alright!?" Trevor said.

"You're dead!" another of Mike's friends snapped. The new guy didn't seem to listen to the TA, or acknowledge Mike's friends who were relaying a later death sentence. The new guy looked at Jane, and smiled rather cruelly.

"You shouldn't pick fights," he said eventually, looking at Mike. "I won't hold back next time."

Mike lunged for him again, and would have hit the TA were he not restrained by his buddies. Jane thought the world felt a little different, like it wasn't real for a moment. The new guy made his way from the fight, and began to walk towards her. There were raised voices, she could hear the principal, but the crowd seemed to part for him. He normally had so much attention, but now, no one looked at him, or saw him go – except for her. "Sorry you had to see that," he said quietly to Jane, and continued down the hall.

She didn't care where he went. Jane heard the word 'expulsion' as several younger students said that Mike started it, and the other guy was acting in self-defence.

"He was being a pervert!" Mike snapped.

"Where'd he go?!" Trevor demanded. "He was right here a minute ago!"

"Go find him," snapped the principal to several teachers. "Get him back here!"

"Does anybody know his name?" Trevor asked.

~*~

Chloe heard 'fight' but she and Bethany weren't allowed out of the band room because they were girls and 'hey might get hurt' as the substitute band teacher went to break it up, a bunch of guys following after him, chanting. A few of the guys came back and one said, "Two seniors. Blood everywhere."

"We missed it," Bethany muttered. They weren't allowed out of the room until several of the students were taken to the principal's office, and one of the janitors was cleaning up the rather small amount of blood considering earlier oral reports.

"As if we'd join in a fight," Chloe said. "Jane and I are doing pre-cal after dinner. You wanna join us?"

"I don't have math until next semester," Bethany said. "I may come over when you're done!" She waived good-bye and continued to the math wing to her locker.

I would have waited for her, Chloe thought, surprised to see her locker punched in. *Great, the only excitement around here in ages happens at my crappy locker, and I miss it.*

Not only was their locker unlocked, but Jane had left her jacket and tupperware – a cardinal sin in her family. Chloe didn't see a note. *Maybe she got into a fight and broke Natalie's nose,* Chloe smiled to herself.

"Your friend left here not long ago with her boyfriend," said a voice that Chloe had thought she'd only have spoken to her in her dreams. "If you hurry, you may catch up with them."

Chloe went to stand and banged her head on the shelf in her locker. "Ow!" Chloe rubbed the top of her head. "Do you know where they went?"

He shrugged. Even his shrug was hot.

"Poo. Hey, what's your name?" she asked. He went back to his notebook. She didn't see a textbook, so Chloe figured he was either an artist or a poet. Chloe tried not to show embarrassment when he ignored her. After all, he was a senior, and he was probably just trying to be polite.

"Neil."

"What?" Chloe asked.

"You asked my name. Neil," he said, closing the book. He clutched his left arm with his right hand when he stood.

He was better than a dream. "Chloe. I'm Chloe." She wasn't sure if she was telling him or reminding herself. She then saw the way he held his arm. "You... are you hurt?"

"Not really," he said. He wasn't wearing his jacket. He had on a simple black t-shirt that seemed just slightly tight across his chest and at his biceps. She could see rips in the fabric of his sleeve. "Nothing I couldn't handle. Your friend's boyfriend is powerful, but slow. He should practice more often, or pick opponents he's sure to defeat."

"You... were in a fight with Mike?" Chloe asked. That wasn't right. Neil shouldn't have been able to fight Mike. Not that she wanted Mike to hurt him. She remembered going to her cousin's judo match, and figured it was possible for someone smaller to win against someone in another weight category. "You don't look like much of a fighter. Not that I'd know. Fighters usually have that look to them. Um..." Why was she babbling so much? "My friend's mom's a nurse. Want me to take a look at that?" Jane was the one with the first aid training, but Chloe knew enough to tell if something was bad. He let her touch him. She rolled up his sleeve. His skin was very firm, and slightly cold. Chloe realized her palms were sweaty.

Neil's arm was swollen and bruised at the back of his elbow, only the bruise was slightly grey rather than purple or blue. Chloe found it odd, but pinched his fingernails. "You got circulation – it doesn't look broken. Does it hurt? Is it sore?" she asked.

"You're shaking," Neil said. He was so close she could smell his breath. Vanilla cookies.

"Low blood sugar," she lied.

"You don't like the sight of blood, do you?" Neil asked.

"No," Chloe said, "I don't like it when people get hurt."

She wasn't expecting him to take her chin in his hand. "You don't look well. Can I see you home?"

Chloe forgot that she had the car, and tried think of the most refined way to accept. "Okie-dokie," she managed.

~*~

Mike opened his left eye briefly, and put the piece of raw steak back over it. Jane wondered if his parents were still going to eat it for dinner. "I can't believe that little pisser got me."

"He's not that little," Jane said. "You know how skinny guys are."

"No. Do you?" Mike asked.

Jane frowned. "I'm just trying to make you feel better."

"Mission accomplished," he said, rolling his good eye.

Jane kept trying to throw her hair back into a pony, but it was being even more stubborn than usual. It wouldn't stay, and the holder kept falling out. What was even weirder, was that it seemed to be behaving while it was down. She didn't leave his side since the fight, but she cast a glance in the office mirror – she was still sweaty from gym, but her hair looked fantastic. Still, she wasn't used to it loose and she kept thinking about what that new kid l told her about her hair. It seemed softer and shinier than normal, too. "Is there a bathroom I can use?"

"Yeah, it's by the front door."

He didn't have to be rude. Jane didn't bother to use the bathroom, but slammed the main door on her way out. As if on cue, the sky thundered. She was half way down the street when she heard a familiar ring tone. Mike had given her his cell phone when he was pulled into the principal's office to explain himself – so the principal couldn't get his parents' work phone numbers, Mike said. She grabbed Mike's cell from her Capri pockets. She glanced at the number. "Hey Trevor, it's Jane."

"Can I speak to Mike?" Trevor asked.

"I left him at home. I forgot I had his phone," Jane said.

"Careful, it's his lifeline," Trevor said. "You should take it back to him. I'll call his house. Are you alright, Janey?"

"Uh huh," Jane didn't feel like speaking to him. "Bye Trevor." It was spitting when she made it back to Mike's house, but there was a black van in the driveway that wasn't there when she left. Jane knocked on the door, and was greeted by Mike's older brother. "Here's Mike's cell. How's he doing?"

"Do you know what happened?" he asked.

"Earl! Invite whoever it is inside, it's raining out!" Jane didn't listen. She quickly raced down the driveway, and tried to think of a route that wouldn't involve her getting soaked by the time she got home. She looked up at the sky, and figured it was only a matter of time before the skies opened up. She didn't make it down the block when she was nearly run over by a brown pick-up truck.

"Get in here!" Mike hollered from the driver's seat.

"I'm fine!" Jane shouted back.

"It's gonna pour!" Mike yelled. "Get in here now!"

"I'm not gonna melt," Jane snapped.

He swung the truck in front of her path, and got out. "I ruined dinner, we're ordering pizza now," he said. "I need you to convince my mother that it was the other creep's fault. Can you do that?"

"I'll have to call my mother," Jane said. He had her at *we're ordering pizza.*

~*~

Jane was going to kill her. Jane really needed a cell phone. Chloe wished she had someone to call besides Bethany, because Janice was going to be livid. Upon entering her empty home, she swiped a diet soda and her puppy and plopped down on her bed. "Bethany, you wouldn't believe who asked me out this weekend?!" Chloe said right after she recognized Bethany's *Hello?*

"Is it Todd?" Bethany asked.

"What?" Chloe asked.

"He dumped me," Bethany said. "He said my preference for the force interfered with the prime directive."

"Oh, that's too bad," Chloe said, puzzled but wanting no explanation. "You're putting a damper on my news."

"He had a camera," Bethany muttered. "Now I have to rewrite this script and turn it into a musical."

"Well, I hope that works out," Chloe said, unsure how to proceed with the breakup until what Bethany said sunk in. "Wait, you want to make a musical with zombies?"

"Why not?" Bethany asked. "I'll write the story, and you can write the music."

"I'm not a composer," Chloe said. "I just play the flute! You play the oboe."

"Badly. You also play the piano!"

Chloe thought of a terrible zombie scene with some classical Bach – Double Violin Concerto in D minor. She pushed the image from her mind. "Are you okay, Bethany? You want me to come over?" Chloe asked.

"I'm as good as I'll ever be. May need to go up to the cabin one more time to wallow in misery," Bethany said. "You going to keep me in the dark about this mystery date, or what?"

"Neil asked me out!" Chloe said. "We're going to an instrumental presentation!"

"Who is Neil," Bethany asked, "and what's an instrumental presentation?"

"Neil's the cute guy in Span- wait, you don't take Spanish. He's really, really, really gorgeous! And a musical presentation is just us in a bookstore while several people play music," Chloe said. "We're going to talk about literature and film." She giggled when Shiloh licked her nose.

"Chloe, can you name a film?" Bethany asked.

"Yes!" Chloe was relieved when Bethany didn't call her bluff.

"Ask him to come to the cabin with us on Saturday," Bethany said.

"What's the weather supposed to be like this weekend?" Chloe asked.

"Hot, like summer," Bethany asked.

"Sounds good to me. I got Friday and Saturday off from the restaurant," Chloe said. "Are you inviting Jane and Mike too?"

"Whoever," Bethany said.

"Mike and Neil were in that fight at school today," Chloe said.

"The one in the cafeteria or the one where we had to stay behind in band?" Bethany asked.

"There was a fight in the cafeteria? The band room! My locker got punched in. Oh! I need to go get my car!" Chloe realized.

"Where is it?" Bethany asked.

"At school," Chloe asked. "Neil took me home on his motorcycle."

"Wait, Mike got into a fight with someone?" Bethany asked. "And he was able to walk you home afterwards?"

"Neil said they hardly touched each other," Chloe said. "His shoulder was a little bruised, but he was alright. I asked him what they were fighting over, and he said that there was a misunderstanding. Jane's not home yet, though."

"So will you write the music for me?" Bethany asked.

"Will you make it about something not weird?" Chloe asked.

"I'll think about it," Bethany said.

They chatted for half an hour about nothing, about how the bathing suits were on sale but Chloe never really wore anything cute anyway, just a one piece and a sarong or some shorts. Chloe had already gotten the car, changed from her wet clothes, phoned Janice, consoled Janice, said she'd put a nice word in with his two friends, and scolded her puppy for tearing up her magazine before she did any of the quizzes. Shiloh was sleeping on her sweater and Chloe was sick of practicing the flute when Jane decided to grace her with a phone call.

"Hey Chloe, sorry I didn't wait around," Jane said. "Mike got into a fight today, and he kinda needed me. You mind if we study together tomorrow? It's getting late."

"I heard," Chloe said, "the guy he tried to beat up is taking me out on Friday."

"What?" Jane asked.

"Neil said it was a misunderstanding and Mike attacked him. He says he could have paralyzed him, so he just taught Mike a lesson. Chivalrous, no?"

"How could you go out with that creep?" Jane asked.

"He's a perfect gentleman, Jane," Chloe said. "We're going to a literary musical festival at a bookstore. Where's Mike taking you, bowling?"

"Mike's grounded for the next two weeks."

"Grounded?" Chloe asked. "He turns 18 in January!"

"His father pointed out that's still several months away," Jane said.

"Why did Mike try to fight him, anyway?" Chloe asked.

"He hurt Mike a lot more than Mike hurt him!" Jane said. "Mike's face was all swollen, and I think he may have hurt his wrist when he punched that locker."

"Our locker," Chloe said. "Neil and I talked about Shakespeare – his favourite's *A Midsummer Night's Dream* – just like me! I forgot to ask about Mike."

"I thought you liked Romeo and Jul-"

"No! Juliet is like, kinda fickle, Jane. The more I think about it, the more the entire plot could have been avoided if she told her parents about Romeo and not went along with his being a dummy. I mean, he was totally into her cousin-"

"Can we get back to the real problem?" Jane asked.

"We have a problem?" Chloe asked.

"Chloe, this entire thing is weird," Jane said. "I mean, this all started because I thought I hit him with my ponytail, and he... well, he took my hair down, then he touched my face," Jane said.

"Mike is facing suspension because Neil accidently pulled your ponytail?" Chloe asked.

"Chloe, it was weird," Jane said, "and he was creeping me out. I think he startled me, and Mike jumped to my rescue."

"A real knight in rusted armour," Chloe said. She stuck out her tongue, and wished her best friend could see it over the phone.

"Hey, at least he has his own ride," Jane said. "And that's not the other weird part. During the fight, Mike couldn't hit him. It was so weird. And then, when the TA came, it was almost like Neil wasn't... really there. He was, but he wasn't... I don't even know how to describe it. You know how in movies, sometimes people move in regular motion, only the world's in slow-motion? It was kinda like that, only he wasn't moving super fast or anything. Everyone was watching the fight, only they moved out of his way when he was done. They didn't turn their heads to watch him go."

"Did you?"

"Yes. He singled me out," Jane said.

"You saw him, so it's not like he turned himself invisible," Chloe said. "You sound like Bethany."

"Chloe, it was weird," Jane said. "And... there's more."

"Oh?"

"My hair looks fantastic."

"...did Neil attack you with some conditioning cream?"

"Don't be ridiculous, Chloe."

"I think you're the one being ridiculous. What could he have possibly done just by touching your hair?"

Jan hesitated, then said, "I guess you're right. Maybe I'm just having a good hair day for once."

"Bethany's inviting us to her aunt's cabin for the weekend," Chloe said. "The one at Lester Beach. I'll invite Neil, you invite Mike, and the two can make amends."

"I don't think they'll want to be buddies," Jane said. "Besides, Mike's grounded."

"It is a big beach, if that's the case. Talk Mike into it," Chloe said. "I'm sure his parents'll give him another chance if he tries to act like a grown-up."

"I dunno," Jane said.

"Phone Bethany up anyway," Chloe said. "Todd dumped her."

"Is she alright?" Jane asked.

"She was too good for that loser," Chloe said. "If we go on IM, we can console her together."

"Our computer is being used by my sister," Jane said. "We all don't have personal laptops."

"I don't know how you survive some days," Chloe said.

"You're telling me."

~*~

It was hard to get a hold of Mike. Jane assumed his line was busy with his parents probably arguing with the principal and Mike was probably trying to quench the bloodlust of the troops. Jane had to explain to her little brother that Mike didn't want to have the fist of death descend upon Neil. "The beach? With him?" Mike asked.

"Chloe likes him," Jane said. "You don't know Chloe. Once she has her mind set on something you can't argue with her until it blows up in her face. Think about it: if he tries anything, you can beat him up and get everyone to apologize to you."

Mike paused for too long. Eventually, he asked, "What if I can't beat him up?"

"What do you mean?" Jane asked.

"I've been looking up different fighting techniques online with my brother," he said, "and we can't find what he did."

"Well, he was moving so fast-"

"I'm not allowed to do anything extracurricular for two weeks because of him," Mike said. "I'm lucky they're not kicking me out of class!"

"So try to tell your parents that you want to make nice with this guy," Jane said. "Please? I'd feel better if you were there."

"I have the morning shift."

"I can wait for you, and we can drive out together."

"Nah, there's only so many nice days left where we're not chained to our desks," Mike said. "Besides, I'm grounded, remember? I have to talk to my parents. If I tell them I'm concerned for your safety, they might go for it. I should be there by four. In time for a late swim, dinner, fire on the beach..."

"When you know for sure, I'll call Bethany and let her know," Jane said, "You ever been to her aunt and uncle's cabin?"

"Nope, but I like the challenge of finding places," he said, "I'm walking you home every day from now on. No excuses."

Jane tried not to sound immature and giggle. "Alright," she said, "Bye, Mike."

4

Pearls

Pearls

Despite being back in school for a week, it still felt like summer as they made the drive to Lester Beach. It was more than warm enough to swim in Lake Winnipeg, but Chloe didn't feel like putting on a one piece in front of Neil, much less that cute little polka-dot number she spotted in one of the shops when they gassed up in the beachcomber town of Grand Marais.

Bethany had a large, extended family that all used the cottage. Bethany was the oldest child of three, and her sisters had invited their friends, and her cousins had invited their friends – there was no shortage of teens trying to fit into the tiny cabin's parking space and use the bathroom, though Bethany's uncle was taking his middle-school aged kids and their friends out on their boat out to go fishing, and Chloe ended up with live bait all over her towel.

Chloe would have preferred they go to Grand Beach or even Gimli, but then one of Bethany's cute neighbours came over, and suggested they go down to the beach. Chloe may have been taken, but he was in his first year of university, and she saw it as a chance he'd drop some terminology that Neil would eat up.

Seadoos raked the distance, and Chloe could see tubers and water-skiers from the cabin porch. They'd have to walk down to the beach-front, but it was more than easy to see the beach from the cottage patio. She watched Bethany's uncle take off in their old jeep with the youngest gaggle to head towards the docks and launch the boat.

"No sign of your boy yet, hey?" Jane asked Chloe.

Chloe knew she was jealous. Mike had managed to convince his parents to let him come to the beach, but he was still grounded. The closest thing to a date Jane had last night was a movie night with Bethany.

Chloe and Neil spent the entire evening with college kids and a real writer even – discussing politics and the state of art. Chloe hadn't realized how dismal the world had gotten, but now that she was properly educated, she was going to do everything in her power to stop a certain zombie musical from ever being seen by the public. Neil even got her a glass of wine. She didn't like it, but Chloe didn't want to act like a child, and besides, her parents gave her a drink last Christmas. Jane just went, "Yeah. Uh huh." The entire car ride out. Bethany at least was a good listener – or she was working on her script in the backseat. Chloe was driving, so she couldn't tell. Jane's hair looked nicer - maybe she'd finally admit that she tried to give herself a perm a few years back and it finally grew out. It was nice to see her dark hair cascading over her shoulders rather than look like she was just stepping off a Hudderite colony.

Chloe heard an engine. Neil pulled up on a sleek black motorcycle, and took off his helmet. "Sorry, had a hard time finding this place," he said, and ran his fingers through his hair. "Is it alright if I park here?"

"How can you afford one of these?" one of Bethany's cousins asked. Several of Bethany's cousins lost interest in the beach preparations and went to inspect the bike.

"Discipline," Neil shrugged. "I packed light, if that's alright." He shrugged off his backpack and put his helmet on the red leather seat. "It's alright if I park here?"

"Yeah," Bethany said quietly, before looking at Chloe, her bespeckled eyes saying *I see what you mean.*

Eventually, everyone made their way down to the beach. When the blankets and towels were set, there was a lot of sand kicking and people vying for choice space and someone set up a volleyball net.

"You coming swimming?" Jane asked Chloe, taking her shirt off, revealing a navy bikini top. Jane had no curves, instead she was blessed with natural skinniness, and her sportiness had given her a trim abdomen and toned shoulders. It was easy enough to add a little bit of padding, rather than cover up problem areas.

Chloe shook her head. "Not right now. Maybe later."

"Care for a walk along the beach?" Neil asked Chloe.

Chloe tried not to get too excited, or too proud for the offer. It wasn't like they were avoiding the others, merely hanging out in different areas. It's not like everyone was in the water, or playing volleyball.

"So, what do you think of Manitoba so far?" she asked.

"When I first came, I expected polar bears and beavers," Neil said.

Chloe had seen both in Winnipeg's Zoo, though she'd accidentally stumbled across an old abandoned beaver dam on a class hike back in grade four. "It won't last long," she said. "It's green now, but the leaves will be red and orange and we'll have snow before you know it. Is it cold, where you lived before?"

Neil looked out towards the floating dock where the others jumped and splashed. "My home can be very warm, or very cold, but not much ever changes. It must be beautiful, when the leaves begin to die."

Chloe opened her mouth, but paused. She never thought of autumn like that. "So what made you move here in your senior year?" she asked. "Especially to come to a place like Winnipeg."

"My parents," he said.

"Yeah, I know completely. They think we're kids and trying to run our lives all the while telling us to grow up," she said.

"What are your dreams, Chloe?" Neil asked.

Chloe opened her mouth, but closed it just as fast. There was the stereotypical, "I just want to be loved." But there was more to it than that. She dreamed of a career of film, to sing. Everyone wanted that. Those sounded childish. What else was there to say? To travel, to see the world? How was she any different than anyone else?

"You're thinking too much."

"There's more to my dreams that can be said in a single sentence," she said, blushing. "I suppose I want to dance. How about you?"

"A dancer?" he asked. "What sort? Ballet? Hip-hop? Not ballroom?"

"No fair," Chloe said, "tell me yours."

"You must have danced when you were younger," Neil said. "You walk like one who danced, but is scared to now."

Chloe tried to see his eyes through his shades. His slender lips revealed nothing. "What do you mean?" she asked.

"I mean, Chloe, you're scared to follow your dreams," Neil said. "You live life for someone else, the way others expect you to. Isn't that right?"

Chloe looked out to the lake, and then back to her friends. "I gave it up when I realized I wasn't very good at it," she said.

"I'm sure you were good at it. You have the passion for it," he said.

What to say? When she hit puberty so young and she no longer looked good in their outfits? There wasn't enough exercise in the world to keep her looking like one of them. She'd seen old family portraits. No grown woman had the body of a real ballerina. She might as well slap on the babushka and be done with it. All the hours she spent in dance studio meant nothing. "Passion doesn't mean anything," she said. "It doesn't matter if you're not right for it."

"You're wrong. Passion is a light in the darkness, a flicker of fire against the cold wind in a storm. It stands out, but only too easily its snuffed out," he told her, looking out to the water. Chloe tried to follow his gaze, and thought he was looking at two people kayaking in the distance. "What do you know about pearls?"

She didn't know anything about pearls besides that they came from the ocean, and living in Southern Manitoba was just about as far as one could get from an ocean. She stopped thinking when he started taking his shirt off. She was expecting him to be slightly skinny, but his back and shoulders were incredible, a perfect mix of musculature and lanky grace. He tossed her his shirt, and began to unzip his pants. Chloe turned her head. "It's hard to find real pearls, they're very rare. You see, in the past they were considered a luxury. Many oysters had to be brought up by slaves. Pearl divers used to drown in the pursuit of something so rare, and so small. Now, pearls are bred. While one can say beauty is now in common supply, it's truly never captured. It fades only to hate its replacement." He waded out to the water, and paused when it became knee deep. "You can watch." He had trunks on. He tossed his pants to the shore and waded out to about waist high. Chloe felt her cheeks burn. "What would you give me in exchange for a pearl?"

"I haven't gotten anything." She left her purse in her trunk. "Besides, where are you going get a pearl from?" He certainly couldn't have one. She could see quite clearly he had no pockets. Besides, pearls weren't found in freshwater – were they?

"I'll think of something," he said, and dove.

Chloe didn't think the water was deep. The muddy Manitoba waters meant that she couldn't see past two feet in the water. She waited. "Neil?" she asked. She had her suit on underneath, but despite her clam diggers waded out until she was knee deep. "Neil, this isn't funny." She took off her own shirt in a hurry to dive. She knew a little about pulling people out of the water, but she didn't think she was strong enough to do much other than maybe drag him back to the beach – maybe, and the others were far away. "Don't tell me you hit your head!" He surfaced suddenly. He rose too high, the water seemed to propel him up. Chloe dropped her belt and her pink clam diggers fell to the water. Neil looked amazing wet.

"You have tan lines," he said with a grin. "Now that you're in the water, you might as well come here."

"You scared me!" Chloe shouted, annoyed that her pants were wet.

"We should have brought towels," Neil said, running his fingers through his hair.

Chloe threw her soggy pants back to the shore and waded to him. There was a sudden drop off, but Chloe could swim easily enough.

He put out his hand and she saw a mussel. "They don't have pearls," Chloe said.

It did. He made her put out her hand and he plopped it out. "Too bad it has to die for us to get the beauty within, but I suppose that's the way of this world," he said. He put a hand on her cheek and stroked it, and kissed her. Chloe almost pulled away, almost objected, but he felt so strong, and she felt safe in his embrace. She nearly dropped the pearl, but he clasped a hand about hers and said, "You need to take care of something like that."

"What are you?" Chloe asked, her voice quivering. She felt faint suddenly, but she was alright. She was with Neil, and he carried her out of the cold water, back to the shore. She heard Jane's voice, but Chloe couldn't be bothered. She had Neil, and everything was perfect.

~*~

Jane almost didn't buy the sunstroke excuse, except that it was Chloe. Chloe was the first to sit in the shade and still complain if she was uncomfortable. She'd find a needle in a haystack because she'd sit down on it, and would need stitches.

"We should take her to the hospital," Bethany said once they had Chloe in the relatively cool den and on the couch.

"That's a good distance from here," Jane said.

"Then we should call the mounties or whatever they got round here," Bethany's neighbour said. "They know first aid."

"I know first aid," Jane muttered. "If we keep her cool, she should be alright."

"She will be fine," Neil said.

Jane heard a can pop from the kitchen. She didn't think anything of it at first, but Bethany got up. "What are you thinking? Give that here!"

"It's open!" her cousin snapped back at her. "Learn to live a little, nerd!"

Bethany continued into a rehearsed drill about the likelihood of an aunt or uncle returning anytime now, and it would be a shame if no one was allowed to use the cabin – ever again – so if underage drinking was to be done, *do it on the beach.*

Chloe stirred and Jane should have retaken her spot instead of watching the drama in the kitchen. She turned to see Neil in her spot right next to Chloe, assuring Chloe that she was going to be alright. "I feel so dumb," Chloe said.

"Don't," Neil said.

Jane glanced at Bethany, who had gotten flack from the three teens. A shout came up when Bethany's aunt's Chevy drove up. "Real macho," Bethany said as the unopened beers were quickly thrown back into the fridge and the open ones were guzzled, though most of it ended down the kitchen sink.

"How are you feeling?" Jane asked Chloe.

"Terrible," Chloe admitted, sitting up. She smiled at Jane, and then looked back at Neil. "What happened?"

"You just rest now," Neil said. "Do you want something to drink?"

"I'm not thirsty."

Heatstroke! She should have been aching and asking for water. Jane didn't try to mask her displeasure while Neil shushed Chloe, and after she sipped from his water bottle, she settled back down and closed her eyes. Neil caught Jane's eyes, and smiled, before standing. "She should be alright after a slight rest." Jane took his spot and checked Chloe's temperature, made difficult by the icy cloth. "I should go. It was good to meet all of you," he smiled, "but I've duties to attend to."

"I suppose they teach medicine at the country club," Bethany muttered after he left the room. "Mind watching him?"

Jane pretended to need to use the bathroom as Neil changed in it, but once he left she grabbed a tissue and quickly followed Neil outside. He was putting on his helmet just as Mike arrived in his truck. The two acknowledged one another by nods. Jane watched from the patio. "How's your arm?" Mike asked.

"How's your eye?" Neil asked.

Most of the bruising had disappeared, though there was still a sign of slight purple mottling around his eye. Trevor hopped out and slid the seat forward, letting the third rider out. Jane smiled when she recognized her little brother. "Who said you could invite the geek?" she asked.

"I thought this was geek central," Paul said, climbing out of the back. "This the tough guy?"

Paul was the tallest in Jane's family, at fifteen he was almost the same height as Mike. "That's enough, Paul," Jane said. "Try to be friends."

"Yeah right," Neil said, revving his engine. "See you around, Jane." He pulled out.

Jane watched him disappear behind a cottage, and then looked back to the newcomers. She didn't like Mike's expression. "What?" she asked.

"Stay away from him," Mike said.

"It be easier if he wasn't dating my best friend," Jane crossed her arm. She invited Mike and Trevor into Bethany's family cabin and was glad her little brother managed to follow without being misled by the underage drinking taking place at another nearby cabin. "Chloe got a bit too much sun."

"She alright?" Mike asked.

"She's cooled down," Bethany said, "You guys just got here?"

"Just as Neil left," Trevor said.

"Neil left?" Chloe bolted upright. Jane didn't think she was awake.

"Yeah, real hero, leaving you while you're down-" Jane said.

"But we had plans for later tonight!" Chloe said.

"I thought you were going to be with us," Jane muttered.

"For the day!" Chloe said. "I have plans with him tonight! Let me up!"

"Chloe, I think you need to rest. What time were your plans?" Bethany asked.

"Tonight, at eight," she said. "He said to dress nice and not to eat."

"I'll drive you back to the city if you calm down," Jane said, catching Mike's frown. "You're not in any shape to go anywhere."

"But he said-"

"Jane's right," Bethany said. "You should cancel."

"But he's been planning this night! That wouldn't be fair to him!" Chloe said. "Besides, Mike just got here, you should really spend time with your boyfriend!! I'll be better in no time."

Chloe was never one for doing as she was told to improve her physical well being if it involved anything more then aspirin, but she listened to Mike's advice and seemed better by five. "Are you sure you have to go?" Bethany asked as Chloe packed up her parent's corolla.

"I'll be fine," Chloe said. "You guys have fun tonight. I have to work tomorrow – see you at school on Monday!"

"What about tomorrow night?" Jane asked. "I thought we were watching movies at my place!"

"We can do that anytime," Chloe said. "Later!"

"I'm glad you're not like that," Mike said as the blue toyota sped down the gravel road and roared back towards Winnipeg.

"Is it almost time to start having fun yet?" Paul asked.

"You guys hungry?" Jane asked. "Bethany, what have we got to eat around here?"

"Chips and stuff. Maybe if my cousins manage to catch something, we'll have something that resembles dinner," she said. "Hope nobody's allergic to fish."

"They have to catch it first," Jane said.

Bethany shrugged. "If not, we pop over to my cousin Hannah's place." Jane had no idea what neighbours lived in which cottage, just the general zone of 'okay to hang'. "I smell burgers."

"This place is like a food court," Paul said, popping a root beer he'd brought from the city. "You don't like what they're having at your house, you go bug your neighbours."

"Bethany can, not so sure about us," Jane said, helping herself to a cream soda from her brother's cooler.

They nabbed burgers and ketchup chips just in time for one of Bethany's cousins to shout, "Hey, the boat's back!" They'd been more successful than Jane had anticipated, but the pickerel would no doubt be divided among the young fishermen. As they began to filet the fish, Bethany's uncle tossed her the keys to his boat.

"Sweet," Bethany said, licking her fingers clean. "Anyone here have their boater's license besides me? I want to use my kneeboard."

5

My Best Friend's Keeper

Jane found Chloe the next day at her hostess stand, mall entrance, trying to stay awake after the lunch rush. "I thought you had no money," Chloe said with a yawn when she saw Jane.

"I'm putting out resumes," Jane said.

"Do you like them?" Chloe pointed to her new tear-drop pearl earrings.

"Where did you go last night?"

"Paddleboat cruise," Chloe beamed. "Neil gave them to me. I thought my dad was going to kill him when we got home so late."

"I thought you had to be eighteen to go on the paddleboat," Jane said.

"He got us on," Chloe said. "Besides, I look eighteen, don't I?"

"If you were eighteen, you'd be serving tables, and making tips," Jane said. "At least, that's what I'd be doing. Not everyone has parents who give them everything."

"Hey, I pay for my own gas," Chloe said, digging into her private den in the hostess stand. "Wanna see the bathing suit I bought for next time?"

"You bought a new suit?" Jane asked. "A bikini?"

"Shush!"

It was unsurprisingly pink with a few silver flowers that screamed *sexy*; whenever Jane bought flowers on anything they tended to scream *Grandma called*. Jane looked for the skirt bottom, instead found something that resembled a normal bathing suit bottom. Chloe wasn't fat, but she was always complaining that her hips and thighs were too big. Jane had no real opinion on her friend's body other than that Chloe had cleavage and she didn't loom over half their class, and that was what all guys wanted anyway. "What sarong will you wear with it?"

"I dunno. Neil liked going to the beach, and he wants to go again soon," Chloe smiled.

"It's September."

"It was on sale and when we go to Australia I want to look good! I wish we were hiring here! You could take my shifts!"

"Are they hiring?" Jane asked.

"I dunno," Chloe said with a shrug.

Jane handed in a resume, hoping for something better than dishwasher, but continued into the mall and handed out at the places she wanted to work first, then realizing a job was a job until she could be choosy, and handed out in some of the other places that she could never afford, but it was nice to dream of a discount.

She spotted Neil right after she handed in a resume in one of the shoe stores. Jane did a double take; they didn't sell men's shoes in the boutique. "Looking for something to match your belt?" she asked.

Neil looked at her, smiled, and then said, "Thank-you for taking care of Chloe yesterday after I left."

"Somebody had to," Jane said. "I didn't see you before I entered the store. You're not following me, are you?"

"I'm shopping, Jane," he said simply. Jane wondered how he could be so condescending without using sarcasm. "That is what this place is for, is it not?" He showed her a pair of bronze-coloured high-heeled sandals.

Jane felt crimson rise in her cheeks when she saw the number. Jane knew Chloe's size was 6 ½ wide, but he shouldn't have known that. "You know that Chloe works in this mall?"

"I thought I'd surprise her."

"You started dating five days ago," Jane said.

"I'm very much in love," he said. "Are you angry it's her, not you?"

"Excuse me?" Jane felt herself ask.

"Try these on." He handed her a pair of turquoise open-toed sandals, size 11.

"Pardon me?"

"You heard me."

"Why should I?" They were very pretty sandals, but Jane knew the store as one she'd never actually shop in because the shoes could be several hundred dollars. She wasn't going to put on anything she wasn't going to buy.

"Humour me."

Jane didn't know why she consented, perhaps she was tired of walking around in her too tight older sister's black work shoes and needed to air her feet. Her toenails definitely could have used a new coat of glitter polish, the day at the beach had softened her rough skin but she had definite tan lines from her flip-flops.

"You're doing it wrong," he said.

"I think I know how to put on a pair of sandals," Jane said, and nearly kneed him in the head when he knelt down.

There were definitely people looking when he slid the first sandal on. "Like this."

"I was doing fine on my own!" she snapped.

He took her other foot and slipped the other sandal on. Jane frowned and crossed her arms, and glowered as harsh as she could, despite remembering Bethany told her she looked like an angry kitten when she tried. "Aren't you going to stand up?" Neil asked.

"I'll be surprised if I can walk in them. I'm too tall as it is already," she said, but he grabbed her hands and Jane kept herself from toppling onto him.

"Take a step," he said. "I won't let you fall."

She wrenched her hands away from him and plopped down to get the shoes off. She looked at the price tag, and hoped she didn't scratch them or do anything that warranted a mandatory buy.

"I knew you were jealous," Neil said, before looking at the nearest clerk. "I'll take them in 6 ½ wide."

"You're a jerk," Jane snapped. "Besides, Chloe doesn't have a shoe fetish." Chloe liked hats, but he didn't need to know that. "What sort of high school boyfriend goes out and buys their five-day girlfriend a pair of expensive sandals? You hardly know her!"

"You're cute when you're angry."

Jane had just about enough of handing out resumes at the mall, and decided to call it a day and dipped into her university fund to get herself an ice cap. *It would be easier if I could just get a job in a restaurant where I can make tips*, she muttered to herself, determined to see that brat Chloe flirting with all the cute guys at the mall, instead saw her bussing a table and narrowly avoiding a tray-laden server. Jane also spotted Neil waiting to be seated.

"She's not a server," said another young hostess at the stand.

"That's who I'd like to be served by. You've enough other girls to clean," Neil said, and then motioned with his head, giving his hair a casual flip. "In the lounge."

"Chloe's only sixteen," said the girl, who was probably seventeen.

"She doesn't look sixteen," Neil said, leaning in, and smiled.

The hostess smiled, batted her eyes, and twirled her hair around a finger. "I'll see what I can do," she said.

Jane felt disgust, mostly from watching how the hostess reacted. Most of the women in the mall – young, old, with boyfriends, or with their small children - were casting glances or openly gawking at him. Neil looked over his shoulder and caught Jane's eyes. "Care to join me?" He had a gift box with a giant pink, sparkly bow tie. "My treat."

"I'm going to enjoy this blowing up in your face," Jane said.

He blew Jane a kiss as he was led to the lounge, where he sat, almost posing like a man much older - it was almost like he was leaking refinement. He treated his onlookers to undoing the top button of his collar. Jane found a table in the food court where she could watch unobstructed, and stirred her ice cap like a witch ready to cast a spell.

"Neil!" Chloe squealed when she saw him. Jane had to reposition herself when a gaggle of fourteen-year-old girls sat in front of her, one started to snap pictures of Neil on her phone. "I should have known when they said a customer insisted!"

"Hello Cinderella," he said, "I suppose I must order something so they don't throw me out. What do you recommend?"

"Um... you like sushi, or a full dinner?" Chloe asked. "We can do soup and salad, something spicy, a sandwich, or pizza...?"

"Spicy."

"The curried chicken's really good," Chloe said.

"I'll get that and a sparkling water," Neil said. "Hurry back."

Chloe, you're making an idiot out of yourself, Jane thought, and then noticed the mall population about her. *Why is everybody watching?*

Chloe came back way too soon, complete with straw, slice of lemon and a chilled mug from the beer cooler. "Thank you, Chloe. Sit down."

"I can't," she said, "I'm working."

"And I'm a paying customer," Neil said, standing up and getting the chair for her.

"Neil, you can't do this," Chloe said with a big dumb grin on her face and letting him spoil her. "You're going to get me in trouble."

"I'm starting to think you rather adore trouble."

Chloe giggled as she sat down. Jane looked for the general manager of the restaurant – he would put an end to this. The general manager was out, but the supervisor that was in was about twenty-eight years old, and gawking from the bar with the rest of the female staff. "I really had fun last night," Chloe said.

"I want to take you out again, tonight."

"It's a school night!"

"So? I won't keep you forever," he said. "Dancing starts at seven, though I expect you to be fashionably late." He slid the box across the table. "When are you done here?"

"Oh Neil, they're beautiful," Chloe cooed, then looked thoughtful. "Dancing?"

"Yes, at the Pavilion downtown," he said. "I've never been, but you know where that is, I hope."

"You're talking about dancing in the Forks Market Square," she said. "People will see, Neil."

"You danced with me yesterday," Neil said.

"Nobody knew me on that ship," Chloe said. "Have you ever been to something like that here in the city? There's always a lot of people, and someone I know might be there."

"People noticed last night, Chloe. Come on, Cinderella. Don't you want to go to the ball?" Neil asked.

"I don't know," Chloe said. "I mean, I have an essay due on Tuesday and I haven't even started..."

"Do I have to buy you an entire outfit?"

"Stop it!" Chloe said. "Fine, I'll go. But my father's forbidden me from riding on your motorcycle. He says they're dangerous."

"He has no idea," Neil said, and grinned.

"Alright," Chloe said. "Let me go check on your curry."

Neil watched her go and then went back to a book he brought with him – a notebook, though Jane doubted he was doing anything scholarly with it. Another server came by to ask him if he needed anything. Neil didn't look up at her; he merely waived her away.

Jane had been in Chloe's staff bathroom before. It was small, but relatively classy, for the girls in that restaurant were expected to look good. Jane was never sure what the perfume was but it always smelled expensive. She didn't get near it when she heard the combined squealing, and recognized Chloe's excited squeal above them all. Jane shook her head, and checked the time. The bus would be coming soon. *I think I'm done,* she figured, and made her way from the food court, and wished she had a cell phone, but rationalized Mike would be at work, and if he wasn't, he was grounded. She made it to the bus loop in time to see her bus leave. It was Sunday so the next bus wouldn't come for an hour. She was tempted to walk just to enjoy the air, or head over to one of the other stores in the parking lot to waste time, but her feet were tired of being pinched, so she made her way back to the bus stop, and plunked down on the least scabby-looking bench and rummaged through her purse for her copy of *The Simarrilion*.

She heard the roar of the motorcycle before Luthien gave up her immortality. "Get on," Neil ordered.

"I have bus tickets, thank you," Jane said, trying not to look at him.

"I have an extra helmet."

"I'm fine waiting for the bus," Jane said.

"I have to go to Charleswood anyway," Neil said. "Do I have to get off and beg you? Get on."

There weren't a lot of people waiting for that bus, but the last thing she needed was someone noticing and making a scene, especially after what he did in the shoe shop. If the foot court was any indication, he might cause a car accident. Jane put the helmet on, and slid behind him. "Hold tight," he said, "You don't live far from Chloe, right?"

"About six blocks away. Head over the bridge, and I'll tell you where to go once we're closer," she said. She couldn't help but hold tight as he accelerated. Jane felt as she was flying as he sped across the four lanes way to quickly, zig-zagging in and out of traffic as they made their way over the Assiniboine River, over the bridge and turning right at the entrance to the Assiniboine Park. He took the scenic route and slowed down.

"Did that scare you?" he asked.

Jane decided he couldn't flirt with her if she didn't give him anything to work with. When they stopped at a red light, he lifted his visor, but she kept hers down. "You are most ungrateful for the ride home."

"I told you I was fine with waiting for the bus."

"I wasn't about to leave a lady I knew at the bus shelter when I was going the same way and had a spare seat," he said. "I can take you back to the bus shelter, if you prefer."

"Please just take me home," Jane said.

"You want to try driving?" he asked, pulling over, and stepping off, then sliding behind her despite her protests. Jane had always wanted to ride a motorcycle, but it never occurred to her it might become an economic reality. The downside, was that it was Neil's motorcycle. "I won't let you kill us. It would spoil my date with Chloe tonight."

"I don't know how to-" He wrapped his hand around the accelerator, and did all the driving for her. It felt strangely safe. "I don't have a license for this thing!"

"You have to learn somehow!"

It was much better than being on the bus. Neil knew just when to accelerate and make her nervous, but he eased up and let her squeal the brakes more than once. She was starting to get the hang of it when she realized he was not making an effort to leave the park – just circle round it, the slowest way possible, of course, but given the late summer weather, with people with their families and dogs soaking in the last summer days. Neil suggested that they do another lap, but she said she needed to go home.

He stopped near the top of her street near the bus stop. "Let's keep this our little secret? I don't think your mother would approve of you riding home with a friend on a motorcycle, though heaven knows it's safer than Mike's truck," Neil said.

"Thank you for the ride, Neil. It was fun," she admitted, handing him the helmet.

"We'll have to do it again some time," he said. Jane started to walk away, "You forgot something." He said, kick standing his motorcycle and following after her. Jane turned and he grabbed about her waist and pulled her to him. Jane initially struggled when he kissed her, but upon realizing he was stronger than she was, stopped fighting. "Not a bad toll, eh?"

She slapped him once with the front of her hand, "That's for Chloe!" and then struck him again with the back of her hand, "And that's for Mike!!" She just about balled her hand into a fist for herself, but instead Jane stomped off, wishing her hand didn't hurt so much.

Bethany's line was busy, but Jane knew she could find her online. Jane just wished the family computer wasn't the family computer, but fortunately, her mom and dad didn't know enough about the internet to properly snoop. Carol couldn't finish her essay quick enough for either of them, and it took Bethany a few minutes to realize Jane messaged her.

Jane: Bethany
Jane: BETHANY
Jane: BETHANY LOUISE PELSHMIDT
Jane: Are you playing a game? Pay attention to me
Bethany: My middle name is Dana
Jane: Get on the phone.
Bethany: Why???
Jane: I said so
Bethany: I'm having another convo. BRB
Jane: AM HAVING ISSUES
Bethany: Mike?
Jane: How you type so fast?
Bethany: It's a gift
Jane: I think I just may have done something bad.
Bethany: I do bad things all the time.
Jane: With a boy?
Bethany: BRB RL

Jane expected the phone to ring. Instead, three minutes later, a very red-faced Bethany nearly crashed her bike into Jane's family car. "Jane! What did Mike do to you?" she wailed for all the world to hear.

"You're worse than Chloe," Jane said. She waited until they were safely in her room before explaining. "I was at the mall and I saw Chloe. Neil was there too. He made a big deal out of getting her to go to some dance with him tonight, at the forks-"

"There's dancing at the forks?" Bethany asked.

"How should I know? Neil sorta flirted with me at the mall. I didn't think he was at first, let me finish," Jane said, knowing that if she were Bethany she'd be interrupting all the time and asking, but her mind raced. This wasn't at all sounding like she had rehearsed it in her mind while she waited. "Please listen to me the whole way through, okay?"

"What was he doing?" Bethany asked.

"Making me uncomfortable! After he asked Chloe out I figure the bus is coming, so I should go, right? I miss the bus, I wait for the next one, and Neil pulls up in his bike, and makes me uncomfortable again. I don't know why, but I got on the bike with him and get him to take me home."

"Was it fun?" Bethany asked.

"You're not helping!" Jane snapped. "He made this big deal about how special she is and how much he likes Chloe and all that, but then he drops me off at the top of the street – because he knows mom and dad will kill me if they see me on a motorcycle – and I think he's just being a bit of a flirt – and then he grabs me and then he kissed me!"

She didn't expect Bethany to be silent. Finally, Bethany said, "What did you do?"

"I smacked him and said I'd tell Chloe," Jane said. "Only, he bought her a pair of really, really, really nice shoes. I think she's going to blame me. I accepted the ride from him. Is that... did I mess up?"

"Jane, if Mike started to... even flirt with me and I didn't tell you, would you be more or less mad at me when you found from someone besides me?" Bethany asked. She gestured, and Jane followed her into the hallway and back to the family room, which was mercifully vacant. Jane's family was all outside. Jane signed in online, but Chloe and Mike were offline. She messaged both, kept it vague.

"What am I going to even say?" Jane asked.

"I wish I could have been there," Bethany said. "Maybe you shouldn't have accepted the ride home," Bethany shrugged, "but I invited him out to my cottage and you were just trying to be friends with her boyfriend. Not that Chloe makes much of an effort around Mike."

"Mike's not like Neil," Jane said. "Neil's... it's like he flirts with everyone, except when he's around Chloe. Does he seem strange around you?"

"Normally I'm the one people consider strange," Bethany said. "I have a hard time putting my finger on it, but yeah, he is kinda weird. Like... I don't even know what it is. Like he's too good, or he's playing a game, or something. Well, prince charming or not we need to tell Chloe. No, you need to tell Chloe."

"What if she hates me?" Jane asked.

"How long have you two been best friends?" Bethany asked.

"You're our friend too."

"You've been friends longer. I moved here in the sixth grade, re-member?" Bethany asked. "Chloe's been mad at me lots, but she comes around." Someone binged. "We got Mike."

"I don't want to tell him," Jane said.

"He's going to think you flirted with Neil if you don't."

"What if I did? I didn't, but what if I accidentally did?" Jane asked.

"Neil knows you have a boyfriend," Bethany said, "and he's with Chloe! Just don't tell him in by computer or over the phone. Ask Mike to come over, and tell him gently as possible."

"I think Mike's dad's takes him hunting next month," Jane said. "What if he...?"

"Jane, I don't think you did anything wrong," Bethany said. "And Mike is responsible for Mike."

"I guess," Jane said, and took a moment to start.

Jane: Mike you there?
Mike: Hey babe
Jane: Hey. You home or at work?
Mike: Work. Had a lot of fun yesterday.
Jane: Me too. Can you come over after dinner
Mike: What 4 din din?
Jane:?
Jane: Who's got Mike's phone?
Mike: I'm Mike
Jane: LOL you one of his brothers?
Mike: I'm Mike!
Jane: Hope you're his older brother LOL
Mike: Mike should be home soon. Forgot his cell. I'll tell him you wanna chat

Jane picked up and her brother was on the line, and told her to hang up. Jane flung herself on the couch. "What am I going to do?"

"Does he live far away?" Bethany asked.

"It's about a fifteen minute walk," Jane said. She glanced back at the computer screen. Bethany started posting pictures of cute bunnies and kittens. "Stop that! They'll think that's me!"

"They're not that stupid. Sorry, Janey. I wish I had answers for you, but," Bethany said, paused, then continued, "seriously, he came onto you?"

"What's that supposed to mean?" Jane asked.

Bethany frowned, then looked out the window. "Do you think he'd cheat on Chloe with me? She's really pretty."

"You're taking his side now?" Jane asked.

"I didn't mean it like that," Bethany said, "I believe you! I just... why would he do that? It's not like he doesn't know you're friends and wouldn't say something to her."

"Bethany, thanks for coming over," Jane said curtly, "but I think it's getting close to supper time."

"Jane-"

"Wouldn't wanna miss whatever's on cable tonight dealing with my stupid problems that don't involve spaceships or gremlins," Jane said.

She wasn't expecting Bethany to be gone when she raised her head. Bethany usually took a little more abuse. Jane grumbled, and signed off the computer and walked to her room and threw herself on her bed. She wasn't done moping before her mother knocked on the door. "Can I get you to clean out the dishwasher so I can make dinner?"

"Mom, I'm not feeling good," Jane said, burying her head beneath her pillow. "Can't you get Paul or Carol to help you?"

"Is it something to do with Bethany Pelshmidt doing donuts in our drive way?" Mom asked.

Jane could hear the preteen skaters jumping over milk crates and plywood from her open bedroom window, but hadn't thought to inspect the antics. Jane wasn't surprised when she looked out to see Bethany doing a few jumps with her bike, even though she was older then the others by at least three years. "I thought you said she was doing donuts."

"I thought you weren't feeling well," Mom said.

"Tattletale," Jane said, and stuck her tongue out at Bethany. Bethany saw it, and stuck hers back, and ran into a block, wiping out. Jane covered her mouth and was about to charge down the hall and out the front door, but Bethany got up and brushed herself off. "Why do some people get all the luck?"

"Sometimes all you need is a change in perspective," Mom said, sitting on the bed. "Is it boy trouble?"

"Yes and no. It's about a boy, but it's not Michael," Jane said. "Chloe's got a new boyfriend. Remember when I went over to Mike's house and we had pizza? There was a fight at school. Her boyfriend touched my hair and Mike got jealous. They got into a fight over me."

"Why didn't you say anything to me?" Mom asked.

"You've been so busy with Carol's schooling and your sister's kids you hardly have any time for me!" Jane snapped at her mother. She saw her mom's brow and calmed down a smidge"Maybe it wasn't really about me at all. He didn't really do anything bad the first time. Chloe had this massive crush on him, and the next day they're a couple."

"Is this putting a rift between you and Chloe?" Mom asked.

"Not like how you're thinking. He's... his name's Neil. I don't know what his last name is. She keeps going on and on like how he's unlike any guy she's ever met – that's what gets me. He's different. In a lot a good ways, I guess, but it's creepy," Jane said. "Like, he shouldn't be in high school."

"People come from different families, and people sometimes grow up quicker than others," said Mom. "Look at Chloe and Bethany compared to you."

"That's not a good comparison," she said, "Chloe's an only child, and Bethany's got two little sisters."

"So these boys are hurting your friendship," Mom said.

Jane fiddled with her braid. "I was at the mall and I saw Chloe, said hi. Normal, right? He was there, and he buys her these expensive shoes and makes a big deal out of asking her out while she's working. Half the restaurant saw it, and I think some of the kitchen staff came out to see what the fuss was!"

"How do you know they're expensive?" Mom asked.

"Because of the store," Jane said.

"Maybe they were on sale, or he gets a discount," Mom said, "It's normal for boys to buy their sweethearts presents. Jane, it's also normal to be a little jealous-"

"I'm not jealous!"

"Then what are you angry about?" Mom asked.

"Because he came onto me!" Jane snapped. "He offered me a ride home – I assume if Chloe's dating him he's not a complete weirdo, but he took the slowest route possible through the Assiniboine Park to get me home, and just when I think he's cool and not a creep, he grabs me and... he tried to kiss me!"

"What did he do?" Mom asked. "I'll call the police!"

"I didn't let him do much," Jane said, "Just... now I have to tell Chloe. And Mike, who nearly got suspended for hitting him the first time."

"No wonder Bethany's still hanging around." Mom said. Jane thought she spotted her blonde head buzz by the window. "She really is a good friend."

"Yeah, who thinks I'm ugly," Jane muttered.

"Pardon me?" asked Mom.

"She made it sounds like Chloe was the prize, and that I'm like the jealous ugly stepsister. You made it sound that way too," Jane said.

"Chloe's... well, she is very feminine and pretty. Men like that in general," Mom said. "You have your good points as well."

"Like what?" Jane asked. "Chloe gets everything! Her family lets her use the car whenever she wants, she's got boobs, and the job where as soon as she turns eighteen she's going to be serving. She makes friends with everybody and she doesn't even care! Me, I'm wearing hand-me-downs and the only jobs I can get are ones where it doesn't matter what I look like."

"Does Mike care about that?" Mom asked. "And it sounds like this other boy doesn't, either. And you are beautiful-"

"On the inside," Jane said, "you know, where it doesn't count. I'm taller than most of the boys in our school, my hair's usually a nightmare, and I got giant feet. I'm not pretty at all."

"Jane, stop feeling sorry for yourself," Mom said. "You're tall – most models strive for a body like yours! You have beautiful eyes. No, you don't look like Chloe or Bethany, but you had no trouble getting Mike, did you?" Mom asked. "You're not an ugly duckling. Besides, your hair's been looking much nicer in the past few days."

"Why's it all gotta be so stupid?" Jane asked. "Should I have accepted that ride?"

"Probably not, you don't know that boy very well at all, but I'm glad you told me about it," Mom said. "Maybe if I get this promotion, the hours won't be as bad and I'll be able to take the bus to get the work. That way your sister isn't spending all day getting to the University of Manitoba, and you can get a job where you can stay later on the weekends if need be."

"I'll be in University in two years, so maybe we can carpool," Jane said. "It was fun being on the motorcycle."

"You were on a motorcycle?" Mom asked.

"Mom, it wasn't a big deal-"

"Those things are dangerous!" Mom shouted before Jane could defend herself.

"You and dad had bikes before you had Carol!"

"And we sold them as soon as I was pregnant with your sister!" Mom said.

Jane knew it was best to let her mother rant a moment. "Aren't you supposed to be consoling me and giving me advice?" she asked eventually.

Mom bit her lip. "No more motorcycles. Is that understood? I don't care if your father is driving-"

"Yes Mum. I'm not going anywhere with that asshole if my life depended on it," Jane said.

"Watch your mouth, young lady," Mom said, "As for advice... NO MOTORCYCLES!"

"MOM!"

"Just listen to your heart," Mom said, "Chloe's probably going to be mad at you. This.... Neil is probably going to blame you. Mike may get mad at you," she said, "but this Neil will show his true colors, and they'll know you were in the right. Do right, the rest will follow. Alright?"

"Alright," Jane said, hugging her mother. "Thanks Mom. I... wanna tell him and get it over with, I guess."

"Alright," Mom said, not letting go until Jane did first. "I'll get your sister to help me. You let me know if you need anything, alright?"

"Alright. Kick Paul off the phone, I need to call Mike's house and go and talk to him in person."

~*~

"You skanky-"

"He came on to me, Michael," Jane said. She wanted the door to be closed, but his parents had strict rules about doors and girls. At least his parents were downstairs, and his room was on the second floor. His older brother was probably getting an earful in his room down the hall. "I shouldn't have taken that ride, I know-"

"What do you expect when you give that kind of signal?" Mike demanded.

"What? I caught a ride from Trevor on Friday!" Jane snapped.

"That's different!" Mike shouted.

"Just promise me you won't do anything stupid at school tomorrow," Jane said, "You're a senior, the last thing you need to be is expelled and screw up your chances getting a scholarship."

"Thanks, Ste. Jane," Michael muttered. "Good to know you're looking out for me."

"Michael, I'm sorry," Jane said, "I messed up. I have to go tell Chloe about that creep, but I wanted to tell you first."

"Hey, you go do what you want," Mike said, looking out his bedroom window. "We're through."

"Michael!" Jane said, almost a question. Mike stood, looking out the window, his pale knuckles clenched at his sides.

Jane wished she knew her way around his house better, but once she found the stairs she found the front door. She grabbed her shoes and managed to keep from bursting into tears until she stopped to put her sneakers on at the end of his driveway. She glanced back at his bedroom window, but he wasn't there anymore. She walked with long strides, half-hoping that there'd be a roar of engine behind her, but there was nothing. Just a too-pleasant Sunday afternoon where people started up their BBQs, and some kids running through a sprinkler, and some old guy telling said kids to get off his property. She saw Bethany on her bike at the top of Mike's street. "How'd-" Bethany's smile dropped when she saw Jane's face.

"I don't wanna talk about it," Jane said, walking briskly. Bethany followed, eventually she had to hop off her bike. "He blamed me."

"It's not your fault!"

"That's what I tried to tell him," Jane sniffed.

"My house is closer," Bethany said. "Come on, let's go."

Bethany's room had too much stuff. She had her own desktop, which shared her art supplies, where old pencil crayons and older paint brushes spilled over from old jars. Jane saw a half-finished page of a comic inked, evidently Bethany'd given up on the musical. She had a lot of comic books and no shortage of fantasy serials stuffed into several bookcases along with random science-fiction action figures guarding them with old stuffed toys that Jane had never seen her play with. Bethany got Jane some tissue and a face cloth. "I didn't think he'd be such a jerk."

"He didn't even listen, he just assumed the worst," Jane said, trying not to cry and failing, "and now the whole school is going to know!"

"No, I'm sure he's just angry. It's not online," Bethany said, looking it up. Mike had already changed his status. "Oh no..."

"I don't want to think about tomorrow," Jane said between sobs, "Wanna transfer with me?"

"I don't think we'd last a day in Shaftesbury, and I don't want to take the bus to Grant Park," Bethany said. "We gotta tell Chloe before she finds out."

"All she cares about is Neil," Jane said. "She'll be just like Mike."

"She's been your friend forever. She should be home by now," Bethany said. "We shouldn't let her go out with him."

"Where's your phone?" Jane asked. Bethany texted. Still no answer. Jane decided to try the landline. She knew Chloe was out before Chloe's mom picked up. "Hi, Chloe's not answering her cell. Do you know where she is?"

"She's getting her hair done," Chloe's mom said. "I didn't think she'd find a place on a Sunday, but you know Chloe's got a friend for everything at the restaurant."

"I'll try her cell again. Thanks." She decided to skip texting and went right to calling. To her surprise, she picked up. "Chloe?"

"Hey Janey! I know you know, but isn't it awesome!?" Chloe asked. "Ow!"

"Are you alright?" Jane asked.

"Yeah, we're just teasing my ---hair!"

"Chloe, we need to talk."

"I'm kinda busy right ---now!" Chloe grunted. "Can I call you back in five?"

"I'm at Bethany's."

"Cell or home?"

"Home, I guess," Jane said.

"Tell her to call my cell," Bethany said.

"Call Bethany's cellphone. Bye," Jane said.

"You alright?" Bethany asked as soon as Jane hung up.

"No," Jane said, feeling her eyes start to water once more.

"Want something to eat?" Bethany asked.

"No."

"Wanna lay down until she calls back?" Bethany asked.

"Okay," Jane said, realizing she was already lying down.

Bethany typed on her computer while Jane hugged a pillow. Bethany's mom called them for dinner and Bethany asked again, but Jane knew she couldn't have eaten anything if she tried. She left Bethany's phone by her head, knowing it would go off and wake her.

Jane's awoke to Bethany shaking her shoulder. "So?"

"So what?" Jane asked, yawning. "Did Chloe call back?"

"No. You sure you're not hungry? We got barbequed chicken, potato salad, and asparagus," she sung the menu.

Jane glanced at the time. Her own family would be done having dinner. "It's been over an hour. I'm gonna call home."

Paul answered the phone and eventually got mom. "Hi Jane. I made a plate for you."

"I ate at Bethany's," she said, glancing up at Bethany, who frowned. "I'm at her place now. I'm... I haven't talked to Chloe yet."

"How did Mike take it?" Mom asked.

"Could have been worse, I guess," Jane said. Mom probably wouldn't find out until Paul logged online. "Is it okay if I stay at Bethany's for a while?"

"I suppose," Mom said. "Don't stay out too late. You have school in the morning."

"Thanks mom. Bye."

"Get out of Jail Free?" Bethany asked. "You wanna sleep over?"

"I dunno," said Jane. She knew better than to ask right away, pretend it was a last minute thing once the sun started to set. "Will your mom mind?"

"She'll understand." Bethany disappeared into the hall as Jane tried Chloe's cell. No answer and a full mailbox. She left her three text messages before Bethany reappeared.

"Yeah, it's cool. Special circumstances," Bethany said. "Wanna watch bad sci-fi on cable with us? It'll be fun."

"Chloe's not answering," Jane said.

"She's probably already on her way there," Bethany said. "This is going to break her heart, but you have to tell her. You up for a drive, or do you want to wait until she gets back from her date?"

Jane looked at Bethany's cell phone in her hands. "Let's go."

~*~

Chloe didn't expect all the girls from work to pitch in and get her ready. "I got just the dress for you, Chloe!" "I can poof your hair up, real nice!" "You need protection?" Chloe wanted to invite Jane, but remembered Mike was still grounded.

"Salsa dancing at the Forks Marketplace?" Janice asked over the phone. "Tonight?"

"I know! Isn't it awesome? One day we're discussing politics and art, the next we're on a boat, and now we're dancing!" Chloe said.

"Sounds incredible," Janice said. "You sure you're up for it?"

"Yeah," Chloe said. "One of the girls loaned me this great dress and it's got satin gloves – I'll post some pictures online later! I gotta go. Bye, Janice!"

Chloe wasn't a fan of the Forks Marketplace. Bethany liked to walk along the river walkway, and Jane preferred the winter when they got to go skating. Chloe found it slightly touristy and kinda grimy, but there was no shortage of free entertainment, buskers, live events and restaurants once you found a parking spot. She hoped she looked alright as she locked the doors on her parent's corolla, and made her way to the outdoor venue lit up with DJ and all the accessories.

Even though she was back in school, it still felt like summer. Winnipeg was an old city, the high rises behind her, after she passed under the old railway bridge he was in the expanse overlooking where the two rivers, the Red and the Assiniboine, met.

Chloe froze when she saw cameras. Just a local TV station, but nonetheless it made her nervous. Did her hair hold its curl? Was she going to klutz out and make a fool of herself? She'd seen videos of her schoolmates online – she didn't want to have an Epic Fail go viral. "Chloe?" She heard a familiar voice.

Not Neil, one of his friends. She had a hard time telling Terrence and Nigel apart save in good lighting, for Terrence had the black hair, Nigel the chestnut (twins, Neil said) but she smiled at seeing a familiar face. He motioned for her to follow. Chloe tied to hide behind other people when she came into view of the camera. She knew it was salsa dancing, and she wondered if she dressed alright. Many had costumes that looked the part of professionals. She had a flirty dress she borrowed from someone slightly older and thinner.

"You look lovely, Cinderella," Neil said.

"My Prince," Chloe smiled, spinning around to see him when she heard his voice. She had a thrown together outfit, he looked the part of a professional salsa dancer, the plunging neckline highlighted his sculpted chest. "You know I studied ballet."

"I know you enjoy dancing so much, it doesn't matter." It wasn't a live band, but they might as well have been in front of an orchestra. Chloe thought she spotted several of the girls from work, strangely without their boyfriends. "I'm a gentle teacher."

Chloe wanted to watch the others first, it was enough to see some of the more professional dancers in action, and she was quite interested in many of the girl's fancy outfits, but instead found herself being led to the round stone dance floor that served as a skating rink in the winter. It wasn't how she envisioned Cinderella would have won the heart of the prince. There was too much garbage, and a train whistled, but she couldn't care less, even as the cameras focused on a reporter doing some sort of special she hoped no one would see.

"You're a natural dancer," Neil said.

"Me? You're the one doing all the work!" she said, trying to master some of the more simple steps. He would twirl her unconventionally, she tried to keep from falling and mooning the world. He picked her up suddenly. "Neil! Don't!"

"As you wish, my princess," he said, putting her down. "We'll have to practice before doing it in public."

"I'll give it a go, Neil," a familiar voice said. Chloe almost didn't recognize her; she looked like she belonged with the professionals. Janice, from school? What was she doing here? She looked amazing, her dark hair running past the small of her exposed back. "Neil Darling, I've been tossed a lot – that is, if I can pry you from Chloe's grasp."

"Chloe, perhaps you'd feel more comfortable if you were to watch first," Neil said, "Janice?"

Chloe didn't want him to abandon her on the dance floor, but he took Janice's hand and she did prove herself to be a better dancer. Defeated, Chloe went out to the side, and watched, waiting for Janice to screw up and fall. Janice was a gorgeous dancer, and she knew the exact moves and when to make them, improvising only slightly – no doubt the cameras and crowd would be watching her. Chloe wondered what Neil ever saw in her. Janice moved Neil's hand from her hip to the lower curve of her bum. Chloe felt heat rise in her cheeks. "Where are you going?" Nigel asked Chloe.

"Just for a drink," Chloe said, trying not to get upset where anyone would see.

~*~

Although they'd never been, both girls knew there was dancing at the forks, but they weren't expecting there to be so many cars on a Sunday evening. Bethany dropped Jane off by the main buildings. "I'll go find parking," Bethany said. "Wait for me."

"How am I supposed to find you?" Jane shouted. Bethany had no idea. She had to hoof it a good distance, and by the time she found a spot and got back, Jane had disappeared into the crowd. Most of the crowd watched the dancing, but there were people in the restaurants and other people enjoy the last light of the day. Bethany scanned the crowd for a familiar face. Bethany recognized Neil right away, and if she wasn't mistaken, she recognized Janice on his arm, hip, and anywhere else he let her touch him. The crowd had their favourite, and it ended with her jumping him, kissing Neil passionately. Bethany thought Jane's job was too easy, except that Chloe was nowhere to be seen. Janice swooned suddenly, and Neil caught her.

"She's fainted!" someone shouted.

"It's alright, I've got her," Neil said. "She just needs some air."

Bethany scanned the crowd for Jane, but didn't see her or Chloe.

Neil had henchman #1 bring the car around. "She won't pass the test, but she is fair to look upon. She'll make a fine bauble for the garden if she will not serve as a handmaid," Neil said, sliding her into the passenger seat. "I'll retrieve the mark now."

The goon nodded, but then saw Bethany watching them. Bethany froze, and both of their eyes fell upon her. She thought Neil's friend's eyes were yellow. "Take care of her," Neil said. Bethany sprinted through the crowd. She made it into the main building and the closest womens' washroom. There were too many people around. He wouldn't dare follow. She realized she was alone in the bathroom, and upon trying the door again, found it locked from the outside.

~*~

Chloe tried to console herself in a diet cola. She was tempted by mini donuts when she heard her name. "Chloe!" At least Jane didn't come to steal her man. Jane looked like she was ready to go on a hiking trip – casual daywear for Jane. "Chloe, I'm so glad to see you!"

"Jane?" Chloe asked. "What are you doing here?"

"Are you alright?" Jane asked.

"I'm just plotting against Janice," Chloe said.

Jane didn't appear to notice what she said. "There's something you should know about Neil," Jane said. "I know you're going to get mad, but please know I can't possibly feel worse about this than I do right now."

"What?" Chloe asked.

"He came onto me after he gave me a ride home from the mall," Jane said, "I told him to back off. Mike broke up with me, and Bethany's here, and-"

"How dare you, Jane!" Chloe felt all the anger she had at Janice boil over. She didn't care that there were people looking towards her raised voice – a camera just outside, people everywhere. "Do you think I'm stupid? You think I flirt with Mike when I think you're not looking?"

"Chloe, please-"

"I'm sick of you skinny girls always trying to hurt me!" Chloe snapped. "I know Neil's amazing. You can't handle that he would pick me over someone like you!"

"Chloe-"

Chloe didn't mean to throw the cup at Jane. Chloe ran from Jane, not sure where she was going, except away from the music, the dance, and the liars. Someone grabbed her arm, and she found herself being dragged through the crowd. Neil had her. "Neil-"

"Come along, we don't have a lot of time," he said. "Where are you parked?"

"Where's Janice?" Chloe asked, letting him lead her.

"I sent her away for now. I noticed quite a few of your other restaurant friends showed up," Neil said. "I'm sorry, I wanted tonight to be special."

At least they had some privacy in the parking lot. She wanted to trash everyone, but paused when her thoughts came to Jane. "Wait Neil. Jane said something to me just now."

He paused, and let go of her arm. "It's true. I offered her a ride, and she did kiss me, Chloe. I'm sorry. Please, get in the car."

Chloe felt tears form, but blinked them back as she unlocked his side first. "Why would she do that?"

"It's not her fault, it's my glamour," Neil said. "It makes women automatically attracted to me. That's why even Janice came and did what she did. Did you ever imagine she'd do something like that before?"

"What are you talking about?" Chloe asked. "What's glamour?"

"Chloe, I need you to listen to me for a minute. Let's…" He looked nervous for a moment, when an older couple walked by. He waited until they passed by before continuing, "Let's talk inside the car."

Chloe nodded. "What is it?" she asked once they were inside the cab.

"I'm not who I said I was," Neil said, his face illuminated by sun as it dipped beneath the high-rises. She'd never seen anything so beautiful. "In fact, I'm not fully human."

That sounded like something from one of Bethany's books. He put his hands out, and she took them in hers. "If you're not human," she said, "what are you?"

"A Prince," he said, "My kingdom is far from here. I am under a curse, Chloe. I need your help. This glamour casts a spell on all women who see me, making it difficult for me to judge women, but you're different."

"You need my help?" Chloe asked. "What could you need me for?"

"Every ten years, I can walk this world," he said, "for ten of your days, and in that time I need to find a mortal who can break the chains that bind me and my world." He took her face in his hand, and lovingly stroked her cheek. "I have searched for so long, but I think you could be the one that breaks the curse."

"Me?" Chloe asked. "What's so special about me?"

"Chloe," he said, bowing his head, "do you trust me?"

He reached into his pocket, and took out at first what Chloe thought was a silver butterfly. She saw the slight, tiny yet elongated humanoid figure kneel and stand, expand its wings, and upon fluttering, gave off glittering dust in her wake. "It's alright," he said. "She's ruled by me."

"Will I hurt her?" Chloe asked, scared to move once Neil put the small figure in her palms.

"Doubtful," he said. "She's stronger than she looks."

She was very beautiful, but her face was anything but human. It had the proper shape and proportion but it had no real nose to speak of, and large eyes that seemed a mirror. It was naked but without genitals, androgynous in form. It flittered around Chloe quickly, faster than she expected. Chloe looked about, trying to see what it was doing, but Neil squeezed her hand.

"This isn't real," she breathed. "You're-"

"The Prince of the Faeries," he said, "and I only have a few more hours before I am bound again. I need your help to free me, and restore my kingdom. I believe you can help me become king."

"For ten years?"

"Yes, ten of your mortal years," the Faerie Prince said, "did you want that time to think it over?"

"What kind of curse is this?" Chloe asked. "Why haven't you spoken of this before?"

"I wish it would affect only me, but it is my entire kingdom," he said. "There is little time. I wish I could have told you everything - but I had to get to know you. Chloe, I understand if you don't want to come with me. You are an amazing young woman with your whole life ahead of you. This is something far bigger than anything you ever dreamed of."

Chloe felt the little faerie land on her hair. She was slightly warm to the touch, not at all furry, but slick. She buzzed again, looked Chloe in the eyes, and landed on her nose.

"Do not be a nuisance," the Faerie Prince said.

"It is alright," Chloe said. "What is her name?"

"Yvara. She likes you," the Prince of the Faeries said, "Chloe, I cannot be for certain, but I have been searching for someone like you for centuries, and I think you could be the one to break the spell. All I can offer in return is a place for you at my side."

"Will I be stuck in your kingdom for ten years?"

"No," the prince said. "Your race – mortals are not bound to our world and can travel freely between the realms. If you are the princess I am searching for, you will be able to let my kind do so once more as well. Chloe... I'm asking you to come with me, and be my princess."

Chloe's heart raced. "How many days do you have left?"

"Until the rising of the sun," Neil said, "But..." He leaned in as if to kiss her. Chloe closed her eyes, waited. He didn't kiss her, but she could feel the heat from his lips, and taste the sweet vanilla scent of his breath. "...what does your heart tell you?"

She kissed him. He wrapped his strong hands around her head and shoulders, and pulled her close. "How do we save your kingdom?" she breathed.

"I'll tell you everything in time," he said, "this curse runs deep. There's no time; start your car. The sooner we make for my kingdom, the sooner I'll be free."

Chloe started the engine. "What about Terrence and Nigel?"

"They'll meet us there."

~*~

Jane went to the nearest bathroom to try to clean up and found the door locked. "I think they're fixing it," said an old woman at the beginning of the line.

Jane found the nearby key ring and unlocked the door, just in time for the other person to hit it with their shoulder and for Bethany to land on top of her. "Jane!"

"Get off!" The two were nearly trampled by the line of stampeding women who just couldn't wait. "I've got pop stains all over my front, and now I've got garbage and dirt on my back!"

"Something weird's going on," Bethany said as Jane picked an old ketchup packet out of her elbow. "Know Chloe's new best friend Janice? Neil was dancing with her too – yes, you were right, shut up. She was practically raping him on the dance floor and she passed out. He put her in a car, and *nobody stopped him*," Bethany said the last part like each word was its own sentence. "He said something about her being pretty and that she'd make a bauble, but they needed Chloe for something. Have you seen her?"

"That's like something I'd expect in one of your screenplays," Jane said. "Chloe ran out that way, but she could be anywhere by now!"

"This is bad," Bethany said as they made their way back outside. The dancing had continued on. "I don't see Neil, or Chloe..."

"There's Lurch!" Bethany pointed to one of Neil's followers, who was sitting on Neil's motorcycle and putting on a helmet.

"Don't let him know that we know!" Jane grabbed Bethany's hand. "I"ll keep an eye on him. Where's the car?"

"I'll be right back."

Jane hoped he wouldn't leave until Bethany got back. Chloe had said their names before, but she couldn't remember them. He seemed to be taking his time, adjusting his cuffs. He drove off just as Bethany pulled up. "Buckle up and hold on," Bethany said. "Should we call the cops?"

"What would we tell them?" Jane asked. "Are you sure they kidnapped Janice?"

"No," Bethany said.

Jane ran over the call in her head before saying to Bethany, "*Hi, my best friend's boyfriend is a creepy stalking cheating douchebag. She's known him for a week and is already planning the wedding, but I think he's up to no good. Can you spare a dozen cop cars while I explain this to her?*"

"Touche," Bethany admitted.

"Let's follow him and see where he's going. I'll bet he's going to the same place as Neil, and then we can talk to Chloe. She can hate us forever, but she has to know the truth."

They followed the motorcycle out of the forks, out of downtown, across the river and to Assiniboine Park, which was easy to do with the light Sunday traffic. Parts of the Park closed down after 7 pm to traffic, so almost everyone left in the park were on their bikes, blades, or walking. The sun had just begun to set but it was still light out. "If he speeds in the park he's going to get a ticket," Bethany muttered, following the hog, but it seemed that when he got too far ahead he slowed down, so they could catch up. "Wouldn't it be great to have a cop when we need one?"

"Where's he going?" Jane asked.

"I dunno," Bethany said. He parked before the pavilion, among several other cars. Jane recognized Chloe's parent's corolla, but saw no sign of her. He turned to smile at them, and motioned for them to park. "This is weird."

"He led us here," Jane said. "I'll get out and talk to him. Be ready to ram him."

Bethany went to object, thought about it, then enthusiastically nodded and hopped the seat and kept the car in drive as Jane got out.

She could never tell Neil's minions apart. "I'm sorry, but this is by invitation only." He bowed his head, and after taking off his helmet he opened his eyes to reveal he had very yellow irises. Jane wondered why she had never noticed them before. "You will go no further."

"Who are you?" Bethany asked, calling through the open window of her car. She grew impatient and parked and got out.

"I am Moaz, sworn to the service of my lord, Prince of our Kindred, and I am one of his chosen guard," he said. "The Prince of the Sidhe has made his selection of Bride from your world. We will see if the one you call Chloe is indeed worthy to be The Faerie Queen."

"I'll keep him occupied," Jane said to Bethany. Bethany nodded, put the car into park and turned off the ignition. Jane walked towards Moaz. "I want to speak to Chloe."

"She will answer only to her lord," he said. "If she is unworthy, he may expel her back to your world, however she is fair to look upon." He looked over at Bethany creeping around the other way, for there were two ways around the pavilion, towards the lyric theatre, and at once his shirt ripped at the back and gossamer wings of gold shot out. They reminded Jane of a dragonfly, six slender glistening blades, almost transparent when they fluttered. They were beautiful and scary at the same time. "I warn you, maiden, do not vex me further!" he snapped at Bethany, his complexion growing eerily fair.

A nearby rollerblader, watching, collided into a tree.

Unlike Chloe, Jane had thought about protection – in the form of her brother's Lil' Slugger. Jane pointed the baseball bat at him. "I want to speak to Chloe. Now," Jane said, trying to gain Moaz's attention.

"Maiden, I have been given powers from the Prince of the Faeries himself, and–" he narrowly dodged an aggressive bike rider.

"Passing on the left!" shouted the second biker.

Moaz waited for the five cyclists to pass before continuing to address Jane. "-and as such have great stake in this–" someone hit him with a Frisbee. His eyes sparkled and Jane thought they turned red. "Who threw that?!" He faced away from her and Bethany and shook his fist.

"Shakespeare in the Park freaks?" asked a teenager, laughing. His collie went for the Frisbee.

"You will show me the respect due–" the fae turned in squinted as someone moved their drone towards him. "What in the nine realms is that?" he demanded, but the collie barked at him despite the young teen telling his dog to get away from the weirdo.

Moaz had enough, and showed the youth and his dog just what a chosen warrior of the Prince of the Faeries could do. He called power to his hands and light came to his fingers, causing his hair and clothing to swirl despite the lack of wind, a display seldom seen by mortals in centuries. The drone started recording.

"Fireworks!" a young girl clapped, eating ice cream with her parents and younger siblings on a nearby bench.

"Don't stare, Breanna," her mother said, grabbing her hand, and making them get up and hurry along the path. "You're just encouraging him."

"As I was saying," Moaz said, slightly humbled, before realizing both Jane and Bethany had run off while he was distracted. "My master is not going to like this…"

"I can't believe that worked," Bethany said as they rounded the pavilion pathway. The pavilion had an art gallery and a restaurant. Jane had always wondered about the stonework that made up the patio of the restaurant, it had always reminded her of old roman temples, only with a wooden roof, and served no real pattern or purpose, just decorative. There were people eating inside the restaurant, but the tables and chairs outside had been put away for the season. Jane spotted Chloe right away, with Neil, at the restaurant patio. The patio was not open, but they were being ignored by the staff inside.

"Chloe!" Jane shouted.

"Jane?" Chloe asked, but Neil grabbed her arm.

"Chloe, listen to me," Neil said. "They're affected by the curse and they're going to try to talk you out of coming with me."

"I want to go with you," Chloe said.

"Chloe, wait!" Bethany said, and then yelped in surprise. Jane looked over her shoulder, and was almost surprised to see the small swarm of silver pixies hurtling towards them. Jane lunged forward, and the dozen or so pixies encircled her, shouting little pixie chants and curses. Jane raised her bat – the pixies backed off.

"If I'd had known, I'd have brought a fly swatter. Chloe, let me talk to you," Jane said, trying to edge around the pillar, trying to get close to her and Neil. "Bethany, are you alright?"

"I'm fine," Bethany said.

"Moaz, I thought I told you to keep them back," Neil snapped.

"I am sorry, my lord," Moaz said, appearing at last, tossing a rather sizzled drone away like a Frisbee. "I was distracted."

"Neil, you let her come here right now," Jane said.

"Must you use force to get your way?" Neil asked.

"Jane, you don't understand. He's a prince, and I'm going to help him," Chloe said. "Believe in me!"

Moaz leapt into the air and his wings hummed, and Bethany shouted and dodged. Moaz could not watch them both at once, and Jane reached up and grabbed onto his belt. "Only my lord is allowed to bring back mortals," he said with a cruel grin.

Jane didn't think his wings were strong enough to fly with him, let alone her weight. Instead, he flew upwards and her fingers burned, and jarred unexpectedly. Jane fell into the bush; trees breaking her fall. She lost the bat before she had a chance to swing it, and she heard both of her friends scream.

~*~

"She is alright," the Prince of the Faeries said, holding Chloe's arm. "Your friends are merely confused."

"Let me go to her!" Chloe said.

"She is alright," he said.

Nigel – or Zilare, her prince had said his name was, touched down. His brilliant wings were a deep turquoise, as were his eyes. Chloe almost squinted when she recognized the dress of the figure draped over his shoulder. "Is that Janice?" Chloe asked. "What is she doing here?"

"Yes," her prince said, "she has been deeply affected by the curse – it would be best to bring her with us, and have the spell removed."

"If you say so," Chloe said, "but Jane!"

Her prince nodded, and Zilare put Janice down, and spread his wings again before taking up to join his twin in the sky. Once in their faerie forms, their faces were quite dissimilar from one another – still handsome, but in a way that would make most people stare at the alien, not the beauty. Janice looked as if she was in a deep sleep. Her prince let go of her, so Chloe touched Janice's cool cheek. "Don't worry, you're going to be alright," she said.

"Let go of me!" Jane shouted. Moaz on one arm, Zilare on the other, they flew Jane over to Chloe. Her hair had no shortage of twigs in it, but she looked alright, save for a bloody scrape on her forehead.

"See? She is alright," her prince said. "The spell has affected her less than Janice." Her prince's servants put Jane down and Chloe could have swore she saw a thin chain attach at both of Jane's wrists, to the ground. Jane thrashed against it. "Come, my servants. It is time, before any other-"

He called out and fell forward. Chloe screamed. Her prince coughed silver blood, which looked almost golden in the dying light of dusk. Bethany stood triumphantly over the Prince of the Faeries with the bat. "You call them off or I'll hit you again!"

"No!" Chloe tackled Bethany. Both girls rolled in the grass, Chloe trying to knock the bat away. "How could you?"

Bethany was the better fighter, but she was no match for Moaz and Zilare.

"Are you alright?" Zilare asked, helping Chloe up once Moaz had Bethany's arms pinned behind her back.

"My prince!" Chloe squealed.

"It will take more than that," her prince said, standing. He bled silver, but he remained beautiful. Chloe expected to see a disheveled look, or a broken nose, maybe even missing teeth. Instead, he spat silver blood onto the grass, and took her hand. "Though I do appreciate your concern, Princess."

"What's going on here?" Janice asked, waking up, and backing up suddenly. She let out a blood-curdling scream.

"My lord, this one?" Zilare asked.

"There is a crowd coming," her prince said. He bent down to the grass, channeling magic and opening the barrier between the worlds as light spread from his fingertips. "Take Janice, leave the others."

"Chloe, please!" Jane called, the magical chain on her wrists thinning with each yank.

"I'm sorry Jane," Chloe said, and taking her prince's hand, followed him into the white space her prince created.

~*~

Jane continued to fight against the chain. The small pixies had returned to torment her, as well as harass the passerbys, stealing watches, hats, and ice creams. Several faeries tried to steal a baby stroller, only to be squashed by a very angry mother. There wasn't much of a crowd, but there were people gathering, panicking in the restaurant, and several had run off. Jane was sure she heard sirens in the distance, but they were far away.

Chloe was already gone.

"Leave her," Moaz told Zilare.

"Why should our master be the only one deserving a mortal soul?" Zilare demanded, not letting go of Bethany. "He may have his princess and handmaiden, I will have-"

Moaz went to grab Janice, and she punched him repeatedly, leapt over his head and knocked him over with a jumping kick, then dug her impressive heel into Zilare's foot. Zilare howled, and Janice let out a throaty yelp, rolling for the bat and threw it, striking Moaz in the head. They were tougher than any man ought to be, but they seemed hesitant to attack Janice. "I don't know what sort of freak show this is," Janice said, posing like someone who had several black belts, "but you got my dress *dirty*."

Moaz and Zilare looked at one another briefly, and then bolted for the portal. Bethany went to follow them, but Janice grabbed her shoulder, and plucked one of the many faeries out of the air as they retreated to their world with their stolen treasures.

"Janice, you saved me," Bethany said.

Janice didn't notice. Jane gave a final yank and the magic no longer bound her. She fell forward, and scrambled towards the white space as it faded into stone. There was no sign of a doorway, a portal or even a lousy magic carpet to follow, only a high-heeled open-toe sandal that had gotten stuck as Chloe stepped from one world to another.

Janice, on the other hand, had something sparkly between her fingers. "Alright you," she said, shaking the little silver faerie, "where is Neil?"

"Our prince has selected his princess," said the fae, "he takes her now to his palace!"

Janice raised an eyebrow. "Okay, whatever." She tossed the tiny faerie to Jane, who hurriedly caught the pixie. Janice reached into her cleavage and took out a tissue to absorb the slight perspiration she'd worked up, and then dug deeper to get her cell phone. "Brad? Hey, it's Janice. Change of plans: I am available. Come pick me up. Now." Janice then got into a bit of an argument.

Jane looked to her hands. The pixie made an unhappy face as Jane pinched his little wings together.

"Let's get out of here," Bethany said, putting a hand on Jane's shoulder before she picked up the bat. "Janice, are you coming with us?"

"...I don't care, I'm at that lame Pavilion at the Assiniboine Park..." Janice said, before catching Bethany's eyes. "Just a second. What do you geeks want?"

"Are you coming?" Bethany asked.

"With you two?" Janice asked, and went back to her cell. "Hi. Brad's grandma? Listen lady..."

"I have a lunchbox in my car, maybe that'll hold him," Bethany said as they retreated from the growing scene. Jane glanced into Chloe's family's car – the keys were in the glove compartment, where she usually left them, passenger's side back door open. Jane discarded the pixie to an almost empty take-out container and climbed into Chloe's corolla. "Meet you back at your place?"

"Yeah, let's hurry," Bethany said as the four cop cars and fire truck pulled up, and an only slightly disheveled Janice took an interest in said young firemen.

6

Pixie Sticks do not Equate to Pixie Dust

Jane felt like nothing was right. The world was too sharp, the wood on the desk was too hard, the chair in Bethany's room was too soft, her tea too hot and she bit her tongue as if that would cool it.

"It just boiled," Bethany said.

"You could have warned me," Jane said. "Think we should pickle him?"

"I don't think that's appropriate," Bethany said. "He'd hardly make a mouthful."

Their little guest continued to thrash against the sides of the glass mason jar. He seemed to generate his own light and sparkles whenever he came into contact with the sides. One of Bethany's sisters poked her head in the room. "You're out late on a school night," she sang.

"Go away, troll." Bethany threw the expensive sandal at her sister's head. The younger teen yelped and disappeared into the hallway.

"Which one of your sisters was that?" Jane asked.

"The annoying one," Bethany said, before picking up the jar. "I'd give this thing to her if I wasn't against torture. How are we supposed to talk to him? He can't hear us through the glass, and I'd rather not punch holes through the lid."

"He'll run out of air eventually. Can we put him on a leash or something?" Jane asked.

"What if he uses magic on us?" Bethany asked.

"I think any magic we'd be scared of would have started with breaking that jar," Jane said.

Bethany consented, and they found an old cat leash and collar – the collar was too big, but they found a way to wrap it around the pixie. It proved in vain, for it wriggled free, evaded both girls, rebounded off the ceiling, shot off the book case, knocked over one of Bethany's action figures, and came to a rest on Mr. Fluffybunny's head.

"Ooooooh…" it groaned, got up, and fell into the wastebasket.

Jane fished him out. "Ouch!" She nearly let him go when it bit her. "Do that again, and back into the jar you go!"

"I have a fishbowl with a lid," Bethany offered. "Well, my sister does, anyway. We just need someplace to put the fish…"

"Stop biting me! You're drawing blood!" Jane said, trying to hold it so that it wouldn't bite her. It was much more passive in the park, Jane figured it was probably scared of Janice. She finally got it pinned by its wings. "Stupid thing doesn't understand!"

"Yes I do!" it squealed. Although rather squeaky, she thought the voice male.

"Stop biting me!" Jane ordered.

It looked at her with eyes full of understanding, and then began to sway, until it got hold of Jane's hands, then posed its little teeth over the webbing between her fingers and thumb.

"Pop you like a little pimple! " Jane threatened.

It looked fiercely at her, but turned to Bethany like a wounded puppy. "Save me from this wretched one!" it pleaded. "I must hurry away."

"Tell us why we should do that," Jane said.

"Because with the coming of the dawn, I will fade and die," he said. "I have no soul, like mortals. To let me die would be most cruel. Let me flee."

"It's only ten," Bethany said, "We've hours until dawn."

"He's lying," Jane said. "Even if he's telling the truth, why should we help him? What is he?"

"A faerie," he said. "A pixie, to be more precise."

"There's no such thing as faeries," Jane said. "Isn't that supposed to kill you, just by saying that?"

"I don't think it works like in books," Bethany said. Her eyes lit up suddenly. "Books!"

At once the computer was on and Bethany pulled out several books from her shelves. Jane wondered what good that would do: the pixie in her grasp certainly didn't look anything like anything out of an animated movie. Jane fastened the cat leash around the faerie again and it thrashed, throttled and tried to bite at her. Jane assumed it must be like taking a bat for a walk, and when he got too frisky, treated him like a yo-yo. She was never any good with a yo-yo, except for Around the World.

"What are we looking for?" Jane asked after several minutes.

"Clues," Bethany said. "Hey, you have a name?"

The faerie landed on Bethany's desk and picked up the pencil. "Maeld," he said eventually.

"Maeld, I'm Bethany, this is Jane. I need you to help us," Bethany said. "If you do, we'll think about letting you go. Alright?"

Maeld started to gnaw on the pencil's lead.

"Let's start with the basics," Jane said. "What was all that about? He was taking Chloe to be his... princess bride?"

"Our Princes have been cursed to never leave our lands again, so we too are locked from your world," said the fae. "Only every ten years, may the Prince of the Sidhe come forth."

"Never and every ten years ten years are not the same thing," Bethany said.

"Our Prince had a mortal dame," said Maeld, buzzing over to Bethany's backpack. "He alone can come – and his power allows his servants to enter your realm. Every ten years, he can search for the one who will free us."

"He can only come every ten years? We have stories like that," Bethany said to Jane. "About faeries stealing people and bringing them back to the faerie realm, and if they come back it's like they think they've been gone a few days and it's been years. There's gotta be clues somewhere."

"I think the clue is in your backpack!" Jane gave the leash a yank and he came flying out, holding onto Bethany's uneaten sandwich, between the slices of bread. "What are you doing?" Jane demanded.

"Oh, such sweat, loving, great nectar!" squealed the fae.

"What is he into?" Jane asked.

"Peanut butter and honey?" Bethany asked. "Do you like honey?"

"Such greatness," Maeld chirped, "to find such a thing with no bee in sight!"

"How about you help us out," Bethany said, "and I get you a little more... honey?"

"Oh, most beautiful flame-haired keeper of the light box!" the fae sang, landing on her computer. "Take off thy mask so that I may gaze into thy beautiful orbs!"

"Alas, without this mask my eyes would turn you into stone, little faerie," Bethany said, but stopped embellishing when she saw Jane's expression. "I'll go get some crackers."

"Bethany," Bethany's dad poked his head through the door. "It's getting late."

"We're working on a project," Bethany said, "Besides, mom said Jane could stay over. We're having a sleepover. Very important for school."

"I see that," he said, wrinkling his nose at the little faerie shoving the bread into his cheeks. "This isn't for another stupid writing project, is it?"

"No dad," Bethany said. "Drama class."

"The things I pay taxes for..."

Bethany came back with the crackers and honey. "Alright. What's our Prince's name?" she asked.

"I cannot say," Maeld said. "It is not fit to be spoken by mortals."

Jane took away the cracker. Their faerie wailed. "So much for that,"

Jane muttered, conceding. He gobbled up the cracker lickity-split, and sniffed Jane's fingers. "So what's Chloe gotta do that helps you guys? Couldn't he put out a want ad? And why are you so much smaller than him?"

The little creature stuffed another cracker in his cheeks, much like a squirrel. He licked his fingers and began to lick the desk where the cracker had been before gathering the crumbs into a neat pile. "My master seeks mortal blood to break the seal that blinds him, for though silver is eternal, it is garnet that gives spark. There are many types of us whose blood runs silver; I am pixie."

"Mortal... Jane, he said he has no soul," Bethany said. "What does that mean?" The pixie continued to stuff his cheeks. "I got it!" Bethany turned to her computer and quickly googled. "Here we go! Hans Christian Anderson's *The Little Mermaid...*"

"We're talking about faeries," said Jane, "not talking crabs."

"According to the original story, the little mermaid traded her tongue to be human. Humans had souls, but mermaids didn't. They lived for a few centuries, and then became foam," Bethany said. "If we go into folklore, a lot of times we see faeries as malevolent spirits – ones that didn't side with good or bad, being in the between. Selfish creatures who don't see anything wrong with stealing a human child and leaving a changeling in its place. That sort of thing."

"Wait wait wait," Jane said, "You mean to tell me, souls. He's after Chloe's *soul*."

"Maeld," Bethany sauced up another cracker, "tell me about this bride business. What curse is he under? If he has a mortal... mother, then is he mortal? What is an immortal?"

"You are mortal, he is not," Maeld said, "You live, and you die, but you can create. The prince has kindred sire, and is raised in our realm. He is Fae. He seeks the one who is worthy to be the Queen of the Fae – so that he may be King. And if he shares soul with a mortal, he may come to this world not every ten years, but when he so chooses, and walk here freely."

Jane didn't understand. "How long has he been after a Queen?" she asked.

The little fae looked confused. "I... do not know mortal years," he said eventually. "He has come to your world more than forty times, seeking his bride."

Jane looked at Bethany. "Why so many?" Bethany asked.

"He has not found the one who can be queen."

"So why not just pick a girl and share her soul, and then when he can come freely, find the queen?" Bethany asked.

"If he does that, he can never be King," Maeld said. "By sidhe law, if the prince takes a bride who cannot master our magic, he loses claim to the throne. He is not mortal. He has time."

"Time for what?" Jane asked.

He didn't answer.

"You said he had a mortal dame," Bethany said. "Doesn't that make him half-mortal?"

"Silver is stronger," he said. "A touch of silver in the garnet yields Silver. Ah, for us to be able to fly in this world once more, without the prince! To not worry about the great sleep he prepares for us." He looked at the girls sadly.

Bethany cleared her throat. "You are a slave to him, aren't you?"

"Yes," Maeld said.

"It must be dreadful, doing what he tells you to," Bethany said, "and for him to abandon you."

"Yes," Maeld said.

"Can you get back to your world?" Bethany asked.

"Yes," Maeld said.

"Can you take us there?" Jane asked.

He looked at the leash and glass jar before looking back to Bethany and Jane. "Yes," he said eventually.

"Watch him for a moment," Bethany said. "I'll be right back. I have an idea."

Jane didn't know if she liked the idea of faeries being able to freely come and go in their world. Every ten years seemed like plenty when you had Zilare and Moaz to deal with. Neil wasn't any better, and Neil wasn't even his real name. She looked at Maeld. "Moaz said that he may expel Chloe, if she wasn't the one," she looked at him to make sure he was listening. He blinked. "He also said that he likely wouldn't."

"He seldom expels princesses," the pixie said.

"What happens to them, if they're not the queen?" Jane asked.

"He keeps them, of course," Maeld said.

Bethany came back with her Oma's silverware. "I heard that silver has an effect on these creatures." She handed Maeld a spoon. He looked at it, licked it, gnawed on it, and then made a sour face. "Maybe that's just werewolves."

"Maybe iron?" Jane asked.

"Maybe," Bethany said, resorting to the internet. Jane looked down at Maeld – he had taken off the antique salt-shaker lid, had it on his head, and was smacking it with a spoon, dancing around and generally enjoying himself.

"You ever get the idea that we caught the 'special' faerie?" Jane asked, before bending down and talking loudly to the pixie. "Hey! Do you have anything useful to say? Like, how I would go about defeating him and saving our friend?"

"His mother defeated his father and his brothers by wielding the Silver Staff," Maeld said. "She locked away us all, save for her son, whom she could not kill. If you were to wield the staff, then you could defeat him."

"And how would I go about obtaining this staff?" Jane asked.

"You would have to go to his realm and seek it out," Maeld said. "I know where it is, but you would not make the journey, much less gain the staff!"

"Bethany, search Silver Staff," Jane said.

"Will do," Bethany said.

"Does your prince have any weaknesses?" Jane asked.

"Only for pretty girls," Maeld said, and bared his teeth.

The little pixie buzzed around and left a trail of sparkle in his wake.

Jane tried to dust it off, and it bunched into globs on her fingers. It had a runny texture; squishy, like an uncooked egg white. Her dry hands absorbed most of it, and it gave her skin a pleasant look, like a high-class eye shadow.

"We could try iron, but maybe we should be careful not to hurt him," Bethany said before Jane could decide how to make money selling pixie dust as a cosmetic. "It's a good thing I have so much iron kicking around here."

"Sounds like we just need to find this staff," Jane said. "Anything on Silver Staff?"

"Let's see..." Bethany said. "A million hits, none of which looks like they pertain to a silver staff of the faeries. Why?"

"He said that it might be how to defeat this guy."

"Woah, calm down a moment," Bethany said. "How do we know he's telling the truth?"

"Because we'll shake the sparkles out of him if he isn't," Jane said. "Maeld, how do we go to... where you're from?"

"Listen to yourself!" Bethany said. "Jane, I agree, we gotta do something. Let's just stop and think about this, okay?"

Jane tried to keep her cool. "Chloe doesn't need good girls who stop and rationalize the danger! She needs help!"

"Running after her unprepared – and I'm not even sure how we're going to go after her except through that thing-" she pointed at Maeld, "-is not going to help her. We need to do this together. It might even take more than just us."

"Who are you going to ask for help?" Jane asked. "Janice? How about Mike? I know, let's invite your little sister! And let's get our parents involved next!"

Bethany looked as if Jane had struck her across the face. "We can't fight each other, Jane. We have to help each other if Chloe's got any chance."

Jane didn't want to look Bethany in the eyes. She was mad. Mad at who? Neil? Bethany? Chloe? All of them. "Fine. Research on the internet, and maybe they've got a train that runs to wherever Maeld's from.

We can have breakfast served to us by a singing badger en route to his magic castle."

Jane couldn't concentrate as Bethany searched and emailed and badly filmed videos. Bethany had her read through different versions of old tomes of faerie tales, and Jane commented how few faerie tales actually had actual faeries as characters. Bethany had an old bunk bed, one that Bethany still fit into but Jane's feet dangled off the end. Jane as surprised Bethany's parents said nothing about her staying over, other than her mother popping in to offer them cocoa around midnight. Jane glanced through Bethany's genre magazines, the ones with monsters holding unconscious nakedish women on the cover, as if the human standard of beauty was the same for swamp monsters. "You'd think she wouldn't go tromping into the jungle in a ballgown," she said eventually, and when Bethany didn't respond Jane realized she was asleep.

Jane couldn't sleep. The digital time read 3:42 AM. Jane wondered if the excuse 'My friend has been kidnapped by her faerie boyfriend, we're trying to research what we can about the fair folk' would be a good enough excuse to skip class.

Maeld was at the computer, watching old animated fairy tales on-line. "That's not right," he said when she walked over.

Jane shook Bethany's shoulder, forgetting past sleepovers. Bethany whacked Jane, saying something about someone named Riddick, and went back to dreamland. "I suppose we forget the way the story goes over time," Jane said. "Whitewash everything, and make it easier to understand. The good guy wins in the end. I mean, that's what Faerie Tales are, right? Stories about happily ever after?"

Maeld blinked at her. "More honey?" he ventured.

He licked the knife clean when he finished the soda cracker Jane gave him. "There's nothing there that can help us, is there?" Maeld shook his head. "But you'll help me. For honey."

"I don't like bees," Maeld said.

She wondered if there was a Faerie Land, why everything wasn't made of honey and rainbows and temperance. Why fae would want into their world anyway. It seemed like their world had plenty of problems. "Tell me about his mother, the mortal," she said. "Who was she?"

"Red Queen," he said, "when at last one prince rose above his brothers, he took a mortal queen as his bride. She defeated them all with the staff, and returned to her world – bore her son, and banished him to ours."

"So this is all about your kind coming to our world," Jane said. "He's using her. I... I can't believe Chloe just went with him."

"She is to be made beautiful."

"Chloe's already beautiful," Jane said.

"She is merely pretty," Maeld said, "she will be beautiful."

Jane bit her lip. She looked at the fae at the end of the cat leash. "Alright, let's go."

"You won't bring your friend?" Maeld asked.

Jane thought about it. Jane didn't want to see her get hurt. It was bad enough one of them was trekking into the unknown. "How do we go there?"

He flittered his wings. "Shouldn't we bring some provisions?"

"Then get back into my backpack and we'll make s stop at the nearest twenty-four hour wallymart before we transverse to Pleasure Island," Jane said.

"We're not going there," Maeld said.

The only perk to Chloe's disappearance was that Jane now had access to Chloe's parent's car, which was good because it was lightly raining. Bethany's family had a cat, which was much quieter then Chloe's dog would have been if she snuck out in the middle of the night. Maeld seemed enchanted by the magic Jane could use, making the great beast roar and move backwards, and open and close the windows from afar. "So how does this work? We need to follow a white rabbit down a hole or something?"

Maeld kept trying to feed the bobble head dog bits of cracker and would ignore Jane any time she tried to be funny. She detoured to the nearest store she knew was open and bought things she knew she'd need:

A bigger backpack, a pair of sandals in case her shoes got wet, a bunch of bottled sports drinks and energy bars, some candy, and a pocket knife – the biggest she could purchase given she was only sixteen. As luck would have it, as soon as they made it to the park there was still a cop car present, but Jane spotted them off in the car, drinking coffee. The park was supposed to be closed after ten or so, but she turned her lights off and parked at the conservatory, and there was more than enough bush to hike around the pavilion without being spotted.

She knew if she called the landline her parents would ask too many questions. She called her mom's cell. Mom thought she was sleeping over at Bethany's. Bethany thought she was still at Bethany's. She knew voicemail would pick up. "Mom, it's Jane. I know this is hard to explain, but I'm going on an unexpected trip. I think Chloe's in trouble. It's boy trouble – Bethany'll tell you what she knows, but I don't think you'll believe her. Don't blame her. She doesn't know I'm going on my own. I left her behind. It's my fault." She paused, wondering what to say. It didn't feel like good-bye. Nothing would worry mom and dad more than, "I wuv you!" "Chloe's car is in the Assiniboine Park near the Pavilion with her cell phone, and her keys are in the glove compartment. I'm not coming home without Chloe. Bye Mom, tell dad I love him."

When he knew where he was, Maeld seemed very eager to go. "Slow down!" He tugged on his leash. "You better not try anything sneaky." She didn't know what good a bat would do against a Faerie Prince, but Bethany had knocked him down with it.

The park seemed eerie in the dark. She'd been there hundreds of times when she was a kid, playing in the fields or biking on the trails by the river, or crossing the bridge for ice cream. Jane knew where she was, could see the duck pond in the distance, the bridge leading over the Assiniboine River to Portage Avenue. "So how do we open a portal into your world?" she asked.

Maeld perched on her head and emitted what she at first thought was a cry, but then she had to shield her eyes from the light. When her eyes at last focused, she saw that the light ran deep – it was a portal, but with depth, from up close, looked more like a tunnel. She wondered what sort of white rabbit the pixie was. He tried to make a dash through the portal that was once concrete. Jane held tightly onto his leash. "Where are we going?"

"You want the staff, do you not?" he asked. "Come, come!"

Jane closed her eyes, and wrapped her fingers around her mother's rosary. She shivered one last time in the wind, before taking a deep breath, and wrapping her knuckles tightly around the bat and following the fae.

7

The Faerie Kingdom

Going through the portal was like stepping through a thick cloud, but Jane stepped off from concrete and touched down on a marble platform. It was dawn in that world, for the sky was yellow. Jane saw two crescent moons though she could make out no stars. The world was cooler than she expected, probably because she was damp from the rains from her world, and there was a slight wind in this one. She stood on a raised black marble platform, the steps leading down before her, and forest all about her. Jane looked over her shoulder. There were only trees behind her, marked by two stone satyrs holding trumpets. She tried to remember where she was, and wondered when she'd return home.

It didn't seem that different than Winnipeg in the early autumn, only most of the leaves were still a lush green with only a few starting to turn red and amber. Jane shifted her backpack, nearly squishing Maeld in the process. "Where are we?"

"I took us to the Dawning Burrow," Maeld said, "it is a good distance to where we need to get the heartstone, and further still to find the Staff of Silver."

Hesitantly, Jane released the pixie from the leash. He didn't fly off, or even seem to notice. "I thought you said we needed the Silver Staff," Jane snapped, following after Maeld and descending the steps. She could see a path in the near distance, and what looked like a renaissance village up ahead.

"We do," he said, "but you'll need the heartstone to break the barrier to enter the floating castle. There, you may find the staff."

Jane wondered about the village. It seemed rather clean and quaint, and she stepped onto the grass to hear a most unpleasant crunch. "Oh!"

"Use the path," Maeld said.

Jane bent down to pick at the grass. It was well manicured and had good color, but it wasn't grass at all. It felt rough and it was brittle, breaking easily in her hands. She looked at the nearby trees. "What's wrong with this place?" she asked, walking to a nearby tree. The poplar was thin, and she could break through the bark with her hand. It was hollow on the inside. She didn't mean to knock the tree down, which smashed into another but they came to a rest onto the third.

"Break not the forest!" Maeld said, flittering about her head. "One of The Prince's uncles thought this place needed trees," he said, "so he made them."

"None of it is real?" Jane asked, "It's all an illusion?"

"What is real?" asked the fae. "You mean, trees that grew from seeds? There are growing trees, here and there. Many mortals and other trinkets have been brought over. The kingdom sleeps undisturbed."

Jane hated to admit that the fake trees looked more like trees than the real trees, which seemed sickly, but when she put her hand on a real tree she thought the color perked up slightly. "Maybe they don't grow here so well," Jane said, running her hands down the bark of a real and fake tree, careful not to press too hard. The fake tree she could damage quite easily, whereas the real tree seemed to flourish when she touched it. "Are we going to that village?"

"That village sleeps," he said. "It is safe for you to pass through."

He flew above the cobblestones, and told her not to leave the path. Jane expected to see fae workers zonked out against their shovels and market sellers asleep, with cobwebs in amusing places, but instead she left the path as soon as she spotted the first cocoon.

They were everywhere. Silk white cocoons, they were large and in clumps. Jane put her hand out to touch the first one that didn't involve her leaving the path.

"Leave it!" Maeld snapped.

It wasn't sticky, but had a very hard texture, not soft like she expected. Jane took out her pocket knife, but Maeld buzzed around her head. "What happened here?" she asked.

"The Red Queen defeated all the princes, slaying the ten and locking two in their castles," Maeld said. "They ruled the land chained to their thrones, until the Red Queen's son came of age. He cursed his uncles, for they wanted to use him so that they may walk free." Maeld flittered and landed on the cocoon. "The Prince could not rule all the land properly, so he put most of it to sleep. He will awaken his people when he finds his queen."

Jane was tempted to cut some one out, but decided against it. There was no way to tell if Maeld was being honest or not, but he seemed to wish her no harm so long as she had honey. Besides, she didn't want to damage the knife. She looked around the village. Besides the movement of water and the slight wind, it seemed frozen in time. There were no spider webs, though there was dust. "Where are all the insects?"

"There are none," the pixie told her.

"Where are all the animals?" Jane asked.

"The Prince keeps everything from your world for himself," said Maeld. "Very few villages outside his castle have life. He keeps many moo-cows and there some mortals stay, so that the vines of his labyrinth may grow. No wretched bees to be found."

Jane never thought she'd miss the sounds of birds or squirrels in the trees, or even swatting bugs. She walked through the small village, which seemed to function without its inhabitants quite nicely. "So the plants and the animals all came from my world?"

"Yes."

"How do you eat?" Jane asked.

"We can create food with magic," Maeld said, "though, it doesn't taste near as sweet as the nectars from your world."

Jane stomped on the ground. It felt real. Some of the trees were real too, and she wondered if the wood used on the houses was real, or if some of the buildings were decoration. She looked at the watermill; when she stopped to drink the water was cool and refreshed her. "So, what's this about needing a heartstone?" she asked.

"The staff is guarded," the fae said. "The Red Queen had the heartstone. It is said that it is essential to free the staff. Hurry! We must hurry if we are to save your friend."

Jane knew he wasn't going anywhere while she had honey. She let him off his leash and he buzzed around her. She looked around the small village, tempted to look for more provisions, but decided no good could come of lingering. "Lead the way," Jane said.

He flew ahead of her, and so she jogged after him, but that just made him speed up, and after half an hour, Jane slowed to a brisk walk. "Would I know this Red Queen? Is she famous?" Jane asked when she saw him perched on a branch.

The fae ignored her and flew ahead, buzzing, landing on low branches, and telling Jane to follow. *I should have brought Bethany with me*, Jane thought, *it would be nice to get a second opinion.*

She was tempted to ask how big his world was, and if there would be any shortcuts. She kept her eyes peeled for cottages made of gingerbread, or golden haired girls being chased by bears wearing hats or even a spare red cloak hanging to dry. She spotted blueberries on the side of the road. She thought about the food she'd brought with her. The berries looked ripe and juicy. She wondered how anything got pollinated if there were no bees, but figured that the prince probably had pixies to do it. "Will I be cursed if I eat the food here?" she asked.

"Why would you be?" Maeld asked.

"Better not chance it," she said. "Do all faeries hate the prince?"

"We do not hate him, but we fear him," Maeld said. "There are those he has not put to sleep, and those who wish for his uncles to be restored."

"Did they take people from our world as well?" Jane asked.

"Of course they did," Maeld said.

Jane spotted flowers in the distance, off the path. Flowers by themselves were not enough to make her stray from the path, but she saw gold and glass underneath a dense collection of vines. The thick green vines were very real. Maeld had flown ahead, but he'd be back. Jane grew curious, and left the path.

A glass coffin! Jane cleared the vines and flowers from the top. Inside was no sleeping maiden, but a man who had looked like he might have been a viking. He wore armour that had been well-used, a mix of polished metal and stained leather. He had an axe in his hands with its head across his breast, and a sword on his hip. His hairy face and hands looked well preserved. Jane cut away the vines and looked for the hinges and latch, and found there was no lock on the coffin.

It opened easily once the plants were cleared away. Jane expected it to stink. She gagged, but saw no signs of rot. "Sorry, but I'm not a princess." The axe was heavy! Jane managed to put both of his weapons over her shoulder. "If I happen to see a spare one, I'll send her your way."

"Water," he breathed.

"Oh!" Jane fell backwards, dropping her looted provisions. "You're alive!"

"Water, please," he said.

Jane went through her backpack, and popped open a sport drink. He drank it greedily. "Give me food," he said.

"Alright," Jane said. He was a strong-looking fellow. He might be willing to pay her back for freeing him, and he looked like he could use the axe. Jane's thoughts raced as he slowly ate the energy bar. "Sorry I took your weapons, but I thought you were dead. I thought I could use them to defeat the Faerie Prince. Who are you, and what's your story?" She put the backpack back over her shoulder.

"Meat?" he asked.

"Nothing resembling real food," Jane said, shaking her head.

He sniffed the air, then growled. "Meat," he said. Jane watched in horror as his beard became thicker and spread all over his face, the hair on his arms become more numerous and bushy. He descended upon all fours. "Meat," he growled, his face lengthening, his clothes melting into the brown and grey fur sprouting all over his body, his hands becoming great clawed paws. "Meat..."

Jane screamed and dropped the weapons, and ran back towards the path. The great wolf howled behind her and she heard it shed its armour. Jane didn't know why he didn't catch her, but she made it to the path and he was suddenly before her, growling.

"Stop this!" Jane shrieked. "You're a man, not a beast!"

Drool poured from his mouth. He leapt at her and Jane swung the bat. The wolf yelped, and Jane smacked him again. "Meat!" he barked, circling her.

"You have some sort of curse on you!" Jane shouted. "Stop! I can help you, but you must-" He leapt at her again, and with great yellow teeth ripped the bat from her hands, and pinned her down with one paw. Jane felt hot drool on her face. The wolf looked up suddenly, and ran off. Jane saw only a flash of brilliant white, like some sort of horse chasing after the wolf, but she was alone in the too-still forest.

Jane lay on the path, her heart racing. She wondered what had really happened, but then she saw teeth marks in the bat, and saw the man's weapons in the fake grass not far away. "I should have brought my dad's hunting rifle," she said, gathering her backpack and collecting his weapons.

"What's taking you so long?" Maeld asked once Jane caught up. "Did you stray off the path? Monsters roam these woods!"

"Anything I should be looking out for in particular?" Jane asked as she continued to follow the pixie deeper into the forest. "Hate to cause any more trouble than exists here already."

8

The Prince's Castle

Flight was more than a little terrifying. Heights scared Chloe; she never let her parents make her sit by the window when they flew out to see family. She should have felt safe in her prince's arms, but instead she gripped around his strong shoulders tighter. She hazarded glances down, but never for long.

Her prince had silver wings, like his eyes, and his hair had lost the slightly yellow tinge, instead appearing stark white once they were back in his world. Moaz and Zilare flew behind him, they too appeared different than they had on earth and gained their faerie faces – brilliant golden and turquoise eyes and they were paler, though she recognized them easily enough. She felt Yvara in her hair, and watched the other pixies fly. *I wonder if I'll ever fly,* she thought, looking down at the kingdom. It didn't look like Faerie Land; there appeared to be a dense forest beneath them, white mountains in the distance, and they flew over several rivers. Chloe saw no sign of habitation, until she spotted a white castle in the distance. She felt a new sense of wonder when she saw the tall towers before the majestic grey-blue mountains, but they didn't fly to it.

"That is the castle of my uncle," her prince said, "it is cursed, Chloe.

You must never go there. He is a wicked villain. He seeks to steal my throne."

"How terrible," Chloe said. "Is your castle far?"

"I can fly faster if you like," he said, smiling, "Are you ready to see your new home?"

Chloe did. She held on tighter as her prince and his followers flew faster. She saw another castle in the distance. It seemed grander, and looked like how a fantasy castle should be, the other seemed more like a fortress. They flew over a medieval looking town of sorts, Chloe could see faeries below with gossamer wings similar to her prince's going about their daily business, but Chloe's eyes were drawn to the tall marble towers and formidable archways, sculpted gardens and waterfalls running down the sides of the castle. She didn't know where they landed, for they were still so very high up. Chloe wasn't sure what to do, she wasn't sure if she was more captivated by the prince or his kingdom.

"What do you think?" her prince asked.

"It's all so... magical," Chloe said, leaning out over the wall to gaze at the kingdom's beauty.

The Prince of the Faeries laughed slightly. "Come, we have much work to do. After all," he said, "you came to save my people, did you not?"

Chloe wondered what kind of curse he was under. There were not as many servants as she expected, there were guardsmen who dressed in proper military regalia, polished silver breastplates with skilfully crafted emblems of proud and beautiful histories. Moaz and Zilare were dismissed, and she followed him down the steps, into the castle. Her prince took off his shirt once they were inside what looked to be his grand courtroom. He had a large throne of silver wrought with beautiful designs of mermaids and unicorns and gryphons, and quickly he took off the shirt he wore as a human, putting on instead a much finer silk tunic and then an impressive blue cape, and strapped a long sword embedded with jewels to his waist. "Do I look like a prince now?" he asked.

"I never doubted," Chloe said, looking around the room in amaze-ment. The ceiling was painted with what looked like legends of old – Persephone being taken to the underworld by Hades, Athena cursing the spinner woman who mocked the gods, the hammer of Thor stolen by frost-giants, and so many more stories she did not know. "How might I save our kingdom?"

"Our Kingdom?" he asked, taking up the steps to his throne. "I am but a prince. By Faerie Law, until I marry, I cannot be King. I'm hoping you will be the one, Chloe." He sat, and motioned for her to approach. Chloe wasn't sure what to do – to curtsy before him, to ask to excuse herself to check her hair. She was only wearing only one sandal, she'd lost one when she walked through the portal. She curtsied. "You were a good choice." He had her sit on the steps and he walked to a nearby rope and pulled the cord. "The last girl was not near as compliant."

Chloe wanted to ask what he meant, but a beautiful woman entered the throne room. She had no wings. She looked human. Chloe loved her dress, it was a pale pink and had a train Chloe'd seldom seen outside of a movie wedding. She curtsied. "This is Chloe," the prince said. The woman nodded. "I would have her prepared for the test. When she is in Yssa's care, have Hyralie and Ariella come here."

Her prince helped Chloe stand. "I will reveal everything in time, but you must rest," he said. "Keep up your strength. Soon, my princess." He kissed her hand, and Chloe nodded, curtsied, and followed the woman out of the room.

Chloe became uneasy when the woman did not speak, and merely motioned for her to follow. Chloe said, "Do I have to speak to you first?"

The woman shook her head. Chloe thought she was just being rude. Chloe wanted to look around the castle – he was being chivalrous, telling her to keep her strength when there was a kingdom to see!

The handmaid led her down tall, beautiful halls until they came to a large golden door, designed with bas-relief swans – more mythology at a closer glance, she thought she saw the transformation of Zeus, or perhaps it was Odette, the Swan Princess, she couldn't be sure; before the woman passed through the archway. Chloe followed as close to the woman's train as she dared, and heard a most pleasing melody. The girl was about her age, her hair a deep auburn, and she played the lyre beautifully. Chloe then saw the other girl, who looked a little older, about twenty, who was dark haired, slender, and pale, who played the flute.

"Handmaiden, you are dismissed," another woman said. The woman in pink bowed, but did not leave. The tall woman directed her attention to Chloe. "I am Yssa. You are?"

"Chloe," Chloe curtsied, embarrassed by the attention. The other two had ceased their playing to look at her. The woman in pink continued through one of the other elaborate doorways.

"Did the prince make a request?" Yssa asked.

"I believe he called for Hyralie and Ariel," Chloe offered.

"Ariella," Yssa said. "Wait here." Yssa followed after the handmaiden. Chloe looked around the room while they were gone, amazed at how beautiful quarters the servants had.

"Practice your playing still," Yssa said to the brunette when she had returned, another beautiful girl behind her. The brunette nodded, and went back to her flute, the auburn-haired girl put her lyre away. "I will show her around."

Yssa motioned for Chloe to follow her. There were other girls in the much larger room, and there was an indoor pool of sorts, as well as fountain. One painted, while another worked on a loom, while another braided another's hair.

"Sisters, make yourselves beautiful, our prince has returned," Yssa announced, "I would like you all to see his selection, Chloe."

They gathered round to look at her. The women ranged in size, shape and race, but all were young; not one of them looked a day over twenty-four. Some wore elaborate ball gowns and others, simple dresses, but Chloe could not say any was more fair than the last. "She's got grass stains on her feet," one of the girls said. She thought she heard two talk in a different language, giggling, though they all appeared to understand her in English.

"That doesn't matter," Yssa said. "She is candidate to be our queen, the prince will have her join us as one of his dancing princesses."

Chloe's heart raced. "I didn't know he had other... princesses," she said.

"Neither did I," said one girl, "but is not his love worth more than mortal love? Is it not the better to be shared by something greater?"

"Has he called for me?" one of the girls asked Yssa.

"He has called for Hyralie and Ariella," Yssa said. "In the meantime, we have to turn this into a proper princess."

The other girls quickly lost interest in Chloe, but she saw their eyes follow her and Yssa around the room. Chloe saw caged songbirds, chosen for their plumage rather then their ability to carry note. The walls were tall and the room spacious. There were no guards, but there was no reason to go anywhere but the room. Yssa instructed three girls to bring Chloe something to eat and drink, and the others returned to their activities.

"The prince has taught me little of what it is I must do to save his kingdom," Chloe said after it was clear that Yssa would not tell her anything unless she was asked.

"Save his kingdom? You are naïve," one said.

"Hush, she may very well be the queen," said another.

"I have been here for three hundred years," said the first, "I do not think there will ever be one to pass the test."

"Not now!" snapped a third. "I hope that you are the one," she said, and curtsied to Chloe.

"Come, dear, let us get you out of that, so that we may teach you to dance properly."

Chloe thought her outfit fine enough, though not in character, she wanted to ask them to care for it, after all, it was a loan from a friend. She though about that friend. At the time, she didn't think to go home, though she left a message on her father's cell. She was sure once her prince was free, and it wouldn't take long, she could explain everything. She hoped her friends and family wouldn't worry. She hoped that the glamour wouldn't affect Jane once her prince was no longer around to enchant her.

Chloe wanted to wear a green dress, as she'd been told green brought out her hazel eyes, but Yssa chose instead a pale lavender. It was a good second choice. She half expected a medieval ball gown, but the dress was strange in design and she had no idea whatsoever on how to put it on, but it was lovely and minimized her shoulders. When she caught a glance at her reflection, she expected a transformation. She was still not akin to the ladies.

"Do not worry," one said, "I was the same. You're aging slightly. It hasn't taken place yet."

"What hasn't?" Chloe asked. The princess didn't answer.

"Come, now we will teach you how to please our master," Yssa said. "He is so very kind of us, to give us this large chamber, and all we need do is delight him with our dancing. Come, I shall show you how to kneel properly, and perhaps the others will favour us with their dancing and song."

Chloe wondered how she could ever walk as gracefully as Yssa. The second princess she saw upon entering their home played the flute better than any she'd ever heard, another a harp, and she had a lovely voice. All the princesses danced. How beautiful and how wonderful they danced! They would switch from something that looked like ballet to something more tribal and mystic, and in an instance more they were beautiful ballroom dancers. What they lacked were the male partners, of course, but on occasion two would meet and dance and twirl, as if the other were the prince, and she his chosen princess.

"You looked scared, my dear," Yssa said. "Is something wrong?"

"I thought I was coming to save the prince, to set him free," Chloe said. "I was not expecting this."

"You are," Yssa said, "but we must first prepare you for your trial."

"Every girl here has failed?" Chloe asked.

Yssa smiled not unkindly. She had the most amazing, beautiful brown eyes. "All of us here have failed," she shook her head, "but you, who come willingly, may succeed yet."

"Willingly?" Chloe asked. Yssa's smile in her eyes died, as if she was remembering something from so long ago. "I am sorry, I didn't mean to-"

"It is best to forget that world. There are a few here who cling to what they were," she said, "It is best not to hurt them that way."

Chloe wanted to ask about the trial, about how it was she was to save the kingdom, but she felt like she was breaking some sort of rule by speaking out of place. There was much to learn about being a princess, she found, and found herself wondering why her prince, who said he loved her, called two of his other princesses to his side when he returned.

9

The Prince and the Weavers

The river the pixie led Jane to was beautiful. Most of the willow trees were fake, but looked pretty. The path split at the river, which edged about a steep rocky mountain. She wasn't sure which direction to take. Jane felt like taking a dip, but she figured she'd likely disrupt the sea hag or be turned into a frog. Her feet ached, and she was hungry. "Maeld? Where now? Maeld? Maeld!" She put the backpack down and looked for her guide, half expecting to see him in her bag. She looked through the energy bar supplies. She wished she'd bought more, saving 35 cents no longer felt like such a great idea. She peeled back her boots and let her feet air out, as she looked at the lily pads. The water seemed very clean and clear, so unlike the murky lakes of Manitoba. She cupped her hands and tasted it. Jane had never tasted anything so sweet in her life. The two suns were now high overhead. Jane yawned, and felt like a nap, but figured that would be the best way to end up captured. "Chloe, you better appreciate all of this."

She almost nodded off underneath a willow tree when Maeld landed on her nose. "Ah!" she yelped in surprise.

"Ah!" he squealed.

Jane shot up. "You were about to steal the honey," she accused.

"No," he said.

Jane grumbled and stood up. "Where to next?"

"You must swim," he said.

"Great." Jane looked at her provisions. She hadn't thought to bring a swimsuit. She figured it would be best not to be weighed down, and took the knife, sword, and a bottle of water, and gave Maeld a tablespoon of honey before she stashed the bag under some heavy rocks.

"What are you doing?" Maeld asked.

"I can't swim with all that stuff," she said, "and I'm not about to have you steal the bag and fly off. Why do I need to swim?"

"The path to the heartstone is underground. I will show you to the path you must take. It is a long swim – can you make it?"

Jane didn't know how long constituted as a 'long swim'. Jane took off her shoes and tied the laces to her belt. It was awkward to swim in her jeans, but she managed.

The water was so different than home, and relatively warm. Jane could see where she was going in the clear water. She could see the deep ponds and rocky surfaces. *I wish Mike was here. He'd be swimming to the bottom no problem. I wish Bethany was here. She could keep an eye on Maeld and make sure he's not going to fly off. I wish Chloe were here... ditz.* She looked at the glistening stones at the bottom of the rocky lagoon. She wondered how deep she could dive, and going down she saw a dark tunnel leading under the rocky cliff. She surfaced, and kicked closer to the tunnel and dove again to take a better look. It looked long, and she couldn't see where it went. She surfaced again.

"There you are!" Maeld chattered above her, circling.

Jane positioned herself to see the tunnel. "Are you coming with me?"

"I cannot swim! You need to find the heartstone! It is in the chest!" the fae told her.

Jane sighed. It would have been nice if he told her before - she could have got an airtight container for him. "There's not going to be a chance that any of these quests will specialize in piecing together fashionable hand-me-downs or playing lacrosse or anything, is there?" Jane asked. Maeld looked at her quizzically and landed on a nearby rock. "Where can I find the chest?"

"The minotaur guards it," he said, "Defeat him, and steal the heartstone."

Jane paused her dive. "I could have swore you said, 'minotaur',," she said.

"I did," he said.

"I thought a minotaur was some sort of Greek myth."

"You assumed there was only one?" the pixie asked after an awkward silence.

Perhaps it's a mini-minotaur. "What does this look like?" Jane asked. "Is it in the shape of a heart? A cartoon heart, or a real heart?"

As Jane had determined earlier, Maeld's usefulness was quite limited. Jane sighed, and taking a deep a breath as she could, dove. The tunnel was narrow, she mostly had to kick and was scared of touching the walls, but soon she swam in darkness, and had no choice. She spotted light up ahead. Jane wondered if there was a monster up ahead or someone waiting to slam a rock down, trapping her under water, but Jane was glad she didn't have far to swim to surface when she reached the end of the tunnel.

Her lungs craved air as she surfaced. As she looked around the chamber, she heard the running water of underground rivers, and was only slightly surprised by the glowing vegetation and fungus ahead of her. "Where's the light coming from?" she asked, and heard only a slight echo.

The cavern seemed to glow, though at closer inspection the rocks reflected the light given off by the moss. Jane poked a patch, and it grew dark as if annoyed. "Now I'm cold," she muttered, putting on her sandals so her wet shoes could dry. "I should have asked Maeld for more information. Or grabbed him and made him come along." Jane considering diving back and getting him. "He's probably getting an army of annoying little leprechauns to move those stones." She reached into her pocket, surprised she still had the lighter on her. She lit it, but it made next to no difference in the tunnel, so she put it back in her pocket before she wasted any more fluid.

Jane knew enough B-movies and old textbooks to know what a

minotaur was: a bull-man thing that haunted a labyrinth of sorts, but she couldn't remember the story. The tunnel was narrow and didn't seem fit for someone to walk, and given that it was supposed to be a labyrinth, she expected a choice. After several minutes, away from the water, the glowing mosses grew more sparse. Jane felt her way through the tunnel, though she could see where it would lead there were few markers and she had no rope or even bread to mark her trail, but there were few breaks in the path. *A lot of good that would do*, she thought. *Probably attract some sort of giant rat to follow me. Then again, a magical rat might be more helpful than Maeld.*

The stone beneath her feet crumbled and Jane kept herself from screaming. Jane scolded herself. "Calm down, Jane. You're going to be alright. You're going to be fine..."

Jane closed her eyes, and listened. *Just the cold, running water of the river behind me and... well, above me. We're underground, Jane, this is insane.* She listened again. Something else was making the rocks stir. *Something's here. Of course something's here, it's probably a rat, Jane. The big stupid rat you were just wishing for.*

Jane eventually found several forks in her path, but came to the conclusion that it was worse, because there was no way for her to mark her trail, save to leave her equipment behind. She used the knife to cut her socks into little pieces, and used scraps of fabric to mark the way she went. The corridors of stone grew narrower as she continued, until she came to a dead end. She continued to the dark corner, just in case it was a trick, but all she found was solid, unmoving stone. "Well, one way down. I wonder how many dead bodies there are at the end of these paths. It would be nice if I had a map, or something."

"My dear, are you lost?" The sudden voice spooked Jane. She turned around quickly, and despite the darkness, Jane could make out a kindly old human face. Definitely not one of the fair folk, she looked ancient. The old woman leaned on a cane, evidently blind. "I can help you, if you are lost," said the old woman. She dressed simply, with a long jacket that reached to the rocky floor, though she was mostly hidden in shadow.

Jane walked towards her. "I would love some help! Do you live here?"

"That I do, my sweet," said the old woman, "I live here to avoid that nasty prince's spells. Those who will not serve he would send to sleep for all eternity! Come."

"I don't even know where I'm supposed to be going. Maeld said I needed the heartstone, so that I could wield the Staff of Silver-" Jane rounded the bend, and saw the woman's lower body extending from behind the turn in the path. She thought the woman tall, and Jane tried not to stare at the eight spindly legs and large bulb proceeding out the bottom of the old woman's tattered coat. Jane froze as the woman's long legs circled round her, and brought her closer, and inspected Jane with her cane.

"Ah, I see. Are there any others who came with you? No? Pity," the spider-woman said. "Ah, you are rather thin, are you not? Come my child. I must fatten you up."

"Let go of me!" Jane squealed. Jane tried to struggle, but the woman was quite strong, and already had sticky webbing on Jane's arms, dragging her back as she tried to escape. Suddenly, the woman lifted Jane off the ground and wrapped the sticky silk around her legs. "Somebody, help me!" Jane cried.

"Shush!" The woman spat the webbing from her mouth around Jane's lower face. Jane found it hard to breathe. She went for the sword she had taken from the wolfman, only to have one of the spindle legs relieve it from her, and smash the blade upon the wall.

"Sister dear?" another asked. Jane had to look up. She could see the outlines of another old spider-woman above. "You were planning on sharing, I hope."

"Of course, sister dear," said the one who had Jane. "With my favourite sister, of course."

"Sisters," another said. Jane would have screamed if she could.

"Of course," the first muttered.

The second examined Jane with her tendril. She was a larger spider, and much fatter, and examined Jane. "With mortals like this, it's almost worth it to sneak to the palace. Can you imagine, what powers we'd gain from one of his pretty princesses?"

"Come child," said the third, "it has been more than ten years since we've been properly fed."

While Jane was slow in the tunnels, these women were not. They moved in complete darkness easily and scale the walls like they walked on flat surface, Jane did not think to climb up through this anthill like maze, nor did she think she could without rope. *How did Maeld expect me to do this?* Jane thought, but most of her thoughts were: *I'm going to die.*

Jane's initial captor weaved along the passage, and upon making a big enough web, put Jane on it. She opened the gag on Jane's mouth, and strung her up better. Jane strained for the knife in her pocket. The spider women had already stolen her sword, but Jane wondered if it could do anything against the webbing. Try as she might, the webbing did not release, instead it stretched and the moment Jane gave it snapped back into place. Jane could not reach into her pocket.

Jane did not expect the women to work so swiftly, for all their bickering they were quick. She'd seen her grandmother crochet many afghans, but what should have taken a spider a morning they did in a matter of minutes. Jane would have marvelled at the complexity of the webbing were she not their captive, and they made themselves walkways, for they while they scurried about the rocky surface, they were much faster on their own webs. The third hurried away to get them tools, though Jane wondered if the others would wait for her to return.

"Spoils, what would you like?" the second asked.

"The eyes," said the first. "Mortal eyes are very lively."

Jane fought against the sticky webbing. "You must not get a lot of mortals that come down here!" Jane told them.

"Not yet!" the other snapped and hit the other. Jane thought they would fight amongst themselves and she smelt venom from their stingers, but the first said, "There is fight in her still! Submission is key here, I think."

Jane felt reinvigorated when they said that. *If you want submission from me, you've another thing coming,* she thought as they argued what they'd take for themselves. The third came back too soon, and in her arms was an assortment of tools and bottles, charms and books wrapped up in a faded leather casing. Jane tried to figure their plan when the first turned to her, "Ah yes, the hair. Good choice."

Jane thought she'd be bald, but instead they cut her braid right close to her scalp. She felt a twinge of relief, than anger. The first giggled, and threw it onto the fire. "What was the point of that?" Jane demanded.

The one who did it embraced the smoke, and Jane realized for the first time, the pair were blind, and could not see, for their eyes were slashed out. "I feel her mortality already!" she breathed in the smoke, "Oh, sister you must have a taste!"

"Of course!" the other did as well, and she too inhaled the smoke.

"Her eyes!"

"Not yet!" the third said. The third picked a bottle from the assortment she'd brought. Jane had thought it empty at first, but it was translucent, and that there was some sort of liquid inside. The third spider-witch opened the bottle and sniffed it as if it was fine perfume, before turning her empty orbits to Jane.

"Now, my dear, you smell like fear but you taste like anger," said the third, "why did you come to this place?"

"I-" When Jane opened her mouth, the second used her spindle leg and forced Jane's mouth to open wider. Jane screamed as the first said, "That will hardly fatten her up at all."

"You would do it with sweet nectar, or perhaps faerie flesh?" the other asked. "Come my dear, you know a woman is only desirable if she is full of body. It will be easier for you, and tastier for us!"

Jane tried to close her jaws, to move her head but the second added another leg and finally a bony hand was on her face. Jane couldn't move. The liquid was cold and disgusting, tasting of old rot and beer. Jane tried not to swallow, but the third sister used her hands to wrench Jane's mouth shut, and then another to close her nostrils. Jane swallowed and then wretched, but the spider woman forced the concoction down her throat again, forcing her to drink the contents of the entire bottle. When the bottle was empty the women cackled, and Jane breathed, coughing, her eyes tearing up. She didn't understand, not until she felt her body grow heavy. She hurt all over, like she was swelling. Though scared, she looked over to see her arms grow fat, like a hog, and the webbing about her break as her clothes stretched and grew holes. She looked down, and though her breasts grew massive, for the first time, but she could not see her enormous feet past her belly. Her sleeves broke open. The spider witches cackled. The webbing began to loosen its hold, and Jane fell down. Jane tried to get up, but her muscles could not lift her immense body, the fat effectively captured her. The spider-witches laughed, and Jane could not tell which one spoke.

"Shall we take her eyes now?"

"One moment more. The pig needs to know what she is."

Jane clenched her eyes, and told herself it was all a bad dream. She knew no story where the maiden was turned into something so grotesque. She'd read myths where the gods' lovers had been turned into an assortment of livestock to keep their jealous wives from destroying them, but she did not imagine this. Jane felt herself be turned over to her back by the spider legs. "Open your eyes, what need you of them? You are helpless, give them up."

Jane used the last of her strength to strike at the face breathing down into her, ordering her. Jane was surprised she could reach across her chest to hit the spider-witch. The spider-witch screamed in surprise, and her sisters cackled at her. The closest said, "I will take her tongue instead of her heart, I think."

"You made your claim!" another snapped.

Jane hazarded a peek when she heard a roar down the chasm, especially when the three spider witches grew just as scared.

"Brace sisters, he is but moving," said the second. They waited in silence, and the sound came again - much closer. "Ward him off."

"You ward him!" said the first.

Jane had never felt so disgusting in her life, her cheeks were fat and swollen and she could hardly move. Breathing was hard. She stopped feeling sorry for herself when she felt the rocks rumble beneath her. She didn't have the strength to do much, but she managed the strength to roll over, and lift her fat neck up.

The minotaur was *huge*.

The spider witch women crawled over Jane and began to hiss. "Be gone, mindless beast!" said the third. "You'll not have our spoils!"

He roared and swung a massive grotesque hand, sending one against the wall. The other went for her potions, but he grabbed her. She flung green dust in his eye and he cried out and released her. The spider-witch sunk her teeth into his arm, but he grabbed her again, and threw her into her wicked sister. The third spat webbing at him, but he growled and grabbed it and swung it round, raking the spider witch into the stone walls. He looked at Jane, and she thought she saw smoke come from his great nostrils. He moved towards her, and picking her up with no less ease then were she her thin self, carried her down a stone chamber.

Jane felt like a cheesy 50's unconscious heroine, being dragged off in tatters kicking and flailing, save for she was a disgusting pig rather than a ravishing beauty. The beast had her over his shoulder, she didn't know what was worse: eaten alive or basted and prepared.

"Mortal girl," said the minotaur, "stop kicking me."

"Let me go!" Jane hollered.

"Not until we lose them. I will drop you if you pull on my nose ring again. What are you doing down here? What are you doing in this land? Did the Faerie Prince steal you?" he demanded as he jostled her down the cavern.

"No, he stole my friend, and I came for her!" Jane said. "Why do you care?!"

He looked at her, and eventually put her down. "That is a nasty spell," he said.

"How do you know I'm not really like this?" Jane asked.

"You really are mortal," he said, picking her up again. "Do not make me linger; one witch I can handle, but not three at once!"

Jane had ridden horses before, but never a bull. At one point, the cave was so narrow he warned her to press close to him, and he went on all fours. She wondered if she was too heavy for him, though despite his great muscles, he seemed gentle with her.

His home looked like a grandmotherly cottage, on the other side of an underground lake he had to leap across. "You... you'd think this was a human's home," Jane said.

"I was human, once," he said, putting her down at a large expanse of the room and finding a blanket for her to wrap herself in. Jane found the strength to sit up and cover herself. "My name is Bijan," he said.

"You were human once?" Jane asked. "What happened? What do you know of the Faerie Prince, what-"

"Are you hungry?" he asked.

She was famished, but did she dare to eat any of the food in this land? Persephone was condemned to live beneath the earth for six months of the year for a little pomegranate. She looked down at the expanse of her body. She wasn't sure she'd ever eat again. "No, I'm alright."

"Suit yourself." He lumbered into the back. She heard chickens clucking. He came back with a wheel of cheese and a dozen chicken eggs, and began to boil the eggs over the fire.

"Where do you get the cheese from?" Jane asked.

"The prince is quite fond of it," he said, "I help myself. He should have made me less powerful when he cursed me. What is your name, maiden?"

"Jane," she replied.

"You seek your friend who was taken by the Faerie Prince?" Bijan asked. He chuckled. "I was a prince, once. I don't look it now, do I?"

"No," Jane said. "I've never heard of a Prince Bijan."

"You wouldn't have," said the minotaur. "I was third son of the king's youngest brother. No one mourns me now. Do you have any news of my homeland? Persia, it is called."

"Persia? The middle east is... well, I know a bit about Israel," she said.

He frowned. "Israel has not been for more than a millenium, girl, I doubt it would ever come to be again," he said. "I know not your coloring. You must be... Canadian?"

"How do you know about Canada and not about Israel?" Jane demanded.

"You are not the first person I have met from this century. The world is strange from when I left it. Every time I can't tell, I just guess Canadian.".

Jane crossed her arms. "I'm actually First-Nations Canadian, if you must know. On my mother's side we're Metis. Mostly French on my dad's, but I've been told I look most like my great-aunt Lucy, who I've never met. She lives in BC."

"Just because I have heard of Canada, does not mean I know your meaning, small one. Though I have heard of *French* before. It is just good to speak to another human, though now, only my mind is human. What Kingdom is Metis?"

"It's not a kingdom, it's a people," she said. "More than a hundred years ago, white fur-traders went trapping and hooked up with native women. We're recognized as distinct from white, and native." She frowned. It was the briefest history she could manage, her heritage wasn't what mattered at the moment. "Did the Faerie Prince kidnap you to make you guard his heartstone?" she asked.

Bijan shook his massive head, and snorted. "What do you know about the heartstone?"

"It sounds cheesy," Jane said.

"I was a foolish prince," Bijan said. "Rather than love the daughter of a king, I loved her handmaid. Stupid was I, when all she loved was a figurehead."

"You were to marry a princess and instead wed her servant?" Jane asked.

"No. I married the princess as I was told, secured a treaty between our people, who were once our enemies," Bijan said. "Had I loved my wife, perhaps she would not have been seduced by the same cur that stole your friend."

"But, that would make you hundreds – if not thousands – of years old," Jane said.

"Hundreds," he said, "I have marked the time. The days pass here like they do at home. Home," he mused, chuckling slightly. "I've spent most of my life here – and I don't know if you can call this life. I have been here for well over three hundred years, young one. I followed after him, much like you did," Bijan paused, his eyes looking distant. "I loved her not, but had duty to her. Her treacherous handmaid told her of our affair. The prince came for her then - I followed after my wife, and he turned me thus. To be treated as a monster, should I find my way back among our people." His great ears moved like a cat's when he talked. "I had hoped to be free of this spell and return to my kingdom, but I am likely not remembered by any historian – just a foolish, spoiled prince, lost to his time and people."

"You seem but a beast in body," Jane said. "We speak the same language."

"Yes," he said. "I learn the languages of those who seek the heartstone. I thought it best to learn the language of the Red Queen first, and I think I speak it well."

Jane wasn't sure what questions to ask first. "You give this heartstone to some who come looking for it," Jane said.

"Yes," he said, "the heartstone is a concentration of power. Those of us who have no power can wield some magic against the sidhe and their wicked kin. Many seek me out, but I will admit you are the first female I have seen in these caves," he said. "Parties of men would not have attempted what you did."

"When I journeyed here, I saw a man in a glass coffin," Jane said. "I didn't mean to wake him, but when I freed him, he... turned into a wolf."

The minotaur laughed. "He cannot stop those who truly love the morals he abducts from coming, so he seeks to turn our passion into our undoing. When I came for my wife, I joined forces with another who he had locked away in a castle of sorts for what he claimed was a century, though he later admitted it became difficult to tell time. We made it to The Faerie Prince's palace, and The Prince cursed us both, turning us into monsters," Bijan sighed. "My friend became a beast. I cling to my humanity now."

"I thought you were his guardian over this stone," Jane said, "a monster to guard this treasure so that he would not be undone."

"Many have thought that," he said. "You would not believe how many young princes would not stand to reason, even after I explain thus to them."

"I was told the heartstone was somehow related to some staff that could break his power," Jane said.

"That is true," the minotaur said. "Jane, I would not send a woman to fight where I have seen great men fall. He has taken many, and many times have fathers, brothers, lovers, mothers and sisters gone after to free the dancing brides. With few exceptions, when the one who is stolen escapes and the heroes flee. We have all failed to defeat him. I would know this better than any, I think. None can break his power – he is heir to this world, and he is not bound as his uncles. If you were a warrior, perhaps I would aid you, but you are but a young girl who very nearly got eaten by Arachne and her sisters. They quiver in fear of him."

"There is a chance," Jane said, "you yourself said you could not handle three of them."

"I've never gotten caught by them," he said.

"Perhaps not alone," Jane said, "but what about together? I could use a friend."

"I will not deliver you to death, nor give you hope lest you become one of his toys. I fear I exist only for his amusement. Would you be a beast to remain hidden, knowing death will not come for you? Would you suffer a fate worse than the princesses?" Bijan asked. "He can keep you alive, Jane. You will be forgotten, neglected, and death's embrace will not find you."

"I will not abandon Chloe," Jane said. "Tell me about the heartstone. Tell me about his power. I can stop him. I know I can. I have to."

He snorted. Jane wondered if he had his moments where his mind became more animal, but the look in his eyes told her he was deeply contemplating. "I have taken others to get the staff," he said, "but they have all failed to take it. I fear..." he paused. "I fear if someone does take it, and the prince defeats them, and takes the staff for himself. He is very clever."

"What about if he succeeds?" Jane asked. "I don't think anyone else is coming for ten years, Bijan."

He snorted. "Every ten years I fear he finds the one, and every year he rages when the girl is not the Queen. I have waited this long, I will wait longer."

"Bijan," she said, "We're on the same side here. I came for my friend. Please."

He snorted, and bowed his head. "Very well. I will keep being the guardian of the stone, and I will accompany you on this quest."

Jane nodded and he went back to his cooking. She looked around his home. He had plate and utensils – crude ones. The food did smell good. She looked at her disgusting body. She had fat on her fingers and on the back of her arms. He said little of the spell, she wondered why; if anything, her lack of mobility would cripple the quest. She noticed a good many barrels by the doors.

"What are those for?" she asked. "Rainwater?" She frowned. "But for a few small things that grow, there is no need for rain."

"Smart girl – the water in this world is good, but alas, I keep my water elsewhere. The barrels are full of oil."

"For what?"

"Pest control. Are you sure you are not hungry?" he asked.

"I've only got faerie tales and mythology to help me out," Jane said, "there is a story that there was once a... god who took a girl to be his bride, and she had to remain by his side half of the year because she ate a bit of pomegranate."

"Ah, you are a hellenist then," he said.

"No," Jane said. "I'm Catholic, but I like to read about other religions. I kinda know some mythology. I am scared of getting into trouble. I did not expect... this."

"It is not the food that will trap you, but your actions. Come, eat something," he said. "The food that the fae make looks pretty but has no substance – it tastes like ashes. I grow my own corn, I mind my own chickens, and I do not feel bad about stealing the rest from the prince's warehouses."

"I cannot walk," Jane said.

"You cannot break the spell if you do not fight it," he said, making himself a plate, but instead of sitting down to eat walked to a door. "Come."

Her legs were heavy, but Jane found that she could stand. The chickens at least looked like normal chickens – Jane had some family who kept a farm, but she'd only visited a few times and been told not to go out and bother the cows. She was allowed to help gather eggs, but that was years ago. He had a patch of open sky and had orchards growing in addition to rows of corn, as well as feed for the chickens. She wondered where exactly in the mountain chain they were. "You don't eat the chickens?" she asked.

"Their eggs have yet to hatch a single chick," he said, "were I to eat one, I'd likely gobble them all up on a single meal. It is better, I think, to eat their eggs rather than prey on spider witches." He reached into a tree and gave her an orange.

"These trees are real," Jane said, running her hands over the bark.

"They grow on what remains of my mortality," he said. "This world feeds off of it. The things that came from our world seem to need us. And, I feel better around them."

Jane peeled back the skin and sunk her teeth into the sweet nectar of the orange. She felt heat coming to her eyes. "Jane, are you alright?" Bijan asked.

"Am I going to be like this forever?" Jane asked.

The minotaur knelt, and spoke kindly, "Jane, you are speaking to a man who has lost everything but his mind. There are worse curses, I can assure you. Perhaps you should think about returning to your home."

"I can't abandon Chloe! It's-" Jane paused. She didn't know what to say. "I can't let him win."

"Finish your orange. I'll find something more suitable for you to wear," he said.

"You have something that'll fit?" she asked, before looking down at her orange to see that her arms were much smaller. "Huh?"

"Keep fighting, lest you be turned into a pig permanently," he said,

"You are lucky, they never went after your mind. The weavers wanted the maiden. He wanted a beast."

Jane was tempted to ask if they could bring oranges with them on their journey. She was upset that her hips and breasts shrunk down much quicker than the rest of her, her belly seemed to be the last thing to return to its original shape. As soon as she was normal again, she felt ashamed that she had ever felt so disgusting in her own skin – she wasn't the vain one, after all.

Bijan returned with clothing befitting a boy. "It will be big on you. You are a slender thing, and tall besides! We were almost the same height!"

He gave her privacy to change. The clothes were a bit big, but of good quality, if only ancient. She ran her fingers through her hair, and wished it would return. It was so short. She looked at her reflection in the water. She looked too much like a boy. Jane looked at her old clothing, and rolled them together. They'd go at the bottom of the bag when she got back to the surface. She'd lost the sword from the forest in the tunnels, but the clothes came with a lighter sword with a leather scabbard. She fastened the sword to her hip as her guardian returned. "Not the sword," he said.

"Why not?" Jane asked.

"Because I am going to do any fighting that will be required," he said. "You need not carry a weapon."

Jane thought about it. He might have been cursed, but he was exceptionally strong and tough. \him holding a sword would be like her wielding a toothpick. "My guardian may need help. Besides, we're to defeat him together are we not?" she asked. "We'll be a team, alright? I can carry it, and maybe if you get transformed back into a human, you'll need it." Jane secretly hoped she wouldn't cut herself drawing it.

He snorted, and quickly left her in the orchard. *Perhaps he thinks the staff will make him human again. Perhaps he thinks he can kill the prince this way,* the word kill echoed in Jane's thoughts. She didn't come to kill anybody. She came to save Chloe. She thought about it, looking at the clothing he'd given her, and the old blade.

Jane heard a beastly yowl. She quickly sped back towards his cottage. She didn't see him inside, and looked outside the window. Faeries! He had been consorting with them all along! Jane looked around hurriedly, until she saw webbing overrun his arms and legs, and he quickly smacked the faeries backwards. A large spider jumped on him, then another, the cottage shook as he fought them off.

"Run, Jane!" he cried when he saw her. "Make for the orchard!"

Jane didn't know what to do, at first, but he'd mentioned that there was oil in the barrels. She found a barrel, rolled it out, and set it on fire and kicked it towards the group. The fae and spiders retreated, and Bijan managed to scramble into his house just as the tunnel before them erupted into flame.

"You've quite the following," he breathed, bolting the door behind him. "You should have fled."

"They were going to kill you," Jane said.

"They'd torment me and grow bored," he said, "I am a beast, remember? You must go, quickly. They will be back."

"I scared them off," she said, before recognizing the smell. "Bijan, you're hurt!"

His blood was red. Despite his hooves and beastly features, when he was in pain he looked the most human. Jane put pressure on the cuts, and used his rags to try to make a bandage. Bijan breathed heavily, hairy hand over his woollen chest. He closed his eyes. "I smell smoke."

Jane wished she knew an appropriate swear. Either they had set the cottage on fire, or they were trying to smoke them out. "To the orchard," he said. "It's our only chance."

"Is there a way out?" she asked.

"Yes," he said. Jane helped him, surprised that she was strong enough to help the massive beast. "The water here: there is an underground route I can divert it long enough, you can ride down, but then you'll need to keep running."

"Not without you," Jane said.

"I will not fit, Jane!" he told her. "I'm sorry your guardian turned out to be of no help to you. Go release the chickens," he said, "The spider witches are blind. The chickens will distract them. I will stop the flow of water."

"Can we not fight them off?" Jane asked.

"I've been here for so long," the minotaur said, "and now, time is so precious. A moment."

He ripped open his shirt. Jane started to shake. "No, Maeld said the chest. That's not-"

"He turned me into a beast. I swore I would see the Prince of the Faeries demise. I will do what I can do have it happen, even if it must take place at the hands of a young girl," he said. "Lady Jane, I do not give this freely. I would not normally give this to a woman. Do not let him take the stone. Absorb it yourself. You must go, and go quickly. Release the chickens; they will buy you time. Hurry!"

Jane didn't know what force commanded her, but tears filled her eyes as she ripped open Bijan's chest. He let out a cry befitting a beast, not a man, and she saw the jewel embedded in his ribs. "Take it," he ordered.

"You'll die," Jane said.

"It's not my heart. Besides," he said, "he won't let me die."

Jane pulled the large stone from his chest and he let out another horrible cry. "The chickens, go!" He was in obvious pain. Jane wondered if the stone in her hand was what kept him safe; it felt warm in her hands. It was not shaped like a heart at all. He put a hand on hers, and forced it to her own skin. She felt the heartstone mesh against her clothing, as if wondering how to join with her. Jane staggered towards the chicken coop, and pulling a hand away saw it had already started to merge through her clothes. Jane put a hand over the stone and forced it in, and nearly fell down as she felt the heat overwhelm her body. She looked over at Bijan, he was already on his feet, making his way towards the watermill. He had only a dozen chickens, and their cages were crafted in care and were quite clean, so far as chickens went. Jane forced herself to move, and opening the chicken hutches she saw a long spindle tendril and closed the door.

"Hello little pig," came an old woman's voice. "Won't you let me in?"

Jane kept herself at the door; barring the witch entrance. "You are trapped, little pig. Come now, before the faeries come. Would you be the prince's toy, like the minotaur? He is in our web – we will enjoy the flesh that will not die, but we prefer *you*. Come, let us end your suffering!"

Jane took Bijan's sword and slashed through a leg, and the spider witch screamed and Jane ran. She felt a leg on her back and she fell, dropping the sword. "You've grown skinny, little piggy. But I won't have two sisters to share you with."

The Spider opened her fangs and another spider tackled the one pinning Jane down. Jane got up, and had no time for the sword. Faeries were with the other spiders, she saw Bijan fighting them off, and smelt the burning of the orchards. "There she is!" shouted a fae.

Jane made it to the water, and looked back one final time at Bijan, and dove in, swam, seeing the bare patchwork of narrow space he meant for her to follow down into the depths. She plunged into water and swam until her lungs gave way she kicked for the surface, only to feel the swift current pull her down with barely a gulp of air. She coughed and struggled to the surface for a breath, and keep from being dashed against the hard rocks. Eventually she was blindly swimming, gasping, until she saw light, and the sensation of falling. She didn't know where she was, but as she kicked and gasped for air, and in the bright day light she suddenly knew she was outside of the caves. She recognized the forest, and she quickly swam for the side. She recognized the cobblestone path, but didn't know where she was. She thought she heard a cry up high, as she searched the path. "How did they find me so fast? Maeld?" she called. No answer.

She put a hand over her own chest, and thought it felt strangely warm, despite her wet clothing. When she was still, she could feel a strange sensation, a second pulse. *Bijan, I hope you are alright. You're more human than most.* She recognized the fork in the road ahead, and made her way back to where she had begun her quest into the caverns.

She went to the rocks to get an energy bar, only to find the rocks disturbed and her backpack missing. "Maeld?" she called, looking around. He didn't seem strong enough to lift any of those stones, but she didn't doubt it was him.

The bright sun was still high in the sky, but one of the moons seemed fuller. She thought she heard another monstrous cry in the distance. She tried not to think about Bijan. She could do nothing to help him. "Maeld!" Jane called. "Maeld! Where are you?"

She didn't know which way to go, and was getting cold. She decided since she'd already come from the path, she might as well continue and follow the river downstream.

She followed the path along the river and followed the current, and kept her eyes skyward, in case she spotted any pixies.

Floating castle. How am I supposed to make it to a floating castle? She heard a low horn in the distance, in the trees – Jane thought the sound more akin for hunting than summoning the prince's guard. *I better get some cover,* Jane decided, and hurried down the path. After a sharp bend, the path ended before the rock did, but just barely. Jane saw a cliff ahead and she spotted a castle hovering above the horizon. Literally, floating higher than anything else in the distance, and Jane saw a great expanse of forest in the valley before her. She stood at the tip of a waterfall, and looked at the distant floating castle. "How am I supposed to get up there?" Jane muttered, realizing how high up she was, and how much higher still the castle was. "This doesn't make any sense. Dorothy, Alice, even Lucy Pevensie had it easier than this."

Jane knew the direction she had to go; the problem was she needed to climb down to the valley floor. She couldn't tell which vines were real, and which ones would crackle and tear when she touched them. She contemplated going back the way she came, when someone nearly bowled her over the edge.

"Hey!" Jane shouted at the fellow wearing a red fox's tail and fake ears. He was about her size, perhaps an inch or two shorter, slightly chubby he looked like the eternal youth that plagued this land had managed to avoid him. At first she thought there was mud on his face, but someone had smudged black make-up on his nose and had made messy stripes to serve as whiskers on his flushed cheeks. "Watch where you're going!"

"Out of my way!" He pushed Jane again, this time deliberately, and continued to the river, and plopped in, and tried to hide among the reeds.

Jane was about to question him, but she heard another voice come from the forest. "Tallyhoo! The fox has gone this way!"

Jane looked back to the woods to see a good many deer bounding through in the woods, and mounted riders atop the deer. She wondered how light they must have been until she saw the deer, which were thick and red and had great curved horns on their heads, with golden hooves and proper saddles and many wineskins on said saddles. The riders varied in size, many her size, some smaller, several exceptionally tall, but they all seemed to be enjoying themselves. Behind them trailed the pixies, who paid her no attention. She thought them to be all fae at first, but then she saw among them those with hooves on their feet, and others who were furry, centaurs and satyrs and enchanted folks all, while others appeared to be no different than a larger fae with strange antlers coming from their foreheads.

"Maiden fair!" said one of the riders, dressed in too bright and gaudy a garb to be taken seriously at any play, let alone a hunting trip. Jane had never gone hunting, but her little brother bored her with details. "Have you seen a fox come this way?"

"I saw an individual with what looked like fake whiskers on his face and a fox tail jump in the river," Jane said, pointing.

"So close to the fall! Huzzah!" he declared, and had his deer trot towards the river.

"I saw him first!" another declared, and crashed his deer into the first. A third joined the fray, Jane was unsure if she should continue to watch or leave before it got sillier.

"Enough!" said another. Though he wore muted colors compared to this party, he looked the most strange. His deer was white, and he had large antlers coming from atop his head, like a deer she'd see at home.

He was actually kind of good-looking and seemed the least buffonish. "I am sorry, mortal, but we get excited easily." He trotted his deer to the river and withdrew a large sword. "I have you now, Fox!"

"Have mercy on me!" the drenched fae wailed.

"You may keep your skin, Fox," said the antlered-fae, "if you're able to pay for it."

"Is that what this is about?" demanded the fae in the river. "Why didn't you just rob me of my money and send me on my way? Why did you dress me like a fox?"

"We haven't had a fox chase in many moons," he said, swiping the man's bag of coins. "This will do nicely, sweet Fox. You may keep your skin, in case we meet again."

"I never–"

"We have caught our fox, gentlemen and notsogentlewomen!" said the leader, ignoring their fox's exasperated monologue. The hunters cheered, and wineskins were opened and horns of wine and ale passed to the victorious. Jane only accepted a drink because she thought it was juice. "Let us hope that the others have made good use of the prince's guard tower this day!"

Jane went to help the round fellow out of the stream, as he was having a hard time crawling up the muddy side on his own. "A lot of help you are," he snapped, squinting at Jane as she helped him. "Oh, a mortal!" He seized her, and fell on top of her. Jane tried to breathe as he picked himself up. "Oh no! I have squashed you! The prince will be most upset with me!"

"Let me go!" Jane snapped, punching him.

To Jane's dismay, it turned out striking fae was akin to slapping one – once again, it felt like she just punched a brick wall. He massaged his face as Jane massaged her knuckles. "That was uncalled for," he said, rummaging through his pockets, "Here we are! This will put you to sleep for a hundred years!" He threw the dust at her before she had a chance to move. Jane tried not to breathe, but eventually smelled the strange concoction and felt its power.

"Hic!" she covered her mouth. "Hic!"

"Curses and drat! I must have something in here that will render you harmless!" he said, searching through his many pockets.

"You- hic! Idi- hic! Ot! Hic!" Jane hiccupped, though all things considered hiccups were more of a nuisance compared to a century long nap. She stomped off from him as he rummaged through his pockets, back towards the cliff face. "If it wasn't for- hic! Me, you'd have tumbled off the- hic! Side!"

She wasn't expecting him to clasp a manacle around her wrist. "Now I've caught you!"

"Give me the- hic! Key this instant! Hic!" She was surprised that he was the stronger of the two, for he looked like he never did anything physical in his life. It couldn't have been more humiliating if he had used a butterfly net. "I aught to – hic!"

"Come along, mortal maid! I'm going to take you to meet a prince. You mortals dream about princes, don't you? He'll teach you some manners," he said, and dragged her from the side of the cliff.

The leader of the merry band came to Jane's aid. "Fox, what are you doing?" asked the hunter.

"This doesn't concern you Sylvanos," said Jane's captor. "You have all my money already, we have no more business."

The antlered-fae looked at Jane. "I am Sylvanos," he said as if it weren't obvious, "the leader of this humble band, and The Great Hunter of the Wood." Sylvanos seemed like the boy your parents would hate, not so much because he kept you out late, but because he wore more make-up than you did.

"Well, great hunter, you've had your fun. I'm off to be a proper citizen-" the fox-fae began.

"The Great Hunter of the Wood. If you chose to call me that, please say the full thing, every time," Sylvanos said. "Fox, not all of us are so scared of the prince that we'll happily drag the first bit of life to him in exchange for a nice pat-pat on the head." He pat-patted his fox on the head. Sylvanos turned his grey eyes to Jane. "Are you are a prince, here to save your princess?" he asked Jane.

"I am a - hic! Girl seeking my- hic! Friend," she said, "are you- hic! Friends with the Faerie- hic! Prince?"

"That I am not, mortal... hic girl," said Sylvanos. "In fact, I seek to be his bane in all things. Come with us! Those who have not hunted the fox are getting us sustenance for this evening, and you look like you would enjoy some very fine cheeses."

"She has a previous engagement," puffed the faerie with a fox's tail. "You know the law! All mortals in our realm are to be brought to the prince! Not even you rebellious scum are willing to take away one of his treasures until he's done with them!"

Sylvanos drew his sword and cut the chain that kept Jane prisoner, unceremoniously grabbing her by the belt, and pulled her onto his deer's saddle. "Yes, we serve a prince who has locked most of our world in endless sleep. Yes, we will bow and serve him no matter what madness takes him," Sylvanos said. "Did he not try to put me and my followers to sleep, Fox? I woke my friends when his magic could not bind me. No matter what Prince Nyveo does, or thinks he may do, his servants brews the finest of beers, and makes the most exquisite of cheeses. And we will be there, to steal those flagons and sample his dairy!" His followers cheered, and finished their drinks. "Come, we have tarried here long enough! Good-bye, sweet Fox! Be sure to have more coin on your pelt next time! Huzzah!"

Jane thought they'd take her just out of sight to annoy the fox, but instead he whispered, "Hold tight, hiccupping heroine," into her ear. Jane felt the white deer's powerful legs move beneath the saddle, and leap from stone to fallen tree to patch of grass, not so much running but bounding through the forest. It might have been exciting if she wasn't constantly whacked by wayward branches. The other hunters bounded and laughed as they raced. Jane simply held her breath in an attempt to stop the hiccups.

It didn't work. She hiccupped as they came across a score of hooded caravans, Jane thought them more like gypsies than Robin Hood in his crew, for they had many deer hooked up to covered wagons and caravans, fry pots and clotheslines hung from every available spot as someone made music from a washing board and an empty jug.

"Sylvanos!" said a woman with much bravado, "have you caught the fox?"

"And sold him back his pelt at a bargain! In our travels, I also found this strange creature," Sylvanos said, slipping off the deer. Jane didn't like being on the deer, and dismounted just as quick. "Seems to be cursed with hiccups."

"Hic! They're getting better!" Jane said, "Thanks for your- hic! Assistance, but I really must be- hic! Going!"

"The prince's men are thick in the woods along the river, all the way to the castle's crossing," said one of Sylvanos' female hunters. "You won't get far."

"We may not look like much, but we are a kindly lot, always willing to help the less fortunate," Sylvanos said to Jane, "you seek the floating castle, yes?"

"Hic! Yes!" Jane said, "How - hic! did you know?"

"Our much-beloved prince has only been at this for... let's see, about four hundred years," Sylvanos said, "I will hear your story when we feast tonight! My men, let us be ready to travel at once!"

Jane was adopted by the female hunters the group, who directed her to a covered wagon and gave her an elixir to cure her hiccups, and proper clothing like they wore, only Jane was given no knife or bow like they had on their backs. "Your hair is so short!" said one.

"The spider witches cut it off," Jane said.

"You defeated Arachne and her sisters?" asked one of the pixies, kicking a pet bird out of its nest.

"I eluded them," Jane said.

"I have always thought those they caught they ate," said another fae. "We can fix your hair!" She one dove into a nearby chest and flung out a wild assortment of herbs and bottles and dried berries, until finally she emerged triumphant. "Drink this potion."

"What is it?" Jane asked.

"You'll like it, trust me," she said.

Jane didn't know what to do, but felt obligated. "I won't turn into a pig?"

"No," said the fae before adding sadly, "I don't think I have the potion for that."

It couldn't be worse if I'm bald, she figured, and downed the bottle. "Just a sip!" said one. Jane's scalp felt strange, and thick hair shot out, nearly knocking several of the pixies back. "Oh!"

The weight on the back of Jane's head was immense, she had a hard time moving her head.

"You took a lot!" said a pixie. "We'll have to cut your hair!"

"I'll weave it into a lovely scarf," said a sidhe, beginning a spinning wheel.

"Let us cut it off her first," said a huntress with scissors.

"Now wait just a moment," Jane said, alarmed from being so short-haired to her hair sticking out of the covered wagon. "I have a say in this." The wagon began to move. Jane directed them to cut it about the same length as it was before - maybe an inch or two shorter. "Where are we going?"

"Wherever our fancy takes us," said one, "and Sylvanos's fancy is doing whatever would annoy the prince best! We have got a lot of treasures from the prince's watchtower, so we should go deep into the woods for the time being."

"But Sylvanos said he'd help me to the floating castle," Jane said.

"He will," said one of the girls, "Sylvanos will help. He is good at helping." They rode for a while, Jane commenting while one of the girls cut her hair to a manageable length and then braided it back in a fashionable style that was common among the huntresses – much better than the single braid that Jane was used to wearing.

"You hardly look human at all now!" she smiled. "And look at all this hair!" Jane got a good look, and was disgusted in the hair that could have made up three Janes. The fae fought over it as the matron of the group began to work the hair at a loom.

"You look like one of us!" cheered another. "You look ready to grow antlers, like Sylvanos!"

"I will grow antlers before this mortal!" another boasted.

"Prince's men! Inspection!" came from a faerie's voice outside.

Jane's heart raced as the caravan stopped. "I thought the prince's men couldn't find us," she said.

"It's more fun this way!" another cheered, and they quickly opened drawers and donned outfits, with fake noses and warts, covering their otherwise beautiful faces to make them appear as dishevelled, bypassing ugly for hideous. As soon as each was finished they left the wagon, the last locked Jane in, but she could easily see outside through a small porthole as their leaders pretended to stumble and be drunk. Her friends cooed and welcomed the prince's men into their wagon.

"I think there's a mortal in my wagon," one sashayed her hips, "if you'll but come in, I'll give you guardsmen the royal tour. Ha cha cha!"

"You pathetic vermin make me ashamed to share the same realm with you," said the captain of the prince's men. "You will, if you spot any mortals, bring them at once to the nearest representative of the prince."

"We do everything for the prince!" laughed one.

"Good luck on finding her, sirs!" said another.

The women came back before the wagons started to move again. "If is a shame they didn't come into the wagon," said one, "must have been something I said." She pulled out a frog's leg from between her front teeth and cackled.

"Can I come out now?" Jane asked. They let her, and Jane was almost enchanted by the way the hunter's caravan moved among a fae village. It was bigger than the sleeping one she'd passed that morning, and she could see an assortment of people, everyone seeming to be working – she saw what she thought were regular cows and someone played a lute by a large fountain, but for the most part the sidhe were busy at a variety of crafts – this place in particular seemed to be alive with industry, she thought she smelled something wonderful – her stomach growled in hunger. Several fae who were not of her companions spotted her from their cottages, but did not point and cry human, so the disguise seemed to work. Their pace was slow enough to walk, so she hopped off the wagon and jogged ahead, looking for Sylvanos. "Where are we going?" she asked when she came upon his deer.

"We are stopping for supplies, and then we will go deep into the forest," Sylvanos said. "You should go and rest. You look like you've had a trying journey already, and I think you will need your strength."

Jane did feel sleepy. She was comfortable with the women she was with, and so she made her way back to the wagon, and curled up on a free mat, and missed the terribly exciting adventure involving coating the mayor of the city in feathers, all the while stealing the most fabled cheeses before disappearing into the deep dark woods.

10

The Hunters of the Wood

When Jane woke up she was alone in the covered wagon, and it was darker than she expected. She sat up when it stopped moving and she heard voices ordering about a camp. She felt like she slept too long, but upon looking saw the sky darkening, but the forest was well illuminated by the two quarter moons. One of the hunter women came into the wagon to get cooking utensils. "Where are we?" Jane asked.

"Deep in the forest," she said. "No one will be able to find you. Go, stretch your legs, but don't wander off too far from the camp."

Jane spotted Sylvanos atop his white deer, barking out orders of tents to be set up and food to be prepared, though as soon as his back was turned his comrades fell onto one another, and there was no shortage of bad comedy to be found as they tried to set up camp. *Rebels indeed,* Jane thought as she stretched her legs. She looked to the woods. They seemed darker, and more sinister in the dying daylight. She watched her companions at first, but her eyes drifted to the many fae in the company. There was great assortment of enchanted folk who rode with them, Jane wanted to ask some of them what they were, but decided it might be rude to do so. "Are you hungry, mortal?" asked one of the pixies.

"I haven't worked yet," Jane said. "And I've nothing to trade for food."

"You are guest among The Hunters of the Wood," said the pixie, dropping a cheese sandwich on Jane's head.

Jane picked the sandwhich up, sniffed it – it didn't smell that bad. She took a bite – it could have used something besides bread and hard cheese. "I thought Sylvanos was The Hunter of the Wood," Jane said.

"He's The GREAT Hunter of the Wood," the pixie said, "and we're The Hunterzzzzz of the Wood. You have to say the entire thing, every time."

Jane walked through the camp and offered to help, but they seemed to be managing just fine without her. Before the sun had finished setting a bonfire was set up, and a fiddle player began a tune to which several other less conventional instruments joined in. Jane marvelled as the faeries danced around the fire, and tried to clap her hands along to the beat. Her stomach growled as she smelt fresh meat over the fire. "Do you dance?" one of the female fae asked. "Come, join us!"

"No, I don't-!" Jane said, but someone grabbed her hand and had them join in their circle. Jane found if you didn't know, it wasn't so much dancing as keeping up and not falling and causing a pile up. She found out the hard way.

"Perhaps in a little while," another said, picking herself off the ground. "You'll be a great dancer next week."

"Where is Sylvanos?" Jane asked, dusting herself off.

"Sylvanos dances now," said the first, pointing across the large fire where several hunters performed a merry jig. "See how fine he dances!"

Jane heard a pan flute and crude drum joining in the washboard and nearly-empty jug, and everyone danced in much merriment. "Ah, the mortal has woken up," Sylvanos said, leaving the dancers who continued their celebration. "Come girl, I will like to listen to your story while we sup."

"Alright, I'll do my best to tell it," Jane said. Once the dancers broke for their dinner, Jane happily accepted the fresh breads and cheeses she was offered when she sat Sylvanos's right hand. She asked for something to drink that wasn't alcohol, but they claimed to serve nothing of that variety, and she was told often times among brigands and rebels that water was precious, but they eventually gave in.

Jane told her story as best as she could, aware that more and more of Sylvanos' people listened in as the story continued. She did not mean to make Chloe sound as bad as she did, and tried to make Bijan sound more like a man, less like a beast. She felt embarrassed telling the story of how fat she'd gotten, and her own despair.

"I like a woman with a lot of body. It shows she knows how to cook. You did well all things considered," Sylvanos said, before looking to his own men. "Us, why, we think it appalling for the prince to turn mortals into monsters! We wouldn't know if we were eating you right now!" Jane glanced at the great slab of meat on the table and pushed down a sudden burst of nausea. There was a good amount of cheering after he said that, but those who rode the great deer seemed to cheer after Sylvanos said much of anything. "We who hunt do so to rid our world of monsters, and keep the trees in line. Tell me, Jane, how do you intend to reach the floating castle?"

"I have no idea," she said, "I was hoping to find Maeld, and he would know the way."

"And how do you plan on learning to use the staff?" asked another of his men.

"I don't know," she said, "Bijan was supposed to be my guardian, but he made it possible for me to escape. I wanted to go back and save him, but he told me to flee."

"It seems to me," Sylvanos said, "that you are in need of help, my dear mortal." Sylvanos took Jane's hand. "I pledge that I will see you to the staff, and I will help you overthrow the prince." His men cheered and more wine was poured.

"You'll help me?" Jane asked. "You really mean it?"

"Of course," he said, "Why, with you as my queen, our illustrious prince will stand powerless before us!"

"What?" Jane asked, drawing back her hand.

"Come now! You need help, and I am willing to help you," Sylvanos said. "Are my men not better than the those the Prince of the Faeries? We turn no one into beasts, except in sport! And in marrying you, I will be free to return to your world, and I will allow my servant to ride free through the night! A real fox hunt, except perhaps when we spot a mortal who deserves it! I'm sure you know a villain who deserves to be hunted down in your woods at home! We will have access to exotic cheeses and fine wines. Oh, the brie!"

"That's what this is about, isn't it?" Jane demanded. "You just want to return to our world, and you need a mortal to do it! Well, I have news for you! I don't think I need your help, Sylvanos. I'm going to defeat the Faerie Prince and make sure none of your kind can ever return to my world!"

The fiddle player looked at Sylvanos nervously. Sylvanos finished his mug, motioned for the nearest hunter holding a pitcher of ale to fill it, took another sip, leaned towards Jane, said, "What makes you think you have any say in the matter?" and went back to his drink.

A cheer went up through the crowd, and wineskins were handed out. Jane stood and stomped as she made her way from the group, but a strong hand gripped her waist.

"Where do you think you're going?" a centaur asked. "It's your engagement party!" He pushed her back to the group, a hand grabbed her arm and spun her and then another grabbed her and the next thing Jane knew, was that she was dancing with several faerie women, one of whom adorned her with a collar, and the next put a bell on it. Sylvanos caught his bride-to-be when she swirled again, the bell rang a most definite *tingle*.

"Ah, you're ready," he said.

"You've got to be joking!" Jane said, trying to stop dancing. She kept tripping over boots and nearly landed on top of one of the smaller pixies several times. "Stop this engagement at once!"

"You're very right. Ladies, do your thing!" Sylvanos ordered, and snapped his fingers, and several of the fae Jane thought were her friends descended upon her.

"That is not what I meant at all!" Jane snapped, but someone put a stone anklet around her boot, another a seashell comb in her hair, another put feather earrings through her ears, another puffed her face with white powder, and another nearly choked her with too strong perfume. Finally, someone clipped a stained kerchief into her hair, and one faerie on each arm continued to make Jane twirl as Sylvanos approved.

"There, you look marvellous," Sylvanos said. "Take her out into the woods."

The faerie women continued to dance, Jane tried to break free from their circle, instead they pushed her in the general direction they desired, but the one time she nearly broke free, they picked Jane up and her bridesmaids broke into a run, leaving the partying camp behind. "Wouldn't one of you rather marry Sylvanos?" Jane demanded, as one of the women smeared her lips with berry juice.

"Oh, what's the fun in marrying him?" one laughed.

"I think she needs horns!" one said.

"We'll give her horns later," said another, "The only potion I have on me is for fox tails and I'm not wasting it on her."

Jane didn't think she looked the part of any bride she'd ever heard of. She heard the sound of the hunter's horn, and started to tremble. She looked back toward the faint light of the camp. At least she was getting further and further away, but she did not know where she was. "Think about it: Woman of the Hunter of the Forest. You'd really be the one in charge," Jane said.

"Why? If he marries you and gains the staff and becomes King, do you have any idea how angry the princes will be?" one laughed. "What am I saying? He will lose interest as soon as he gains the power to return to your world, and we his riders will enjoy hunting mortals once more! I think he will like best to return to your world and leave his half-brother behind! I will bring only the most handsome of young men to this place! Why have Sylvanos, when I can have a harem?"

"Who cares about keeping them? Mortal men make for the most excellent sport, but I would rather enjoy the treasures and fruit of their homes! Tipping cows and swapping babes - Oh, to run free in your world again!" another said. "I think this is silly, giving her a chance to escape."

"Chance?" Jane asked.

"Why, Sylvanos has to catch you, of course," said the faerie who had Jane over her shoulder. "It's in the rules."

"Who makes these rules?" Jane demanded.

"Why, Sylvanos, of course. He decided on them while you slept." When Jane could no longer hear the music she found herself on her feet.

"You can't do this!" Jane snapped.

"Sylvanos is a great huter," the huntress said. She looked unhappy. "Will you treat your maidservant well, Lady Jane, or must I throw your children into the well?"

"I'm sixteen," Jane said, "I can't get married."

"You will be by midnight," she looked at the sky, "you better run, or it will be earlier than that. Come girls, we must make ourselves beautiful!" They began to smear themselves with berries and perfume and powder.

Jane didn't know where to run, but the faeries blocked her path towards the camp – not that she wanted to go back. She ran through the forest, and wondered how she'd hide, if she could fight, and what she could do. *I need to get to that floating castle*, she thought, *and I have no idea where I am.*

The wood was surprisingly well lit from the moonlight, and Jane knew that no matter how light her tracks were, she'd leave some sort of trail. *What I need to do is calm down and think*, she told herself as she ran. She was glad she was athletic. If Chloe had to save her, Chloe probably could only run about three minutes before getting winded. Not that she'd make it much passed the spiders, she'd be calling Bijan wicked and would have given up. *You're probably sitting on a soft pillow complaining about the lack of your favourite kind of chocolate.*

At least the bell around her neck was somewhat muffled when Jane clasped a hand over it. Jane wished she'd pay more attention as to the direction they traveled. *I can't save her if I can't save myself*, she decided.

She found a stream and took off her boots and travelled along the stream, hoping that in the darkness he wouldn't see her tracks. She considered herself clever, until the bell around her neck started to sound. She didn't jingle, and was extra careful to try to keep it muffled.

No, she clasped a hand over it, but still the little bell chimed, an 'I'm here!' resounding through the wood. She'd already tried to get it off when she was taken from the camp, and she tried again in frustration.

The bell stopped suddenly but she didn't dare take her hand away in case it suddenly began again.

She heard the grunt of the deer in the woods and the sound of hooves on grass. Jane's heart sped. She couldn't outrun a deer. It was very hard to run with one hand trying to mute that bell, with varying success. *He might have others helping him too, probably to herd me back to the camp,* she thought to herself, and she decided to leave the stream and go for speed and perhaps den with a bear when suddenly a brilliant white pelt appeared before her.

"What do I see before me?" Sylvanos asked. "In all my years of hunting, I've only seen this a handful of times. Are you feast or prize, madam?"

"Sylvanos, enough of this nonsense," Jane snapped. "Tell your men I ran off, and perhaps after I defeat the Faerie Prince, I'll let you be a prince provided you promise to stay in your realm."

"Oh, dear mortal, your passion makes my heart a flutter," he said, "from the first moment you hiccupped, I know I had to make you mine." He posed, paused, and then looked down at her. "Please run, you're making this too easy."

Jane didn't know why she listened. She ran into a thick briar patch that must at least slow the deer down, and jumped down a small ravine cut by an old creek. She landed on her back and looked up. Sylvanos looked nervous, as if he was about to lose his quarry. Jane picked the narrowest pathway, and though she heard the hooves on the stone above, eventually it died down. *He can't continue this way,* she thought, finding a clear opening. She looked around, and saw no sign of Sylvanos or his deer. She was not expecting a net to overtake her from above to make her stumble and fall. Jane thrashed about to free herself from the net, only to have her hands seized and bound while she tried to free herself. Sylvanos tossed the net off of her once he had captured his prize.

"Let me go!" Jane shouted, "Let go of me!"

"Ah, my spirited wifeling," he said, hoisting her over his shoulder. "You run like the wind! You are sure you are pure mortal?"

"I play soccer," she muttered as he tied her wrists to the saddle. She dug her heel into the deer's ribs as Sylvanos went to fold his net, but the deer merely snorted and waited for his master. "You can have any of those girls back there, who are much more fair than me, Sylvanos!"

"So?" he asked, sliding in behind her, "Do not worry, I am an honourable villain, I will play everything in its proper order."

Jane tried to steal his dagger or kick him off his deer, but Sylvanos kept her close and kept one hand over hers. She did not think there would be a mock ceremony ready for them when they returned.

"What about the engagement party?" Jane asked.

"Engagement's over," Sylvanos said.

"Mortal, make an honest man of this scoundrel!" shouted a pixie.

Sylvanos lifted her off the deer but kept her hands bound. He did look handsome, he changed his coat and someone had combed his hair, but Jane didn't appreciate it as he dragged her down the aisle of twig and grass to the small satyr in the oversized friar's outfit standing before the fire. The satyr most definitely did not look the part of catholic clergy, save the very large hat, likely stolen from some poor bishop seven centuries prior.

"Dearly gathered, we are here to make our beloved Sylvanos married to this mortal," said their satyr priest, "In doing so, he will be able to take us with him to her world. Our Sylvanos will accomplish in one night what the princes of this realm have not been able for centuries!"

"Cheers!" came from one of his riders, to which everyone, save Jane, emptied their goblet, horn or flask.

"Stop squirming," Sylvanos said, holding Jane tight. "I know you are excited, but we must be solemn for the time being."

"Sylvanos, what do I have to do to make it clear? I will never marry you!" Jane snapped. "And that is final!"

Sylvanos finished his drink and ducked his head between her bound arms, and scooped up her legs. "Do you mind speeding it up? My bride desires to dance."

"Of course, Sylvanos," the Faerie said, tossing the very large book into the fire. Jane had thought it a bible, but it was a cookbook. "Of course, there are no objections from anyone..."

"I object!" Jane shouted.

"No objections from anyone whose opinion counts," the satyr added. "Sylvanos, do you take this mortal to be your bride?"

"Yes," Sylvanos said, "so are we married now?"

"Patience Sylvanos. Patience," the satyr said, finger in the air, as if checking the wind. "...there. Now you're married."

"Hurray!" the crew cheered, and Jane found herself being twirled around.

"That doesn't count! I didn't say I do!" Jane snapped.

"Didn't say what?" Sylvanos asked.

"I do!" Jane shouted at the top of her lungs.

"You've come around! I'm glad!" he said, and kissed her cheek and put her down.

Jane tried to knee him in the groin, but he caught her and picked her up again. "You're right, my darling, but my wagon's busy right now. Give my cousin a few minutes more, and then we'll celebrate properly. We should dance with my men first anyway. I'm a stickler for tradition."

"You just made up the tradition!" she said.

"And I like to see people do what I tell them," he said.

Sylvanos put her on her feet and pushed Jane towards the celebration. She found herself being twirled and spun. Jane was given more wine, and offered a wheel of cheese cut like a cake – Jane liked cheesecake, but what was being served was complete havarti. She was congratulated and well wished and someone threw up on her boots. Her boots were removed, and then she was given a fresh pair of sandals. Jane tried to escape several times, but each time someone would grab her, and throw her back into the dancing circle. Jane eventually stumbled into Sylvanos' arms. "Good timing, my dear, the wagon's finally free," he said, before addressing his band. "Excuse me for a minute. My bride needs my attention. I won't be long!"

"You never are!" cheered one of Jane's bridesmaids.

"Wait," Sylvanos paused. Jane thought he'd come around. "This night is special! Roll out the cheese wheels we've been saving!" The group cheered once more as he started up the steps to his wagon, dragging Jane behind him. "And spiced rum for everyone! Spare no expense!" More cheering. "And I expect wedding presents from everyone!" No cheers. "You have time, this is rather unexpected!!" More cheering. "That doesn't mean they can be cheap!" A slight 'Aw...' was heard. "They can all be from the mortal world!" The loudest cheering was heard throughout the camp, Jane wondered if anyone from her world heard the noise.

"Sylvanos, no. No no no. A million times no," Jane said as the party once more became oblivious to her plight. "If you drag me in there, I'm going to murder you."

"Most of my men are quite enjoying your performance, but I think, my dear, that you think too much!" Sylvanos laughed, hoisting Jane over his shoulder and climbing on top of the wooden frame of the wagon, twirling about. "Here you are, at your own wedding feast and not enjoying a moment of it!" He put her on her feet and swiped a goblet from a serving centaur. "Let excitement lead you for once in your life!" She didn't take the drink, so he drank it for her. "Duty is a thick shackle that will drag you down and make you old before your time!" He grabbed her arm and Jane fell onto him he jumped back to the steps leading to his wagon. A scream echoed through he camp. Sylvanos' smile died, and he shoved her inside. "I will be back soon. Feel free to take your shoes off, I try to keep it clean in here."

Jane wasn't sure what to do, save get her hands freed. He had several swords and knives – perfect. She heard screaming as she cut through the bindings and looked for something more suitable to wear to flee. Jane found a bow and quiver and peeked out the window, and only saw chaos outside – and several of Sylvanos' party pinned under heavy barrels of ale, as well as a pixie screaming as it ran before a large wheel of cheese, forgetting it could fly. *It must be the prince's men*, she thought, cutting the stupid bell from her neck. She belted a sword and dagger around her hip and slung the quiver over her shoulder. She'd only some archery lessons a few years ago and had quite enjoyed them, but her consistency wasn't as good as Carol or Paul. This bow seemed more curved and these had feathers probably taken from some magical bird - she hoped they were magic arrows and would explode on impact. Sylvanos didn't lock the door, which was fortunate, and Jane left the wagon to aim the bow at Sylvanos, who bore blade at something brilliantly white under the moonlight.

Jane thought it was Sylvanos' deer at first, and then a horse. It was slender and tall, white like snow, save for the bronze cloven hooves and horn a deep yellow. It looked at her with golden eyes, and said, "I trust I am not too late, mortal."

Jane thought her aim most poor at Sylvanos, for she could not help but stare at the unicorn. Sylvanos' proud band of brigands had left him and a few loyal followers to the mercy of this brilliant creature.

"My men will be back, horse," Sylvanos said.

"Horse!" chortled the unicorn, "Mortal, stain not your hands with his blood."

"This does not concern you, unicorn," Sylvanos said, "be gone from this place!"

The unicorn reared and those who remained loyal to Sylvanos fled into the woods in terror. Sylvanos fell on his backside, no longer looking the part of the proud hunter-warrior, but a rather pathetic frat boy.

"Mortal," the unicorn said, "if you would leave this place, climb upon my back."

"Let me kill him," Jane said.

"Is that what you want?" the unicorn asked. "Do not let him defile you. I can only defeat villains, I cannot stop you from becoming one yourself. I am sorry I took so long to find you, these woods are thick."

Jane didn't know why she didn't fire at Sylvanos. She found herself stumbling towards the unicorn, feeling unworthy to touch it. Her hands were grass stained and hadn't been washed properly since she left the river, her skirt had picked up leaves and other dirt during her flight, and she didn't want to think about what her sandals had stepped in. The unicorn knelt, and said, "Please hurry. His stench bothers me."

And mine doesn't? "What do I do?" she asked, sliding onto his back.

"Hold onto my mane," he whinnied, "and hold on tight." Jane thought she'd cry out when he moved, and never had she felt something so soft when his hair entwined her fingers.

"You can't do this," Sylvanos said, still on the ground, "I married her."

"She did not marry you," the unicorn said simply, before muttering "great hunter indeed." It reared and charged into the woods. Jane clung to the unicorn's soft velvet neck as it carried her away from the Great Hunter of the Forest.

I I

To Dance no More

Chloe tried to remember everyone's names but she couldn't even get that right. Yssa was her principal teacher, but another served as her principal dance instructor, another excelled at telling her to fix her posture, another taught her how to eat with courtly grace

"You are learning too slowly," Yssa said, "Practice until you get it perfect, Chloe. Hyralie will play for you until you can master it."

Hyralie was easily gorgeous enough to be Miss Universe, but the other princesses tended to dump whatever they could on her, and their chores were few. The others went back to what they considered important: their paintings, their own dancing, the composing of music and song. One of the princesses seemed to always be designing and making outfits for the others, and had pixies bring in beautiful fabrics, the likes of which Chloe had never seen before.

Chloe wondered why he princess made their clothing, so she asked Hyralie. Hyralie explained as they left the room to find a quiet spot, away from the others. "Bryne she is our most skilled seamstress, and it pleases the prince to see his princesses so finely adorned."

"I thought the prince would forbid the princesses such labour," Chloe said. Yvara, the pixie she'd been shown back on her world, buzzed by, and nestled in her hair. "I was wondering where you'd gotten to."

"The others say Bryne was picked not as a princess, but because she was so skilled at her craft. The prince does truly love us, and he will not take away her love of the craft," Hyralie said. "You are so lucky if you are the one."

Hyralie began to play her harp and did not criticize Chloe when she obviously messed up dancing. Even Yvara flew off in frustration, but returned half an hour later to sleep in a bed of scrap fabric from Bryne's latest creation.

Hyralie had a bit of calm and kindness that Chloe found genuine. "The others say you are learning slowly," she said after Chloe stopped to massage her aching toes, "but you must take heart. You are learning much faster than I did when was brought here."

"I think my feet are going to bleed," Chloe said.

"It is best not to think about the pain," Hyralie said. "After all, it is only after the caterpillar sheds the cocoon that it may be a butterfly."

"I've not seen any butterflies here," Chloe said. "Are there many in the garden outside?"

"I never go to the gardens without the prince," Hyralie said.

"Does the prince take you to the gardens often?" Chloe asked.

"Sometimes," Hyralie said, "but I am not one of his favourites."

"Who are his favourites?" Chloe asked. "Besides Yssa, of course."

"Yssa is not one of his favourites. She is his guard dog," Hyralie said. "She keeps us in line, and he pretends like she's one of his favourites. You will see later, at the ball tonight. You will always see Yashiako on his arm, and Ariella at the foot of his throne. We are all favoured in different ways. I exist to bring his more beautiful princesses water."

Yashiako and Ariella were incredibly beautiful, but Chloe didn't see them as being fairer than Yssa or Hyralie. "Did he speak of me, when he called for you yesterday?" Chloe asked.

"No," Hyralie said, "but the others are jealous of you. I think that Yssa and the others never want him to find the queen, never-" she stopped. Chloe followed her eyes. Several pixies watched them from the window sill. Chloe didn't know why Hyralie seemed nervous about the pixies. Chloe was only scared of squishing one of them by accident. "Play the harp, and I will show you again."

"I do not know the harp," Chloe said. There were other instruments, and her eyes were drawn to a lovely wooden flute, with vines and flowers carved into its body. It seemed only slightly different than the old metal one so far away, stuffed in her locker. "If you will play the music by the harp again, I think I can learn it by the flute."

Hyralie nodded, and she began to play, and after she repeated the verse Chloe joined in, and they played together. She laughed when Chloe messed up, and the Chloe couldn't help, but join in the giggling. Chloe wondered if this was what it was like to have a sister – not a sister like Bethany's little sisters, or even Jane or Bethany. They played again and eventually Hyralie stopped playing, and began to sing along. Chloe mastered the chorus before Yssa broke in. "That was lovely, Chloe," said the princess. "Where did you learn to play the flute?"

"Jr. High," Chloe said. "I'm not very good, am I?" She was going to say she thought she played the piano better, but Yssa seemed uninterested.

"I think it would be better if you tried the lyre," Yssa said, taking the flute from Chloe. "Osophene will teach you."

"I rather think you play the flute lovely, Chloe. Besides, we're going to be here forever," Hyralie said. "I've not been here half as long as the others, and-"

"She cannot sing and play the flute at the same time," Yssa said, "whereas she can enchant with both her voice and the lyre at the same time."

Chloe felt the urge to protest, but she picked up the lyre dutifully. "Where is Osophene?"

"She is getting ready for tonight," Yssa said, "The prince is holding a ball, and the ten of us will accompany him. Hyralie, Chloe needs further dance instruction. See that she is ready."

"I am sorry you cannot go to the ball," Chloe said as soon as Yssa left them.

"Sorry?" Hyralie asked, "We have balls so often. Like I've told you before: I am not one of his favourites."

"But you're one of the dancing princesses!" Chloe said.

"And how can he pick a jewel in his crown?" Hyralie sighed. "Yssa's definitely the biggest ruby. And Bryne? The shiniest diamond. Arialla is an amethyst, and Osophene is an emerald. Me, a tiny sapphire, making them glitter more brightly, and reminding them that they're more precious."

"That can't be true," Chloe said.

Hyralie looked at Chloe, then smiled, "I hope you're the bride," she said quietly, "if you are, please ask our Prince to make me your handmaid."

"You'd rather be servant to the queen than a princess?" Chloe asked.

"I... live to serve the prince," Hyralie stammered, "in serving the queen, I can do just that."

She went back to playing the harp. Chloe found the lyre quite difficult. Hyralie showed Chloe how to play the harp instead, although they received a sharp look from Yssa when she walked by, she said nothing. "When the others are gone, you must show me how to play the flute so beautifully," Hyralie said.

The others left as night fell, and they still practiced for many hours, only breaking for their dinner, a feast of fresh breads, spiced wines and cheeses, of which the two princesses ate dainty portions. As soon as they were satisfied, Chloe stated that her toes were very sore, so she and Hyralie soaked their feet in the bathing pool.

"Why aren't we allowed to talk about our old lives?" Chloe asked.

"The prince doesn't like it, even if we mean to complain about how horrible our lives were compared to how it is here," Hyralie said. "I didn't leave much behind."

"You can tell me," Chloe said, "I won't say anything."

Hyralie looked up through the open balcony, to the night sky. Chloe thought the stars themselves were painted against the two moons. They didn't twinkle like they did back home. They could hear the music and festivities despite being so far away. "We lost everything because the Czars didn't like our people. We fled to the Americas, and I had to give up my name when I got there. We found so much hardship," she said, shrugging her shoulders. "Then my brother took sick, and papa was willing to sell me to an older man because he was rich!" Tears came to her eyes suddenly. "Sasha died, and they still…"

"I'm sorry," Chloe said, and put a hand on top of Hyralie's.

"It is alright," Hyralie said, tears running down her cheeks. She squeezed Chloe's hand. "It was so long ago. But I still remember…" She shook her head. "They're all dead now, aren't they? The last girl said it's probably been almost a hundred years since I've been gone."

"The prince goes back to our world every ten years," Chloe said, "Yssa said you were the latest."

"That he keeps here," she said, "sometimes he brings back no one. Sometimes, the girl escapes, or is rescued. Most times, they're taken to the labyrinth in the garden."

"What happens there?" Chloe asked.

"Mortals help the flowers grow," she said, "Immortals – this world, almost everything stands still. Even though we stop aging, our being here helps give life to the kingdom. We are different than the fae here – something about us makes this world flourish. So we serve the prince or his kingdom, whether we wish to or not." She bit her lip.

"Some girls do not wish to come?" Chloe asked.

Hyralie shook her head. "One of the last girls was angry and tore up a dress Bryne had been working on for a year when they tried to put her in it. There was no pleasing her, or talking to her to accept her place. To be fair, I did not expect this when I was brought here. He made it sound like I was the only one, like I was special. Like I was-"

"Hyralie, the prince has called for you by name," a voice, one of the princesses Chloe should have known. In the beautiful ballgown and in the heavy shadow, it was hard to tell them apart. "Are you weeping?"

"I am alright," Hyralie said. "I just need to put on something to make me suitable for the prince. Chloe, please help me."

Her tears made her no less lovely. Hyralie donned a silver gown, and Chloe helped her put the appropriate hair clips into her auburn hair. "You look beautiful," Chloe said.

Hyralie frowned. "He will not call on you. You may rest. We will be late, Chloe," she said.

Chloe did not know what to do when she was alone, but she bathed quickly and found a suitable garment for sleeping. She woke early, in her assigned spot, and rose before any of the others. The other princesses snored around her, and many had yet to shed their exquisite gowns from the night before. Chloe took some solace in how some of them deteriorated in their sleep.

Chloe looked about the room for Hyralie. She could not help but feel slightly jealous that her prince didn't call for her.

One of the princess' eyes opened when she walked by, but she closed it just as quick. "Your lesson will take place later today," she said. "You should rest."

"Where is Hyralie?" Chloe asked.

The princess muttered and covered her head with the silk blanket.

Chloe tied her hair back into a braid and put on a simple dress and walked to one of the adjoining rooms, and played the flute quietly, as she'd little else to do, and her feet were still sore. A pixie she didn't know rose and watched her play for several minutes, before fluttering off to the garden. Chloe walked to the window to watch where it flew. She looked back at the princesses. Chloe assumed the castle would sleep until noon. She wouldn't be gone long, just long enough to see the garden. She could see the pixies shimmer in the distance. She started into the hallway, and a voice caught her off guard.

"Who braided your hair like that?"

The prince! Unlike the princesses, he looked as handsome as ever. Chloe felt suddenly guilty for going into the hallway unescorted. She bowed her head. "I did," she said.

"It is beautiful, Chloe," said her prince. "You rise early?"

"I was not out as late as the others," she said quietly. "Where is Hyralie?"

"Come," he said, "walk with me."

There were more servants and guards than she remembered. Chloe wanted to see the castle, the great art painted on the walls and sculptures and the majestic garden out front. She was not at all surprised to smell the fresh water – the castle had no shortage of growing green things, the garden, more labyrinth than sitting area, bloomed many roses in addition to the assortment of running water trellises and fountains, and many sculptures of fantastic things.

"Yssa has talked about you," he said.

"Has she said anything good?" Chloe asked.

"She is jealous of you," he said. It was unlike how they walked before, he led her and she pretended she was the one who would break the spell.

"Janice was jealous of me," she said, "No, the whole school was."

Her prince smiled. "Now it's the whole world," he said.

"Your world," she said. "This place is beautiful. Everything is."

"I shall have to give you a tour of the entire kingdom," he said, "though I fear, with this curse, the castle is the only place safe for you for now."

"I want to know how to break the spell, so I'll work hard and learn. Yssa says you go riding often," she said, "perhaps I could go with you."

"Perhaps you could," he agreed, "we will cover more ground on the back of a horse."

He took her to the stables and Chloe was amazed at the beautiful horses. Most were a solid color, and everyone was strong, beautiful. He selected a white one, Chloe didn't know why, but although they were horse in shape, they looked different. Their legs were sleek and muscular, and their manes and tails adorned with ribbons, and each had silver shoes on their hooves that she thought cloven, and each had a metal covering atop their brow and a bit in their mouth. "Come."

"Which one shall I ride?" Chloe asked.

"We will ride together, my princess," he said.

She felt safe in her prince's arms. She was glad that he treated her like a child, for the horse was very strong and she felt queasy when he burst into a run. Her prince never made his mount leave the castle grounds, but the gardens were huge, the hedges were well manicured and kept, the cobbles a glistening white, and she had never seen so much detailing on the marble statues that heralded gateways into the labyrinth. Chloe looked for their keepers and servants, but she had seen so few people in the past few days, save for the princesses. She thought of speaking of Moaz and Zilare, but she often wondered she might make her prince jealous, so she pushed the thought from her mind.

"Are we going anywhere in particular?" she asked as their mount slowed.

"Yes," he said.

Chloe heard a woman singing. Then another. Then another. The horse paused, and perked his ears. "What is that?" she asked.

"I take all the girls here the day before their trial," he said. "You understand because I am a prince, that I am in a most difficult situation?"

"Yes," Chloe said. "Hyralie said that some of the girls who-"

"Those who would remain grains of sand rather than pearls," he said, "I have them kept here, where they are treated like queens! I ask them again and again to be one of my princesses, but they will not come. Come with me, Chloe. You will see."

He helped her off the horse, and led her down the path. He seemed to know where he was going, but she knew she'd never find her way through the labyrinth. He took her to what she could only describe as large birdcage at first, though vines and flowers covered the bars. Inside seemed smaller than the outside, where a running waterfall kept a pool in the middle of the room, and while the furniture was sparse, there were songbirds that could fly through the bars and would come and go. A girl about Chloe's age sat facing away, on a silver chaise with silk padding, while several pixies brushed her hair. She wore a simple dress, but she looked no less lovely than one of the princesses in all their jewels and finery. Her prince put out a hand, and the vines and bars folded, making an opening. "Hello again Kildare," he said, gesturing for Chloe to go in first. The pixies flew off they entered the room. "You look beautiful today."

"My name is Karen," the young woman said. "Everyday your servants come and dress me up like some doll, even if I see no one for weeks." She looked at Chloe. "Is this another girl you've spirited away?"

The Prince of the Faeries said, "Chloe chose to come."

The girl said, "You look the type that would eat up his nonsense."

"Kildare, you be nice to Chloe," the Faerie Prince said. "She may be your queen soon."

"Karen! If you had any power, you'd send me back to my world," the girl snapped.

"I see you haven't touched the harp in ages. Have you learned any dancing?" The Faerie Prince asked. "You have a most beautiful voice. Won't you sing for me?" Kildare faced away, and crossed her arms. The Faerie Prince put a hand on her shoulder. "Kildare, your world has forgotten you. There's no place for you there." He took out a glass ball. "Shall we see what has become of your friends and family?"

"Stop it," she said, trying to face away, but he had her by the neck and forced her to face the ball, and used the other hand to show her visions of the mortal world. Chloe felt a sudden longing for home.

"Your sister's children are grown. Her son is engaged. A spring wedding next year. They'll have everyone you knew in attendance, only they'll not mention your name. You left your sister more than ten years before her first child was born. We were engaged once," he said, "and I would have given you everything you desire." The glass ball floated up from his hand, and changed in a burst of light. Chloe saw a beautiful crystal tiara in place of the magic ball.

"I desire my family," she said, moving her head as he went to crown her.

The Prince of the Faeries smiled, and said, "That world is lost to you."

"No, it's not," she said, blinking back tears. "I am nothing to you! Send me back to the mortal realm."

"My beautiful Kildare, you thought that someone would come for you, but you have no prince but me," he said, taking her in his arms. Chloe couldn't help but feel a little jealous – this creature had been seventeen for so long. She had her time with him. She obviously didn't deserve him. "Need I give you to a monster, and I come to save you for you to know how much you mean to me?"

"I'm already prisoner to a monster," she said. He seized her neck suddenly, more violently than the first time. "No!" He put a hand over her face.

"Sleep," he breathed.

She struggled, but Chloe felt the prince's power from across the room. The unworthy princess crumpled in his arms. He picked her up, and put her down gently on the chaise. She breathed deep as he put the tiara in her hair. He suddenly turned his silver eyes on Chloe. "I did not mean to upset you, Chloe," he said.

"What did you do?" Chloe asked.

"I simply reminded her that my princesses remain my princesses," he said. "Do not worry; only the prince's kiss can wake her. I will let her sleep for a few years. Perhaps a century. She will be more agreeable when everyone she knows has passed on. It is most difficult, hurting those whom I love," he admitted, "but I will not throw my pearls back into the sea. Are you happy here, Chloe?"

She didn't realize how faint she felt. She gripped the golden bars of the wall for support. "Of course I'm happy," she said.

"You are shaking," he said, touching her cheek.

"I am sad for her," she said, "but I see what it does to you, my prince."

He smiled, and kissed her. Chloe felt weak in his arms, but did not fall to enchanted sleep like she thought she would. He led her back to the horse. "I am so happy to hear this! I hope you are the one. Perhaps if Kildare were to see you, crowned in glory, she would change her mind."

Chloe let him lift her onto the horse. "You said she had no prince but you," she said. "What did you mean?"

He paused, and then mounted behind her. He put an arm around her, and pulled her tightly to him. "There are robbers who come into my castle. Those who would steal you away. Those who profess to love you. Not everyone desires to be a pearl, Chloe. They would keep you as common sand. Not just knights and princes, but sisters, brothers, fathers, mothers, friends, lovers; all have all come to steal away my princesses."

"But who can fight against you?" Chloe asked. "You have no weakness."

"From the mouth of babes!" he laughed. "I will show you."

They were not sculptures. Chloe saw flight. She saw embracing. She saw men and women covered in vines. Calla lilies, hyacinths and birds of paradise bloomed overtop of their frightened and determined expressions. "They tried to escape," Chloe said, touching the face of a small barefoot child of eight or nine leading a maiden of fourteen dressed in finery. "She tried to take her sister home."

"I have turned many to stone because they sought to steal my treasures," the Faerie Prince said. "Others because I could not bear to see them in the cages, like Kildare. Some jewels are to be enjoyed; others should be displayed, for they do not know how to compose themselves. And others," he said, "you can see for yourself."

Chloe felt as if they rode through a cemetery. She spotted a majestic fountain, and saw figures dancing about it, and there were not just humans. She saw a unicorn fighting a centaur before the fountain, their battle frozen for all time, and several faeries, some of which were chained, pleading, while others seemed happy, as if in jubilation to be an addition to the garden decor. Chloe walked to the fountain, looked in to see a marble mermaid at the bottom. She looked back at the prince sadly, but looked up at the sky, and saw a figure atop the fountain, in mourning. "Hyralie?" she asked.

"She became no longer fit to serve me," he said. "At least, not in court. It happened before you came, my love. I just could not bring my heart to do this to her before..."

Hyralie was no less beautiful as a statue, she knelt in the shallow part of the fountain, and her tears trickled down endlessly. "Is there anyway to undo the magic?" Chloe asked.

"You will have the power to, if you are the Faerie Queen," he said, arms over Chloe's shoulders, and then taking her hands in his. Chloe felt a sudden coldness wash over her as he led her into a path crested with every sort of flower imaginable, leaving his horse behind. He led her to a hidden sitting place of sorts, a hidden grove surrounded by water, with water lilies and several stone satyrs playing near the water. Carp and koi lazily swam. Chloe wished the swans were real, and not marble. He led her to a seated bench. "I will deny you nothing if you are worthy to be my bride," said her prince.

"And if I am unworthy?" she asked as he bent to kiss her.

"Then you are happy to be one of my princesses?" he asked.

"Of course," she said, and let him kiss her.

<h1 style="text-align:center">12</h1>

Heart of Stone

Jane stirred from slumber, remembering something about spiders and a beast in a labyrinth. She wondered why she wasn't in bed until she realized she had a unicorn's head on her lap as she lay against a tree with silver leaves on a small grassy island surrounded by green-grey water.

The sound of rushing water was almost loud, but it was soothing and she did not notice it until she looked around. What looked like a strong current pulled past the island, to what looked like the edge of the world. To Jane's left, she saw land, though she doubted that she could swim to it with such a strong current, and she couldn't tell how deep the water was. The grass looked sickly, but real. Jane touched the bark that she had laid her head against. The tree was real. Wondering how all the water didn't run out, Jane looked to the land. In the distance was a constant shower, a wall against the castle she could hardly see from where she sat, thickest around the base, though she could see the tall towers looming high. The thick black clouds overhead gave a constant downpour that flooded the land. Jane wanted to stand, but remembered she had a unicorn's head on her lap.

Jane hesitantly pet the unicorn, who chortled in his sleep. She flicked its horn with her fingers. It sounded hollow. The unicorn opened one eye, caught Jane's gaze, and said, "I would appreciate it if you didn't do that." The unicorn then shuffled his head off her lap, and went back to sleep.

Jane stood up, to look at the island they were on. It was no more then a few paces from the tree. The grass seemed greener where they were, and didn't break the way it had before, when she stepped from the path in the forest. The water tasted fresh when she drank. "I suppose the unicorn's got some sort of sinister fate planned for me as well," she said to herself as she looked up at the tree with silver leaves. "Is this the tree of good and evil?"

The unicorn yawned and stretched. "That tree, last I checked, was made into a desk, a wardrobe, and many very poorly written novels," he said.

Jane asked, "How did we get here? Where are we?"

"At the floating castle," he said, pointing with his horn, "where we will find the Staff of Silver."

Jane climbed the lone tree to get a better view. From the cliff where she met the hunters, she thought she could see a castle, but here, all she thought she could see was water moving quickly and the generating mist, masking the castle in the constant downpour. "How did you know?" Jane asked.

"You told me before you fell asleep that you sought the floating castle to save your friend." The unicorn sniffed one of the apples on the ground. He bit it, and made a face. "Disgusting! Maiden, please pluck me some apples! Toss them down, and I will catch them."

"You just said they weren't good!" Jane shouted. They looked shiny, red, and perfect for putting girls to sleep.

The unicorn replied, "You'll make them real!"

Jane decided not to argue. She tossed down three apples and he speared two on his horn and munched on the last. "A little help," he said, trying to get them off his horn.

Jane slid down the tree and hesitated.

"Are you scared of me?" asked the unicorn.

"Yes," Jane admitted.

"Why?" he asked.

"You're a unicorn, and," she paused, "no offense, but I'm kind of scared of everything right now. So far fairyland has been the opposite of sunshine and rainbows."

The unicorn chortled. "Rightly so! There is much danger in this kingdom! We unicorns do not come here often," he said, and munched on the apple. "Eat the third one, you made it very sweet."

Jane bit into the apple. It did taste good – much better than those energy bars. The apple suddenly reminded her of the orange in Bijan's grove. The sweet taste in her mouth went bitter. "Do you want more?" she asked.

"If you're offering," he said, finishing his second apple.

Jane climbed the tree once again and picked several, and hand fed the unicorn. "I'm surprised I didn't fall into a deep sleep," she said as he ate his third apple.

"I wouldn't let a curse befall you," the unicorn said. "It would shame me!"

"Thank you," she said, "for saving me from Sylvanos."

"You're welcome," he said. "I think you were handling yourself quite nicely with that bow you found. I raced to find you as soon as I discovered your quest. You were difficult to find, for that scoundrel half-brother hid you deep in the forest."

"Brother?" Jane asked.

"Half-brother," the unicorn said, "Sylvanos and the Prince of the Faeries are the only two with claims to the throne, for their uncles are all destroyed or locked away. Fortunately for all concerned, Sylvanos has next to none of his brother's power."

"Why not?" Jane asked.

"Because Sylvanos came from a mortal who was not the Queen of the Faeries," the unicorn said. "He has no claim to your world."

"But if he has a mortal mother–" Jane began.

"You have eluded them so far, yet seem to know so little of faeries!" the unicorn said. "I know little of the pixies, but for all their magic, they can create food and trees, but they require mortals to give the food taste, and make the trees flourish. I believe they require mortal blood to make more of them. The Prince of the Faeries, unlike Sylvanos, is legitimate. He has claim to this world's throne, and one of the thrones of your world."

Jane wondered which one only briefly. "His mother was important, then?"

"I do not know," the unicorn said. "What I do know, however, is that Sylvanos is the truest sort of sidhe! He is but a shadow to his brother, if what the other unicorns have said is true."

"I thought I could trust them," Jane said.

"The worst kind of villain," the unicorn neighed.

"So... is this what unicorns do?" Jane asked. "Run around rescuing maidens?"

"We aid mortals," he said, "I prefer the quests of knights, for they are always trying to slay some sort of monster and usually enjoy it when I leap."

Jane began to shake. "Sylvanos married me," Jane said. "Can his followers return to our world?"

"I doubt any of his followers could conduct a successful tea party, let alone a wedding," he whinnied and pricked his ears. "Did you at any time give in to him?"

"No," said Jane. "I went with them because he helped me get away from another faerie, but as soon as Sylvanos told me what he wanted, I tried to get away from them."

"You didn't marry him," he said, "you never gave in, Jane. That is what matters."

"Is that why you couldn't go save Chloe, instead of helping me?" Jane asked. "She seems like the type of girl who would get a unicorn's help."

"All girls deserve the help of unicorns," the unicorn said, "but too often they give into despair. Chloe? Is that the name of the girl he spirited from your world? That poor girl." He whinnied. Jane liked horses, but when he neighed and whinnied, it sounded different. It was like every dream she had as a small girl made real when he moved his head or looked at her, let alone speak, but rather then sounding calm and serene, he spoke and it was like kindling some sort of fire from deep within Jane. "Many unicorns have tried to free the mortals he's stolen from your world, and he traps us here. He lures us with maidens singing their sad songs in their cages, and no sooner do we free the maidens and we discover the trap, and then out come the golden reins and silver shoes and he makes us submit. If we do not, he cuts off our horns! Were I fully grown, I would still be wary of approaching his castle."

"You are not a grown unicorn?" asked Jane.

"I am but a colt," said the Unicorn. "What is your name?"

"Jane. Yours?"

"Sedolei," he said.

"So... if unicorns are against the prince..."

"Not all of us are," he said. "I was warned not to come – this world traps more than human mortals, but when I learned one from your realm dared defy the prince, I decided she need not do it alone. I defied my parents and made the journey into this realm."

"I wish you would have come earlier."

"We unicorns are proud, and rather than protect maidens and knights from those who would cause havoc, we enjoy our victories! Because so many children have real reason to cry, we become indifferent to tears. We all seek out the greatest monster to defeat. I am no different than the others, but if you would have me, I will help you as best I'm able. You will need more than an untested unicorn to defeat the Faerie Prince."

"I have the heartstone," Jane said, placing her hand over her heart. "Bijan said the staff was on this floating castle. But..." Jane looked to the rushing water about the island. It looked deceivingly calm, then it looked like it pulled right off the edge of the castle grounds. "How do we get to land?"

"Get on my back," he said. Jane did as he told her, and he leapt across the water quite easily, Jane looked down in their reflection in the gray-blue water and expected him to spout wings, but instead he landed on the grass and said, "You are sure you have never met a unicorn before? You ride well."

"I've never ridden a horse before," Jane said, looking up at the castle walls. "Why is it I'm getting a sinking feeling?"

"I should hope that we're not sinking!" the unicorn said. "Stay on my back, Jane, we will cover more ground." He did not run as fast as he did when they fled the forest, but it was still much faster than Jane expected. She looked for sign of a door, or way to pass through, but saw no break in the wall of water.

"How do we get in?" Jane asked.

"I do not know," he said. "This is your quest."

"Do you know anything about this staff?"

"Very little," the unicorn said. He slowed suddenly, and perked his ears. Jane tried to follow his gaze but saw nothing unusual – just a wall of water surrounding the castle. She felt her heart start to race. "How deep is the water? Can you charge through? When I climbed the tree, it seemed thinner in spots."

"Have you no magic of your own?" Sedolei asked.

"No," Jane said, and felt heat coming from her chest. She couldn't help but cry out, not in pain or fear, but surprise. The power expelled from within her very suddenly. Jane had no idea what to expect, and felt almost powerless at her sudden command of the magic. The unicorn reared, and suddenly, a path opened before them, as if an invisible force shielded the water so that Sedolei and Jane could ride through. "How...?"

"It seems we found the path," the unicorn said. "Are you ready?"

Jane wasn't expecting the heartstone to do anything without her activating it – a little bippity boppity boo would have been a nice warning. "No wonder he didn't just want to give it to me," she said between breaths. "I guess I'm as ready as I'm ever going to be."

Sedolei didn't charge, but walked. Jane was glad they didn't try to jump the wall of water, for the tunnel, while not extremely deep, continued to fall about them, cold rushing water lapping to their sides, and to Jane's displeasure, closing behind them. They were on a stone bridge of some sort, and once past the wall of water there was a moat, and no shortage of brown ducks swimming in it. Jane expected a black cathedral, but instead, she saw something that looked more akin to a squat fortress than a gothic castle.

A woman stood at a black door atop several steps. She seemed slender, insofar as the blue robe with white trim allowed. She was older, Jane would guess about seventy, but it was hard to tell, for a prince could come to their world every ten years and look no older than twenty-five. The woman stood no taller than Chloe did, and only her moving eyes showed Jane that she was real.

"Who are you?" the woman asked as they neared.

Sedolei stopped before the steps, and Jane dismounted. "My name is Jane," she said. "I was told that the Staff of Silver was here, and with it, I could defeat the Prince of the Faeries."

The woman descended the steps. She was shorter than Jane expected – not even as tall as Chloe. Jane studied the woman's face. Given the woman's robes, and the design of the castle, at first she thought her face Asian, but it was hard to tell. Though she could not put her finger on it, her face was like no human face Jane had ever seen; her face was very long and her eyes were an unnatural blue, so Jane wondered if the woman too was a fae. "You are right on both counts, Jane. I guard the staff here. I am mistress of this castle. I can feel the power of the heartstone from here, it alone can undo my power surrounding this castle," said the woman. "How did you get it?"

Embarrassed, Jane hesitated. "The man Bijan has been turned into a minotaur. He was going to accompany me, but instead we were attacked, and he gave it to me, and told me to flee," she said. "His home is overrun with these... spider women, and there were fae looking for me. I wanted to help him, but he said it was more important that I defeat the prince."

"I know Bijan well. He tends to accompany those who seek the staff," the woman said. "He has never sent a girl on her own."

"I'm not like other girls," Jane said. "Besides, what does it matter if I am a girl?"

"Yes! What does it matter?" Sedolei said, neighing as he spoke. "She is here for the staff!"

"Silence, unicorn," the woman said. "I know why you are here. I just wish to know how those who come for the staff handled the one I entrusted with the heartstone. She is not the first to abandon him."

"She did not abandon him," Sedolei said. "She could not stand up to the likes of them-"

"Excusing her?" the woman asked, before her eyes settled on Jane's. "I'm sure you picked the wisest course of action. You were no good to anyone captured or killed."

Jane didn't know what to say. Bijan was bigger and stronger then she was - she took his advice, afterall. "I have been told that this staff has the power to defeat the Faerie Prince."

"Indeed," the woman said, "that is why it is locked away. Come child, walk with me."

Jane looked over her shoulder at Sedolei. The woman waited at the door leading into the castle. "The unicorn may come as well."

"Inside the castle?" Jane asked.

"You mean to take the staff," the woman said, "I cannot allow it to go to someone who cannot properly wield it. I have hosted stranger things. The unicorn may accompany you inside, though you will face your trial alone."

Jane had many questions for the woman, but she waited for Sedolei before following her into the castle. The place smelt too clean, like someone had lived there, a long time ago. There were no decorations, no sign of habitation, no spiders, not even dust. Jane felt like she should wipe the bottom of her sandals as she followed the woman into a long hall lined with many closed doors. "Do many people come?" Jane asked.

The woman betrayed a smile. "The staff was made by the Prince of the Sidhe who became King. It is a symbol of his authority. I have kept it safe from his offspring. The Prince of the Fae is very clever, girl." She caught Jane's eyes, and paused. Jane saw nothing special in the hall, no marker. She made no move to continue further. "Do not think for a moment he has not anticipated what actions those who come to his world will take. If you were a dragon, perchance you could fight him.

A unicorn ally?" She glanced at Sedolei. "You were not able to come to the aid of Prince Bijan against the prince's minions. What chance do you think you have against their Prince?"

"I... don't know," Jane stammered. "I was hoping you'd be able to tell me. There are other methods to defeat him?"

The woman nodded. "Stealing his princesses works best – at least initially. Most don't make it past the castle grounds," she said. "Though there have been many who are successful in racing back to their realm. Once you fail here, it would be the option I would consider if you have not abandoned hope wholly. You have no magic, and you are no warrior."

Jane wished she wasn't talking as if she had already failed. "So what do I have to do to get this staff?" Jane asked.

"In time, girl, in time," the woman said. "Here, I am very powerful. If he were to set foot on this island, I would likely be able to destroy him. However, he knows this, and will not come here himself. However, I do contemplate his actions, and ask myself if he ever sends anyone to take the staff for him."

"I have no wish to aid him!" Jane said.

"And if you are playing into his hands?" the woman asked.

"You're scared," Jane said.

"Of him gaining the staff?" asked the woman. "Petrified. Why do you think I keep it locked away? If I thought I could use it to defeat him, I would have done so long ago."

"But The Red Queen–"

"That mortal was ruled by her heart," the woman said. "She knew what she had to do and she showed mercy. Mercy! How many have died and live on in this stagnant world because she spared her child, knowing the burden would be carried. In saving her child, she condemned so many others."

"Heartstone," Jane said, hand over her chest.

"You have no idea what it is, do you?" the woman asked. "You've access to a unicorn – be gone from this place! Perhaps in ten years, when you have some knowledge of that what it is you would face, then you may return to claim the staff. It would be best if you forget the one you came for. She has likely already forgotten herself."

"So I'm just supposed to abandon my best friend?" Jane asked. "And what about the others he's stolen? I'm to leave them as well? And what about Bijan? The only way to help him is to-"

"Girl," the woman said, pausing, "at the end of this hall is a door. Therein lies the trial. It will cost you nothing to attempt it. I will not harm you if you fail or demand anything from you. I see what you are, and know you will not succeed. I know that you will try anyway, for yours is the type who would live with failure, rather than one who didn't take the chance. Prepare yourself, talk to the unicorn, for all the advice he can give." Sedolei snorted. "I will wait for you at the end of the hall."

Jane watched the blue train of her dress disappear down the hallway. Sedolei whinnied. Jane stroked his nose. "Are you ready?" Sedolei asked.

"No," Jane said, her eyes watering. She wrapped her fingers around the silk of his mane. "Sedolei, what if she's right? What if I'm just a little girl who can't do it? I shouldn't have come. Not alone," Jane said. "Can you get me back to my world?"

"Yes," he said.

"Then you need to go there and find someone strong and wise and daring and who can do these sorts of things," Jane said. "I couldn't save Bijan. I couldn't even save myself from Sylvanos! I couldn't stop Chloe from going with him."

"Jane," Sedolei said, "I am a young, untested unicorn, and most would say I am not known for my wisdom, save for lack of, but I do know that I cannot make heroes, Jane."

"I'm scared," Jane said.

"Of what you have to do?" he asked.

"She said the Red Queen was weak for not killing her own child," Jane said. "I could not kill an innocent little baby – even knowing what he could become. And it's not just that, but... what if she's right? What if I even get the staff, and I can't... I won't do what needs to be done? I didn't come to defeat anyone. I came to help Chloe. I don't want to kill anybody."

"Do you remember what I told you before?" the unicorn asked. "When you were aiming your bow at Sylvanos?"

"Do not let him defile you," Jane said. "It doesn't even sounds like I will get the staff anyway. If this doesn't work, Sedolei... do you know of any other way to defeat him? This was originally just about Chloe... but Bijan... I want to help him, too. I want to stop all of this."

The unicorn looked contemplative. "I wish there was another way," he neighed. "This staff was made when one of the Ten Princes of the Sidhe rose to be king – and it was his queen who took up its power. I know little of this staff," he said, "but I would see the stolen maidens freed."

Jane bit her lip and nodded. "Wait for me. Please?"

"I will go nowhere else," Sedolei said and then neighed.

Jane met the woman at the door. "What is your name, if you don't mind me asking?" Jane asked.

"You may call me The Empress. It will serve for now," the woman said. She put out her hand, and Jane felt a rush of wind as the heavy iron doors opened. Jane saw a courtyard of sorts, a dead patch of ground where the remains of spindly trees and dead grass littered a mist-filled courtyard. It seemed too big, like it didn't belong inside a castle. Jane peered, but she couldn't see through the mist to the other end of the courtyard.

"Empress," she said, "what is this place?"

"We used to plant cherry blossoms and play in the river," the woman said, her voice sounding from far away. Jane assumed the dried up trench was made a long time ago. "This is the courtyard that my sister was taken by the Prince of the Sidhe - one of the ten, before your enemy was born. I have uprooted this castle from our world, Jane, as a reminder that not everyone from that world is weak. That I will oppose him, and should he ever gain one who can be queen, kill her before he can use her."

"You're just as bad as him," Jane said. "Letting the cycle continue, rather than stopping it yourself!"

"So you say, child," the Empress said. "The Staff of Silver is here, someplace. Find it, and take it for your own, if you can."

"That's it?" Jane asked. "No time limit, no hints? Just find the staff? What's it look like? What about the heartstone? How-"

The woman closed her eyes and faded into mist and light. Jane wanted to ask her, "How do I know if I failed?" There should have been a door behind her – there was, and it led out. She could walk back to Sedolei, and go home – however unicorns managed. She wasn't going to fail. Jane quickly started at a jog through the dead courtyard, only slightly encouraged by the smell and feeling of real dead foliage around her.

She saw nothing around her that varied, until she came to the wall she looked back. Nothing - no indication of what to do or where to go. She continued around the perimeter, frustrated she wondered if the Empress should have given her a shovel. Jane looked up at the sky, and saw that there were things in the air, but there seemed to be a mist in the air, and she couldn't make them out.

"Are you lost?"

The voice startled Jane. It was a young girl, looking no older than eight. "Yes I am," Jane said. "I'm looking to find the Staff of Silver."

"It's been another ten years?" The child dressed strangely and had an eccentric hairdo with tassels sticking out to the side. Jane assumed she was the great-grandchild of The Empress. She played in the trench of the dried river, and then walked to a dead tree, and did a headstand against it. "Then again, there's no other reason for her to open the door," she said, clicking her heels in the air.

"Who are you?" Jane asked.

"Call me Winkie," the girl said, bowing her head despite the headstand, and then winked. "I can help you, if you'd like. It's my job, actually."

"Is that cheating, Winkie?" Jane asked.

Winkie shook her head. "Not if I *offer*. You wouldn't believe how many big men refuse my help outright! The staff is up, you got that part right."

"How am I supposed to go up?" Jane asked.

"The Prince has wings," said Winkie. "While you have none of your own, The Empress has decided that anyone who wants to defeat him should lose their fear of heights. You know, overcoming something primal or some gibberish."

"How do I do that?" Jane asked.

Winkie rolled out of her headstand, and giggled when grass and twigs were in her hair and only broadly brushed them away. She motioned for Jane to follow, and lead her into the thickest mist. Jane found the wind growing stronger, and saw a gust of mist propel dead twigs and leaves upwards; she likely would have run into it blindly without help. "That's how I'm supposed to travel up?" Jane asked. "How fast will it go? What's going to catch me?"

"You don't have to do it," Winkie said. "I will do the first one. I know you're scared. That's alright. Just know that the prince will threaten you with worse things than heights. Imagine if he locked you in a tall tower for a century! You wouldn't want to crack when faced with simple fears, would you?"

It was one thing to be scared, but seeing a child leap onto the patch of air and be carried into the air, disappearing into the mist alarmed Jane. She was no coward, but Winkie traveled so high – what if she fell? It was well for sorceresses and unicorns to attempt these things. Jane knew she'd break her legs. She thought of Chloe. Jane felt her mother's rosary, and eyes closed, stepped forward.

It was almost fun. Jane was not surprised that the wind itself was stronger in parts. She looked up and saw a floating patch of rock, and a further one where Winkie did cartwheels. "Thank you, Winkie!" Jane called when she landed.

"You are most welcome, miss!" Winkie said. "I do hate being this guardian, everyone quite enjoys themselves and almost nobody ever fails," she smiled, "but they do fall. Be careful, miss!"

There were several floating platforms. Jane needed to jump and to get to them, and she spotted another gust of wind. "How do you get down, Winkie? Safely?"

"Don't you worry about me, miss!" Winkie said. "If I play here too long, the Empress comes and makes me leave."

Jane glanced down. In the excitement, she didn't realize she couldn't see the ground through the mist. "Aaah!"

"Are you alright, miss?" Winkie asked.

"I'm uh... I'm alright," Jane said, looking for something to grip onto. There was nothing above waist level, and the platforms weren't very big. And stable? Jane started to imagine old video games of a character jumping to platforms like this, only for some of them to fall after lingering on them for more than a few seconds. They did teeter under her weight, but Jane was determined. Heights never really bothered her, but she didn't like how high she was climbing, either. "Has anyone ever died doing this?" Jane asked.

"No," Winkie said, "but there is always a first time for everything."

The platforms became smaller as Jane progressed. She glanced back at Winkie, she wasn't climbing with her, wasn't giving her any more real help. "Is that as far as you go?" Jane asked.

"You're almost to the next level, miss!" Winkie said. "If you win the staff, come back here, and I'll teach you how to really use this place! Whee!" She leapt off the side, disappearing into the mist below. "Good luck!"

"Winkie!" Jane called, realizing she was alone. The platforms became more and more difficult, and Jane found that she would have to pull herself up on the last two.

Even knowing where she must go, and seeing the rifts of wind in the mist did not make it easy. Jane found that there was a long way to go down. Jane saw the next gust of wind swirling the mist, and clenched her eyes. "Chloe, I'm sorry I'm slow," Jane said, "This isn't what I expected."

She held her eyes and leapt, and was alarmed to find there was no wind. Just an illusion. She screamed and fell, and knew she was going to die, as her stomach came to her throat and the mist became thinner and the ground closer.

Jane heard someone cast a fishing rod, and was pulled up by her belt.

"Hello," said another voice. The girl was about eighteen, and was beautiful and dressed like a vogue princess might. "You must be the one the Empress has told me about." She unhooked Jane's belt, and cast back into the mist. Jane nearly kissed the ground. "Talk about your leap of faith. I think it's silly – if you knew it was going to fail, you wouldn't have jumped, but, no one asks *me* what *I* think. Overcoming fear! That's not a challenge, that's an IQ test!"

As Jane crept back to the edge, and peered back down into the mist. She could barely see the dead courtyard so far below. The young woman pulled on her bamboo line and pulled out a seashell encrusted pan flute from the mist. "You wouldn't believe my luck!" She tossed it into a pile with several chests laden with jewels, statues of important people, toy boats, and other treasures hidden in the deep. "I haven't caught anything interesting all day!"

"My name is Jane-"

"I know, the Empress told me," the young woman said, putting down her fishing line. "Not to worry dear, this one is quite simple, pass or fail. You look tired! You have bags under your eyes, and it looks like you're hungry! Are you hungry?"

"I've been trying to avoid the food," Jane said, picking apple out of her teeth with her tongue. "I'm not sure who I'm eating."

The woman laughed. She had a very melodic laugh. "I'd get you a muffin, but not until after you're done your trial – can't have the others making you sick – not that it's much of a challenge! Come, we have time. Soak your feet for a moment, while I prepare," she said, pointing to a nearby river that seemed to flow from even more mist.

"Are you sure?" Jane asked.

"I'm not going to trick you," she said. "The Empress should have had tricks as one of the trials, but she has no sense of humour. She's completely dried up, you know? Never has a sense of adventure or does anything interesting. I can't remember the last time she spoiled herself."

The water did feel good on Jane's toes. Her big feet were surprisingly dirty. Jane relaxed, and was tempted to look through the pile of rubbish, but figured pilfering would at the very least get her disqualified. "The Empress seems very wise," Jane said.

"Yes, but she never lets me have any real fun," the woman said. "What I wouldn't give to be out of this castle once and a while, and meet a good few men! But, rules are rules," she said. "Close your eyes."

"This isn't like 'pick a hand', is it?" Jane asked.

She smiled and shook her head. Jane did as she was told. "Okay, open them."

Jane blinked. The young woman just beamed a smile at her. Eventually Jane said, "Okay...?"

"Look in the river, you silly!"

Jane did, and nearly fell in when she recognized her own face. If it wasn't for the young woman with her, she wouldn't have, for she leaned over Jane's shoulder, her reflection present in the water. Jane saw the soft full lips and slender nose, the smoothed out hair and deep brown eyes. "I'm... you..."

"Let's go for the full effect, Jane dear." She had a hard time pulling Jane away from her reflection. "I know you like it, come on! You remind me of Adonis... no, I never met him, but I had an aunt who did." She conjured water to stand before the two, and formed a mirror reflection. Jane couldn't believe it: not only was her face perfect but so was her body - she wasn't gangly, instead there was a certain amount of perfect softness to her inherent length. Even her fingertips were no longer stubby. She was more beautiful than Chloe – more beautiful than any woman she'd seen before, and she wore no make up, and was still dressed in the grass-stained get up she'd worn while with the Hunters of the Forest. She even appeared to have some cleavage. Her hair looked *fantastic*.

"I should really do something about that outfit," the woman said. "Would you like a dress like I'm wearing? I'm not a prude, so if you want something that shows off your navel-" She walked off and, were

Jane's eyes not glued to her own reflection, Jane would have seen her pulling beautiful gowns and fashionable boots hither and yon from the pile of refuse.

"How did you do this?" Jane asked. "Are you the goddess of beauty, or something...?"

The woman laughed, stopping to toss Jane an ungainly but fashionable hat. "I have made this trial easy. Jane, you have done well to come so far; the prince admires his enemies that are some threat. He will gift you with your heart's desires," she said. "The Empress said you will not succeed. I will give you this gift, if you give up, Jane. This gift will stay with you. I will not make you immortal - you won't like it, believe me - and I will not keep you young forever, but I will keep you looking radiant and slowly age with good grace. You'll be a hot gramma. You can return to your world, and have a career in modeling, acting, and singing – whatever you chose. After all, we women are defined by what we look like, and you my dear, can be the face that men dream about long after you are gone. Your face will be inspiration for a thousand portraits, sculptures, not to mention the tasteless book covers..."

"What about Chloe?" Jane asked.

"Leave her for another," the beautiful young woman purred, putting on her own ugly hat, "eventually, the right prince will come along to save the princesses. I will tempt him with something else, but he will already be handsome and have a different sort of temptation. I know what it's like to not be pretty, Jane. It hurts to be judged when it's something you have no control over. It's not your job to save them. She chose to go with him." She admired her own reflection in the water mirror. "Take your time deciding."

Jane's heart raced. "I came for Chloe," she said. "Take this back."

The woman frowned. "Are you sure?"

"Yes."

The woman tore at her own hair and gown, "This is the thanks I get! You think I deserve this? I offer you the chance to be something great, and you scorn it! Do you not think that stronger people, smarter people, better people haven't made it this far? That they failed in the next, the most difficult task? Pah, you humans!" she roared, and flung her hat back into the mist.

Jane felt a whirlwind about the woman, and Jane fell backwards as the woman disappeared. She touched her face, and looked down. Definitely no cleavage, and when she touched her face she still felt the traces of acne, and the general size of her nose. Her hair was misbehaving. *I hope she didn't make me worse*, Jane thought. There was no magic mirror behind her, but when she went to the river to check she was appalled. Her teeth were worse than if she'd never had braces, and her lips were thin, and cracked. Back to her body resembling Olive Oyl. She blamed her adventure for the bags under her eyes, but she knew she couldn't blame everything on her quest. *It's just the river, Jane, calm down*, she told herself.

"Am I supposed to swim up the river?" she asked. She had no answer, so she did. It was most difficult to swim up, but she found a rope, and pulled herself up and then struggled against the current until she found a flat expense where she could stand. When she spotted land she made her way, and expected the next voice.

"You didn't take it, did you?" She didn't offer Jane a hand up out of the water. "I suppose you consider yourself noble."

The woman dressed like one suited for battle. Jane wished she knew history better to determine what period she was dressed for. She had a long sword at her side, a quiver at her back, though she bore no bow, and wore a plumed helmet. She almost looked like a man. Her face was exposed, unmarked by scars or injuries, but lined with time. She was dressed akin to a general, not a heavy-skirmish fighter. "I didn't think women went to battle," Jane said.

"You haven't figured out that I am not a woman yet?" she snapped. "Desire said you will not be swayed easily. Come. Before we begin the next trial I would learn more about you."

Jane wrung out her hair and stumbled after her. The world was dark, but there was only small stones and a cobbled path, no dead grass or riverbanks. The mist was still heavy. They walked through darkness,

Jane thought she saw distant towers and castles that they walked towards, but the woman didn't so much as look at them, instead keeping to the path as Jane tried to dry off. Jane wanted to talk to her, but even addressing her seemed to be somehow wrong.

They came upon light suddenly, and from the dark Jane recognized real trees and the sounds of birds and human voices. They were home – at least, back on earth. Jane knew where she was. "Can they see us?" Jane asked.

"No," the warrior said. They were in a refugee camp. Jane had always changed the channel when she saw those commercials. She didn't know how people could make other people suffer. She knew she was in Africa someplace, but suddenly it changed. She was on a Manitoba reserve. The condemned houses, terrible poverty, the stuff her grandma told her about and she didn't want to hear. It changed again. They were in North Korea, seeing the starving bellies of those worshiping their president.

"Stop getting teary eyed, you emotional twit," the warrior snapped. "You're as bad as Winkie and Desire! Crying doesn't solve anything!"

This one seemed the most like the Empress. At first Jane thought she was the Empress's daughter, but perhaps she was a much younger sister. "This is all wrong," Jane said, as the world changed again. A boy of six was being outfitted with a gun, and made to serve with several other children – a girl of ten being sold for less than a bag of groceries. "What am I seeing? What does this have to do with the Prince?"

"This has nothing to do with the prince, this has to do with you," the warrior snapped. "Let us pretend that the staff lets you take it for your own – let us say next that you save your friend, you right the wrongs. You defeat him, you save your friend and every other pathetic wretch who has been defeated by him thus far. You do the unthinkable. Now," she said, gesturing at an old woman with a bruised face in a nursing home, "what will you do with that power?"

Jane didn't know what the staff could do. She didn't know what to say – Sedolei said that unicorns wanted to fight monsters rather than help people. She didn't think about after fighting the prince, she just thought about being able to stop him. Everything the woman showed her broke her heart – a failed family business after forty years because a Walmart moved in. A woman who wouldn't leave her abusive boyfriend, thinking that he'd change once the baby came along. "The staff would give me power," she said, "you're saying that it could make me fix all of this."

"In the wrong hands, the staff could make the one who bears it rule your world," the warrior said. "Think about it: no more war. The world would be scared of you. You could rule the world as you saw fit, and make it better."

Jane looked at her, then at the images, then said, "Do I need magic to make the world a better place?" She crossed her arms. "I used to laugh at my dad when he said that power corrupts. I used to think that wouldn't be true in my case; that if only people listened to me, the world would be better. And I... I want to help everyone you showed me. Part of me wants to hurt those who've hurt others, but..." she paused, "...but I've hurt people too. I don't know how to help everyone," Jane said. "It's funny. When my brother Paul went for a course on guns so he could go hunting, he laughed, because he said the gun laws only really applied to people who followed the law." Jane hugged her ribs, and didn't hold back her tears when she saw a girl in college overdose on Tylenol because she failed a course. "I don't want to rule the world; I don't think I can do it. Not if I was the smartest, most fair person born," she said. "Winkie was fear – Desire, she was selfishness, wasn't she? Temptation, maybe. You're harder. Is it wrong to want to help them, but know that there's no way that I can ever do it without becoming...?"

"Why do you think you can't do it right?" asked the warrior. "Isn't peace worth an iron fist? You made it this far. You have discipline. You can surround yourself with wise people. Strike down the tyrants."

"The Faerie Prince has power," Jane said, "and everyone's scared of him. I'm sure he'd put an end to some of this, if it suited him. What is this trial? Morality? How can you tell me what's right and wrong?"

"You're the Catholic," the warrior muttered.

Jane opened her mouth, but shut it just as quick, and tightened her already firm grasp on her mother's rosary. "So what do you think I should do with this staff after I defeat him? I want to stop the evils that plague this world, but the staff is not of my world. I would want it to be destroyed, if it can be."

"The Empress has not succumbed to its power," the warrior said, "she knows that she is better guardian than champion against the prince. She is very powerful without it. With it, she knows she would succumb and make many worlds hell. Jane, the other tests were straightforward, this one is more complicated. I wanted to hear what you would do before I took you further. Can you give yourself the power to stop injustice, and give it up so easily? It will haunt you for all of your days."

Jane bit her lip. "The only power I can think that I want to do with it," she said, "is to save Chloe. If that means I have to kill the Prince, I will, but I will not enjoy it. I prefer to save him and the others. I will make sure they can't come to our world. And Bijan... I'll break his curse. That is all I want. Maybe I'm being stupid, but..."

"You're being honest," she said. "There are times when we must permit evil so that others can freely chose good. I will permit you to take the trial now."

"What was that for, then?" Jane asked.

"You want a selection of answers?" the warrior asked.

Jane saw an aged knight in armour, world weary and tired, faint in the light. "People suffer all the time," he said. "It is the way of the world. I do not like it, but neither do I pretend that I am to be its savior."

An older looking woman appeared, Jane assumed she was someone's mother. "I don't want it for myself! But these children... I'd do anything to save these children..."

Another, this one looked like he was a poor youth. "You mean, I could save our people? I could even be king, if I wanted?"

A young girl, maybe fourteen, "World peace, naturally. I would make them get along."

An older man, kneeling, his hands praying. "Tempt me not..."

Jane thought she saw the Empress, "How many worlds will I destroy if I take this abomination? I will not defile myself with Faerie magic."

"The Empress is very wise," the warrior said, "Come Jane. The staff must accept you. There are few heirs left in your world."

She walked through the darkness, Jane felt guilty at wanting to leave behind the voices. "This is where everyone fails, isn't it?" Jane asked.

"Few give into Winkie – they wouldn't have made it here if they were not brave already," the warrior said, "Most give into Desire. They know that they're being selfish, but selfishness is the way of most worlds – we all acknowledge goodness, but fall short of it, knowing our flaws make us unworthy. When the Empress made this trial, I thought it was too close to Desire, but Desire always gives something personal," she said, "a dream unfulfilled, typically. Most women of your world are vain to some degree or another - men desire power. My domain is external, not internal. You can deny your own pleasures, but you cannot deny your soul."

"But I never dreamed about being beautiful," Jane said.

"Not even when you were a small girl?" the warrior asked.

"How would she know?" Jane asked.

"The Empress is very wise," the warrior said, "she tells Desire."

"Do you all wait for ten years, or however long it takes?" Jane asked.

"Others come, from many worlds, seeking the staff. The Empress lets us do as we will in the castle," the warrior said. "You mortals would find our interests trite."

Jane wanted to ask about immortality. "I thought you came from Earth," Jane said.

"We consider Earth one of our homes," she said. They came to a door lit by two torches on either side of the archway. "Faerie magic can be wielded by mortals and humans – it is more difficult for us who have our own magic to learn fae magic; not so with humans, though there are so few of you who can wield their magic, and less still who can call upon the staff's power. Use the heartstone, it is of a different magic," she said, "and see which flows better through you."

The warrior put her hand out, much like the Empress did to open the first door. "What is your name?" Jane asked.

"Ambition," the warrior said, bowing her head, "I wish you well.

If you take the staff, remember your words here, when you had no power. Do not let it corrupt you, or you will have more enemies then a single Would-Be King. This is the only trial where you may come out changed."

Jane felt uneasy when the great stone doors opened. If the Empress wouldn't take up the staff for fear of corruption, why should she? Jane didn't know what to do, what to expect, but she could feel the heartstone racing ahead of her own heart as she entered the doorway and into the darkness of the next room. The warrior did not follow.

The room was bare, but there was no mist present. Jane saw a door on the other side, and walking to it, found no way to open it. She looked back to the center of the room, and stared up. She saw something dark hovering, but couldn't tell what it was in the darkness. "I can't fly," she said to herself. "Is this a test to see if I can use magic?" No answer. No door closed behind her; she wasn't trapped. The heartstone still beat uncontrollably. "Don't just beat and give me nausea, do something. We have to do something. For Chloe," Jane said.

The dark shapes drifted down. Jane thought they were jewels of some sort, black crystals, perhaps. They reflected the light from the open door behind Jane. They were large, bigger than Jane's hands, and in different shapes. *I don't understand*, Jane thought. *Do I touch them? Do I pick one?* She hesitated. Was hesitation a sign of temptation, or a sign of the virtue of patience? She thought perhaps it was a puzzle. "Empress," Jane said, "I don't know what you expect of me. Enough games, I came to help my friend."

The beating of the heartstone ceased, and Jane saw the crystals fall. She knew they'd shatter if they touched the ground, and put her hand out.

The crystals hesitated. They rotated slowly, and she wondered if she was supposed to fit them together somehow. She was tempted to touch the sleek surfaces of the black crystals, and she did not know how to control them, only wishing for the staff, and wishing for them not to break. *The heartstone has power, not me*, Jane realized. *Do I?*

Jane let the crystals fall, and closing her eyes turned as they shattered behind her. "Enough of these illusions and trickery! Enough tests of my bravery! Open, and let us see if I can use the staff!" she ordered the door. The heartstone was silent, but Jane felt the power come from her hands. The door slowly creaked open.

The warrior stood on the other side. She smiled.

"You can wield Faerie magic," The Empress said, appearing in the midst of the broken crystals. "Are you hurt?"

Jane shook her head. "That was it?" she asked.

"Yes," The Empress said, moving to the next room. The Empress and The Warrior put out their arms, and the floor in the middle of the room sank, and then rose. Jane saw the staff encased in dark crystal. It did not look silver, but rather it appeared a tall twisted branch.

"Have I won the staff?" Jane said.

"Yes you have," said The Empress. "Only you and one other have made it this far. Break it from its protection and take it," she paused, waiting for Jane to extend her hand, "but know this: if you take the staff for your own: Fear, Desire, and Ambition, die."

Jane paused from touching the crystal encompassing the staff. "What do you mean?"

"It is quite simple, miss," Winkie said, appearing from the shadow.

"We are guardians bound to the staff," said Desire, descending from the mist.

"And we will not see it in the hands of the prince, or one who is unworthy," said Ambition.

"The Prince of Faeries does not hesitate to kill," the Empress said. "How about you?"

Jane clenched her fists. "This isn't fair."

"Life isn't fair," said the Empress.

"I'm not about to kill them to prove anything to you!" Jane snapped.

"Innocent people suffer all the time," the Empress said, "do you not think the Prince will throw innocents at you? That he may even use the one you seek to save against you? He will trap you, and take the staff as his own-"

"You are insane!" Jane shouted.

"No, I am Wisdom," she said. "If I could wield the staff without it corrupting me he would have been defeated long ago! Instead I linger here, waiting for him to find his queen, and when he finds her, I shall rip out her heart."

Jane looked at the eyes. "They're you... you're all the Empress."

"I have cut off those parts of me," said Wisdom. "I am the only one that matters. Take it. If you need, I can remove your heart, make it easy."

"You are heartless!" Jane said, feeling the strong beating in her chest. She realized it was not her own heart beating that echoed in her ears. Jane let the tears fall, and calling out, fell to the ground. "Aaaaaa!"

"Miss!" Winkie cried.

"Stay back," said Desire, restraining the girl.

Ambition knelt by Jane's side, and comforted Jane as the rival magic expelled from her body. Jane felt the stone warm in her hand. "Another's heart is a difficult burden to carry," said the warrior. "Focus, Jane."

"Ambition," Wisdom said, "do not weaken now. We have to remain strong."

"Isn't this what I said would happen?" Ambition asked, holding Jane protectively.

Jane thought she would pass out. Instead, once the stone expelled from her body, she gripped the warm stone, and held it out for Wisdom. "Don't you want it back?"

"Oh!" Winkie's eyes widened.

"I remember..." Desire said, reaching for Jane's hand.

"Silence, you two!" Wisdom shouted, slapping Desire's hand. "I removed our heart long ago. What good is something that can be broken? Swayed? Fooled and misled? What use is something that can be used against us?"

Ambition spoke quietly, "What good is all the brilliance in the world without compassion? That is the difference between you and I. We decided fear and desire could be irrational long ago, but ambition towards the greater good gave wisdom purpose. Perhaps a heart can be corrupted, but we're stronger with it."

Winkie took the stone in her hands. "We have guarded this staff for so long, divided our self in case one of us decided to succumb."

"Knowing that one day," Desire said.

"We would be whole again," Ambition said, helping Jane sit up, before standing and approaching Wisdom with the heartstone. "One who can bear the staff is with us. A champion from that same world. Let us end this stalemate."

"She is too young! He will destroy her!" Wisdom roared.

"That is up to her," said Desire. "Are are you going to be selfish now?"

"Or scared?" Winkie asked.

Hands embraced hands as Wisdom wept, and the figures finally became whole. Jane didn't know what to expect, save a human. Their blue dresses, armour and robes melded and became long, and the white hair on Wisdom's head and marks on her gown spread. She was long and serpentine, and Jane found herself looking at a sky blue Chinese dragon etched with white markings, massive and long, encompassing the room.

"Oh my..." Jane gaped.

"Jane, at last we meet," the dragon said. "Ah, you seek a different form! Very well!"

She was dragon in human form; Jane did not know how she did not see it before. She had Wisdom's face, Winkie's hair, Desire's voice and Ambition's powerful walk. "I am The Empress," she said.

"You were under a spell, all that time?" Jane asked.

"My sister was stolen by one of the Faerie Princes of old, and I hunted them. I helped the Red Queen gain power, and I cursed her when she did not destroy her infant son, for she saw him as innocent. I told myself I would never allow my petty emotions – my childish fear, my own desires, even ambition for the greater good – control my actions as it did her. I feared I would one day take the staff and become what I hated. However," she said, becoming serpentine once again, "I am at my most powerful when I am whole!" She roared, and the dark crystal protecting the twisted staff shattered. "Take it!"

"But you–"

"I am a dragon!" the Empress roared. "Take the staff!"

It felt strangely warm in Jane's hand. The dragon roared, and Jane felt wind gust about her. She found herself standing in the hall before the door, the Empress in human form.

"Jane!" Sedolei neighed, running to her side. "Are you alright? You have the staff!"

"Yes!" Jane hugged Sedolei's neck. "I don't believe it."

"Child, you have gained mastery of the staff, but I will give you a warning," the Empress said, "and a final plea. You and one other have made it to the final part, and the other refused the staff, not willing to destroy the three bound to it. If you find him, tell him the Empress would have her son back, for she is whole again."

Jane didn't know what to say. Sedolei spoke. "And the warning?"

"That should you become what you told Ambition what you'd never be, you will have to deal with The Empress! I do not wish to make you doubt yourself," she said. "Just know he will offer you everything. You may have to kill the one you came to save to free her."

"Your sister," Jane said, "Whatever happened to her?"

"My son went to save her, and in doing so, he thought he would save me," she said. "They are both prisoners in this world. Do not worry about them, for they are dragons! Destroy the Prince, and save your friend. Know that if he falls, that they will be free. They will all be free. I wish you luck Jane." She caught Jane's eyes a final time and smiled, before turning into her serpentine form, and flying off through the castle halls.

"Eccentric dragon," Sedolei whinnied as Jane climbed onto his back. They found the castle gate open, and the wall of water vanished. Jane looked up to see the blue dragon dancing in the sky, the terrific roar a beautiful song that renewed Jane with strength. "Are you ready to free your friend, or shall we rest, Jane?"

Part of her wanted to stop and rationalize their next move, but with the staff in her hands, Jane felt a strange sense of vitality. "Do you need to rest before we save Chloe, Sedolei?"

"You will not see me put to shame," the unicorn said, and leapt from the castle grounds into the sky.

13

On These Broken Wings

"Are you ready?"

She didn't remember when they stopped saying her name. Chloe knew all of theirs: Mediala the Graceful; Osophene the Songbird; Bryne the Illuminated; Yssa the Beauty; Zyeth the Enchantress; Cideo the Lovely; Ariella the Fair, Yashiako the Solemn; Jasmite the Spirited; Deliath the Tall.

They were missing Hyralie.

The Exiled.

All chosen.

All failures.

Chloe stared at her reflection. She recognized it, but she didn't look much like herself. Maybe an improved version – one with less flaws. She felt her flaws all the more. When they should have been preparing her for the trial, they fussed about themselves, as to what shoes went with which necklace and how they should fashion their hair.

"Three days is not a long time to learn everything," Chloe said, trying to get some attention.

"Being one of us is very difficult," Deliath snipped, "you either can do it or you cannot. Why waste time striving towards something you can never achieve?"

"You are one to talk," Zyeth said.

"Enough," Yssa said. The two stuck their tongues at one another behind Yssa's back. "Girl, are you ready? Our Prince is waiting."

Chloe, she thought. "I'm ready," she said.

Chloe followed the princesses into the court. Her prince sat on his throne, clad from neck to boot in brilliant white silk, looking the part ready to take up his mount and rescue her. He barely cast a glance in her direction. "Yssa, you have done well," he said, taking Yssa's face with his hands. Yssa closed her eyes and he breathed on her neck and kissed it lightly, before turning to Mediala and kissing her hand. "Choosing among you is like choosing a star in the heavens, or a pearl on your necklace." He touched Chloe's collarbone and put a black pearl necklace around her throat. "I hope you are indeed the one, Kasmodiah."

"A lovely name," Yashiako purred.

"Wear it well," Cideo said.

"Come now." The prince had her on his arm. They walked from the throne room, Kasmodiah/Chloe looked behind at the other princesses where they waited, save for Yssa, who followed. Her prince led her down a staircase. Kasmodiah/Chloe felt humidity, and saw a great marble pool of sorts that smelt strange. The prince let go of her hand, and put it in Yssa's. Yssa led her forward. "Here you will begin the process. Are you ready?"

"This isn't going to mess up my hair, is it?"

Yssa sighed theatrically, and gestured. Three pixies buzzed over, one brought a crystal goblet. "These waters have strange properties - they will help you harness any powers you might have in this world." She dipped the cup in the water, handed it to Kasmodiah/Chloe. "After this, we'll see whether or not you can wield the magic of this world."

Kasmodiah kept both pinkies out and wished she'd been told ahead of time so she could pick something smudgeproof for her lips. The water tasted funny - almost like it was carbonated, light. She felt strangeness on her back, and she lifted herself up with a flap of silver wings.

"Oh!" Yssa exclaimed.

"Her?" a pixie asked.

"Could it be?" asked another.

Kasmodiah felt strange as the magic overtook her body. She was not sure what to expect, for she expected the trial to be a dance, or an act of humility perhaps. She did not know how to fly, but that didn't matter.

"Leave us now," the prince said. He met Kasmodiah in the air, and took her hands.

"I have wings," she said.

"The pool grants many gifts," he said, "I have not seen such a gift before. Follow me."

They flew, the room was high-ceilinged and Kasmodiah felt strange. Was she magically transforming before him? They flew through a window and above the castle, until he led her to a balcony, before they went inside a tower.

Kasmodiah landed and looked over her shoulder. They were beautiful and like light. Touching them, she thought she'd never felt anything so fine. "Did I pass?"

"No," he said, "that was preparation. I have never seen this happen before. Be still." He circled her.

Kasmodiah smiled until she saw his face. She did not expect anger. "Perhaps this is a sign that I am the one," she said.

"I fear you will fly away and leave me, Kasmodiah."

"I could never do that." She touched her wings. They shimmered, and were not at all like his which were like that of a dragonfly, but hers were like a butterfly's in shape and form. They twitched as if tempting her to take flight.

"Wings make you want to test them, wings make you want to fly," he said.

"Your men all have wings and fly with you," he said

"I have granted them wings for my service," he said, "and the pixies fly under my orders."

"Perhaps I have been granted wings for your pleasure," Kasmodiah curtsied. She felt pain suddenly at her back, and she fell forward, and tried to keep herself from screaming from the strange pain – it was not pain in the classic sense, but almost like she was losing a part of herself.

She saw the first wing fall, and then the second; she tried not to let her tears fall as he cut the wings from her back. "Why...?"

"They would interfere with your dancing," he said, "and I could not bear to leave you in one of the cages in the garden. Am I not worth more than wings, Kasmodiah?"

"Of course," she said, shaking. "It just hurts."

"Not near as much as it would hurt if you were to ever leave me," he said, bending down and taking her quivering face I his hands. "And now, the test."

Kasmodiah didn't understand. She existed in this place because of him – she wouldn't be here if it weren't for him. How could he say she'd fly away? Where would she go? The pixies were everywhere, always watching. As for the dancing, she'd find a way. He took her arm and made her stand, lead her up the staircase. They came to a room in the tower, Kasmodiah saw suspended crystals hovering a foot from the tall ceiling and light came from them. "What is this place?"

"If you can control my power, you will pass the test," he said. "Do not hold back, Kasmodiah."

She put her hand out the way he did. The crystals began to shake. "What do I do?" she asked. "Are they a puzzle? Do I put them together?" She saw the first one drop from the hold and shatter. "No!" She shouted, kneeling as if to put it back together, cutting her hands on the rough shards as the rest of the crystals fell and broke.

"Another failure," said her prince.

Tears came to Kasmodiah's eyes. She thought about her wings, thrown to the wind. What was the point, if she was not the Faerie Queen? "I am sorry, my prince." She lay prostrate at his feet. "I thought-"

He took her chin and made her look up. "Like all the others," he said, "useless."

"No, I'm not useless!"

"You're not?" he asked.

Her mind raced. Hyralie, Kildare, and Yssa. She did not want to end up like Hyralie or Kildare. "What must I do to serve you?" Kasmodiah breathed.

"You know," he said.

She kissed him and he kissed her back forcefully. Kasmodiah's mind raced. She was a failure – one of many. She'd have no special privileges. Only death in the garden waited for her. She had to have some worth, somehow. There were the others. He loved them. She could be one of *them*.

He ran his hands through her hair. "Your sorrow is intoxicating, Kasmodiah. You may take your place among my princesses. You may dance for me for all time."

"Of course, my lord," she said, and drank in his kisses once more.

14

The Night Garden

Even on the back of a galloping unicorn, Jane had no idea how large the kingdom was, or how long it would have taken her to get to the prince's castle by foot. She felt the staff in her left grip, the magic had a strange sensation at the best of times, enticing her to use it. It made Jane very afraid. Jane was tempted to ask the unicorn to stop so that she could practice, but she thought of The Empress and Bijan as they raced through the fake forests, catching glimpses of the sleeping villages in the distances as they rode towards the prince's castle.

Sedolei stopped suddenly, unmoving except for his twitching ears. "What's wrong?" Jane asked. "Are you alright?"

He did not answer. Jane followed his gaze, and looked up. A large shadow swooped overhead, and Jane saw great copper and golden feathers and yellow-brown wings before the long tail ending in deep red, and the magnificent black beak.

It landed on the path before them. The gryphon was smaller than Jane thought they would be, though its wingspan was much bigger than Sedolei. "Where are you going, unicorn?" the gryphon asked, her voice regal.

"I am on a quest," Sedolei said, "where we go does not concern you."

The gryphon caught Jane's gaze with topaz eyes. The magnificent gryphon flicked out her tongue, as if tasting the air. "I am Sunsoar – there are whispers in my mother's eyrie. I had heard that The Ancient Empress has finally left her castle. At last, someone has taken the staff. Human girl child, we are most interested in these events."

"*We?*" Jane asked, wrapping her fingers tight in Sedolei's mane.

"You do not think such events would go unnoticed," Sedolei said.

"Because the last person to take the staff was the Faerie Queen," said the gryphon, "the mortal queen from your world. Until her death, they were forced to stay here, but for-"

"Every ten years, the Prince of the Faeries may walk our world," Jane said. "Her son."

"The Empress has told you a little," the gryphon said. "Both Prince Altroine and Prince Nyveo of this Kingdom seeks the staff in your hand, a sceptre of every ruler of this land. Altroine remains bound, however when Nyveo learns you have taken the staff from its sanctuary, he will hunt you. Have you mastered the staff's power?"

Jane shook her head. "The Empress didn't tell me how to use it."

"You will master it, Jane," Sedolei said, "We are on our way to the prince's castle now, Gryphon, and we mean to defeat him! Do not hinder us."

"You would race her to the main gates and challenge the prince?" the gryphon asked. She sounded like she was laughing. "Don't waste your time with that colt, mortal. He is rash and only seeks glory for himself. He accompanies you now only for his unicorn pride! He thinks that you may be the one to defeat the prince, but I know better."

"She has possession of the staff," Sedolei neighed. "No one else has done that besides the last Faerie Queen!"

"That Queen knew her enemies!" Sunsoar snapped, before focusing her yellow eyes on Jane. "You are too young to know any better! All you can think of how wonderful it will be to save those girls – girls who are out of their own time, and who live only to serve him! Most of which who are happy to be possessions." She stepped closer, extending brilliant brown claws as she strode. "I know you think yourself brave, but let me assure you there is much foolishness in directly confronting the Prince! You have much valour, but you do not stand a chance against him. He will take the staff from you, and if he does this, he can claim this realm."

"I will not let him!" Sedolei said.

"Girl, your quest is now something bigger than the reason what you started," Sunsoar said.

"How do you know what it is I'm here for?" Jane asked.

"The prince will allow you entry to his castle, and use every trick to take the staff when he learns that you have it," said the gryphon, "and I believe he will know soon."

"Then why do you make us tarry?" Sedolei demanded.

The gryphon roared and the unicorn reared. Jane merely clung to Sedolei's mane. "There is a way," the gryphon said, "use the staff's power to confine the prince! Trap him in his castle, where he will never bother anyone again!"

"What about Chloe?" Jane asked.

"Is she one of his princesses? Her fate has already been sealed," the gryphon said. "Do you not think he will not use your friend against you? He will kill her to slow you down! He will throw all of his princesses and servants and his castle and the kingdom itself into the sea, for he knows that if he gains the staff, he can replace it all!" She cawed loudly, and Sedolei backed slightly. "You must have some wit to have made it this far! Come with me, and we will lock the prince away forever! He may never come to your world again, for now, he alone can walk your mortal pathways." She smiled as best as gryphons can. "Unless a unicorn is foolish enough to come this way, of course, and bring one of them to your world, they will be forever barred. We can end this now."

"There are many who should know better than to set foot in this world – unicorns and gryphons alike," Sedolei quipped. "Jane, do not listen! Gryphons think they are wise, all the while all they think about is themselves! They would smash their own eggs to further their own ideals."

"As unicorns would sacrifice maidens to do battle with gryphons should they offer up the slightest infraction," the gryphon hissed. "Is it not what you want, unicorn?"

"Jane, get off my back," Sedolei said lowly.

"You can't be serious!" Jane said. "We have no reason to fight!"

"She has insulted my honour," Sedolei countered.

"No," Jane said, "You said you'd help me! Fighting her doesn't help Chloe!"

"The girl is not to be harmed," Sedolei said, kneeling, and shook Jane off, "under any circumstance."

"Unicorn, do not make promises you yourself cannot fulfill," Sunsoar dug her talons into the rock and soil. "I will not harm her. I cannot say the same for the prince."

"Wait!" Jane hollered, only to see both cast magic at her. Jane found herself in a clear magic bubble, which suddenly floated several feet above the air. She pounded the jelly-like walls with her fists. "You can't do this!"

The gryphon and the unicorn talked for a few minutes more, but in her confinement Jane couldn't hear what they said.

Sedolei reared and light gathered to his horn, a powerful burst of lightning temporarily blinded Jane. Stones shattered under his powerful hooves, and he met the harsh winds created by the wings of the gryphon head on. He went to strike through her heart with his horn, and the gryphon slashed at him with her talons. Sedolei fell back, but rebounded just as quickly, and ran at her again. The gryphon took to the air, and he reared, challenging her to come down and face him.

Jane felt a sudden large POP. She found herself falling, and someone gripped underneath her armpits. She did not expect to see Zilare, one of the prince's servants that she'd tried to fight off in the Assiniboine Park.

"Take the staff," he told another she did not recognize.

There were over a dozen of them, all in the prince's guard, judging by their blue and silver uniform and ornamental swords at their sides. Jane tried to keep the staff in her hands, but when there were five arms forcing against hers, the best she could offer was a classic, "No!" while three pairs of arms pinned her.

"What about her?" another asked.

"That is for the prince to decide," Moaz said before catching Jane's sour expression. "Thank you for the staff. When the prince said to lead you to the gate, I thought you were the most unlikely to succeed."

Jane tried to kick him but he flew out of range. "Sedolei!" she called, looking below and realizing that while she struggled for the staff, they had flown her above the canopy.

"Jane!" the unicorn cried.

"The staff!" the gryphon cried.

The fae sped over the tops of the trees. Jane could see a castle in the distance. The pixies and sidhe flew much slower than the other two. Though she struggled to free herself, Jane could tell the fae were nervous – glancing over their shoulders and, if they weren't so white already, they might have paled. "Moaz, use the staff, and hold them off," Zilare said.

"I cannot wield it," Moaz said. "Such an action would be treason!"

"If you do not, the gryphon will be upon us," said Zilare.

"Then I will vanquish it by sword!" Moaz said, drawing his blade.

"All the gryphon cares for is the staff!" Zilare shouted.

"Then give her something else to chase!" Moaz snapped.

Jane realized she was that something else.

They were very high. Jane wondered if the fake trees would do much to slow her down. They let her go very suddenly, as if the two holding her were of one mind about the matter. Jane screamed and looked up, to see the gryphon make no move to save her, but toward to the fae, who attempted to fight her with their curved blades and faerie magic. Jane felt a sudden cushioning, and felt her left leg slam against it; only it wasn't real, just a puff of unicorn magic trying to slow her fall. The unicorn had bounded into the air, and caught her almost instantly after; Jane grabbed his neck and held on tightly as he landed.

"Are you alright, Jane?" Sedolei asked.

"The staff! They have it!" Jane cried, not waiting for him to kneel so that she could get on his back. He could bound much higher than the height she'd fallen, but he tried not to do so, as while Jane was a good rider, the unicorn seemed to know that humans tended to break easily. She watched the figures above battle with the gryphon, and she focused on the staff. She felt a strange sensation well up within her, and closing her eyes, let the power flow. Sedolei reared, but she did not hold onto his mane, for the Staff of Silver flew to her extended arms.

Jane felt strange, whole with the staff. "How did I do that?" she asked.

"You're the staff's master," Sedolei said. Even despite the noise, their antagonists had noticed above. "Hold tight!"

The fae and gryphon had assumed where the staff had gone, and Jane had no idea what to do, save that Sedolei couldn't hold them all off at once. Jane felt compelled by the power at the end of her arms, and she raised the staff above her head, and just thought of protection for her and the unicorn. Silver light came off the staff, like the sun on a mirror, blinding Jane, but she felt the power of the staff resonate throughout her body.

The surge of power left Jane breathless. Sunsoar landed before her once the prince's men fled from Jane. "You are learning quickly," said the gryphon, "but Prince Nyveo is much older, and much more practiced."

"So that I may give you the staff for safe keeping when I am done defeating him?" Jane asked. "You would have let me fall!"

"I knew the unicorn would have caught you," Sunsoar said. "Unicorn, we have business to continue. That is, if you are not winded."

"Sedolei, if you fight her, I won't have you accompany me anymore," Jane said. "Both of you! Your stupid fight nearly cost us everything! Put your pride aside, both of you, we have a common enemy!"

The gryphon chuckled after Jane's outburst. "I like your spirit, human, but it needs to be tempered. Once we defeat the Prince of the Faeries, I will teach you to hone that spirit, to become something great."

"Gryphon, be gone from this place," Sedolei said.

Sunsoar roared and spread her wings. Jane was not expecting the gryphon to knock Sedolei to the ground and steal her off his back. The gryphon kept the staff in one talon, and held Jane in the other, and flew away from the castle. "Do not worry, the unicorn will be alright," Sunsoar said as they climbed above the tree line, "they are stronger then they appear. Your compassion is admirable."

"Stop this! I want to free all of them!" Jane said. She struggled, and with each wriggle the gryphon's talons closed tighter around her rib cage, making it more difficult for Jane to breathe.

"Will you climb onto my back," the gryphon asked, "or must I carry you in my claws?"

"I did not come all this way to be the possession of anyone, least of all yours!" Jane said, and she felt the power once again. She didn't know how she did it, for the staff could not be contained by the gryphon, for all the gryphon's strength it wrenched itself out of her claws and flew to Jane. She cawed and dove to the ground.

"Little fool! Must I kill you to take what it rightfully mine?" the gryphon demanded, letting go of Jane when she neared the ground. They were on a rocky, elevated surface, and the gryphon showed her claws as she skulked towards Jane. Jane knew she couldn't get down easily without the gryphon's help. "When I took the Empress's test I knew she was a fool to say the third stage was the most difficult! Wisdom indeed!" Sunsoar roared.

"You would have easily killed anyone to take the staff," Jane said.

The gryphon cawed so loud Jane thought that the Empress would hear. "You are a stupid little girl who got lucky," the gryphon hissed. "You have not had your species hunted to near extinction by the Prince's forefathers! I will not allow him to do the same to your kind!"

"Let her go, Gryphon!" Sedolei whinnied, charging through the woods, though Jane could only hear his voice.

"Unicorn, the staff is mine!" the gryphon yelled, diving off the rock to battle him in the forest.

"And I am hers!" Sedolei whinnied, and charged.

Jane scurried to the cliff side to see them battle below. The gryphon clawed and hissed magic out her beak and Sedolei seemed to break it on an invisible shield that reflected it in a dome spanning from his horn. Jane called out, and shielded herself with the staff's power as magic struck magic, claw and hoof and talons and teeth and horn met. Both bleeding, they backed from one another, circling. Jane could see Sedolei limping. "No Sedolei, run," Jane said when she saw that unicorns bled red.

He met her eyes, and perked his ears, then reared, and charged the gryphon.

The gryphon crooned and called out, "Fool! Use your magic to save yourself!"

"Unicorn pride," he grunted, and struck her belly with his horn.

Jane covered her mouth as the gryphon fell back, then took to the sky in retreat.

Jane navigated the rock to the forest floor. "You did it! You won!"

Facing the direction that the gryphon had fled, Sedolei reared and neighed victorious, but he staggered backwards before falling to his left side. "Sedolei!" Jane screamed, running to his side. "Why? Why? How could you do this, you stupid unicorn?"

"I told you," he said, struggling to get up, faltering, laying back down, "we become indifferent to tears, and seek to defeat monsters. Are you any different, Jane?"

"Don't! You're hurting yourself!" Jane screamed. She used the pocket knife to cut loose a strip of fabric from her skirt. She tied a bandage around his leg, tried to stop the bleeding. The cut ran very deep. "Why if you know, do you do it anyway?"

"Unicorn pride," he said. He whickered as if in a laugh. "Let me rest, a moment..."

Jane led his head to her lap and she hugged him. "Please don't die. Sedolei, please..." She let the tears flow. She didn't care if the prince's men came, she would stay with him. She had the staff; she would defeat them. *What if that gryphon's right? What if it's too late for Chloe?* She couldn't think like that. Not after everything she had been through. Likely the prince's men would be upon them soon. She would stay with her friend – defend him. Jane held onto his neck. "Will this faerie magic help you? Or hinder you?" she looked at the staff, before closing her eyes and hugging him tighter. "I can't use it for everything. It's not right."

She sat with him, stroking his head for hours. The sun set before he opened his eyes again. "You stayed with me?" Sedolei asked.

"Of course I did," Jane said.

"The dangers of the forest – the prince's men...!"

"I see what the Empress said before, about abandoning Bijan," she said, "I assumed because he was so much stronger than me, that he'd be alright," she shook her head. "Maybe if the prince didn't make him look like a monster, I would have tried harder."

Sedolei slowly rose. "You cannot undo what you have done," he said. "Only go forward. Defeating the prince defeats the spell on your friend, does it not?" he asked. "I... I can run, I think." He staggered to kneel. "Get on my back."

"Sedolei, you're still weak," Jane said. "Leave this place. Get as far away as you can."

"Jane, after we defeat the prince, I will take you home," he said, "and perhaps, when you are finished being grounded, I shall take you to where we unicorns run. If you are strong enough to continue, then so am I."

Jane wondered how quickly unicorns could heal. "Then let me lead you," she said, "together."

"Together," the unicorn agreed.

He limped but did not complain as they continued down the path. They were closer to the prince's castle grounds than Jane would have liked, but it felt good to see their target in sight. "It's beautiful," she said, overlooking the castle from the edge of the forest.

The castle was large, with many towers and high walls, the green garden labyrinth sprawling out before it on all directions. "Do you feel strong enough to charge through the garden?"

"That will alert the guards," Sedolei said.

"He knows I'm coming," Jane said. "Are you sure you want to come?"

"I won't abandon you," the unicorn neighed. "You need not face any more of this world alone."

Jane wondered about the guards. She saw light ahead in the castle windows, but no one in the garden. She wondered if there were little pixies with trumpets ready to sound the alarm. She didn't know which way to go, but neither did Sedolei. "You could transverse this entire place in three bounds," Jane said.

"Two, if I were running," the unicorn said, "and feeling better." He perked his ears suddenly. "Can you hear it?"

Jane listened. She thought she heard a woman singing, so she slowly nodded.

"Not everyone stays freely," the unicorn said, "those who he doesn't have locked in towers, or under spells awaiting him to rescue them, he keeps in his garden here," he said. "We should free these maidens!"

Jane grit her teeth "We need to focus on the mission – not rescue random princesses. She'll be more of a hindrance than help. The world is dangerous, not to mention the prince may have her under a spell of some sort."

"You have the staff," the unicorn said. "Come, this way."

Jane followed him down the path of perfectly manicured hedges, difficult for Jane to landmark, save for the life-sized statues marking the paths. Sedolei seemed to have no problem deciding where to go, and led her to a silver gazebo. Jane saw no door, but the unicorn tapped the wall with his horn. Jane stepped back when the silver vines and coiled back, making an entrance inside. "Hello!" Jane called. "Anybody in here?"

"Go inside and look around!" Sedolei whinnied.

"Are you nuts?" Jane asked. "She can come out!" They didn't hear the song anymore. "Maybe this one is empty. "

"Perhaps," the unicorn said, "but I could have sworn I heard..."

The song again, away from the cage, though without lyric the melody was mournful. Sedolei perked his ears and trotted down the path, showing little sign of his injuries. "Don't get too far ahead!" Jane shouted, following him.

They went down a dead end in the maze, and Jane was surprised to see a beautiful young woman sitting, chained on a pedestal. "Who goes there?" the beautiful girl asked. "A unicorn?"

"And me," Jane quipped as the unicorn appraoched the girl.

"Oh!" the girl said, touching Sedolei's nose. "Have you come to free me? At midnight, the prince is coming to turn me into a statue!"

"Who are you?" Jane asked.

"I am Osophene, and the Prince of the Faeries has tired of me," the girl said. "He has ordered that I be taken out to this garden, so that others may see my beauty for all time. Please, release me!"

"Jane, the staff!" Sedolei whinnied.

"Have you seen a girl by the name of Chloe?" Jane asked.

"She is one of the dancing princesses, and no longer goes by that name," Osophene said, "I think she has his favour – for the time being."

"If we help you," Jane said, "can you help us find my friend?"

"I dare not," the woman said, "Please, have mercy!"

"Jane," Sedolei said again.

Jane wanted to tell him to use his horn to free her, but she had no idea what unicorn magic was good for. Jane hoped she wouldn't toast the girl, and tried to imagine the shackles unlocking. She wasn't sure how she summoned the power, but truth be told, it was becoming second nature. The staff made the silver shackles fall off her wrists. Osophene smiled at Jane, then embraced the unicorn's neck.

"I don't suppose you'd rather save her, deliver her to safety, and then come back?" Jane asked flatly. "If we have to do that every time we come across a damsel in distress-"

The princess' shackles moved suddenly, on their own, and clasped round the unicorn's forelimbs. Sedolei tried to rear and the girl stepped backwards. "Maiden!" he neighed.

"I am one of the prince's, how can you call me maiden?" Osophene asked, taking a golden bridle from the folds of her skirt.

Pixies exploded from the petals and foliage, carrying slender ropes and chains. Sedolei snapped the chains that bound him, his magic initially blinding Jane. He reared and charged, past the misleading princess and Jane. Ropes came from over the hedges, Jane knew at least one rope circled his neck, but the unicorn still charged. "I will free everyone here in the garden!" he declared. "Jane, go to the castle! Save Chloe!"

Jane aimed the staff at Osophene. "Where is the prince?"

"You came to save us," she said, "but did you ever think to ask yourself if we desire to be saved?"

Jane wanted to strike her with the staff, but she heard someone behind her. She turned to see the Prince of the Faeries walking towards them, as if he'd been a row or two over all along, but he paid Jane no attention. "Well done, my princess," he said, taking Osophene in his arms, "has Jane been threatening you?"

"She hasn't hurt me, my lord," said Osophene, swooning in his arms. "Am I still required to catch the unicorn?"

He shook his head, poised his lips just above the hollow of her collarbone. "You must hurry and join the others, I will not have you any less lovely for the ball. When the unicorn is broken, you may be the first to ride him."

"I am most content to be by your side," she said, "but I am content still to do as you will."

He kissed her forehead and the briars opened before her, allowing her a direct path to the castle. Osophene obediently left and the thorns closed in behind her. The Prince of the Faeries looked to Jane. "I couldn't have caught him without you."

"You won't catch him," Jane said, aiming her staff at the prince. She could hear Sedolei thrashing about several hedges over, and many faeries sounded like they were in pain. "I've come for Chloe."

"Perhaps I would trade her for the staff," he said, "but, perhaps not. After all, why must I give up something of mine, for another that is rightfully mine? Do you want to kill me, Jane?"

"No," Jane said, "but I will."

"It's not time for us to fight yet," The Prince of the Faeries said. "Chloe is not here – but a young, foolish unicorn is. We will battle soon enough, Jane," he said, and spread his gossamer silver wings, which sparkled in the rising moonlight. "In the meantime, I will add the unicorn to my collection."

Jane felt the power of the staff surge through her body, across her arms and to her heart, but the prince leapt into the air before she had the nerve to strike. The ancient talisman and insignia of his power made a good ray gun at least, and toasted through four rows of flower and stone. She wondered if she could fly with the staff, and focused. She had no wings, but she could at least chase the Faerie Prince. She levitated, and focused. She wasn't quite used to flying.

He flew over to where Sedolei was charging through the maze. Jane found she could only muster one spell at a time, and could not attack him while she flew. Jane felt nausea as she found that she did not know how to land, and ended up in a sprawling koi pond. Clambering to her feet, she rushed to where she assumed the prince was. She stopped when she saw the Faerie Prince atop Sedolei, the unicorn trying to buck the prince off.

The Faerie Prince held onto the horse's mane like an expert rider. "I think a black saddle will be most fitting," he announced to his servants, though Jane suspected it was aimed at her, "and hooves of silver!"

"Get off my back!" Sedolei whinnied.

The other pixies did not help their master, even the larger sidhe did nothing to help. The Prince drew his sword, and pressed it against Sedolei's brow, the sharp edge against his horn where it met his fur. "Stop this, I would have a unicorn, but you will make a magnificent horse."

Sedolei looked at Jane, and stopped struggling when his horn was threatened, though when the prince gestured he still tried to fight off the bit into his mouth. The prince only dismounted when a black saddle was brought forth.

Jane felt the power build into her hands. She couldn't hit him without hitting Sedolei.

"Your friend has told me several times that she only desires to be my princess," he said. "I think she will like this present very much. She loves to ride with me; I think he will be a fine mount for her, once I ensure his silence."

"Let him go," Jane said, "I'm warning you."

"I have told you, now is not the time," he said, and remounted the unicorn once Sedolei was properly fitted with the saddle. He made

Sedolei rear. Jane thought with every step he took, Sedolei looked more horse, and less unicorn.

"Let him go!!" Jane shouted.

"Jane, you're getting ahead of yourself. You and I will fight, but in my castle. You still have a long way to go, and now that you'll be walking, it'll take a lot longer," said the Faerie Prince. "Don't worry, about me; I'm having a ball tonight. I will keep busy until you arrive."

He made Sedolei bound towards the castle, his pixies and fellow Sidhe flying after him, leaving Jane alone in the garden labyrinth.

Alone, Jane thought she was going to cry. Then anger took her, and gripping the staff she wished Winkie had dropped her a lot harder and faster, for she could not summon the magic to fly fast enough towards the castle. She looked down at the many fixtures, and was tempted to smash every silver gazebo and marble statue below but she knew it would take too long. "I've had enough," she said to herself. "Nobody steals my unicorn."

She did not see where the prince and his men took Sedolei. Jane forsook planning and went straight to the main gates of the majestic castle. The guards saw her flying, and bowed their heads as she stomped up the impressive steps.

"He's been expecting you," said one.

"Would you like an escort?" asked another.

"Where can I find him?" Jane asked, wary that they were a trap.

They opened the great arched door. She could hear faint music from somewhere inside, , and thought she heard the sound of struggled whinnying, and the sound of hammering against metal. A pit rose in Jane's stomach. Part of her wished she still had the heart of a dragon to give her strength.

Though the exterior of the castle was fairy tale classic, the interior took Jane's breath away. On the one hand, it was very beautiful, like something she'd expect out of a storybook. Everything was taller – leaner – gleaming. The strange decorations, white at a fleeting glance were pleasing, but she saw strange monstrosities carved into the marble of the walls – humans in servitude, of great stories she tried to remember from when she was a child, of fae triumphant and cruel. She shuddered, thinking about the fae versions of the same stories. She saw no servants, no guards, only beautifully decorated archways and staircases, and windows feeding in pristine moonlight. Jane looked for a reference to a Red Queen as she walked. She found none.

Instead, she heard muted struggling. She detoured into the small room, and recognized her knapsack. "Hello, Maeld."

Many pixies buzzed off at her advent, leaving behind several incredibly tiny pixie-sized pick-axes and other implements, that had ultimately failed against the plastic containers in the shape of honey bears. Maeld squealed in fright when she plucked him up by his wings. Then he looked back at the sealed honey container. "Help, please?"

"I should have brought a flyswatter," she muttered, picking up the knack sack, and wondering if she still needed it. She quickly ate a candy bar, and didn't give Maeld a crumb as she put the backpack back down. She had the staff. It had to be enough.

"I hid everything, waited for you. Knew you'd come this far," Maeld said. "Honey, please!"

"Do you know your way around this castle, Maeld?" she asked. He nodded vigorously. "Then take me to Chloe."

He nestled in her hair. "And then we get honey?"

"And then I won't think about feeding you to Chloe's puppy when we get home."

15

Faerie Queen

Jane expected a court of woodland fae similar to those she'd seen with Sylvanos' troop, but there were no centaurs or satyrs here, the tall sidhe guards merely bowed their heads as she advanced. She saw a few pixies fluttering about the castle. It seemed too empty, like there should have been more servants, or at least guards in the tall cold halls of the castle, silent save for the distant sound of music. She thought the music sounded like it was getting closer. There were a good many stairs, which she thought strange for beings who could fly. She batted Maeld out of her hair when he started demanding sustenance. "I'll get you a beehive when we get home," Jane said, "even though you don't deserve it."

"Bees!" he squealed, and flew into the nearest stairwell and buzzed up the stairs.

"Wait for me!" Jane shouted, running up the spiralling stairs. She wondered how many stairs there could possibly be, until she looked out a small window, and realized she climbing a tower. "This isn't funny. Maeld! Come back here!" She held onto the staff tightly as she continued up the steps. "I know you can hear me, Faerie Prince. A gryphon wanted me to seal you away, but I'm here anyway. You're scared of me, or else you would have taken the staff before – when we met in the garden. I'm not scared of you."

At the top of the steps Jane found a door. A sleeping princess was on the canopied bed. "Chloe?" she asked. No, the princess was taller, and slender, though it was hard to tell from the garb she wore. Jane almost screamed when she recognized herself on the bed.

"Are you almost ready to wake up, princess?" the Prince asked. Jane turned around and he was at the door, and locked it behind him.

Jane edged from him as he advanced. Jane wasn't sure if she should hold the staff like a sword or a shotgun. "Enough illusions!" she shouted.

"Give me the staff, Jane." The Prince extended his hand. "Princesses don't need to fight."

Jane glanced over her shoulder. Her false self was gone from the bed. He still advanced. She couldn't go any further back without climbing onto the bed. Jane felt the staff's power, and stepped forward. He paused. "Where is Chloe?" Jane demanded.

"I will show you."

The world changed. Jane blinked, and found that she was in the middle of an elaborate ball, everyone wore an elaborate fantasy outfit and proper colourful mask wrought in jewels and feathers, and almost everyone danced in much too elaborate choreography. The prince and Jane alone were out of costume. Jane looked around the throne room that doubled as a ballroom. The instrumental music was enchanting, and the prince put his hand out, gesturing for Jane to make sure she didn't miss a thing: the crisp sounds of perfectly dancing feet to the sound of enchanting violins and harps, the intricate decorations, the smells and sounds of what she knew was all a show. "She's here, dancing. Do you see her?" Everyone besides herself and the prince wore a mask. How could she? "She is a natural dancer," he said. "Does it make you jealous?"

"Chloe!" Jane called. No one stopped to look at her, though a handsomely masked dancer offered Jane a hand. For an instant, she thought it was Mike. She didn't take his hand. "Chloe! It's Jane! I'm here to take you home! I have the Staff of Silver! I can free you! I can free all of you!"

"I think she likes it here," Prince Nyveo said, making his way through the dancers, and ascending the steps before the ballroom dancers to his throne, pausing only to gesture for Jane to follow. "My newest stallion, on the other hand, is having trouble adjusting." He reached into his pocket, and pulled out a slender, spiralling horn. "Don't think it didn't hurt me when I did this."

Jane felt her cheeks crimson. It was obviously not Sedolei's horn in the prince's hand, for this horn was paler than Sedolei's. Jane felt no less rage at the thought of him defiling any unicorn. "You monster!"

"I'd offer you a drink," said the Prince, "but I'd hate to see your husband show up and ruin the party."

"I didn't marry him," Jane said.

"As if that matters." He took a crystal goblet from a tray suspended by several pixies. "Half-brothers are a bit of a trial, but you can tell me all about siblings. I'll deal with him. When he's dead there'll be no question as to whom you belong. You're not as attractive as the others, as far as conventional looks go, but I can fix that."

He gestured for her to take his hand. Jane didn't, but a satin green-gloved hand took his and passed by Jane.

Jane's heart raced, though she could not see her face behind the beautiful golden mask. Jane recognized a collection of freckles and an old faded scar just below Chloe's jaw and her hair color, even though it was styled so differently then anything she'd seen her best friend wear before. The lovely princess stood passively, one of his arms draped over her shoulder. She looked surreal. "Chloe..."

The princess didn't respond. Jane blamed the mask, though it only covered the top half of her face. The Faerie Prince removed it, to make sure Jane could see. Chloe had never looked more beautiful, her hair piled on top of her head in a curly bun so elaborate nobody could sit still that long (well, maybe Chloe), and her green and gold dress brought out her hazel eyes. Jane thought Chloe's eyes flickered as if in recognition for an instant, but the prince took her chin in his hand, and kissed her. Chloe kissed him back, and patiently waiting for him to continue when he stopped. "Kasmodiah, will you tell your friend that you like it here? That you've never been happier?"

"I like it here," Chloe said. "I've never been happier."

"That you are content to be among my dancing princesses," he said, his eyes on Jane's, "and be beautiful forever?"

"I am your dancing princess," Chloe said, "and I'll be beautiful forever."

"Chloe-" Jane started, but she heard dancers behind her. Ten princesses, like Chloe, save for different style of gowns and each in a brilliant jewel-tone color danced, and Chloe joined them. They danced before their prince and Jane, and though she could not see their faces, each was more beautiful and lovely than the last.

"Are they not beautiful?" the prince asked. "Would you not like to be among them?"

"I don't need you to be beautiful," Jane said.

"You, beautiful as you are now? Are you sure you didn't come because you were jealous I took her instead of you?" he asked. "It was fun to summon you. Now, give me what is mine, or I shall take it from you."

"Summon me?!" Jane snapped.

"You know it's true," he said. "Garnet and Silver: Mortal and Immortal – a mortal who can wield Faerie Magic can wield the Staff of Silver. Every step in your quest bound you further. My mother sought to keep the staff from me, but I knew my bride could bring it to me." The princesses swirled around Jane as she backed from their prince. "Give me your hand, Jane. I'll show you what real power is. Submit to me, and we shall make worlds in our image."

The music stopped. Jane looked at Chloe, and then at the prince, his hand extended. Jane put her hand out, and he rose from his throne to help her ascend the steps, and she struck him in the face with the staff. The princesses shrieked and rushed to their master. Jane raced down the steps and grabbed Chloe's arm, who tried to fight back, but, given that she was Chloe, just came along. Jane used the staff's power to force the other ballroom dancers out of the way. "Run! Couldn't they have given you wings?! Run!!"

They made it out of the ballroom, and ran down the hall. Jane looked for windows to see how and where they should run. Chloe seemed to run in a trance of obedience.

Guards left their posts to impede their flight, so Jane tried to think of magic that would just slow them down. A small pixie burst from Chloe's hair, and tried to bite Jane's fingers. Jane slapped the pixie away, let go of Chloe and shot bursts of magic at the guards – trapping them in bubbles, like she'd been in earlier. She was glad to see Moaz and Zilare among those captured. She grabbed Chloe's arm and kept running.

"This way!" Jane said when she saw a window showing the garden labyrinth. They followed the long hall to a beautiful receiving room. Jane could see an open door leading to the midnight garden. The prince waited for them.

Jane knew she couldn't fight him while holding onto Chloe. "Stay out of the way, stay safe," she said, pushing Chloe behind a pillar.

"Give me the staff," he said once Jane faced him. "I'm its rightful heir."

"Come and take it," Jane said.

The prince was fast, and more importantly, controlled his magic. Jane knew how to shoot the thing off to destroy shrubbery and gardens, but she could think of nothing clever, and did not know the staff's power, or its limitations. She tried the bubble spell that had worked on his minions, but he sliced through it and advanced. Jane used the power that she'd used to clear a path in the labyrinth. She hit him, and the prince shielded himself. Jane saw him stagger under the weight of the spell.

"You are nothing without power," Jane said., "You're nothing but a bully! Stand down. I don't even want this. I just want Chloe and Sedolei to be free – and I want you to transform the man Bijan from his beastly form."

"I will be king," said the Prince of the Faeries. "No one will give me orders, least of all from my own castle!"

Jane focused her energy, and hit him again with the power of the staff streaming through her. She felt her arm and shoulder muscles twitch. He fell back. The path was no longer blocked, if only she and Chloe could run quick enough. "We'll find the stables on our own," Jane said. "Chloe, come on!"

Jane grabbed Chloe's arm, and Chloe sunk her elaborate fan into Jane's abdomen. Jane shrieked when she discovered that it was bladed. Jane fell backwards in surprise, and was even more alarmed when she saw that most of the blood that was spilled was not red, but instead, a shiny grey color that glimmered against the starlight.

Jane released the staff and looked up at her best friend.

"Jane?" Chloe asked. "Jane?" She stepped backwards, and slipping in the blood, fell down herself. Unlike Jane, Chloe rolled over, stood up, ran, and knelt by her best friend's side. "What happened?"

Jane felt a strange sensation. Her blood felt cold. She realized she was being healed by the staff. "My staff," the prince said, "is very dangerous in the wrong hands."

Chloe put her hands on Jane's wound, repulsed, but still wanting to help until Jane pushed her hand away and put pressure on her own wound. Chloe still looked beautiful, but no longer perfect, color drained back into her cheeks. "What did you do to me?" Chloe asked the prince, touching her face, Jane's silver blood staining her face and hair.

Jane grunted and climbed to her feet, gripping the staff tighter.

"What did I do to you?" the Faerie Prince asked. "You did this to yourself."

"Liar!" Jane snapped, attempting to skewer the prince with the staff, but she didn't hear the other princesses behind her. They grabbed her, and dragged her back. Jane struggled against the many delicately gloved and jewelled hands, only to lose her staff to the prince when he walked over casually and took it from her.

"Do not hurt her," the prince said once he had the staff in his hands, "yet."

"Chloe! Help me!" Jane shouted. "Chloe!"

"Jane!" Chloe reached for Jane's hand, but Jane's hand was seized by three satin gloves, and Jane was dragged away from Chloe, further into the castle.

~*~

Chloe didn't know what to do. She felt weak, and like she did something terrible. Her prince simply barred her from following by standing in her path, his back turned, examining the staff in his hands, "Who would have known a paltry thing like friendship would have carried her this far? I'm sorry, Kasmodiah. I didn't think it would hurt you so."

"You used me," Chloe said, not blinking back tears. "You wanted her to get the staff, and you tricked me..."

"I cannot have you in my court," her Prince said. "Please understand."

She heard Jane call for her again. "Jane!" Chloe screamed, and tried to run past him.

Chloe felt arms grab her – arms of the prince's guardsmen. "Be gentle, for I am fond of her. Perhaps in time, it will be appropriate for Kasmodiah to retake her place among my dancers, after the queen has learned her place. Take her to the gardens," said her prince. "She will make a lovely songbird, far from the castle walls, where her mortality will make the flowers real. Do not worry, Kasmodiah. I have a new mount to break in. I will visit you soon."

~*~

Once she was subdued, one of the princesses slapped Jane, and another grabbed the slapper's arm.

"She struck my prince!" said the woman in purple.

"The prince will deal with her," said the one in yellow.

"What do you care if I take Chloe home? Let us go and dance here for all eternity for all I care!" Jane snapped. They pushed her down on a fancy chair in an even more fancy room. She tried to stand up and they forced her down. Though her wound was healing very quickly, she kept her left hand on it.

"We should tie her hands," said the one in blue.

"The prince will decide," said the one in pink.

Several of the smaller pixies came to her and inspected her. Jane batted them away. Eventually the prince himself came, the Staff of Silver in his hands.

"Where's Chloe?!" Jane demanded lowly.

"You should be more concerned with your own fate," her prince said.

"You can't do this!" Jane snapped, standing, only to be pushed back down by several hands.

"I have been planning this for centuries. Of course I can," he said, crouching down slightly to look Jane in the eyes. "Tomorrow, thanks to you, I will no longer be bound to your world but once every ten years. I will reclaim both thrones, as is my birthright."

"You are sick."

"I am your master," he said. "My birthright gives me claim to your world. Yours opens the door."

Jane clenched her eyes and tried to call the staff to her. He laughed slightly, and took her by the chin, and had her look up at him. "You needn't worry, Jane. I will use the staff's power wisely. None may stand against me."

"I will," Jane said.

"You will be my loving and obedient queen," he said. "Do you understand, Titalia?"

"My name is Jane! Plain Jane; Jane Doe; You Asshole, me Jane!"

"Tie her hands and feet," he ordered his princesses, and they took out long strands of silk and did as they were told. An ambitious princess put one across Jane's mouth. The prince smiled, and tightened that one himself before picking Jane up. "You may all wait where she will emerge."

He carried Jane to a nearby room, and put her down on a grate of sorts. He undid the gag, and whispered, "It is over. Surrender."

Jane tried to roll, but she was more or less stuck to the grate when it started to sink beneath floor level. Maeld landed on her nose. "How could you do this to me?" she asked.

"I am what my master tells me I am."

She descended slowly, surprised by the cold and the water. She thought they were going to drown her, she wasn't sure how much water she drank before someone finally raised the grate. She coughed, gasping for air she tried to vomit but she wasn't able. Two princesses cut her free of the binds. When she rose the servants were quick to towel her off. Feeling all the strength leave her, she let the prince pick her up and she put her head on his collar. He carried her to the most beautiful of chambers any woman could dream of. He left her to the care of the women, who brushed her hair and dressed her in a gown more spectacular than one she'd ever seen before, anointed her with perfumes and jewels. Finally, the last thing that came was a silver necklace with a large garnet stone at the bottom.

"Finally," said one of the dancing princesses, "We have our Faerie Queen!"

The dancing princesses were both in awe and jealous of their queen, for she stood taller than any and while all were beautiful, she was the most adorned, her blood the least mortal and her soul to be shared by their prince, whom they all loved.

Titalia obediently rose when summoned, the ten princesses in her wake as she met her lord. "Are you ready to attend our engagement ball?" he asked, handing her a silver mask.

"Of course, my lord," Titalia said. The ten went first, and when it came time for her presentation of the realm, of all the faerie kindred and immortals who made up this static world rejoiced, for the prince had at last allowed the kingdom to begin to wake.

Titalia descended the steps on the arm of her prince, awash in a world of ermine and finery, magic and moonlight.

16

Flight

The cold plants in the royal labyrinth seemed to come more alive when they passed – when *she* passed, they didn't react to the immortals at all. Chloe thought the world of the fae was beautiful until she saw the deepening of color and felt the texture of the rose petals when she brushed her hand against them, and the sharpness of the thorn. Chloe wondered if she'd ever see her world again.

She looked to her captors – they needn't lay a hand on her. She was incapable of fighting them off or fleeing, they marched her down the meticulously sculptured hedges, to find a cage for her no doubt somewhere in the beautiful garden, forgotten, or, worse. She thought the perfectly shaped roses beautiful in the daylight. Now she wondered if they were the last thing she'd ever see. As she walked, she saw signs of a struggle, evidently someone decided to shoot a hole through several rows of the hedges. It no longer smouldered, but it seemed that her captors were not using the most direct route. It was still stinky.

Not that she minded them taking as long as possible. Chloe shivered, remembering the cage she saw earlier. It was beautiful on the outside – and the inside. She slipped out of one of the out the glass slippers, tried to kick it away, into the hedge. If there was a chance for her to run, then she didn't have time to take the time to get her shoes off. One of her captors noticed. "Forgetting something?" one of them asked, picking up the shoe.

"As if it matters," the other said.

"The master lost interest in this one quickly," the one with the shoe said, smiling at Chloe, walking towards her.

"He hasn't lost interest. He's found his queen. Besides," said the other, standing before the other sidhe. "He's about to claim the throne. You'd be a fool to upset him now. He's going to the world of the mortals: her world."

The fae hesitantly nodded. Chloe wondered if she wasted her time watching them when she could have chanced running. *At least I won't be turned into stone*, Chloe thought. They continued to walk the rose labyrinth. "What's he going to do to Jane?" she asked the one who fancied her.

"He's going to make her queen," the one who had taken her shoe said. "He's going to bind her to the throne, and sharing her soul, open the road to your world – claim it perhaps. As his subjects, we'll be free to accompany him there, princess."

"How will he bind her to the throne?" Chloe asked.

"Enough you two," said the stoic one.

"What difference does it make?" the one who still held her shoe asked. "Our prince is triumphant, the mortals are powerless to stop us."

"Fool, he favours this one!" the fae said, turning to yell at the other. "Else he would take no chances and destroy her outright!"

Chloe's heart raced. What if he was planning on destroying her? The fae didn't know the minds of their master. Something whipped through the air above them.

Chloe was relieved when her captors looked away - an alarm went off at the castle. "Already it begins," the stoic fae said, "Take her to the gazebo – it is your life that will be forfeit if she is not found."

The one that still held her shoe grabbed Chloe's arm and dragged her while the other raced off. "I suppose that cuts down our time together," she said to him.

The fae looked down at her, said nothing. Chloe wondered how such a beautiful race of beings could find her species all that attractive. *Then again*, she thought, looking down at her elaborate green and gold ball gown andexquisite jewellery. "Are you not going to answer me?"

"I have my duties to my lord," he said.

"As do I," Chloe said, stomping down hard with the other heel on his foot, "to my friend!"

He yelped and Chloe ran. She didn't know where she was going and she wasn't sure how she managed with the heavy skirt and roses thorns that grabbed and tore at her as she passed. She knew he could fly, knew he was behind her – the darkness was all that she had shielding her from immediate capture. She looked over her shoulder, saw his outline in the moonlight scanning, searching the labyrinth. Chloe found a dead end, complete with bench, and she used it to hide behind, hoping that and the darkness would be enough. The fae flittered over her, and when she began to move, he flew back around.

"I know you're here," he said. "It's only a matter of time; I will find you. You hurt me – you wouldn't want me to hurt you. Your bruises will heal before the prince sees them – and it might be months before he remembers you. Reveal yourself, and I shall be forgiving!"

"Harade!" a voice called. "Help! Help us, the Empress is overwhelming us! Quick, before she frees the minotaur!"

He flew off – Chloe waited, suspecting a trap she waited, but also knew that she couldn't wait. She wasn't in the world of the fae long to realize that there were powers she didn't dare waken. She moved through the labyrinth, the shadows that had saved her earlier a hindrance as she got lost. She found the smouldered blast that led towards the castle, and decided that at least she could see what the guards were doing. Moving back towards the castle, which was lit enough for Chloe to see, over twenty of the prince's men appeared to be fighting off a giant Chinese dragon of some sort. Chained and left on his side was a large beast, his feet cloven though his long torso was human, with horns like a great ox and a hairy body, bound in chains he flailed against his netting, even bound, he was able to knock back half a dozen of his enemies at a time. He scared Chloe to even look upon him, so she continued to run through the labyrinth – getting turned around and twisted as she ran, confused, trying to find her way out. She couldn't decide whether or not she wanted to save Jane or just run away – it was her fault Jane was in this mess, but she felt powerless. She could do nothing to help her friend.

The dragon snaked through the air and landed before the castle – and her prince, who waited on the steps. The dragon was at once in human form – an older, formidable-looking woman looked at the prince, and every ounce of her screamed defiance. "I tire of these games, Prince Nyveo."

"You dare speak my name?" he asked. "Here, where you are at your least powerful?"

"I have greater powers than any prince of this realm," she said. "Be content with your lot that we did not destroy this world outright!"

"I am prince no longer."

"You are not crowned yet," the woman said lowly. "You have been given mastery over these realms – king in every way, save name. Your kind is not welcome in other worlds, Nyveo. In time perhaps we may forgive the sins of your fathers. Give up the staff and the girl. They are not yours."

"Do you forget that I was born of a mortal sow?" he asked. "My dame's blood grants me right to enter the human world – and my sire's blood rule this one. How dare you, an outsider, come to my world and tell me how to govern?"

"Your kind has come and gone into other realms and wreaked havoc since before the time we Dragons began to record our history! Your line brought about your father's destruction! It was not your mother alone who had case against you. We dragons and others would have destroyed it outright if she did not put a end to their wicked rule. The silver dominates you, prince, do not deny it!" the dragon-woman snapped. "You were spared out of mercy! Worlds hounded for the death of your infant self, as well as this world, but you were spared out of a mother's love, and her words that you would not choose the paths of your fore-fathers! Of a chance that you would rise above your legacy. Look to that little piece of yourself that came from humanity - humans are weak and foolish, but eventually they learn from their mistakes."

The prince laughed lowly. "A King that rules by permission is no sort of king at all," he said. "Be gone, dragon – return to your world while you still have the chance. The worlds of Fae and Human are mine by birthright, do not make my next act of war to be conquering the heavens where dragons dream."

The old woman changed in an instant and was again the formidable, long dragon, which launched at the prince. He held the staff like a sword and it powered up, light and sound gathering at the silver staff Jane had wielded just hours earlier. Even from a distance, Chloe was blinded by a burst of bright light. She did not see what happened, but the dragon was gone before her eyes adjusted.

"I trust you will have no more trouble with the monster," her prince said to his fae guard, who bowed. Chloe saw her prince ascend up the steps, several of her beautiful former-sisters waiting for him at the archway. Chloe strained, wishing to see Jane, but she could make few details out as the magnificent ball carried on.

Unsure what to do, but knowing she could not enter the castle without being found, she followed the guards taking the beast-man around the back of the castle. She smelled fire and the forge. She had not been to the royal stables before, though she had seen the brilliant horses of the prince, he and his men would take them out riding. They seemed more spectacular than real horses, and Chloe also thought they were smarter, but she hardly contemplated as to the why until she stumbled across a unicorn chained in a small corral. The creature was magnificent, but seemed diminished – like the silver chains that bound him weakened him somehow. She heard sounds of grunting and a struggle, and found a place to hide. She left the unicorn behind in the corral, and went back outside, to watch the sidhe chain down the beast-man.

"What does the Prince want with him?" asked what looked like a heavy-set smith.

"Bound in chain from head to toe," one of the guards said. "I don't know why – he's let him roam free all these years. The simpler thing to be would be to... you know." He made the motion of a slit throat with his thumb.

"He plans on returning to the world of humans," said another. "Likely, have him thrown back into his own world, still a monster. Who knows?"

The guards stood round one another, chatting, laughing. Chloe wondered if they were looking for her – no doubt, the one who let her go wouldn't want to draw attention to his stupidity – she was, afterall, just one small mortal. What harm could she cause?

The minotaur was too large to enter the smithy, so the guards helped the fae smith bring out what they needed to bind him in solid fetters. Chloe wondered if anything would be big enough to truly keep the beast confined, but decided not to stay and find out. While they were preoccupied, she stole back into the smithy, to the other room with the bound unicorn. Chloe felt stupid going up to something so beautiful and defiling it with her touch, but when she took the blinders off, she knew it was her only chance. She took the key, and released the first chain. He moved the bit in his mouth. "I need your help," she said, getting a saddle. "I need you to-"

Light came to his horn, and he focused it on the chain that she didn't untie. "No, wait!" Chloe said.

Magic thundered into the small corral – Chloe fell backwards with the tremor. She knew the fae just outside must have heard that. The unicorn spat out the bit. "Fake! False! Liars, all of you! Oh, it burns!" he winced as he stepped. He knelt down on his magnificent legs. "What good is it all? I am to lose my horn afterall..." he looked at her – as if asking for help, but she wondered what sort of help she might render such a magnificent creature. "I am no good to anyone, innocent maiden. I haven't the strength to walk, let alone carry you to freedom. I am sorry. Flee while you have the chance."

"I don't know how you can call me... innocent," Chloe said, close to tears as she knelt next to the unicorn. "I've... I've done terrible things." She shook her head. "I didn't mean to. I wanted a fairy tale come true... but... this... this isn't what I wanted. Not at all." She couldn't blink quick enough to hold back her tears. "I don't know what to do. I just want to help my friend."

He nuzzled her hand. "You should go. They will come back soon."

"Why does it hurt you?"

"It is Fairy Silver – the power of the king flows through it – it binds me."

Chloe looked to the horse's legs. They were magnificent and gold, and his hooves were cloven and of gold, like his horn – but beautiful, harsh silver shoes had been nailed to his feet. Though chains no longer bound him, he seemed to grow weaker at every moment. "Please, find the strength to walk. Please," Chloe said. "They'll come back and they'll take your horn. You need to move, now."

The unicorn trudged slowly, weakly. Chloe saw cuts over his body – this was not a soft animal from her dreams, but a wild fighter, a champion of justice that at the same time, gave small woodland creatures peptalks. At least, that's what images filled her mind when she looked into his eyes. "Did the prince give you those cuts?"

"No," he said before wickering. "The wounds you see are from when I was battling a gryphon! Perhaps she was right," he bowed his head sadly. "You haven't seen a mortal girl your age, have you? Of course, they're all about your age... she is tall by your standards – had dark hair, and is of royal lineage. Jane, is her name. Of the Great Wood of Charles."

"You mean, Charleswood? I mean - you know Jane?" Chloe asked. "Jane isn't of royal lineage!" What had happened? Jane had met this unicorn? What, when, how... who...?

"Of course she is," he said. "That was why she could take the staff. That was why she could yield fairie magic. The rules of the fae may seem arbitrary, but they are consistent. The power to rule realms can only be by heir of royalty."

Chloe frowned, looking towards the castle. Jane, of all people – a princess? A real one? "Her dad's French Canadian," she said. "And her mom's metis..." she paused. "You mean to say, she's a French princess?" Chloe admittedly didn't know much about the French revolution, but generally speaking, if a country cut the heads off their monarchy, in Chloe's mind, it didn't count any more.

"Wrong side of the family," the unicorn said. "I... I believe Jane is the great-granddaughter of a chief."

Chloe blinked. "Her grandmother sits on a council I think but, she's been elected to the position. That doesn't count, does it?" The unicorn bobbed his head. "Wow, that is arbitrary..."

"The prince will claim her land when he marries her," said the unicorn.

"That's... Canada," Chloe said quietly.

"Yes – a what is it... colony of the great power..."

Chloe's eyes widened. "You mean Britain."

"In the time of his mother, it was the Americas – Spain conquered the south, while England and France squabbled over the north of a then thought to be new world," the unicorn said. "Jane is an heir of the people of that nation - recognized by the ancient crown. Through her, he will claim that land. My mother said that human wars mean little to the fae. They follow the blood lineage. He will place his stronghold in this Canada."

"We need to go."

They tried to go out the back. Chloe thought they got away undetected, and in truth, given how slowly the unicorn, who said his name was Sedolei walked, she was surprised no one came in to check on them. She looked sadly at the other unicorns, bits in their mouths and horns missing, covered in brilliant horse-headdresses and made to look formidable. She was tempted to save them all, but knew in their eyes that they all bade her to rescue the poor creature doomed to lose his horn should she fail.

They did not get far into the labyrinth, Chloe leading the unicorn into the darkness of the maze. They heard the laughter of the fae behind them in the stable, and Chloe saw the unicorn's expression change from sorrow and weakness to a forgotten rage.

"What are you doing?" she asked as he turned from her side.

"Give me strength," the unicorn pleaded, and turning from her, charged back to the area before the stable where the fae tormented and fettered the great minotaur. He reared, light came from his horn, charging he ran down the fae, sending them running off and stunned by his power that Chloe thought near-lightning. Chloe kept herself from yelping; she thought the creature weak and unable to move, not able to go on without her encouragement, she suddenly realized that the power of the unicorn was considerably more than she had imagined. He trampled the fae – there were but three of them now, for they thought the monster subdued. "Brothers! Sisters!" he called to the stables. Only whinnies met his cry.

"There is no time," said the monster that the fae had been chaining, motioning to the chains that bound him. "Their horns have been cut – the prince will come. we need to escape now."

The unicorn bowed his head, and brilliant gold light came again to the unicorn's horn, and he attacked the thick chain that held the monster back. Chloe screamed as it broke free finally.

"What have you done?" Chloe demanded, but the unicorn fell over as an alarm sounded from the castle. One massive hand grabbed hold of him, and then, with his dark eyes, he saw Chloe, and taking a massive step towards her, bounded. Chloe turned to run, but he grabbed her. "Sedolei! Sedolei!" Chloe screamed, trying to beat her fists into the monster's massive hands. The minotaur leapt over hedges until he was clear of the hedged labyrinth, then he was in the forest where with mighty strides he made it over tall rocks and almost smashed down the trees as he went, taking them further and further from the castle. "Don't eat me!" Chloe squealed as he slowed.

"Why, you look positively delicious. With a side of potatoes, of course. I don't have any, so I'll have to pass," the monster said, putting her down gently once they were deep in the woods. "Unicorn, what are you doing in this place? Do you not know what he does to your kind?"

"And don't eat him either!" Chloe ordered, crossing her arms.

Sedolei slowly opened his eyes. "The silver... it burns..." he looked at the minotaur. "Are you for us, or with the prince?"

"For the time being, with you. Thank you for saving me. You shouldn't have used all your strength."

"I know what it was like to be his prisoner," Sedolei said. "To see my kind, turned into mere horses..." he shook his head, then closed his eyes again. "But, where is it that's left to go? He's won." He almost sounded amused. "I thought I could help her... I thought I could have made a difference. In the end, I wasn't even there to help her. I have doomed her world, as well as my own. I deserve to lose my horn."

"This isn't your world?" Chloe asked.

Sedolei craned his neck and looked at Chloe with all seriousness. "Of course it isn't!" he said. "How dare you think I am one of them!"

"Well, I don't know these things," Chloe said, hands on her hips and trying to give back his tone. "I just found out my best friend Jane is really a princess on a technicality..." She thought long and hard about if any of her relations ever ran for political office.

The minotaur snuffed. "Jane? You've met Jane?"

"She's only been my best friend since before preschool."

"Oh, you must be the spoiled girl she came to save."

"EX-CUS-EE ME-EE?" Chloe found the two weren't sure how to handle her sass, and she liked it best that way. "Number one: I didn't ask for anyone to come and save me, and number two: I got the unicorn out, who by the way got you out. So technically, I saved you both."

"I got us all out of harm's way for the time being," the minotaur said. "We can figure out who owes whom what later. Unicorn, let's see about getting those silver shoes off."

"But what about Jane?" Chloe asked as the minotaur sat down with his pilfered blacksmith's tools and tried to pry the silver off the hooves of the unicorn.

"The Empress could not save her," the minotaur said blandly. "She has been captured herself. What makes you think you could?"

"You mean, the dragon-lady?"

The unicorn cried out as the first shoe came off his hoof. Chloe grabbed his head, and pet him.

"Yes. Jane came for you," said the minotaur. "I had no idea at the time, that the prince wanted her."

"Why wouldn't he have just taken her if that was the case?"

"Because he needed the staff," the minotaur said. He laughed. "She thought she could save you... look where that got her."

"She came to save you..." the unicorn joined in before starting to cry slightly.

"Chloe, is it?" the minotaur asked. "I am Bijan. I have been here for several hundred years and have been unable to escape. I came to save my wife – a princess stolen by that cursed prince. She was of proper bloodline but she would not bend to his will. He killed her and transformed me into this."

"You... you mean to say...?"

"I was not always a monster. At least, not on the outside," he said quietly. "What I did to my wife – perhaps he just let my outside reflect my inside." He shook his head. "Save your strength unicorn. Weep for yourself, and your kind. Then, you must take Chloe home."

"There isn't much of a point." A female voice said from the woods. Chloe and the minotaur stood, though Sedolei craned his neck to see whom the voice belonged to. "I mean you no ill," the voice said again, and the creature emerged. It was taller than Sedolei, though nowhere near as great and massive as Bijan, with a head of gold and copper feathers, and a majestic beak and deep brown eyes flecked with gold. Its paws held massive claws, and she spoke powerfully. "We should not have battled, earlier."

"Why are you still here?" Sedolei asked the gryphon. "Can you not feel this world's end nearing?"

"I saw the prince lock the girl Jane into the tomb located at the heart of the labyrinth," the gryphon said. "I cannot enter there and save her. I have come for the other mortal. She can enter the tomb and rescue her before the dawn. It is our only chance."

"Who are you?" Chloe asked.

The gryphon bowed her head. "I am called Sunsoar by those in my Eyrie. I came to convince Jane to destroy the prince's castle from afar.

She and the unicorn disagreed." The creature bowed regally, and Jane saw the fresh scars and missing feathers along her pelt.

Chloe licked her lips. "Could she have done it?"

"With help, yes," the gryphon said. "There is little time; you must come with me, and then we can free Jane. He has the staff, but if he is bound to this world-" she paused when the unicorn let out another howl, and another shoe let go, "the power will be contained. He will continue to rule this world, unable to return to yours for ten years." The gryphon looked deep in thought. "Though... that might only be buying your world time."

Chloe wrapped her arms around her waist. *She could have stopped him... but she didn't. She was too focused on helping me. She risked everything, for me.* She tried to keep her lips stiff. *This is all my fault.*

"You can't take her to the tombs," said Bijan. "He won't leave her unguarded. You'll be caught."

"The world of humans is a portal to other ones," Sunsoar said. "He will destroy the world of humans, and wage war on others if we do nothing. We must try. I do not see why you try, cursed one," she said to the minotaur. "Take the shoes off, the silver is inside of you, unicorn. Those with silver in their blood are bound to his world. You cannot escape."

"I am not fae," the unicorn gruffed. "I have to try... let me at least save one maiden, and then my failures will not be complete."

"The silver he put inside of you will weaken you. I could open a door – and you would weaken every hour until you returned to this one, if you did not perish the same way the fae do if they stay outside the allotted time," Sunsoar said. "Besides, there is nowhere you could take her that he will not look. The old powers will stir and the prince will be sorry he ever tried to take up his father's mantle. How many worlds must die before the madness ends?" She almost chuckled to herself, but Chloe thought she was clucking. "Girl, are you listening to me? We must go, now."

"Are there others, like you, who can fight?" Chloe asked.

"Rumours will reach the ears of my kin quickly," she said. "As well as where unicorns and dragons roam. Worlds are at stake, young one. I cannot say what their course of action will be. I was called foolish to come, before the threat was too great." She bristled her feathers. "Such are the ways of committees, it seems."

"I'm not a hero," Chloe said. "I don't know enough to save anyone. But," she said, "I do know a sorceress. She might be able to help us. How much time do we have?"

17

The Sorceress of 27 Foxberry Bay

Bethany Pelshmidt just wanted to go to bed. For the past two days, she'd been hounded by everyone – the police, psychiatrists, her parents, people at school, and when she got home, her two annoying sisters, laughing at her, saying that she'd finally cracked.

She was the last person to see Jane. She and Jane were the last people to see Chloe. Janice was no help. She just played stupid. Well, Bethany wasn't convinced she was playing, and there wasn't any cure for *that*.

Bethany was in her room: No computer, no window to the outside world besides the – well, ground-level window leading out but it led to the backyard and the old tire swing and that most certainly didn't count. She wasn't allowed to go out 'until you decide to tell the truth' and her telling the truth sounded more ridiculous as she told it.

She was picked up and dropped off to go to school then brought directly home by her father, and her middle-sister Ava was spying on her all the time at school. Bethany became a social outcast (moreso) and while she appreciated the quiet time to work on her screenplays, when she tried to ask Mike if Jane had said anything weird to him, he ignored her – she pestered him until he told her to get lost – that he didn't want to have anything more to do with that craziness.

Am I the only one who's also wondering where Neil and his henchgoons went? No – several of the girls, including Janice, had lamented his transfer. But a transfer meant he went somewhere else. Gone without a trace, really, but it was almost like the school forgot – like they were under some sort of spell, all except that geeky Bethany Pelshmidt, who couldn't separate fantasy from reality.

The hard part though, was their parents. She'd never seen Chloe's dad lose his cool – but he did when it came to their only child. Jane's parents were frantically looking for their daughter. To hear her own-parents say, "We got Bethany going to the best psychiatrists – she'll tell the truth soon, I promise," crushed Bethany. She wished she could play dumb like Janice. No one expected anything from her.

Bethany was already the weird girl who liked stuff she wasn't sup-posed to – two days prior she got caught trying to take Jane's little brother out to Assiniboine Park with a shovel. A few vandalism charges added to her rap sheet, her father continued to berate her as they drove home from the police station. "I told you we shouldn't have let her read your old books," her mother said as the door opened to their old blue station wagon. "It fills her head with a lot of nonsense. Bethany, you're not the hero in one of your stories. There's no such thing as fairies and cthuthlu."

"What is a slu-slu?" her youngest sister Francine asked, and their mother elaborated on the wonders of Lovecraft. Bethany wondered how they could consider her the geeky one as her parents agued about what exactly an elder god of madness was. Francine went back to her *Teen!Bop* magazine almost immediately while mouthing along to this year's popular Disney song on her iPhone.

Bethany couldn't think of what to say to make it all better. That was the problem, really – she'd clued in just earlier that day that people didn't want the truth, they wanted their suspicions confirmed. If she had said that Neil had kidnapped Chloe, and that his friends grabbed Jane, they rode off in a car, and that was the last she'd seen them, she couldn't remember more, throw in some crocodile tears, she'd probably be given sympathy and left to her own devices. Saying, "They sprouted wings and we caught a little one, but he's gone now, I passed out and Jane left without me," gets you labelled 'nutso'.

Playing dumb seemed to be doing her youngest sister a world of good academically – Ava was able to pick up as many spares as she wanted and got rewarded for just showing up to classes. Bethany went to the bathroom, brushed her teeth and scrubbed her face. Already, the summer freckles were receding. She wondered if it really was all in her mind – in addition to her pulp fiction addiction, she'd read books on criminal psychology. The human mind wasn't to be trusted, afterall – people could hardly remember certain things and everyone had bias besides. What if she *had* imagined the whole thing? People didn't disappear in holes in the ground, and, faerie tales were for children... well, not the original ones that involved cutting off your foot to fit into a shoe or the villain gets shoved naked in a barrel containing nails and glass and rolled down a steep slope into the bay during the happy wedding ceremony, but, people hardly sat around the bar and talked about them now, did they?

Bethany went to her room, and looked at the vintage movie posters of Blade Runner next to her HALO action figures. She frowned at the old Disney stuff that was too young for her years ago. She looked in disgust at her old toy foam swords and came to a realization: Everyone was right. She walked to the wall, and tore off the poster from *Pan's Labyrinth*, making sure to rip it in the process.

"Whatcha doing?" asked Francine, pretending to just be walking by.

"Getting rid of some of this junk. I've had it forever and I think it's time for me to grow up." Bethany realized she had blue walls.

"Oh. Can I have the *Beauty and the Beast* poster?" Francine asked.

Bethany wondered if the little snot would be seen dead with a kid's movie poster in her room. Bethany gave her sister that one and a few others, and her dad told her to be careful with the *Blade Runner* and *Star Wars* one, but other than that said nothing besides collecting them when she wasn't looking. The posters gone, Bethany grabbed her few action figures from her favourite video games, who were ready to fight and defend her bookshelf. She tossed them in a box she scribbled "DONATE". She was hesitant to turn to her library, so instead she went to her video game library. Her parents had taken away her computer, but she could get rid of her games. Almost all the girls in them were horrible role models besides. Finally she turned to her bookshelf – anything that wasn't popular was definitely out.

She was so busy waxing poetic that she didn't notice anybody come in through the window. "Bethany, uh, what are you doing?" Chloe asked as Bethany silently lamented the donation of a Frazetta-covered paperback.

"I decided to put my childish delusions behind me and maybe with a bit of hypnosis I'll find out what happened to you and Jane," Bethany said before gasping (it came out a bit like a squawk) and turning around grabbing Chloe and shaking her by her shoulders, "WHERE HAVE YOU BEEN?!?!?!? AND WHERE IS JANE?!??!?!?!?!?!!!"

"If you don't want it, can I have your *Art of Pixar* book?" Chloe asked. Bethany frowned, there were some things she wasn't willing to give up. They heard a knock at Bethany's window. "OOOoooooOOO... who's the secret admirer?" Chloe asked, walking to the window and opening it, disappointed. "Jane's brother?"

Paul went from his regularly brownish self to Bethany-pale when he saw Chloe. He opened the window from the outside. "Where is my sister?" he demanded, climbing in.

"Bethany you cradle-robbing..."

"Where is Jane?" Bethany demanded, arms crossed. "Everyone has been worried sick about you! Paul and I have been teaming up to try to find you."

"I still think we should have done that ritual in the park," Paul said.

"Could you get a live chicken and four candles made of beeswax?" Bethany asked. "I'd go on Kijiji but my parents took my laptop..."

"I got the knife and salt!"

"That was the easy part! Well, where were you, Chloe???"

"Well," Chloe said. "Don't interrupt, and I'll tell you as quick as I can. Neil – well, that's not his real name – he lied about his entire curse. He's really a half-faerie, half human prince of another realm but for some reason he's mostly faerie and he tricked me into coming back to his realm so that he could get Jane to follow. You see – hey, I guess that makes you a prince!" she said to Paul, who looked repulsed by the idea. "Anyway, this all started after we went dancing - he told me that he needed my help to break his curse. Turns out this curse is what keeps him from coming to our world and enslaving it. Anyway – I heard this all from the unicorn..."

"Unicorn?" Paul demanded. "Of all the girly... where is my sister?!"

Chloe snorted. "Fine – I don't have time for this." She said, climbing out the window and going to the back yard. "I tried guys, it was a waste of time coming here."

"I told you it wouldn't work," said a giant golden cat-bird hybrid to a brilliantly white non-horse waited out by the back of the fence.

Bethany's eyes widened as the formidable unicorn played with her old tire-swing. He looked over, and trotted over, sticking his head in the window. The gryphon appeared to be eating her mother's hydrangeas. "Hello," the unicorn said, with a cheesy grin on its face.

"MOM! DAD! I AIN'T CRAZY!" Bethany snapped, tearing off down the hall towards the living room. Paul followed. Her family wasn't sitting around the tv or playing around on the computer, they were standing on the deck. The gryphon was now pulling up and munching on the lilies. Francine had even stopped texting.

"These are delicious," the gryphon said.

"Hi Mr. and Mrs. Pelshmidt," Chloe said, waiving sheepishly. "Sorry – I couldn't get back here on my own – the unicorn is kind of in a weakened state and the gryphon had to open a celestial doorway. Sunsoar, stop it! We can stop for a burger on the way back."

"The Spirits of Winter will destroy them all anyway in a few weeks," the gryphon said with a full mouth. "I might as well have a full tummy now." Her feathers bristled as Chloe approached her, but she didn't make a threatening motion otherwise.

Bethany's mother, Anne, went to Chloe. "Chloe? Chloe, are you alright? Where's Jane?"

"It's a long story – I don't have much time. Jane's in trouble. I need Bethany's help."

Bethany's father, Henry, was on the phone. "Yes, your daughter's here," he said. "Chloe, you need to speak to your parents."

Chloe nonchalantly took the receiver. "Hi dad. Put me on speaker, I know mom must be upset. How's Shiloh? Did he miss me?"

The unicorn was trotting along, prancing, really, her sisters on his back. "Mom, look at meeee!" The two no longer seemed 12 and 14, but like very small children. "Can we keep him?" Francine asked.

The unicorn trotted over to Paul. "What were you saying about girly nonsense? Oh, you share Jane's garnet. Greetings, favoured prince."

Paul went from pale to completely blanched. "What?!"

"I'll explain later," Chloe called from the phone. "Stop crying, mom..."

"Explain nothing!" the unicorn said, kneeling. "Alright, girls, off my back – I shall show this mortal prince how we I leap!"

"I can't ride."

"You are older than many knights I have accompanied into battle! You mustn't be scared! I shall not leap higher than the roof."

"I ain't nuts," Bethany said to her father. She then started to take pictures with her phone. "Oh, my website's hits are gonna skyrocket!"

"I would appreciate if you didn't post those on social media sites until after we have concluded our business," the gryphon said. "Your so-called scientists are almost as bad as some monsters from the nether-dimensions in terms of what they're willing to do to sate their curiosity. Besides, everyone will just say we're photoshopped." The gryphon had no lips to speak of, so her smile was more creepy then anything.

"Yeah, you do look really fake with this resolution," Bethany admitted.

"I can't talk long, mom," Chloe said on the phone. "Jane's in trouble and it's all my fault. I need to go after her but I need Bethany's help. No, I can't go home and explain everything, it'll take too long. We're having what for dinner?"

"Time is of the essence," the gryphon said. "Fortunately, the brother of Jane is here – with his help, I might be able to convince the elders of my Eyrie to action."

Paul yelped when the unicorn touched down. "My turn next!" Bethany's sisters chorused.

"You can let go now," the unicorn told Paul. "Are you still convinced I am the creature of female-fancy? If only I had a monster to vanquish..."

Paul's fingers entwined with the unicorn's mane. "Are you kidding? I think we're just getting warmed up."

"There will be time for all of this later," the gryphon said. "We have come for the great and powerful sorceress, Be'tty Pel'Schmid't. Hear our plight, famed one: you must accompany C'loe and the unicorn back to the realm of the fae to free Ja'ne before the prince claims her and this world as her own. I must fly back to my Eyrie. P'aul, brother of Ja'ne, must accompany me to my home across the lake of gold and mountains of fire and plead for intervention before the fae lay claim to this world."

"No one's going anywhere," Henry said.

"And you are?" the gryphon asked drolly.

"The father of this 'sorceress'."

The gryphon bowed her head. "I am pleased to make the acquaintance of the great warlock known as Pelshmid't. You must know that the situation is dire – that worlds will end if we do not act, your very own will be among the ravaged. Would you come in the stead of the boy? The elders would accept the wisdom of a sage rather than an untested human prince."

"Of course I would!" Henry exclaimed.

"Now, Henry-" Anne began.

"Anne, how many opportunities to save the world are going to come up in my lifetime?" he asked. "Now Beautiful and Forgiving Ann'e Pelshmid't, Wife of the Warlock, I charge you: Keep this duplex safe from all harm in my absence."

Bethany's mom snorted. "Well, since the world depends on it, I guess it's alright," she said. She gave Bethany a hug. "Dear, as much fun as all this sounds, I want you to think long and hard..."

"Oh, I'm going." Though truth be told, Bethany was silently lamenting being the only character in the history of YA to have their parent come along for the journey.

"Wait, did I just get left behind?" Paul asked.

"I can take two riders, but I fly swifter with one," the gryphon said. "The unicorn must return with the girls now. You must go, now, if there is any chance of saving Ja'ne. I am but glad that Cl'oe knows of such a powerful sorceress. It is this element of surprise that the prince might be caught unawares."

Bethany blinked several times, looked at Chloe, glared slightly, before mounting the unicorn. "Come on, damsels don't rescue themselves in these sorts of stories."

~*~

The Empress snapped at the prince, swirling around in the little glass orb that he had trapped her in. She'd made the throne room rain several times already – the kingdom was now dark and stormy. It had ruined the ball completely, but the prince decided that capturing one of his few equals was worth a delay in festivities. Prince Nyveo lounged on his throne, idly playing with the ball in his hands as the Empress thundered – flying against the great expanse that he could hold in one hand. His power shielded him from the storm inside his throne room.

"You cannot delay the day forever," the prince said, looking at the miniature blue and white dragon inside the crystal ball. There was no land in that realm – only endless sky for her to fly through clouds, lost, forever, unable to escape. "Delay it for a day or a week, or even a year – but your allies won't find her. I do not doubt they shall come, and I shall destroy them, one by one." He put the glass orb on the tip of his silver staff, now his royal sceptre, and watched in amusement as the silver staff bound to it, encasing it. "We shall see the extent of your power. In time, I will add yours to mine. Perhaps, if I am not to wed on the morrow, then I shall bring your castle to the ground? Yes, I think I shall."

He got up from his throne, his magical cover keeping him the only thing from being drenched. As the silver of the staff consumed the ball her power weakened. His court continued to rain – as did the outside world, but the hallway was dry. He walked down the hallway of his castle, wondering if sleep would come.

"My lord?" one of his princesses asked.

"I am busy, do not delay me."

"My lord, it is important. Your queen…" Yssa began.

"I have hidden her, so that neither of my uncles may steal what I have rightfully won."

"My prince, please… I know that we are still your princesses, but I am concerned. Will you not grow tired of us, now that you are able to see so many in the world of the mortals?" she asked.

"You dance for my pleasure, nothing more," he said. "Content yourself that you are in my favour, or you may soon find yourself out of it."

"My lord," she said, bowing her head, and did not address him again.

He didn't mind showing the Empress what his intents were – so long as she delayed the dawn, she showed her power – but he did not mind waiting. He had waited so long, but he reminded himself that he was immortal – he could wait a hundred years and it did not matter. Part of him was sorely tempted to free his uncles, and invite them to the wedding, but a cooler head told him to continue to wait. A younger prince would have had the ceremony immediately – but he knew that everything must be done in accordance with tradition, lest his uncles cry foul and he be denied all of his rightful inheritance. He was immortal – the worlds were his to claim.

He entered his bedchamber, strangely quiet, and he wondered if his fools would tell him that they lost track of his Kasmodiah – and the unicorn. It didn't matter. The Empress, his uncles – who else? Who else could stop him? He was tempted to have Yssa come to him – but then again, it was getting late.

A knock came to his door. His room was large, he wondered if it was another of his beautiful princesses, coming to beg him to still be considered favourable. He snorted. Now that he was able to come and go to the earthen world, the other doorways would soon be open to him. He needn't keep his old pets, however pleasing.

He opened the door and smiled. "It is finished? Put it up there," he gestured. His men brought forth the portrait of his betrothed, Titalia.

They hung it up before his large, canopied bed. "She looks magnificent, doesn't she?" he asked, raising the staff so that the empress might see. It hardly resembled the gawky mortal girl that had come – of her own free will, no less – into this world. In the elaborate wedding gown, her hair done up, the necklace with the garnet stone as the mask of silver waited in her hands. She sat obedient, waiting, almost watching him in the portrait.

"Eventually the dawn will come. If it does not by the time I awaken, I shall first bring your castle to the ground. Then we will hunt my good-for-nothing half-brother. His little farce was never consummated, but I want to make everything clear to all parties concerned. By then, I will have mastered your power, and I will control the seasons, the day and night in this world. I was tempted to conquer the world of the humans first, but," he added with a smile. "The realm of you dragons is enticing as well. So many realms... and all the time in existence to bend them." The only nagging thought in his head was his missing princess. Friendship was a strange bond among mortals. But, unlike Jane, she was weak-willed and a coward.

He summoned a servant. "I will retire and awaken with the dawn. Make sure all preparations are ready for the wedding. Send message to the weavers – that one of my princesses has escaped. The clouds will give them the coolness they've come to expect in the caves. I would have them return my bauble unharmed. They can eat the unicorn and anyone else that happens to be found helping them."

~*~

Riding between worlds was exhilarating, but Bethany expected the Fairie Realm to be... different. It looked at first like the undeveloped Canadian shield, but once the unicorn bounded and leapt high, she saw the majestic castles and a flying one as well – it was a pity that the skies were overcast. She should have brought her rubber boots.

Chloe had at least used some common sense and changed into some jeans and a hoodie and, even though they were different sizes, it fit well. Chloe wondered about that – Bethany wasn't as curvy as her. She wasn't as skinny as Jane, but kind of... normal. *Maybe I'm not as fat as I thought I was,* Chloe thought, but in truth Bethany mostly wore loose-fitting and comfy clothing more suited to twelve year olds then sweet-sixteens. Bethany knew her sisters would be prancing around, taking turns in that giant puffy gown when they got back, but for now, they had Jane to save.

She wasn't expecting the first monster to be a minotaur. "I don't recall this in fairie tales," she said, arms crossed. "This is straight up Greek-Mythology."

"Ah, a pagan sorceress," the great ox-headed beast said. "This is the one who can solve all the riddles?" The minotaur looked at Bethany critically. "She is no wise crone! She is but a girl child, much like you and Jane."

"Unlike those two, I know what you're from," Bethany said. "Theseus was supposed to have..."

"I was once human, like you are now," he said. "My name is Prince Bijan. I was transformed into the form you see before you by the prince of this realm. We don't have much time before the dawn."

"I think we've been bought time," Sedolei said, looking to the skies. "These winds... this rain. The Great Empress is trying to stop the dawn."

"Why does that matter?" Bethany asked.

"The fae wedding ceremonies can be quite complicated," the unicorn said. "To my knowledge, the prince has the staff – he needs no queen for him to become king. He will be crowned with the dawn, but he will have to marry her under the moon's light."

"So we have less than a day to save Jane," Chloe said.

"It's more complicated then that," Bijan said. "Once he is king, he commands this world. I heard that the last king was able to command the rising and falling of the sun."

"Well, technically it's not the sun that rises and falls..."

"Oh, stop nitpicking," Chloe said to Bethany. "Is this... Empress, is she on our side?"

"I think so," Bijan said. "She has fallen, however."

"How can she have fallen if she is causing the rain?" Bethany asked.

Bijan snorted. Chloe hoped Bethany would have sounded smarter by now – Bethany always seemed smart about this sort of stuff. "She is captured – but she is still able to work some of her magic. I saw it with my own eyes."

"Did you haunt a terribly labyrinth and kill seven youths and seven–"

"You are very familiar with that evil. No, I am but three hundred years old," Bijan said. "This place freezes time – the fae destroyed their world, ripping open the gateway to others. They meant to invade and conquer. They see no harm in hurting, changing, using us so that they gain power."

Chloe frowned, watching Bethany's expression. She looked contemplative. "I don't see why you couldn't have told me all of this. I can help too, you know."

"Now is not the time to argue," Bijan said. "Hopefully, this sorceress will be able to defeat the evil of the faerie prince. Tell me, what powers do you possess that could aid in rescuing the Empress?"

Bethany said. "Would you excuse Chloe and I for just one moment? Thank you." She grabbed Chloe's arm and dragged her behind a large treestump to yell at her. "Why do they keep calling me a sorceress?!"

"I had to tell them something!" Chloe snapped. "You were the only person I could think of who knows about this kinda stuff, and besides," she said. "You and Jane were the only ones that came after me when I was being... you know..."

"Selfish? Stupid?? A Grade-A dumba–?"

"Alright already! I could have asked them to bring anyone, and I said you. Doesn't that make me a good friend?"

They heard something running through the wood – something big, with hooves. Chloe looked overhead to see the starless night be bound in what first looked like a centaur – leap overtop of them. She didn't stop to apologize or look back, and just as quickly nets fell over of Chloe and Bethany, and they screamed for help. Bijan moved towards them, only to be caught up in webbing, invisible save for slender threads shimmering against the torchlight. "Ah, if it isn't the oxen again," said one of the voices, which belonged to an old woman.

Chloe strained to see in the dark – to see past the net, and saw it was no net but sticky webbing. "Ignore him, capture the centaur!" another snapped. The old woman rised up high, atop a spider's body. They were very old and a thick sheet wrapped around their eyes, but they ran off. "Don't let her get away!"

"Bethany, I'm stuck!" Chloe wailed.

"Well, so am I!" Bethany said. "I'm trying to get my pocket knife... eww...."

"This is hardly the time to be squeamish!" Chloe said. "Bijan! Bijan, are you alright?"

He lie perfectly still. "Sedolei? Bijan? You need to help us!" She strained against the sticky fibers, getting herself and her hair more messed up with every strained grunt. "Somebody, help us!" she called out.

"Who do you think will help? Be quiet, let's try to get out of here," Bethany snapped, straining with her pocket knife to cut through the sticky webbing. "Before they come back! Chloe, you need to help me!"

"I don't have anything," Chloe said, before thinking about it long and hard. She dug into her pockets, and took out her nail file

"What good will that do?" Bethany demanded.

Chloe reached as far away from the sticky mess as she could, and dug the metal file into the ground. She pulled herself from the webbing, and straining, grabbed hold of another log to brace as she pulled herself out. She felt her arms go rubbery, and the sticky webbing pull against her face and hair, but it did not rip. She pulled herself free.

"Good job!" Bethany said, still almost completely stuck. "Don't come near me! Try to find something to cut me loose!"

Chloe knew she couldn't rest. She raced over to Bijan, and tried to lift his massive head. He looked dead. "Spiders have venom, but it's not like a snake's," she said to herself. "Bijan, please, I can't carry you. We need to go, now!" He didn't move.

"Chloe hide!" Bethany snapped.

Chloe listened, and hid behind the nearest tree as the three gartantuan spider-women returned, bringing with them another mass, but rather than the snow-white fleece of Sedolei, Chloe saw hooves and legs belonging to something brown, and with it, a small satyr. A regular fae was also with them. "It's a pity the unicorn got away," said the first of the spiders.

They surrounded Bethany. "Where did the other one get to?" another asked.

"Does it matter?" said the last. "After he is made King, he will reign unchallenged. The kingdom will wake, and all stragglers will be caught. Better to take these ones to Bulgorio – he will reward us."

"I hunger for their flesh now!"

"The Faerie King will bring back more mortals than even you can eat – we have displeased him, let us find favour with Bulgorio."

Bethany yelped as one grabbed her, pulled her from the netting and wrapped her like a mummy in their slender webbing before tossing her next to the satyr, who was being bound by the other two. Chloe wasn't sure what to do or how to help them, but she watched every moment, shaking and waiting for them to begin work on Bijan. *If only there was some way I could help them,* she thought, looking through Bethany's rudimentary bag of supplies. It was mostly books, and Chloe doubted throwing anything at them was going to accomplish anything beyond her on capture, though reading to them might be the same as a sleeping spell. *At least they're not eating them,* she thought, but kept her eyes peeled, looking for more of the giant spider-women or perhaps if Sedolei came back.

"What if we find the other girl?" one of the spiders asked.

"Well, he'll never know if we eat just one..." their laughter made the hairs on the back of Chloe's neck stand on end. She couldn't help but wonder if it was because Bethany was skinnier than she was. Chloe pushed her vanity to the side, and wondered where Sedolei was – he claimed to be a young unicorn, afterall – would he have abandoned them?

The old spider-women moved quickly, once their prisoners were securely wrapped in their captive silk, they constructed a litter and threw their five captives inside, and began to move on. Chloe chased after them, trying not to let a trace of her give way in the darkness. *Will Jane start to forget herself?* Chloe thought, her mind racing. *No – Jane's strong. He can't make her marry him. Hold on, Jane, I need more time than I thought.*

She chased after the spiders, not sure what she would do if they saw her. Surely Bethany was still busy at work with her pocket knife. She wondered about Bijan, about Sedolei – what went through their minds. *No doubt they don't think Bethany is much of a sorceress.* She blinked back tears, wondering if perhaps she should have given up, and let the unicorn find someone bigger and stronger to save Jane. *No, she came for me,* Chloe thought. *I can be brave.*

~*~

Bethany found herself being cut out of her prison. Tendril-like arms grabbed her, and she was forced to her knees. She wasn't sure where she was, but it was lavish – the colors were more vibrant here than any other place she'd seen since coming to fairy-land. Someone took her glasses before she could make any details, but the smells, the softness of nature, the intricacy of the room's details were fascinating. The centaur was being led away, and someone had given the satyr a little vest and a fez, and told him his job was now to announce people coming and going.

"Are you sure that is wise? What if she turns us to stone?" one of the fae around her asked.

"Red Queen!" one of the guards shrieked, letting go of her. When he did that, her other captor did the same.

"Red Queen!" came the chorus, and suddenly everyone let go of her. Bethany squinted – she was not blind without her glasses, but she wanted to know what sort of beasts she was up against. At least they had her facing an elaborate stage of some sort – steps led up to a heavily curtained throne area, if one could consider a giant lounge chair a throne.

"Red Queen?" asked a deep baritone.

Bethany saw perhaps the most gelatinous creature imaginable, and she had read all the Star Wars expanded universe novels, and was quite familiar with the Hutts. Once she could make out that it was human – rather, fae in form - she determined that it was well dressed in what looked like luxurious velvet draping it from its massive multiple chins. Even though it made the poor saps on TLC look tiny, it still had the general beauty of the fae in its face. "Pah," it said, adjusting the crown of laurels on its forehead. "This is not the Red Queen. I have seen her – the real Red Queen would not be seen in such *ugly* shoes. Tell me, dear, what is your name?"

Nicknames somehow didn't seem appropriate. "Bethany-"

More shrieking, and several fae trampled over one another to get away from her. She realized that there were not just small fae and big fae, but like the centaur and the satyr she had seen, in this court, there were all manner of beasties – some even had the look of humans from another time in this strange and elaborate court. Bethany was somehow unsure if she was captive or if her captors were now scared of her. The massive figure shifted in its E-Z-Throne, the only one seemingly unconcerned while the old spider women cursed, saying how they should have gotten a much bigger reward.

"It is not THAT mortal, but A mortal," said the formidably fat fairy, "Mortals do not live that long. The hair color isn't even close. Let me prove it further. What are the names of your parents?"

"Well, my mom's name is Annette," Bethany began. "And my father's name is Hen- wait." Bethany frowned. "The Red Queen was a character in Lewis Carol's story, but you don't mean her."

The surplus-sized sidhe attempted to sit up, but quickly gave up. "I will ask the Fates later about this joke... you mean to say they weren't invited? I'll deal with you later! Tell me, Bethany, your brothers and sisters, who are they?"

"I don't have any brothers," Bethany said.

"None living?" he asked drolly.

"None at all. Only two younger sisters."

"See, my followers? Stop cowering and wetting yourselves. This one has not a smidge of royalty in her blood. She has no power. " The prince grew quite angry, going so far as to sit up. "And if would be best for you if you did not mention the name of that forsaken opium addict's name in my presence," he snapped, before lounging back again. "Now, what to do with you... no doubt my nephew would reward me greatly for giving you to him. He won't even invite me to the wedding. Tsk. I'm sure they'll have the most exquisite cake."

"You must not want him to become king."

"He finally succeeded – that stalemate between Altroine and Nyveo got boring *sooooooo* long ago," he said, taking a glass of what was likely rich wine from an overly jewelled goblet in his heavily ringed fingers. "My nephew knows I will begrudgingly support, whereas Altroine must be destroyed now that he's fulfilled his usefulness of scaring that over-dramatic dragon. He might destroy me as well, so I might as well enjoy these my last few centuries."

"Don't you want to be king?" Bethany asked.

"Now now, if you are king people expect you to do things for them, now don't they? Bulgorio, I beseech you; Bulgorio, I want you to fix this problem; Bulgorio...! Oh, I couldn't stand to hear it." He plucked one of the grapes from a nearby dish being suspended by four exhausted pixies. "Give edicts and conquer worlds. My brother and nephew won't listen when I said I couldn't be bothered. No, it is far better to enjoy all the perks with none of the responsibility. I think I'll add your head to my collection, Other Bethany."

Bethany saw a large man with a golden-bladed axe step forward. Bethany was going to ask how sharp gold was supposed to be, but didn't want to ask and find out. "I like my head very much where it is right now, thank you very much," she said. Arms grabbed hers and forced her down. "Wait!" she said. "I challenge you!"

"To what?" asked the prince.

"A game of some sort," Bethany said. "For my freedom. What are you good at? I like chess."

"Do I look like the Grim Reaper?" Bulgorio asked. "Though, I do like the idea of humiliating you. My dear, do you know much about trivia?"

Bethany's heart leapt. She was a whiz at Trivial Pursuit and had a fantastic memory. "Alright, how do you want to...?"

"Simple. You ask me a question, I answer it. I ask you a question, you answer it. The first person to lose... well, I'll let you go free. If you lose," he gestured. The guards forced Bijan down.

"No! Stop!" Bethany said, but arms restrained her. The axe swung and Bijan cried out. Bijan yelped, only to blink several times, looking down at his body. "What... the curse..."

"Put the head with the others. I've been told his body will keep healing, and as muscular as it is, I trust my staff will make it quite succulent," Bulgorio said, lounging.

Bijan called out as his head was taken through one door, his massive strong body taken through another. "Now... mortal girl... tell me, have you ever forgotten your head? Ahahahaha!"

His court joined in his laughter as Bethany blanched. She wanted to ask where they were taking the head, but she had the feeling the axe would be quick to fall on her neck, and she wasn't kept alive with any curse. "Who is Altroine?" she asked quietly.

"Is that your first question? This will be an easy game indeed," snapped the putrid pedigreed prince. "You could have at least waited until we were all done laughing," he said, then began to cough. Bethany wondered if fae had ever heard of coronary bypasses, but reasoned she'd worry about their specific anatomical differences later. A walrus couldn't have that much blubber and be healthy. "Altroine is my oldest brother – the cliché ambitious sort, who, when our little brother Kylreas took the throne and became King, went out of his way to help the Red Queen defeat him. You can pick up a map to his castle in the gift shoppe if you win. My treat. Alright, my question: What color are the spots of a Harumen Dragon's egg that is born in the spring?"

"I would have learned this where?" Bethany asked.

"You can also pick up the extended edition of the *Guide to Wyverns, Drakes, and Dragons* in the gift shoppe on your way out – nevermind,

I'll have you be given a gift bag on your way into the head gallery," he guffawed. "We'll make it so you stare at the page with the answer for a few years."

Bethany felt all eyes on her.

"Blue?" she asked.

The prince's eyes narrowed. "Lucky guess," he said, though he strained to sit up and he coughed again. By that time Bethany realized that his lips were turning purple. "It is time again, I suppose." He raised one slovenly arm and pointed at one of his illustriously buff guards. "He'll do."

"My Lord, please!" he said, dropping his spear and pleading, but already his fellows had grabbed his arms. "I beg of you, I have always been loyal."

"You have great discipline. I'm sure you'll be able to make the most of the situation."

The fae pleaded again, but the axe came down all the same. "Oh, nuts!" the fae said after a moment, as his severed head was held up by his luxurious thick curly locks, and the decapitated body dragged towards his lord. Bulgorio glowered at the fae who grabbed his head, and unlocked the collar on his neck. "Be careful!" he snapped, until his head was in place on the very muscular body, and the golden collar was fastened. Bethany wasn't even aware of such a thing, for he had no real discernable neck, and the thought of touching the mounds of flesh gave her chills. It was almost comical, seeing the intensely obese head atop the svelt physique. "Alright, get that out of my chair. I'm going to slip into something more comfortable."

"A marshmellow?" Bethany asked flatly.

"Your questions, my dear, are not very difficult to answer. It's almost as if you want me to add your head to the collection."

He stopped in mid track as the other fellows attempted to move the massive body from the chair. The head of the fae who had so recently lost his body was placed atop the flabby one, and attached with a copper collar, despite his protests. He strained to get up. "It's my chair, now get off," Bulgorio ordered. "As for you," he said, descending the steps, licking his lips, looking at Bethany. "Ask your next question, before I get bored."

"Do faeries always tell the truth?" Bethany asked.

"We of royal blood are bound to our words. While we do not always allude to the truth," he said, smiling as he made himself comfortable on his chaise, "we cannot outright lie."

"So you chose your words carefully," Bethany said.

"My turn," Bulgorio said. "What color socks are you wearing?"

Bethany honestly had no idea – she'd put them on in a hurry in the dark that morning. "Uh... black?" She checked her left leg. Her heart raced. Navy blue, but would that count?

"Check the other one," the prince said. It was checked – fortunately for her, one sock was black. Bethany decided she'd never put on socks without the lights on ever again.

"Alright," Bethany said, "What is the principle problem in the Terminator movie sequels?"

"Are you referring to the time continuity problem?" Bulgorio asked. "Or do we consider the canoness of the mini-series? You really much be more specific, my dear... but really, where to begin. I believe it all started with the megalomaniac director and his problem with that Harlan Ellison fellow..."

"A prisoner! A prisoner! We caught a prisoner!" one of the armed guards said, running into the throne room.

"Good. Bring her in. I'm going to take a break. Think of some good questions, Mortal Bethany, I'm getting bored." Bulgorio's throne was then lifted off the stage and taken out as the prisoner was brought in.

Bethany rolled her eyes when she saw Chloe. "Way to not get captured," she called once her friend was in range.

"Oh, like you're one to talk," Chloe snapped as she was brought in. "Ugh. Who decorated this place?"

"WAIT!" boomed a voice from outside the throne room. The prince was born back to his throne room despite the red faces of his staff. "You dare insult the grandeur that is my throne room?"

"Grandeur?" Chloe asked, snorting slightly. "When did you last redecorate? The renaissance? Oh, I'm sorry; the renaissance wasn't this gaudy."

Bulgorio's his face appeared red and sweaty though the fit part of him seemed to be not even working up a sweat. "And who is this, with her obviously borrowed hoodie, hideous as it is? Are you Another Bethany?"

"This monstrosity to fashion is hers," Chloe said, gesturing at Bethany. "I didn't have time to run home and change. I was wearing something from Prince Nyveo's line. It was fantastic, the way it made my tummy shrink, but it didn't make adventuring practical."

"Nonsense! Beauticians! Esteticians! Gownmakers and wigmakers and general stylists, assemble!" An overly tired group of servants appeared.

"You look fine, your majesty," one tired-looking fae said.

"I want her to acknowledge the superiority of my imperial dressers!" he snapped. "Take two servants, alike in build and grace, and style one in our favoured fashions, and the other that of our beloved nephew."

"I wouldn't mind knowing these treatments first-hand," Chloe said sweetly.

"And so you shall!" he clapped.

Bethany scowled something fierce at Chloe. "What are you doing?"

"Just trust me."

Bethany thought they wasted precious time, but still the game of trivial pursuit continued – Bethany knew she lost with several questions, but Bulgorio seemed to have changed the rules as they went – he wanted her to see the fashion show anyway.

After an hour of Bethany managing to keep her head, Chloe reappeared, in a heart-themed ballgown taken to near cartoonish-extremes, but her hair was styled and her nails had a nice fresh sheen on them. She sat beside Bulgorio, fanning herself. "Is the show about to begin?" she asked. "It would be better if there was a velvet curtain to announce them... ugh, who picked this music?"

"I agree, but it was all I could get on short notice. Do you play an instrument, Bethany?"

"Is that your question?" Technically she played the oboe and Chloe played the flute, she could think of some amusing *wah wah wah* sounds to make with a trombone.

"BEGIN THE FASHION SHOW," Bulgorio ordered, and Bethany tried not to groan out loud.

There was not one simple comparison – over two dozen fae walked down Bulgorio's court in fantastic fae fashions. The servants obviously preferred the slight variations found in the courts of Bulgorio, but it was over-the-top and flamboyant, much like Bethany assumed a real fashion show would be. The fae looked ridiculous, but whenever one of the servants from the other courts appeared, several spectators started booing. One threw a lemon tart.

"Ooh, I like her shoes," Chloe said. "But I wouldn't have done that with her hair. It makes her forehead seem enormous."

"You are very good at this," Bulgorio said. "It is too bad I decided to eat you and the Other Mortal after all." He sighed and it sounded genuine.

"Woah woah woah," Bethany said as the fashion show ended. "Wasn't the minotaur enough food to last you a long time?"

"My dear, sweet child," Bulgorio chuckled. "You had your chance, and I was going to add your heads to my collection, but I don't think I could do without the pair of you as a complete set, and it's obvious that you would just bicker. No, I think we've had our fun. You shall be made into a most succulent meal for all to enjoy. Well, I'll enjoy it, anyway."

Bethany thought she saw Chloe start to sweat. As the fashion show ended and the magic lights were raised, platters of sugared treats and steaming meats were brought forward. Bethany was bid to sample, but she knew somehow that they were really minotaur. She wondered where they had taken Bijan's head – and how much longer they had until dawn. She didn't have long to wait – the servants came, bearing with them a great dark suit of fur, and behind them again, a mirror. Chloe was losing her nerve. "You call that the height of fashion?" she tried her best to sound incredulous.

Bulgorio smiled at her. "Try it on before you judge."

"No no, I couldn't," Chloe said, but the guards grabbed her, forced her down towards the furry garment. Bethany tried to rush forward, to help, but arms seized her and she was forced back. She saw behind her that there was another such garment.

"But the colors clash!" Chloe shouted as the cloak was put around her shoulders, and as the hood went over her head she grew in size, Bethany could not see what happened but she saw a great white bovine where Chloe once stood. "You call this fashion?" she mooed.

"Now my dear, don't be silly," Bulgorio said, grinning. "I think you look good enough to eat!"

"I call bull!" Chloe snapped. "Just be glad I wasn't literal." She twitched her tail into the arm of one of the guards.

"Can this garment turn us into anything else?" Bethany asked. "I have heard of otters who shed their skins..."

"Why would anyone wish to eat an otter?" Bulgorio roared. "Very well, show her!"

The servants pulled off the skin and Chloe was her normal spoiled, ball-gowned garbed self. "How does it work?" Bethany asked, gesturing at the one for her.

"Well, the one who closes the cloak just thinks of the form they'll take on," the servant said.

"Like this?" Chloe asked, grabbing the cape, and she became very small, a black bunny. She sped around the room, and hopped onto Bulgorio's lap.

"How cute!" Bulgorio said, petting Chloe's little twitchy head. "But not very much to eat."

"It's a pity you only have one such cloak made," Chloe said, twitching her little black nose. "I could see something like this being very useful."

"Maiden," he said, "How else do you think I consume those like you?"

Chloe hopped off, and became human again. "You don't think you have enough – what with the meat that keeps growing back?" She batted her eyes at Bulgorio.

"Enough is not a word I use often," Bulgorio said. "Guards, turn them both to swans, then roast them for my snack later. For now, I shall go watch all eight Harry Potter movies in a row. Whoever disturbs me shall lose their head, you know the drill."

Bethany's heart raced as the guards came towards her with the cloak, but Chloe shrugged into the garment and shank again, and a spotted mess hurled towards Bulgorio, knocking him to the ground. The leopard pinned him to the ground. "Polka dots!" he complained. "You see how I put on this robe with the stripes!"

"Bethany, do me a favour, and get the keys from him," Chloe growled. "That is, if the guards don't want me to rip out his throat."

Bethany scrambled to her feet, and took the keys in her grasp she said, "Okay, now what?"

"Now, you go find Bijan and rescue Sedolei and–"

Bethany unlocked the collar that kept Bulgorio's head in place. "Now, you don't want to be doing that," Bulgorio said, but Bethany gave the head a nudge, and it rolled and bounced down the steps, towards the mess of servant fae, looking at it with wide eyes.

"Bethany!" Chloe roared. "What have you done?"

"Oops," Bethany said, realizing Chloe only had the body pinned.

The fae moved, swarming the head they started to beat it senseless. "My body! My poor body!" a familiarly heavy-set fae wailed, trying to snatch the keys from Bethany. "Allow me," she performed a switcheroo, and as his head came near his real body, a neck grew. "Oh, thank you, pathetic mortals," he said, near tears. "I shall have to hate imprisoning you."

"Then don't worry about it," Bethany said, stealing the other cloak. "Chloe, let's get out of here!" She shrugged on the cloak and became a large green thark. "Yeah!" she had imagined having a sword for each of her four hands, and was not disappointed.

"Stop messing around," Chloe said. "Let's get out of here while they're still busy."

They transformed into fae version of themselves – small pixies that flickered and twinkled as they flittered down the hall, to where the heads of prisoners were kept. They found no one guarding the halls, as all of Bulgorio's servants wasted no time dropping their chores to give him a proper licking. The found the room of heads full of glass cases on display, each embellished with a ridiculous amount of detail. Once they found Bijan, they took off the furs and became human again.

"Girls!" Bijan said, though several of the heads began to sing acapella.

Bethany unlocked the case. "I don't think your body's in such good shape," she said. She held him, thought of making a lame Shakespearean quote, but then smiling, put the cloak overtop of him.

"What are you doing?" Bijan asked, but he suddenly became much heavier than a man should have been so Bethany dropped him.

"What did you do?" Chloe squawked, going towards Bijan, but a tall figure rose up. He was undeniably attractive – like they would have imagined a real life Sinbad the Sailor or Aladdin, his mocha-colored skin and dark hair and incredibly toned, and naked, body, save for the fur cloak covering around his waist, censoring any naughty bits the two teens were unabashedly trying to see and pretend they weren't looking for. He looked about nineteen or twenty, and looking at his hands he felt his face, and didn't have to look far to find a mirror. "I'm... you... you are a sorceress," he said, holding the cloak about him tightly.

Chloe frowned. "You couldn't have turned him into something more vicious until we escaped, could you?"

"I guess his being hot and naked is a bonus."

Bijan at least embodied every combined stereotype the two girls had regarding historic princes. He found a sword and took charge. "Alright – we face the monsters head on. Has anyone got any pants?"

"Chloe, do you mind?" Bethany asked. "My cloak's being used."

"Well, I don't think a horse would be big enough for both of you..."

"Give me that," Bethany swiped the cloak from Chloe, and she turned into a large dragon-like creature that was more horse in function, complete with two humps in place of saddles. "On board!"

"How did I know your being a nerd would come in handy?" Chloe asked.

"What monstrosity have you turned yourself into?" Bijan demanded.

"Relax, I got the idea from a video game," Bethany said. "Hop on!"

Bethany loved the way that the cloaks would literally turn you into whatever beast you imagined them to be – the character in the video game was a crude pixely thing from the 80's, but Bethany pretended it was lizard, and the way she snaked along corridors made her giggle – every fae that stood in their way quickly fled at the sight of the large scaly monster. "You don't suppose the other dragons will mistake me for one of their own, do you?" she asked Chloe.

"Let's just get out of here."

They raced out of the castle, over the drawbridge and into the surrounding woods, and as they slowed Sedolei raced to them. "I was just formulating a plan to rescue you when you gave yourself up to the fae," he said to Chloe. "But, why haven't you saved our friends?"

"These are your friends," Bethany said, taking off the skin and becoming herself.

Then, you must be...?" he looked at Bijan. "Quick, we must save Jane! But first, find some pants!"

"They got a 24-Hour Pants Shoppe near the End of the Rainbow?" Bethany asked, looking up at the sky. The sky was beginning to get lighter. "Oh no..."

"We have time," Chloe said. "Oh, and I have pants." She plopped down a bag of elaborate clothing before Bijan. "I didn't really think of getting anything for you, but his staff gave me some of their samples. This moisturizer is amazing!!"

"Did you plan that entire thing?" Bethany asked while Bijan found himself some clothing that fit. He didn't like it, but that was besides the point. Chloe smiled. "You know, I really don't want to know," Bethany said eventually with a shrug.

Once Bijan was adequately clothed, the prince mounted the unicorn, and the girls turned into small squirrels, and hopping onto his shoulders, the unicorn gathered up speed and took them away from the chaotic castle, where the least-powerful prince of the realm became a literal tetherball for his relieved staff.

18

Night Mares

They arrived at the crypt the gryphon had spoken of as dawn crept over the kingdom, the beginning of the Last Day had not yet reached the castle, but they knew that it if Jane was to be found, it needed to be done quickly. No one was sure how long they had until the guards came for Jane – when the prince would be crowned.

The cloaks allowed for them to hide in plain sight – the fae guards were on the alert, but preparations for the day's coronation and evening wedding took everyone's attention, and they were able to enter the labyrinth. Though the last evening's attack from Jane had burned through the hedges and had enabled them to move quickly through the rose gardens, it also made it easier for them to be seen, and it was impossible for the unicorn to leap and not be seen. Sedolei and Bijan both later admitted to wanting to rescue the maidens in the gazebos, but rescuing Jane took precedence.

Chloe couldn't get over just how gorgeous Bijan was. Up until recently, she considered Neil to be the new standard of beauty, but Neil - *Nyveo* showed his dark side. Bijan was a complete knockout. "Did you have a harem back at home?" she asked as she was a small squirrel on his shoulder.

"No, but I was unfaithful to my wife," he said.

"You were married? How old are you?"

"I came to this world at twenty years of age," he said. "I stopped aging shortly thereafter."

"Oooh. So you're not seeing anyone?

"Chloe, focus," Squirrel-Bethany snapped.

"I'm very mature for my age."

"You and your *Hello Kitty* backpack..."

Bijan dismounted Sedolei, and put the girls on the ground so they removed their skins and became themselves again. "Well, Sorceress, what say you? Is she down there?"

"Did any of you see her?"

"Sunsoar said she saw the Prince and His Guard take the coffin containing Lady Jane below," Sedolei neighed. "Though... I cannot enter."

"Why not?" Bethany asked.

Sedolei for once, looked nervous – the crypt hardly looked like one Chloe wanted to enter either. "It's okay, I'm scared too."

"I'm not scared!" the unicorn brayed, then composed himself. "Well, perhaps a little, but that's not why. Fae are immortals - this is where they leave their dead. This place is bound by strange magic... no doubt the prince has safeguards to sense creatures such as myself. I would draw attention to myself."

Bijan spoke, "Do not worry. The three of us shall find Jane and return – we could use a guard anyway."

Chloe looked at the unicorn and the entrance. "Maybe the cloak could make you smaller. You know, a Mini-Uni."

"Or maybe turn you human," Bethany offered.

The unicorn shook his mighty head. "The silver magic that bound me still affects me now," he said. "I do not think I could stand to be transformed by it again. I am sorry."

"I forgot you're a creature of magic," Bijan said to Sedolei. "Do not worry – we shall journey to the heart of the crypt and find her. Give us time – if the guards come, fight them off, to the best of your ability."

The unicorn nodded. "I hope Sunsoar and the Warlock return swiftly. The Empress must be weakening," he looked to the clearing skies. "I feared him when he was but a prince. When he is crowned, his powers will be tenfold."

"Well, standing around talking about saving Jane isn't saving Jane, now is it?" Bethany asked, taking the torch and leading the way down into the crypt. "HURRY UP!"

Bijan followed after her. Chloe hesitated. She felt foolish – she'd seen the crypt during the day. She'd asked the other princesses if the fae were mortal, why they had need of a crypt. She got a variety of answers – faes could kill and be killed, and, another said, some were just sleeping. Chloe knew the kingdom was waking, but would the prince allow everyone to wake before he had succeeded in taking his throne? Or would he have them see him come into majesty?

"You getting used to being weak like a human?" Bethany asked Bijan as they descended the steps. Chloe noticed the lack of spiderwebs and all things creepy crawly expected to be in a crypt, but, thinking back to the monstrous spider-ladies, liked that fact.

"Yes, but I'll give up the strength for better general odour," the prince admitted. So, I have to ask,"what is your plan to defeat the prince, sorceress?"

Bethany frowned, and pretended like she didn't hear him. Chloe caught up to Bijan. "I don't think there is a plan besides grab Jane and run right now. I mean, that's the issue, isn't it? He can't just marry anyone..."

"He has the staff. Even if he is bound for ten years, do you not think that all we'd be doing is buying time?"

"Well maybe with a little bit of proof and some celestial gateways, that'll buy our governments enough time to send a welcoming bomb," Bethany suggested.

"She's older then she looks," Chloe told Bijan. "I know not of what riddles she speaks."

"I'm three months younger then you!" Bethany snapped. "Is there any item of power that can defeat him?"

"I do not know," said the prince. "If there exists such an item, I don't doubt Sunsoar or some others have found it long ago."

Chloe wondered if they were already too late – or if Jane wasn't down here. She didn't want to go back to the castle, to confront the world that she thought was so beautiful. She blinked back tears of shame. Bethany wasn't scared – neither was Bijan. She could be brave. *For Jane*, she told herself.

The crypt was cold – the world of the fae was cool; Chloe often forgot how there was no wind, no sunshine, no real change in temperature, but she shivered as they moved further down the steps, which seemed to lead down too deep. She tried to keep up with the other two. How big could a crypt be, anyway?

There were many coffins in the first room – some glass, others solid but each wrought out of beautiful carved stone, wood or bone. Beautiful sculptures of fae tormenting hideous and terrified renditions of humans and other mythical creatures littered the place, looking more monstrous as the shadows of the bas relief danced in the torch's light. Chloe was just thankful there were no bugs to fall on her shoulder and make her scream. She didn't need much of an excuse.

"Let's get started," Bijan muttered, handing her his torch and moving aside one of the coffin lids. Inside, lay a sleeping fae, beautiful, looking like some sort of elven vampire.

"I left my stake and holy water at home," Bethany muttered.

Bijan frowned, looking at the handsome lord, but despite Bethany tickling his nose, he was not waking up. "For all we know, he's put a curse on her. We might not be able to recognize Jane."

"Well, you are a prince, aren't you? Start smoochin'," Chloe snapped.

"I'm not kissing everyone here," Bijan snapped. "Besides, the last thing we need is for some of these ones to wake up. Sorceress, use your power to find Jane here."

"Uh... too much faerie magic.""Tombs. Why tombs?" Bethany asked. "Fae are immortal, aren't they? You'd think they'd have something different for their dead."

"Yes, but they can be slain," Bijan said, as they walked along, looking at the bodies of the not rotting. Perfectly preserved, some were open while others were wrapped in the spinner's concoction. "That was why the prince ordered the kingdom to sleep. Fae are cruel – they would demand he marry the first mortal that he comes across to open the door once again. He would lose his claim to the kingdom, and then one of his uncles or his descendants would take the throne. As for why this... I have noticed that the fae are always interested in us. They claim to always be our betters, but they lack... creativity, to say the least."

"Will time start to flow, if the kingdom wakes?" Bethany asked.

Bijan looked contemplative. "I'm not sure. I don't believe so – perhaps they are not immortal, the same way that a small bug sees us and our lives. Why us mortals cease to age when we come to this place, I do not know."

"Do you eat any golden apples regularly?" Bethany offered.

"No," Bijan said mundanely.

Chloe wandered around the large room, finding not one but many rooms exactly like the first. Lots of the coffins were glass and gold – she could see they were not Jane. She wondered if any would wake if they were sufficiently disturbed, or if they were awake truly, and were waiting until they were too deep in the tomb to escape. She found one doorway led to a room surrounded with water, with a coffin at the bottom of the pool. She raced back to the other two. "Guys, I think I found something!" she said excitedly, and led them to where she found the submerged coffin. "This is the one! Jane!" She stepped in the water, despite Bethany's protests. She descended, tried to bring the coffin up. She had to ascend to catch her breath. "It's heavy!"

"No kidding," Bethany said, taking off her hoody. Both stared at Bijan expectantly for him to take his shirt off.

"What are you two gawking at?" he asked, ignoring the cue and hopping into the water fully clothed. "Bethany, you stay up there and grab the top. Chloe, I'll gesture."

"I can't hold my breath forever, let's just do this," Chloe muttered at him.

It was heavy – Chloe knew Bijan was doing most of the work, and once they got to Bethany it became easier. Chloe coughed as they surfaced, and Bijan helped boost her out the side of the shallow pool.

Chloe used Bethany's hoodie as a towel but she still shivered. "What if that's not her?"

"I'm not going to be happy," Bijan said. "Break the lock, sorceress."

"Next time we get involved in the quest to save the multiverse," Bethany said to Chloe, "You tell me what supplies we're going to need before we go."

Chloe glanced at the giant backpack Bethany had at her back. She didn't ask what was in there. "Did you really think any sporting goods stores were going to be open around here?" Chloe asked Bethany.

Sighing, Bijan broke the lock with his sword, and opening the casket, they found a human-looking girl sleeping – she was dark haired, but it was not Jane. She held an impressive sword rather than a bouquet of flowers, and she dressed darkly – almost like one of the prince's guards, but different, her gown form fitting – almost like a high-paid ninja on her way to the ballet.

"I've seen this insignia before," Bijan said, kneeling. "I'll take the sword, though..."

"You already got one! I want one!" Bethany said, just before the young woman opened her eyes, and leaping up clear of the coffin, swung her blade at Bijan.

Chloe yelped and ran away. She heard Bijan parry from a safe distance away. "Stay your hand, girl, we freed you," he said, but the girl swung at him savagely. Bijan quickly disarmed her, knocking her sword to the ground.

"I am a master," she snapped. "I have been practicing with a blade for over twenty years." She took a long knife from a hidden place in her sleeve.

"You can challenge me again once you have been for over three hundred years," Bijan snapped back.

"Figures," she muttered lowly.

"Who are you?"

"I don't remember," she said. "The Younger Prince, he named me Wyvarre. Altroine, my master, he took my name, said I'd remember if I..." her eyes suddenly clouded. "You stand in my way!"

"How did you get in the coffin?"

"You waste my time!" the girl snapped. "If you are against the prince, you would not hinder me."

"You were imprisoned in this coffin, unnamed one," the prince said lowly.

"Is it safe?" Chloe called from the doorway.

"Yes," Bethany said.

Wyvarre stiffened, crossing her arms. "Time is short. I seek a mortal girl – to end her life, if need be."

"You're hunting Jane?" Bijan asked.

"Is she to be queen? Altroine would take her to walk the world of ours again. Altroine would be merciful. He rewards his servants."

"Altroine would be a monster," Bijan said. "I have heard of his cruelty – you cannot willingly serve him."

Wyvarre narrowed her eyes. "Altroine has promised me my freedom if I deliver the girl to him," she said. "Prince Altroine is the rightful ruler of this realm – the oldest of his bloodline, first born of the greatest king this realm has ever known. He will reward you if you help him."

"We're looking for Jane. She's somewhere in this tomb."

The girl nodded, and turning, ran from Bijan, past Chloe.

"What are you doing?" Bethany demanded.

"Using her to find Jane!" Chloe snapped, following after Wyvarre.

Wyvarre ascended a dark staircase and from her shadow, creatures emerged, passing through Chloe and causing chill to run up her arms. The figures weren't large, perhaps only her height, but wide, creeping as they skulked along the stone and traces of light, the pair moving around Bethany and tackling Bijan. The shadow creatures jumping in the water and dragged down Bijan. Chloe screamed, Bethany dove down after him, but the creatures had Bijan by both of his arms, and flew above the water, Bethany emerged, wet and shouting at Wyvarre for help. Bijan coughed, and tried to throw them off of him, but there was nothing physical for him to grab hold of.

"Let me go!" the prince snapped.

Bethany dove again and retrieved Bijan's sword. She tried to hand it to him, but the shadow creatures threw him across the room. One struck Bethany, knocking her sword clear across the room. "We have no quarrel with you, mortal," it said, its voice almost like a hundred different voices, male female, young, old; each cold and distant. "Leave us to our prey."

Chloe grabbed the cloak and turned herself into something with wings – a falcon, and she dove at the creatures with her talons, but they batted her away. She slammed against a grotesque gargoyle and fell to the ground, taking off the fur skin she became human again to see Bethany become the lizard-dragon mount beast again, but the shadow beasts turned from the two girls, their focus on Bijan. They were horrid – it was like a being of shadow and flame in one, skeletal-thin and pale-eyed, they combined to form one greater monster of shadow, making Bethany seem small and ridiculous in their presence. It roared at Bethany, and Bethany halted, genuine fear across her face. The being melted, and once again were two, but they multiplied again and were four.

"What are you?" Bethany asked.

"We are what you fear most. We are not here for you," one spoke, the same, strange voice, distant yet near. "He is ours." The one stood watch while the other three swarmed the prince.

"Girls! Run! You can't fight them!" Bijan screamed.

"We can't leave you!" Bethany snapped. "What are they?"

"I have no idea!"

Chloe didn't want to hear that – after three hundred years, he had to be familiar with just about every nasty trick this world could offer. "Bijan!"

"Go!"

The creatures were slow – they could be fast if they so chose, but their lingering essence worsened their presence as they carried Bijan from the room, deeper into the tomb.

"Bethany, what are those things?" Chloe asked, most of her wanting to run and abandon the prince.

"I don't know," Bethany said, taking off the fur, becoming herself again. "Wyvarre! Help us!" There was no reply. "It's like... something out of my worst nightmare!"

Chloe took the torch from the wall and led the charge, thinking of what Jane would do, followed after the creatures. Bethany sprinted behind Chloe, and they entered a room with a great mirror. The shadow creatures pulled Bijan towards it, though he dug his legs into the ground and tried to keep himself from moving, but the creatures entered it, and the last thing they saw was his boot as he was taken into the mirror.

"What sort of prince keeps getting himself captured, anyway?" Bethany demanded.

"So far it's just once more than you since you got here," Chloe said.

"He's been a prisoner here longer than either of us have been alive!" Bethany reminded her. "You'd think he'd be more help then something else for me to babysit."

It took Chloe a minute. "Hey!" Bethany ignored her, and they put the cloaks on again and became fierce dogs, and growling, they rushed towards the shadow creatures as they walked through the mirror. The girls slammed into the mirror one after another, yipping and yelping.

"Ow! Chloe, are you a poodle?"

"I wanted to be a pretty dog," Chloe admitted, pulling off the cloak and becoming herself. "Now what? How do we follow them?" She tapped the mirror, and her finger passed through it. "Okay, now why didn't that work before?"

Bethany became again a fearsome beast. It blocked her. "It must be because the cloak is faerie magic," she said, returning to her natural form. She put a foot through. She tried to bring the cloak through. It wouldn't move. "But... he was enchanted..."

"We used fae magic to break fae magic," Chloe sad. "I don't know – what I do know, is that we can't wait here and do nothing."

"A double negative should cancel that out."

"Shut up and come."

They piled the fur cloaks in the corner of the room. "On the count of three," Bethany said, facing the mirror. "One, two, three!" She sprinted.

Chloe hesitated, just in case it didn't work, but Bethany was gone. Taking a deep breath, Chloe put the flat of her hand against the glass, and fell forward, into the bleakest world she could have imagined.

"I told you on the count of three!" Bethany snapped at Chloe. "What's wrong with you?! You wanted me to get trapped in another dimension all by myself?"

"Sorry – I'm not as brave as you," Chloe said, scrunching her nose. "What is this place? It's like from a Tim Burton movie."

The sky was dark but there were no stars, no moon – the world seemed very cold, but Chloe could not bring herself to shiver. The ground they stood on was like hard rock, dark, the landscape incredibly vast but there seemed to be very little left of it – splinters of the ground seemed to be perpetually falling into the void surrounding them. There was no light, but a brown-green haze seemed to cover everything. Nothing grew here – nothing lived, truly. Everything was harsh rock, and she felt despair as she climbed to her feet.

There was only one castle in the world, and all roads led to it. It felt very wide and very small and cramped at the same time. Clearly, she wasn't the most athletic person in the world, and her idea of an adventure was going to a new restaurant or trying a different hairstyle. She looked at the castle. It was unlike the others – the others felt like they were part of a fairy tale – well, figure that one out – this world felt shallow, different. Real, maybe, at least compared to faerie land.

"I don't think we're in the fae world anymore."

"I guess that's where he is," Bethany said. "Look! Unicorns!"

The creatures were of the same shape and color as a unicorn, but as they neared, they couldn't be more different. Brilliantly white and silver, they radiated with shadow, their faces cruel and seeming more corporeal than solid, their manes flicked like fire and they dashed from the distance. They ran past the girls, almost trampling them as they thundered, the ground breaking beneath their cloven hooves.

"Those weren't unicorns," Bethany said.

"No kidding," Chloe rolled her eyes. "It's too bad we had to leave those cloaks behind. I would have liked to have flown to that castle. Think Wyvarre will find Jane?"

"I don't know," Bethany said.

As they walked, they came across a river. The water was dark, and they saw, submerged beneath the waves, humans, unicorns, dragons. All, petrified, stone creatures, but as they looked to the deep they saw their own reflections.

Bethany saw her manuscripts being thrown out of the editor's office – laughing. Her plays performed, to a laughing, jeering crowd. She saw herself – married to a sports-obsessed man, changing diapers with curlers in her hair when she should have been working on her screenplay.

"How horrible!" Chloe said, looking at her life. "I would never wear orange to grad! Blagh!"

"Chloe, look at this," Bethany said, leaving the river and walking towards a grotesque stone monument. "Welcome – this is the place dreams come to die. Is the 'Welcome' necessary?"

"Oh, as if I'd ever buy a Hyundai..."

"Chloe! Focus!" Bethany said. "Look... we need to either go rescue Bijan, or leave, save Jane, and come back for him later. I don't like this place. I think Bijan would agree stopping Prince Fairy-Pants takes priority."

"I could never be a dog-groomer! What? I might be like, twenty-two and you mean to tell me I'm NOT MARRIED YET???"

"Chloe!"

Hands of stone shot up from the rock and grabbed Bethany's ankles. She called out and tried to turn but the hands held her steady, as a giant stone man emerged from the ground, holding her upside-down. Bethany looked to its wide features and saw the expression slowly move from blank to pleased. "Run!" Bethany shouted. Chloe was already doing so, but stone men emerged from the rock just as quickly, and one grabbed Chloe. They wasted no time in binding their arms behind their backs with stone shackles and blinding them.

A woman's voice said, "Take them to the Queen."

"Who are you?" Bethany asked, but they were silently led away.

~*~

Bijan was brought in unshackled to the throne room of the dark castle, and as he was thrown down his captors faded out of existence in bursts of smoke. Nothing about the world was kind, instead, it sapped his hope that there was any hope of escape. There were many seats – most were simple, though many chairs, and most were vacant, encircling the room. Bijan faced instead a cruel-looking chair that was occupied, dark-hooded figures at her side.

She was undoubtedly a beautiful woman – tall and slender, her hair dark blonde and her eyes cold and grey, she looked down upon him with disdain. "I don't know who you are," he said, relying on his memories of his royal heritage that allowed him to command, and this woman, no doubt a queen, would know she was dealing with an equal, "but if you are enemies with the Prince of the Realm of the Fae, you would do well to release me."

"Are you sure you wish to look upon him in this form?" the sharp-featured woman asked. "I would have him drowned in the river."

The Queen did not move her head, but Bijan knew she spoke to the woman on her left. The dark-clad figure turned, the bottom of her face visible. Bijan's heart raced. "Shakilah?" he asked, standing.

The face he'd thousands of times in his nightmares, knowing he'd failed her. "They said you were dead..." his wife was dressed like the other women of this realm were – dark lace covered their necks to their wrists and their boots. His wife was not a beauty among their people, but this world had managed to bring out her most regal features. She looked at him, her face firm and uncaring. "Shakilah, my love!" he cried, moving towards her.

"Love?" she asked, and he stopped. "You dare say that word to me?" She strode towards him. "All these years I have enjoyed watching you suffer." She looked him in the eyes – gone was the comely, humble woman who he had been betrothed to. She was defiant and cruel. "Or do you forget the charms of the harlot you succumbed to?" she laughed, and as she peeled back the hood, her face changed – to that of fuller cheeks and the tongue of whispered promises from centuries past. "Do you have any idea how much I enjoyed watching her nightmares, watching her charms succumb to age and time?" She aged before him. She struck out a hand – and he saw at once the beautiful young woman age before him, until she all but died before him. She melted back to the princess he married.

"I have done you great wrong," he said, dropping to his knees. "I beg your forgiveness." He knew it was unmanly to weep, but surely that would move her to see he was at least genuine. "I have done to you what no man should do to any woman, much less his wife-"

She struck him across the face. "Death is too good for him. Set him to slumber! Dream of what could have been, and know I despise you all the more for it!"

"Shakilah!" he called as the shadow beasts materialized and grabbed his arms. "My friends will come!" he snapped, as stone golems entered, bringing with them blind-folded and bound teenagers. "Wait!" he called. "What will you do to them?"

"Bijan, is that you?" Bethany asked.

"Told you we should have rescued Jane first," Chloe said.

The stone beasts removed the blinders, and Chloe almost gasped when they looked about the dreary castle. She looked back at Bijan, then at the queen. "We've come for our friend."

"We are aware of your quest, Chloe and Bethany Pelshmidt," said the seated woman. "Welcome, to the land of dreams."

"Uh... good or bad?" Bethany asked rhetorically.

"Is Candy Land a real place too?" Chloe asked.

"We've come for Bijan," Bethany said. "Please, we don't have much time..."

"We are aware of your quest, Chloe," said the eldest of the assembled. "And we support you."

"Are you like, the Unseelie court?" Bethany asked.

"I have told you, this is the Land of Dreams," said the elder woman. "Both good, and bad."

"I'm not feeling the good vibrations," Bethany said.

"Our land is governed by the hopes of those who dream," said one of the dark-clad women, who continued to hide her face. "Pleasant or terrifying, mortals and immortals all dream. The dreams of those who know Prince Nyveo's rise to power show this world to be in shadow. We do not wish to be overrun in terror."

The queen nodded. "This realm relies on eternal balance – hope and sorrow, joy and regret. Too much of one would lead to our destruction, for when nightmares become real, the terrors we keep imprisoned become unleashed." A low roar was heard from the distance.

"If this is the world of dreams, we can kind of expect a good one, maybe? Maybe some sort of avenging angel or hero?" she asked hopefully.

"It doesn't work like that," the queen said. "Dreams inspire. Both good and bad. We must have bad with the good." She looked to the masked figures around her. "We found his wife suffering all sorts of memories. She is one of our finest weavers of terror."

Hairs rose on the back of Chloe's neck at the mention of the weavers. "Not like, those spider women..."

"Arachne, and her sisters," Shakilah said. "They wove the truth in tapestries, and for it, were punished. I weave lies, and for it, I am rewarded. Please, take him away."

"Wait!" Bethany said. "We need his help. Please, if you ever loved him..." Bethany stopped, staring into Shakilah's eyes. She fell back in terror, suddenly, and she backed up from Shakilah.

"I warned you – I weave nightmares," Shakilah said, bowing her head and closing her eyes. "You must hurry if you wish to save Jane. The prince has her under a spell – for now, it is all balls and finery, in a mist she doesn't know – soon, the spiced cakes will turn to ash in her mouth, and the beautiful becomes into the grotesque. She will be bound to sit and see everything around her turn to horrr, and she will be helpless." A single tear escaped her eye. She looked at Bijan.

"If I could take it back, I would," he said quietly. "Shakilah... there is no apology I could make, no action I could do that would redeem myself in your eyes... I thought you were dead! I thought you were gone from me forever, please, show me the terror in your eyes-!" She caught his gaze. Chloe and Bethany watched silently as he began to sweat – as fear took his body, but he did not look away. It was Shakilah that broke their gaze.

"Take him away!"

"No!" Bijan struggled against the monsters, but was taken from the throne room. The girls tried to follow, but the same monstrous creatures appeared before them, blocking them from following after Bijan.

"You must hurry, if you're to save Jane," said the strange blonde woman. "You have no further business in this realm."

"Why do you want us to save her?" Bethany asked. "Don't give me the crap about balance. Do you not want competition for creating nightmares?"

The woman looked solemn. "You assume much for a mortal who has only lived a few short years."

Bethany was frightened, but she stood her ground. "You think you can judge him to have him suffer eternally? I've only known him for a few hours but he's been suffering for three hundred years – and will it please her, to know that he has no end of terror? Where is your balance?"

"Child, you do not understand," the woman said simply, putting her hand out. "Away with you, and consider yourselves lucky to leave; most who venture into this world descend into madness."

At once the world around them moved – at least, that was the way it felt, until their stomachs had a chance to catch up with them. The girls were thrown back to the dark grounds, before the mirror that they entered into the world of dreams. Chloe felt nausea.

"So... that's it?" Bethany asked. "We leave him?"

"I don't know," Chloe said. "We don't have much time. We need to save Jane. She was never in the crypt. Sunsoar was wrong." Tears filled her eyes. They went back through the portal, and found that their cloaks had vanished and, despite leaving the world of terror, the nightmare hadn't ended.

~*~

The monsters chained Bijan's hands to a rock before the void. He thought they would make him sleep or perhaps drown him in a river of misery, but instead the grotesque beasts disappeared. He struggled against the chains – chains that, were he the monster he'd been for most of his life, he could have easily snapped. He did not keep from weeping, staring at the void. "Where is your balance?" he asked himself, staring out into the world, before bowing his head. "I deserve all of this, and worse."

As he stared into the void, he saw again, as if through the eyes of an insect, the spoiled young prince he was – how cruel he was to his younger brothers, how arrogant he was in his studies. Every short coming in his life came streaming back, to see the young arrogance of a prince who thought he was entitled to the world, he hated his betrothed because she wasn't as fair as he thought he deserved – how she tried to be polite and please him, how she never could. How he succumbed to the charms of a woman who didn't love him. He wept. "When you have been here a century or more," said one of the dark-hooded women, "You shall be part of this world. You shall aid in nightmares, for you have known pure humiliation for your actions. You will suffer the terror so that others – like the many you have wronged, will no."

"Is she here because of me?" he asked. The woman was silent. "Let her go! She doesn't deserve to dwell in sorrow and regret!" In the void, Shakilah stood before him, fragmenting away, falling into the void.

He roared and was once again the beast – the minotaur. The creatures of shadow and flame appeared, but he batted them away. They came first one at a time, but then by the dozens, until all the world was the shadow and darkness. Bijan struck them down, but for every one he slew or flung into the abyss, Shakilah became further and further away. "I will never stop looking for you!"

She turned, the terror gone from her eyes, she strode towards him, stroked his furry snout and horns. Only his mind was whole, he was the beast. "Find me, please," she said, weeping.

The world fell away in brilliant light. Bijan sat up, in the tomb, before the mirror, which was shattered and the pieces lay all around him.

He climbed to his feet in the darkness – his human feet, complete with human strength and weakness. "Chloe? Sorceress?" he called, bumping his leg against a crypt in the darkness. But because it was a magical realm, and his eyes adjusted to the dark, he was able to navigate. He knew now why the prince had made him so large and powerful – he would not fit through the crypt doorway. He went through coffin and monument, searching. Until at last he found her – his princess, his wife.

She lay asleep, in a modest dress of harsh white fabric, her hair her pillow, laid out, a single black rose in her clasped hand. She rose to life when his lips touched hers. "I knew you'd never give up," she said, and he gathered her in his arms. "I dreamed... I became..." she wept. "I had no idea my dreams could pull you in."

"I'm glad they did. I found you," he said. "Can you forgive me?"

She nodded. "You must go, and help them."

Bijan held his wife close. "I have been searching for you three hundred years. They are a sorceress and... I don't even know, but the task is theirs. We are together again. I'm sorry it took this long."

For a moment, they were tempted to lay down together in the coffin – to dream and be together, in dreams of a life that could have been or perhaps terror, to let the spell take them both. Nyveo was ready to be crowned, afterall – in all likelihood, it was already too late. They could have dreamed together – in a field of bliss or perhaps they would be weave terror, but they would be together. And that, it seemed, was enough. But instead Bijan carried her from the coffin, back towards the light. "For three hundred years, we've been prisoners," she said quietly. "Where are we to go? Back to the worlds of men? You would not recognize the world we left behind. I'm afraid of the place it will become."

"My place is by your side," Bijan said quietly. "That is enough."

19

The Crowned

Nyveo I, The Youngest Prince of the Realm of the Fae, stood before a mirror, and the tailor finished the last thread. "Shall we retrieve your queen for the ceremony?" Moaz asked, ruining the moment.

The prince looked in the mirror. He thought himself the spitting image of his father – at least the part of a king. "The armies gathering?"

"Even now the gryphons and dragons are pouring in – even the unicorns have grown bold as to come. They still gather. Shall we launch an offensive before, or after your wedding, my prince?"

"King."

"In all due respect," said Moaz, bowing low, "you have not yet been crowned. You are the greatest in this realm, of that, none can deny. You are still not yet King."

"This kingdom has been without a king long enough. Leave my queen where she is - "

"My prince," the fae said, "you would be better to marry the mortal now, to have opened the doorway back to earth, and through earth, we might enter all the other realms. Please, reconsider."

The prince held the staff in his hands. "I need no wife to be king," he said. "I have my father's birthright – I have proven myself greater than his brothers, of any of my bloodline. It all shall be done as tradition demands so that none may say that I am unworthy of my claim." The prince snorted. "Is everything ready?"

"Yes. You waste too much time if we are to wait until night to come again for the wedding."

Nyveo looked up to the picture of his father, Kylreas – regal and handsome, he was older than his son when he took the crown, and had to defeat his monstrous brothers to hold the title. He readied his servants and entered his throne room, dry now, embellished as his servants had worked through the night making ready the preparations. There was no sun in his realm – no light to govern the day, no longer did the three moons watched over the night, but the King could control the kingdom – bring back the stars. He looked to the officient, the eldest of his race. His beautiful princesses waiting alongside the newly woken court. He wanted the ceremony to be grand – knew that more dragons would come, that the wedding would be a spectacle.

Instead he kept with tradition, kept it brief, and when the silver crown wrought with leaves and rubies, garnets and the heads of stags was laid upon his brow, he stood, facing his realm. He felt the power of the kingdom lay down before the one who bore the staff. He closed his eyes, felt the world acknowledge and obey its king.

~*~

Henry Pelshmidt, self-professed warlock and ambassador for Earth, who had up until that point of his life defined himself by being an accountant of the chartered type, could not for the life of him keep in order the amount of gryphons, eastern-style dragons, and unicorns that all assembled on the floating island, and seemingly kept arguing about which course to maintain. There were of course, denizens from other worlds as well (he for one could not see why Unicorns and dragons could not coexist in what he could only describe as fluffy-cloud heaven) but they were in the minority. Still, at least one phoenix went through a rebirth. He wished he'd brought his GoPro.

Henry was partial to the dragons of the western-variation, but there being none of their sort whatsoever, he was most enchanted with the gryphons. They ranged in size, some were a deep roan red while others black as shadows and others white, while others were speckled or striped in variations common to owls and falcons.

The dragons were out of a living tapestry. They would take the form of humans, but when he stood next to them, they were quite different in stature and manner. Both dragons and gryphons were arguing against the unicorns, who generally wanted to charge in and take the castle by force.

One magnificent creature, who was darker than night and with a golden horn crowning him, spoke on behalf of the unicorns.

"Too long have we stood by and done nothing," said the unicorn.

"The prince wishes for us to attack him rashly," said a great gold and purple dragon. "He knows that if we attack him separately, we will fall like waves upon the rock."

"We were foolish to listen to the wisdom of dragons," said a magnificent mahogany gryphon, "who let the threat grow until it is too late. We should have destroyed this realm years ago! Now we are to leave earth to suffer the same fate. It too must be sealed before they break through."

"The fae destroy worlds, not us," said another dragon, this one red and gold, "There is time still."

"The Empress could not destroy him..." said the black unicorn.

"It was not for The Empress to kill him," a purple and gold dragon snapped at the unicorn. "We had hoped that he would have become a king worthy of the throne of this world. You cannot so easily cast judgement on an entire race."

Henry Pelshmidt stood, looking over the expanse of strange worlds that shouldn't technically be existing. He wondered where his daughter was – if she'd any luck finding Jane. His thoughts changed abruptly when the sky brightened, and a great sun appeared in the sky – and just as quick, it set over the land, and three brilliant moons appeared in the darkness, with stars speckling, almost heralding the night.

"That's not possible," Henry said.

"He's been crowned," said a silver unicorn, warning in his voice.

"Did he make a sun, or did he transport us to a star? Scientifically..."

"Warlock Henry Pelshmidt," the purple dragon said, "you can do no more here. We must be ready our attack."

"My daughter isn't back yet."

The old dragon looked not to the sky, but away from the castle so many of the other creatures looked towards – to the far reaches of the world. Henry followed his gaze to the distant expanse of fake forests, which began to fall, but soon Henry could sense a terrible bleakness, when the trees no longer fell but vanished. "What is going on?" Henry Pelshmidt asked.

"He's umaking the world," the dragon said, "likely, he thinks to bring parts of yours back with him."

Henry looked to the ancient dragon, who watched soberly as the world around them fell into darkness. "What was the point of the sun and stars?"

"Proving his dominion," the dragon turned away. "we can delay no further – we must attack the castle now."

"More of my kin are coming!" roared another dragon.

"As are mine," said a speckled gryphon.

"There is no more time. This world has seen its last morning," the dragon said. "Human, stay with Sunsoar. We go now to do what we should have done centuries ago. If there is time, we might yet be able to save this world."

"But, my daughter-!"

"We do this so that no other parent might know your loss."

Henry was about to argue, but the magical creatures began to lift off. He looked away – the world was falling into a void. He wanted to cry out, but the gryphon Sunsoar nuzzled his hand. "They will try to destroy the palace and kill the king. You are fortunate your daughter is such a powerful sorceress. We must fly, now, warlock."

He'd seen worlds from the back of a gryphon – celestial heavens and the rocky Eyries overlooking glistening seas and the gossamer plains. He knew at once that this was faerie land and it was dying – and looking over his shoulder, saw the great floating castle crash at last into the void that consumed the land.

~*~

Chloe rushed from the tomb. "Sedolei, did you see-?" she stopped, seeing his ears twitching, looking away from her. She followed his gaze and saw day turn into night just as quickly. "What is happening?"

"The King is crowned during the day – the royl wedding takes place at night," the unicorn said. "I... I feel... strange..."

Bethany ran up the steps. "Sedolei, did Chloe say that Jane's not..." she looked up. "Woah..."

They looked to the east - sky was thick with serpent-like dragons and gryphons, and she could hear the distant thundering of unicorn hooves. While it they came, they heard stirring from inside the crypt from which they were just in.

"To the castle! Quick! The King is unmaking the kingdom, do not be caught outside!" said a voice from deep within.

Bethany stood, watching the dragons and gryphons. "It's too late, it's over," she said, trying not to weep.

"I'm not giving up!" Chloe snapped at Bethany. She mounted Sedolei. "Come on!"

Bethany looked at her, but the unicorn looked back at Chloe. "No... we must warn them!"

"Warn them what?"

"That they're flying into a trap," said the unicorn. "Can't you feel it?"

Chloe looked back towards the castle – at first she saw nothing, but then, from Sedolei's back, she could see something – she wasn't sure what – surrounding the castle. "He protects the air around the castle, my brothers and sisters run, but they will leap when they near it. They must be warned!" He stepped towards the dragons.

"I'll tell them," Bethany said. "You have to go save Jane."

"How will they see you?" Chloe asked.

Bethany took off her backpack. "Fireworks."

Chloe didn't want to ask. "You just happened to have bought fire-works..."

"I can't buy them - I made 'em at home. Youtube. Don't look at me like that. I'll be right behind you – can they enter the castle by ground?"

"For the time being," the unicorn said. "Good luck, sorceress!" with that, he carried Chloe off towards the castle.

Bethany knew she didn't have much time – it would have been better to set off her home made pyrotechnics at night at any rate, but she couldn't wait for the night to be high. She thought of what night also meant. She released the first – a bit of a dud, admittedly – but the second and the third drew attention to herself, but from the fae coming from the crypt. One handsome sidhe came up behind her. "Hello, human. What brings you to this realm?"

Bethany wished she'd remembered Jane's brother's baseball bat at such a time – it didn't do that much good earlier, but it made her feel better. There were a score of them – most were on their way to the castle, but several looked at her not unlike how a zombie would contemplate its next meal.

She pointed a homemade firecracker at the one nearest her, and put her thumb on the lighter. "I'm warning you," she said, "I have a great and powerful magic not to be underestimated."

The fae laughed, but around that time, a brilliant golden gryphon dove down, as did several dragons and a wyvern. It would have been amazing, were her father not involved. "Hi sweetie!"

"Daddy, I'm a sorceress! You are so embarrassing!!" Bethany wailed. "Oh, by the way, trap." She pointed up towards the sky, where several dragons had already been stunned, sent to the ground in their weaker human forms.

"Oh no!" Several of the gryphons tore off into the sky, to warn the rest of the flying army. Sunsoar bounded ahead on foot with the others, though they moved slow enough that Bethany was able to catch up with them. They found several of the dragons, reduced in their magic to shells of themselves as they lay sprawled in human form. One young dragon, who looked like a formidable warrior, said, "He protects the castle... you must go forward, on foot. Hurry," he said to Sunsoar, "there isn't much time."

A gryphon scooped Bethany up and the army of gryphons raced towards the castle. She looked over her shoulder, seeing at last the armies descend rather than flying too close, where the prince's magic would knock them down and reduce them magically. She wondered if there was another sort of spell waiting for them, but as the darkness overtook the kingdoms, and the three moons grew full in might and majesty, she thought she saw the castle shrink.

It happened very quickly. She was not the first person to approach the hole in the world where the castle was. She thought it was cheating if he teleported away at the last minute – what with the world falling apart behind them. Several unicorns had beaten them, by that time, to the crater – the magical denizens looked into the darkness. Bethany saw a light. Her dad got off Sunsoar, and climbed down the slopes, towards the solid crystal ball. She followed, not to be outdone by her warlock-father. He stopped before the beautiful crystal ball – Bethany thought it was some sort of snowglobe, until she saw very faintly, inside, movement. Her father took the crystal ball back to the dragons and gryphons.

One of the elder dragons took human form, and he took the ball from Henry Pelshmidt. "He has locked his castle inside this orb," he announced. "We must fly, now, before the world is unmade."

"Where's Chloe and Sedolei?" Bethany asked. The magical creatures said nothing to her. She felt the world beneath her crying out – the cruelty of a king destroying what he had taken, and although the creatures had already taken to flight, and one tried to save her, they were too late. The kingdom fell apart, and Bethany fell into the void that the King of the Fae had created.

~*~

The King of The Realm, Nyveo I, felt the darkness of night cover the kingdom, and, knowing that he would rebuild it soon enough, left nothing to chance. The creatures from other worlds had no right to tell him how his kingdom should be run. The King felt the cries as dragon, gryphon and unicorn fell into the abyss, the nothingness that awaited them. They could not outrun it. Once he felt a stillness, he knew that the only thing that remained of his realm was his castle – were those inside the walls that were loyal to him.

He stood from his silver throne, his court bowing, most trembled. Several had pleaded for their kin to be woken, but he assured them he would restore them and the world once he was finished his task. If his uncles had any remnant power to stop the nothingness from overtaking their respective castles.

He raised his silver staff, showing The Empress the darkness. "This castle will remain. I shall merge the worlds, soon enough." His coronation over, Nyveo nodded to his men. "Prepare the wedding ceremony. I shall go and retrieve my bride."

He walked swiftly, feeling what little of the world around him remaining crying out. He had told his subjects that they would merely sleep – he would take great pains to restore the kingdom to its former glory. Nyveo went to his chambers, and, checking himself in the mirror, looking the part of the king, stood before the portrait of his beautiful mortal queen.

Putting his hands on the portrait, before putting his hand through it, he grasped his mortal bride's hand, warm, however enchanted, and pulled her out of the picture. She stepped through – a vision in her white, silver and gold dress, edged with the hint of scarlet that represented her mortality. He took the silver mask and put it on her face – it melted in with her skin, were she not enchanted, the mask would render her silent. The spell would wear off and give her back her mind in time, and she could see – she was fortunate he was so kind.

He took her from the room, to where his subjects were waiting outside the court room. His People, most would still be waking, were they not discarded, would be amazed at the attendance of court – so many had woken from the beds they slept in the palace for the engagement ball. They looked as formidable as they did, centuries before, when he put them to sleep.

"We are ready," he said. The officiator nodded, and the king closed his eyes, listening to the music of the final ceremony begin. The officiator moved first towards the throne. The fae who had crowned him turned.

Each of his princesses walk towards the throne, each wearing the same variation of the same dress, each one could have been the queen, if someone had never seen her. He smiled to himself, knowing that for all their beauty, they would be mere trinkets to the creatures he would take for himself once he was lord of the earth.

His beautiful Ladies were not half-way down the court when a mortal in a beautiful dress attacked the procession. She drew blood on her first strike – the beautiful princesses closest to her fell, one clutched her bloodied arm as they scrambled, and the girl moved forward as the royal guards attacked. His court did nothing to protect their future queen.

King Nyveo's reaction was to strike her down with the staff, but instead he marched towards her, sword drawn. Only his queen remained standing still – the spell singled her out, but before the assassin could strike, Nyveo met her blade.

"Wyvarre," he said, "do you remember how this ended last time?"

She pushed him off and dove backwards, grabbing the wounded princess and putting the sword to her throat. "I'll kill her. I'll kill all of them to get to you."

"My Prince... my king... please..." the princess wailed.

"I am King, and you are wasting my time." He drew back his sword but instead he moved his left hand with his staff, turning the assassin into stone.

"You..." his princess began, but the spell began to consume her as well. "No! Save me!"

He turned, facing the officiator. He glanced back, and his beautiful injured princess was a cowering statue. He walked back to Titalia, and took her arm in his. "Now, let us continue."

They walked to the end of the court, pausing before the steps leading to his throne and they knelt. He felt his kingdom cry out though he kept his hand firm, as their hands were bound in ribbon, hers in his. "Arise, King Nyveo," said the officiant, "And crown your queen."

Nyveo stood, taking the crown in one hand, he bade his queen to stand. He helped her rise to the steps, and had her sit on the throne. She began to change, as did the throne, almost as if she became a living sculpture. Silver vines came from the throne, wrapping around her wrists, binding her to the throne of silver. He put the silver crown upon her head.

"Seal the marriage with a kiss, My King," the officiant said.

Nyveo almost did not feel her breath as he bent down. "I have waited so long," he said, "I do find you pleasing when you are obedient," he said with a smile. Her expression remained frozen until a voice broke the silence.

"JANE!"

The voice rang through the court like a thunderbolt through a clear sky. He saw the queen's brown eyes flicker – but the vines wound tighter around her, and she stiffened.

"You're too late," The King said to the girl riding the unicorn. "We are married. You have no armies left. They have all fallen, and I am a god in this realm."

~*~

Chloe wrapped her fingers into the soft beautiful hair of Sedolei's mane. There was something to be said for a flashy entrance, and riding on a rearing unicorn had to count for something. The scene was as she expected – beautiful fae stood watching the marriage of the king to her best friend who, looked really dazed. "Let her go!"

Small pixies and fae guards moved towards her, but Sedolei charged down the aisle. The prince used the staff and the unicorn bucked, throwing Chloe forward. When she looked back, she saw a magnificent marble statue of the unicorn rearing on two legs.

"Did you really think you could stop me?" Nyveo asked, standing between Chloe and Jane. "It is a pity." He walked towards Chloe gingerly, the silver staff in his grip.

Chloe sprinted towards her best friend but he grabbed her arm as she tried to run past him, trying to grab hold of Jane. "I'm sorry! Jane, you hear me? I'm sorry!" she squeaked the last part out, tears running down her face. "I'm sorry!!!"

Her prince walked her to the foot of the steps, to the guards, who grabbed her when he threw her aside. "I would turn you to stone for this insolence, but I think having you watch would lead to the most fitting punishment. I shall turn you into something in the morning – perhaps a nightingale, and you can sing to the queen for all time. If you'll excuse me," he said, turning, "I'm going to go kiss my bride. I think I shall bring you back with me to your world, Chloe. I shall tell them who made this day possible."

Nyveo walked back to his imprisoned queen. "Now, where were we?" he asked, but as he leaned in to kiss her, he realized that the mask was missing. She met his eyes and turned her head, smiling.

"I believe I was just about to kick your butt," Jane said. He reached for the staff to find she had it in her hands already, and the silver vines had come undone. The King drew sword and went to threaten her with it, but The Staff reacted stronger to its master – to the mortal that had earned it, obeying the law of her birthright. Better to kill her then let her have the power, he went to run her through but the power of the staff enveloped Jane, knocking the King of the Faeries backwards, down the steps. The world obeyed its queen – and, ruled by the night, crowned without the consummation, Nyveo shielded his face as the power flowed through the mortal queen.

Nyveo grabbed Chloe, put a sword to her throat. "Stop! Submit to me now, or she dies!"

The court began to rain. It was a shimmering light shower at first, but then the downpour began. Nyveo had only the power to shield himself and Chloe from getting wet. The Ancient Dragon stood beside the queen of the realm. "Thank you for freeing me," The Empress snapped at Jane, though her eyes were on Nyveo. "You should have done that first."

Jane looked at the King of the realm. "You were a fool to crown me Queen – and you cannot compete with both myself and The Empress. It is over, Nyveo. Give up now, and I shall leave you to this kingdom."

"No one commands a king," Nyveo snapped. "What sort of love broke your spell, when your inactions killed your greatest friend?"

Chloe called out as he impaled her with his sword. She felt no pain at first, just coldness, then weakness. She struggled to stay awake. The King of the Realm ran towards Jane but the kingdom bowed to the mastery of the staff – the staff she bore, and time stood still – only Jane, the Empress, the King, and Chloe moved.

Jane rushed to Chloe, took her friend in her arms. "It's going to be okay." Chloe said. She didn't exaggerate – somehow, she knew. "I... I'm not dying?" Chloe asked.

"This is a magical Faerie Kingdom," Jane said defiantly, looking at Nyveo. "A world that obeys its queen."

Nyveo turned to the gaping jaws of the dragon. He struck back, using his power as the dragon encircled him, snared him, but the prince broke free. "I am King," he said lowly, putting his hand out for the Staff. "It is my birthright!"

Chloe saw Jane grip the staff tight in her fingers. Chloe wondered how much power Jane had – if the queen was really the king's equal. "You would carry on and destroy your own world?!" Jane asked.

The prince halted his attack. The rains became heavier, and the sound of distant thunder made what remained of the realm tremble. "What other way is there? Mortality, which leads to death and oblivion? You mortals claim to speak fair, but you would do the same as I have. Any of you would, if given half the chance." He summoned the power, Chloe saw the staff in Jane's hands grow bright. "And why should I let what is mine fall into the hands of anyone else?"

Chloe blinked, feeling the world pulse with power. And in an instant, it was gone – the castle, the prince, the dragon. Everything.

But she was still with Jane. Jane held her, and Chloe felt the wound heal over. Light came back, and with that, the rains began to fall, and the world breathed itself back to life. She thought she heard singing. The white and blue dragon flew from the castle. Chloe felt her abdomen. The hole was gone – there wasn't even a mark on her dress. "Where... where is he?"

"He tried to destroy the world, rather than let me try to save it," Jane said. "I... I don't know. Perhaps he destroyed himself as well, but, I felt him... escape." Jane said. "It's... it's difficult to understand." She looked pale. Chloe stood and helped her walk.

Chloe wiped at her face, but still quietly wept. "They're all gone," she said, looking around the empty castle. "Bijan, Sedolei, Bethany..."

"No, they're not," Jane said. "They were just sleeping."

A crooning roar was heard. The girls sped from the room, as a multitude of creatures entered to find the castle empty, missing its enchanted faerie inhabitants. "What has happened?" one brilliant black and white gryphon asked the girls. "Where is the Empress?"

"She flew outside," Chloe said. She and Jane ran outside. Jane might have saved the world, but it was dark and grey– nothing grew, beyond rock and stone. The floating castle was gone, as were the distant towns they had seen earlier. It was so different than the beautiful forests, mountains and lakes both girls had seen earlier.

The sky clouded over, and started to rain. Jane and Chloe could see, from a distance, the hedges growing back quickly. "She's... I'm not sure what she's doing," Jane said.

The unicorns and gryphons slowed, while the dragons conversed in the air. Bethany looked overwhelmed, but she ran and knocked over the other two in a hug. "I'm so glad you guys are okay! What happened? Where's the prince?"

"He disappeared," Chloe said.

Jane nodded. "He went to destroy the kingdom if he could not have it, and our world. I think he might have destroyed himself, but..." she looked sadly over the kingdom. A pixie sparkled by her ear. She looked at Bethany and smiled. "The fae... they're waking too."

Bijan and Shakilah rushed over. "You did it!" the prince said, picking up Jane and giving her a twirling bear hug.

"Uh, who are you?" Jane asked.

"Oh, right," Bijan said. After some explaining, Jane's smile was beaming. "It's nice to meet you, Princess Shakilah." She bowed her head.

The woman nodded her head, but rested it on Bijan's broad shoulder. "I am pleased you were able to defeat him."

Bethany's father followed behind shortly after. "Where are all the fae?" he asked.

"How many times are we going to have to repeat this story?" Jane asked Chloe.

"As many times as need be," Chloe said to Jane.

"It does feel like it's been going on too long," Bijan said, sighing. Shakilah squeezed his hand. "I thought I would have to be the one to face him, when all was said and done with. You impressed me – both – all of you."

Jane looked strange as she wielded the power of Silver – no longer human, but not fae, either – but she called all the power back. She smiled at Chloe, and the two began to giggle. "What is with that heart-themed dress you're wearing?" Jane asked. "You are so lame."

"I'm the one who's lame?" Chloe asked, before walking over and tripping on the steps. The two burst out into laughter.

"Woweee, the power of friendship saved the day," Bethany said lamely. "I was expecting something more... *original.*"

Jane sobered up considerably, and, running a hand through her hair, she walked to the balcony, looked up at the sky, then said, "Empress? Uh, can you take the form of Winkie? She's the least intimidating."

The Empress appeared human, as did a tall man by her side. "Please don't bring that up. Jane, meet my son."

"It is an honour, Faerie Queen," sad her son, bowing. He was not as young looking as Jane expected him to be – she wondered how very old the Empress must be. "May you rule this land as a fair and just queen."

"Huh?" Chloe asked as the dragons, gryphons and unicorns bowed.

"You have mastery of the staff, Jane," said the Empress. "It is up to you to rule this country wisely."

"Awesome! Jane, I want a holiday named after me!" Bethany hollered.

Jane looked the Empress in the eye. "I remember what you said," she said. "Can you destroy the staff?"

"Myself no," she said, "but, you are in the company of many powerful beings. This company can unmake it."

Bethany ran up to Jane. "Think about this carefully, Queenie – you're in charge of fairy land – you never grow up, you have zero responsibility..."

"I want to grow up," Jane said. "Well, not get old, but you know what I mean. I don't even have a high school diploma – as if I can rule a magical kingdom." She looked over, smiled at Bijan. "How long have you been here?"

"Lady Jane, you can't be serious," Bijan said. "I am as human as you."

"You've been here a long time. You've lived in this one longer then our world. I think you can do it."

"I was a stupid boy who hurt the person I should have loved most and I abandoned my kingdom," Bijan said.

"You left to find her. You spent centuries as a monster, prince Bijan. I think you can now rule as a man."

One of the unicorns looked thoughtful. "Humans on a magic throne? Well, it worked for Narnia..."

Shakilah bowed her head, and took Bijan's hand. "There are many who do not belong back on earth," she said. "We will do our best, we wish to know more about our... subjects. We cannot control such creatures who have magic if we ourselves do not."

"This kingdom bows to its king and queen," said the Empress. "And besides, we have vested interest to see a world restored, rather than destroyed. Would you sit on the throne, and be just rulers? It would be good, I think, to have a real prince and princess who know the horrors of this world to guard it against future travesties."

"But what about Nyveo?" Jane asked. "I don't know where he is. What if he's gone to earth?"

"He will hide for a century or two, no doubt," The Empress said. "I rest knowing full well that humanity continues to surprise us."

"We dragons shall guard this realm," said the old purple and gold dragon.

"We shall see its majesty restored," said a black gryphon.

"I'm in so long as I don't have to sit on a committee," a unicorn added briskly.

The dragons began to sing, and with them, the unicorns joined in, and the gryphons bowed their heads and beat their wings. With the song of unmaking the staff disappeared from the hands of the new King and Queen of Faerieland, and the grasses began to grow.

Very, very slowly.

"Alright, girls," Henry Pelshmidt said, "time to get you home before your mothers murder me."

"Come on Dad, can't we go save another world? I'm sure the dragons are having some sort of trouble somewhere across the universe..."

"Get going."

20

Return

While most of the mortals who had lived longer in the realm of the fae chose to stay, several wanted to return to earth. Henry Pelshmidt helped one girl get in contact with her family, going so far as to book her a plane ticket to get her back home in Ontario.

Hyralie had nowhere to go. So, she went back with the girls, and became a foreign exchange student. The dragons knew something about forging documents, and while no one wanted to condone illegal immigration, it was the easiest course of action.

Hyralie - *Hilary* looked like a teenager – a worried looking one. "Come on," Bethany said as the four walked together for their first day back at school. "Oak Park's not so bad."

"Will they like me?" Hilary asked quietly.

"What's not to like?" Bethany asked. "Come on." She grabbed her arm and dragged her off, talking about how lame it was to come back after a century to the land of mortals and be forced to go to high school, as if the dragons could forge some things but not others.

Chloe and Jane pretended to be busy chatting with one another as they walked towards the school. People stopped talking, staring at them. Bethany was only gone for a few hours – not that anyone would notice if she was gone for a week – but the two felt having to deal

288

with their social peers less threatening then anything else they'd gone up against.

"Hey," Trevor said, walking in front of them before they got through the doors. "Is it true that the two of you got kidnapped by Columbian Drug Lords?"

"Not Columbian," Chloe said.

"Omigod Chloe!" Janice said, running out and giving her a hug. "Is Neil with you? Oh, did you break up? I'm so, so sorry he dumped you. Come on, let's go talk about it in the forum..."

Chloe wrenched her hand out of Janice's. "Jane helped me dump his sorry ass," Chloe said. "Tell you what though – if I see him, I'll let you know you're interested."

Jane hmmmphed and they continued to their first class. She ran into Mike on the way. "Hey."

"Hey." He kind of smiled at her, kind of looked away. Jane felt the silence going on way too long, but eventually, he spoke. "Look, about what happened earlier..."

"I'm fine, Mike. Maybe let's just be friends for now, take it from there, okay?" she asked.

Mike smiled, and was about to say something, but Billy Isliefson ran down the hall, "Guys, I just saw a unicorn in the parking lot! Said he needs the aid of some Sorceress of Foxberry Bay."

"Was he being ridden by a leprechaun?" Mike asked.

Billy took out his phone and showed Mike, whose mouth became a definitive "o". "Doesn't look like it."

"What do you suppose he wants this time?" Chloe asked Jane.